Adam And Eve Live Again

Adam And Eve Live Again

John Class

Aventine Press

Published by Aventine Press
1023 4th Ave #204
San Diego CA, 92101
www.aventinepress.com

ISBN: 1-59330-438-2

Library of Congress Control Number: 2006937462
Library of Congress Cataloging-in-Publication Data
Adam And Eve Live Again

Printed in the United States of America

Prelude

This book has been preceded by *Alive Again*, *From Ashes to Beauty*, and *Fingers Stained with Evil*. In this series we have lived with Lev and Rebekah Aron through Armageddon into a changed world, the world that has held its dead in the earth and has given them up to a regenerated life. Although those who died in the last few violent centuries were the most numerous and resourceful in doing evil, there was too much hatred and murder for which to take responsibility. Evil, programmed and drilled into society, destroyed character. Yet progress in righteousness can now be made because of the uplifting reign of love.

We share with Lev and Rebekah as they actively deal with the human and scientific problems that emerge as the regeneration expands, until it concludes with the return of Adam and Eve. Over six thousand years of human history are encompassed in bringing the human race from its creation to its ultimate degenerated state and then to a new beginning in the regeneration.

When all men are restored to life again, the first work will be to reconcile mankind with one another. The second and even greater work will be in reconciling men with God. This will take what remains of the reign of Christ to accomplish.

The return of our first parents will be electrifying to the whole world. Everyone will be back to tell his or her own story and to bring wisdom accumulated through time to bear on the new pathways. Adam and Eve bring their experience and knowledge to bear on the issues that confront mankind.

Preface

The regeneration will dwarf history, because everyone who was on its stage will be alive to certify the total truth concerning the past and will enact new scenes producing even greater drama. The winners and losers in history will not necessarily be the same when everyone lives again.

The former life was unequal in many ways. People did not all have the same opportunities. Some were born with physical or mental handicaps through no choice of their own. People expended most of their energy surviving under difficult conditions. Privileges of education were denied the vast majority, and there was an inequitable distribution of wealth. There were droughts, famines, and plagues to cause an even greater imbalance in man's condition, but mostly the power structure of earth favored an elite few and exploited the unprivileged many.

Men and women were often taken in death before they could achieve their dreams, and the music in their hearts went unwritten. No such limitations exist in the regeneration. All hopes, dreams, music, and creative skills will be unleashed so mankind will attain magnificent goals, and none shall be able to take credit for what another has done. Pride will be replaced by love that rejoices in blessing humankind. No one will waste time making things that hurt or destroy.

Evil done in a former life will be the heaviest burden with which individuals will return in the regeneration. Flagrant violations of conscience, sometimes cloaked in religious fanaticism, took a toll on human character until there was such a thing as total depravity, when human virtue was completely suppressed and evil was committed without inhibition. Those returning to life with such loathsome backgrounds face enormous difficulties and need special guidance if any hope of recovery is to be realized. Fortunately, most people intended good and tried to live wholesome lives. These will find the time of regeneration a rich and blessed experience.

When competition is replaced with love, the spread of human happiness will be astonishing. When poverty and ignorance are gone, human life will be more precious than gold, and the joy of living again will grow until it fills the whole earth. Weeping and sorrow, pain and sadness, will be but memories of the past for those who learn to walk in God's appointed paths. Man was not made to live by bread alone, but *needs* the Word of God and the love of God in the inward parts.

For the first six thousand years of mankind's existence, the world was under the wicked rulership of Satan, and the history of mankind was filled with pain, war, poverty, brutality, murder, and mayhem. Yet, even in the midst of such evil conditions, most men and women tried to live on a higher plane. Most people admired love and beauty and made some effort to emulate it in dealing with their fellows. Consequently, we have read countless stories of "good Samaritans" who amazed everyone with their kindness and generosity to those in need. Such will find the time of regeneration heart fulfilling.

How do we explain the great differences in people? Even more intriguing is the question, how is it possible to make humankind bear the image of God in which they were once created? Only God could devise a plan to accomplish such an extraordinary feat.

Our story will continue to unfold through seven thousand years of history, but the crowning moment will be when Adam and Eve make their grand entrance into life again. What a triumph of God's grace this will be! Finally, the human family will gladden or sadden the hearts of our first parents as they learn how their children behaved in their absence. Try as we may, it is not possible for anyone to grasp such a dramatic time when the whole human family is back on stage with righteousness reigning everywhere all the time. Love that was lost will be returned generating boundless growth. We invite you to imagine with us such a time and place in the glorious regeneration.

Remember, this is not some mythical story. We can only guess at the particulars, but Jesus has promised, "all that are in the graves shall hear his voice, and shall come forth" (John 5:28, 29). The resurrection of all the dead is the central teaching of Christianity. But the Bible does not teach a spontaneous emergence of all from the grave in one given instant. Rather, it clearly teaches, "For as in Adam all die, even so in Christ shall all be made alive—But every man in his own order" (1 Corinthians 15:22, 23). Though we can only imagine what this reality will be like, our best endeavors will surely fall short of the grand reality.

*"There is an evil which I have seen under the sun,
As an error which proceedeth from the ruler"
(Ecclesiastes 10:5).*

Chapter One

As time passed, Lev found the pace of his work assignments had diminished. There were many other well-qualified people volunteering to help. The regeneration work had been brilliantly planned and expedited so that the vast majority of earth's population had returned. Society was now stabilized and educated in the ways of righteousness. Only those newly returned to life needed help and guidance, but in most cases well-adjusted people returning to life found conditions superb and fulfilling. When one observed perfect people, such as the Ancients, it became personally challenging to emulate their nobility. There were no shortages of perfect patterns since so many had made enormous strides in righteousness.

As new generations returned, they brought with them the long shadows of sin in every shade of expression. The differences between those newly returned and those who had many years of development were very noticeable. Starting out in life a second time with full knowledge of the past, people were freer to chart a nobler course with their second opportunity. Still, there were some who wasted time and effort, justifying their former evil deeds. It was these that needed special help the most but desired it the least.

Lev was called from his home in Beersheba, Israel, to assist a man named Diocletian, a former Roman emperor. The Ancients felt he would need special help in adjusting to life again. Prisca, his former wife, and Valeria, his daughter, had made all the arrangements for his awakening. Diocletian had been a successful emperor in civil matters and had done much to strengthen the Roman Empire, but he became a monster in suppressing and destroying Christians. For this reason, he would have to face the anger and contempt in the faces of many he had tortured and destroyed. As every person returned to life, so did his or her past. Wantonly taking human life was never anyone's privilege, whatever powerful position they may have held. How would the offender face his crimes against mankind, and how would the murdered and tortured ones resolve the pain and bitterness in their hearts? God provided no magic wand to heal the aggrieved and no magic potion for the perpetrators to obliterate past deeds.

Christianity is unique in that it is the only religion in the world that holds forth forgiveness of sin and reconciliation between men and God. Reconciliation is a goal that can be reached only through effort and true desire. The time of regeneration will demonstrate that no one gets away with anything but in the end must find reconciliation, even if they left carnage in the former world.

Lev made preparations to leave for Split (formerly Salona, Croatia), the home of Diocletian. He knew of this emperor's savage ten years of bitter persecution against Christians (303-313 A.D., Rev. 2:10)*, but admired a few things about him; especially that he stepped down from his office while in full vigor. Most men craved power and having tasted it, they never voluntarily or willingly stepped down. Yet, Diocletian was able to leave his office to another and returned to life tending his own estate.

Diocletian Returns

I awakened feeling strange and knew something was different about this day. I was very comfortable without an ache or a pain. Even the old war wounds seemed to have disappeared. As I opened my eyes and glanced around the room, I could see that this certainly was not

* See www.revelation-today.com

my palace. I decided I must speak to my servants for bringing me here without my permission and especially for leaving me without apparel! I found clothing, not to my liking, but decided to put it on until I could speak to my servants about the liberties they had taken. As I dressed, I noticed none of my scars could be found, and I had not a trace of my rheumatism. Looking into a mirror, I was amazed at how handsome and youthful I looked. This was all very pleasant, but for the strange feeling I had. Something was very different and totally unexplainable. A sense of anxiety replaced my displeasure with my servants. Where was I and how did I get here?

I was about to shout for my servants but decided first to take a careful look around the room. To my amazement, it seemed that while this building might be much smaller than my palace, it was immeasurably more beautiful. The ceiling emanated light that made the cloudy day pleasant. All the furniture was exquisite and there was far more of it than in my palace bedroom. I entered into a small room near the bed and was confused to find different facilities than I had ever seen. I turned a handle and to my shock, fresh water came out. I recognized the large bath, but the metal circle with holes in it above the tub confused me. I sensed the chair with a hole in it was some new tool for human comfort but did not know how it worked and decided not to touch it. I stopped to admire myself in the incredibly clear mirror and could not believe my full head of hair and a smile of sparkling white teeth! My beard was gone...and without my permission! But I decided my skin was so clear and fresh now that there was no purpose in hiding it. I had trouble accepting these new conditions.

Why was I alone? In my palace it was rare to be alone, but now where was everybody when I wanted them? Slowly, I opened the door to see if anyone was outside of it. I felt a sense of fear—a fear of the unknown. What if armed guards waited outside? I knew I had many enemies. My fears turned to joy upon seeing Prisca running toward me, followed by my daughter Valeria.

He embraced them both with a profound sense of relief to find that they had not changed very much, though he did notice his wife looked much younger and more vivacious. He was so happy to see them, it would not matter how they looked. What he needed most was someone he knew and could trust. He found himself more confused by the minute, yet he just stood there embracing them, hoping they would not disappear.

"I am so glad to see you! I awakened this morning and everything is different. Pray tell me, where are we? What happened to our palace? Where are our servants? Please tell me I am not mad. I never felt this way before. I feel good, better than ever, but I don't understand."

Prisca placed her two hands on his face, saying, "My dear, be at peace; you are not mad. We love you, and you must believe us when we tell you all is well. Come, Diocletian, and have breakfast. By eating real food, you will know this is not a dream or a vision. You are real and so are Valeria and I. This is your new home, so do not worry about your old palace. It may have been bigger, but this will be more comfortable than anything you've ever had."

"Oh, *Pater*, you have come to us in answer to our prayers. *Mater* and I helped build this house for you and we know you will enjoy it," Valeria said.

"Where Are My Servants? I Shall Have Them Beaten!"

"This is outrageous. Where are my servants? Why should you have to do such heavy labor? I shall have them beaten for this."

"*Pater*, you have no servants now. Things have changed, as you can see. Don't fret yourself; you do not need servants anymore. Life is so simple."

They entered the cheerful kitchen with white tiles gleaming around the appliances that Diocletian did not recognize. The smell of freshly brewed tea made from the leaves of the trees of Paradise quickened Diocletian's senses. "What smells so fragrant?"

"*Pater*, this is the most wonderful tea! If you think it smells good, wait until you taste it."

Valeria poured him a steaming cup of tea.

His faced brightened as he sipped it. "If this is something new, it certainly is better than anything from the past. Is this from India or some such place?"

"No, *Pater*, it is not imported at all. It comes from your backyard. We will show you all the beautiful trees that once grew in the Garden of Eden."

"Oh, no! You are referring to the Christian Bible, are you not?"

Prisca quickly changed the subject. "Now let us try some of this fruit."

"You know that I like eggs for breakfast. I don't mind trying this fruit for dessert, but fetch me some eggs, my dear."

"I am sorry, *Pater*. No one eats eggs anymore. We don't raise chickens to obtain eggs anymore."

"At least give me some bread. As a soldier, I often lived on bread for days. Don't tell me you don't have any bread now."

"*Pater*, we don't eat bread very often. We eat this fruit. All you have to do is taste it. Once you do, you will never ask for bread or eggs again."

"If you were not my darling daughter, I would have you whipped for insubordination. This is simply outrageous! Don't you know how to make bread anymore?"

"Of course we know how to make bread. However, seldom is it baked now. *Pater*, just try this fruit, please."

"Lies! Lies! I Have Had My Fill of Christ!"

Diocletian's wife and daughter explained to the confused and disgruntled ex-emperor all about the new diet and its benefits. After taking a few bites, he found they had not begun to explain its delights.

"Why is everything different? My clothes are different. My home is different. My food is different. My surroundings are different. Even my wife and daughter are strangely different. What happened? I am a man of authority. Where are my servants? Where are my regal garments? Where is my sword? Where is my palace? I tell you, this is maddening! I wake up from my sickbed feeling wonderful, but assuredly, I am out of my mind. If I did not at least have both of you to identify with, I should be beside myself. You *must* know something more than you are telling me. Nothing is as it was and I want to know why! Now give me an honest answer!"

Prisca knew this was not going to be easy. The reality Diocletian would have to face would soon challenge all he had stood for. She gently held his hand and said, "My dear, everything we told you is true. What we did not tell you is that you died and have been dead a very long time. Centuries have come and gone while you slept in the grave, but today Christ has raised you from the dead."

As Prisca might have expected, her former husband violently banged his hands on the table and stood with a cry of rage. "Lies! Lies!" he screamed. "Christ raised me from the dead! I have had my fill of Christ and his insolent followers. I did everything in my power to rid our nation of the name of Christ and his troublesome worshipers. If there were a Christ, he would certainly not raise *me* from the dead. Do not insult my intelligence, Woman! Now, I ask you again, what has happened to me? And do not tell me I died. Look at me; do I look like a dead man to you? I tell you I am alive and could not have died!"

"*Pater*, please calm down. We know you were a man of authority and we love you. We never lied to you in the past and we would not lie to you now. Besides, only the truth is spoken now, everywhere, all the time. You were raised from the dead this morning. Did you look in the mirror? Did you see the same old man that you once were? No. You saw a more handsome face than you had before. Didn't you notice this? You were always a man careful about details. Why are you ignoring all these obvious facts?"

The steam swooshed out of him as he slumped back into his chair. He dropped his head between his hands, muttering, "I feel so good and should be happy. I fear I am afflicted now with madness. Maybe I would rather be sick than out of my mind."

Prisca tried to divert his focus. "My dear husband, come with us and let us show you your garden and the house you live in now. Everything has changed and you will see how beautiful life is. The walk will do you good."

Quietly he rose and followed Prisca, as she led him out into the garden enclosed with glass. He'd had large gardens around the palace, but this one, though smaller, seemed more full of life. A fragrant aroma from the trees of life filled his nostrils.

"These trees certainly are different! There is the tree whose fruit I ate for breakfast. This is not the place they called Eden, is it?" He sat on a comfortable patio chair to soak up the loveliness. Prisca and Valeria joined him.

"No, the Garden of Eden was not destroyed for many centuries, though it was kept carefully hidden so no one could find it. The angels harvested seeds from those trees all the while. I know you do not know much about the Bible, but centuries before we lived, there were men and women who were very faithful to God. Their lives demonstrated great faith, and as a reward God raised them with perfect human organisms and put them in charge of the government of this new order. We call them the Ancients. They report directly to Christ and his spiritual Body, so they never err in their judgments. When these Ancients came back to life in Jerusalem, they brought the seeds of the Eden trees with them. Since that time the seeds have been planted, and the Eden trees are growing all over the world. *Pater,* these trees are trees of life. You will live forever if you are privileged to eat from them. Adam and Eve died because they were denied this fruit, as much as they longed to eat it again."

"What Happened to My Palace?"

Diocletian didn't even try to acknowledge all this information at once. His interests were more immediate. "Tell me, what happened to the spacious palace we enjoyed so much after I retired from being emperor?"

"Your palace disappeared long ago. There is a new city in Croatia where it once stood called Split, and that is where we are living now, but don't trouble yourself about that. You have everything you will ever need right here. We want to show you your home and all the new and wonderful changes that have taken place. The world is no longer the ignorant and hostile place it once was. Learning is a passion with people today."

Prisca took a deep breath before continuing.

"And my dear husband, we now know that there is, and always was, only one God. God's Son and his bride are in charge of this whole world. Jerusalem is the throne of Christ and his Bride, and the Ancients are his representatives on earth. This is the truth."

"If Christ rules the world, why would he want me in it?" Diocletian asked, full of distrust. "You know that I persecuted Christ's followers without pity or compassion. I was determined to end this insolent religion that denounced the great gods of the Roman Empire. I fear if what you say is true, I am going to be in terrible straits. Surely, if I have been returned to life, it must be to inflict torment on me for what I did to his followers. This is a horrible state of affairs!"

"No, no, *Pater*," Valeria said comfortingly. "Christ is not like that. Those cutthroat rulers you appointed—Maximian and Galerius—now they might have behaved that way. Constantius, whom you also appointed, was slightly more tolerant. You yourself were more generous; but your two appointees were your tragic partners in death to Christians. You denied your native benevolence because of them."

"Strangely, Valeria, you speak the truth. As I recall, I was not disposed initially to persecute and destroy Christians. Galerius and Maximian were the brutal soldiers who feared the gods of Rome and felt that we must preserve our heritage of gods for the welfare of the empire. They were the ones who convinced me that Christians were making attempts on my life. You are right. I was not by nature a cruel man, but once my mind was convinced that this is what had to be done, I relentlessly made war against Christians." Fear enveloped him. "But if I made war against this Christ, your so-called present ruler, what defense shall I find?"

"If he brought you back to torment you, *Pater*, and to destroy you, he would be like you. But he is not like you. He brought you back because he loved you in spite of what evils you did against him and his followers. Christ has no pleasure in human suffering—yours or anyone else's. Under his righteous rule and authority, suffering will end. The only cause of suffering now is the evil that was done in the previous life that people bring back with them from the grave."

"Then it looks as if I am in for hard times. I am a soldier, however, and I will not cower before this Christ. If I die, so be it, I die. I died once and I can die again. Death is not that bad. You know, I did worry when I died if, perchance, I might have to cross the River Styx and enter the Underworld. However, that was a lie. Being dead was absolutely painless. I didn't feel a thing."

"Well, Diocletian, let us not spend the day worrying about so many things. Today you are alive, well and happy. Let us rejoice in life. While the fact that you did not allow many Christians to live and enjoy life is a problem you will be forced to deal with tomorrow or the next day, for the moment let us be glad."

"*Pater*, we must show you some of the amazing things about your house. You will not have to chop wood for heat, nor carry water into your home. All the food you will need is growing in your orchard and garden. Part of the problem in our previous life was ignorance and superstition. We did not know enough to do what was right. We were brought up under false pagan gods who were lifeless images created by evil spirit beings and the devil. We learned a lot of things that were not true."

"How is that possible? I was able to read and write, and that enabled me to become emperor. Why do I need so much knowledge? I am a man of action. I learned to fight and was victorious. I learned to govern and knew how to share power with others. That should be a good record. Now you are telling me I did not know enough?"

"Diocletian," Prisca interjected, "come into the house and sit down. Let us show you an enchanting world of knowledge." As soon as he was seated in the living room, she turned on the large wall-mounted computer screen. When it lit up and people appeared on screen, Diocletian was startled.

"Is this witchcraft?" he inquired anxiously.

"No, you are watching the Ancients. Let us listen to a history lesson on the Emperor Diocletian." Prisca punched up a program that outlined his life, accomplishments, and the terrible persecution of Christians for ten years. A careful analysis was given of how Diocletian was led to violate his native benevolence by his associates Maximian and Galerius. It told everything that he did, and how, through ignorance and superstition, he was led to persecute Christians in a most sanguine manner.

Diocletian was startled to hear his name and everything he did in a new light. Now his deeds were weighed in the light of present truth, and all his ugly actions looked unworthy of a man who by nature was more benevolent than his deeds allowed.

He knew that somehow he had become a monster without a monster's heart. He appeared as a savage and did not like what he saw. Yet he perceived the accuracy of the facts, and in his heart he wondered how and why he had taken such a path.

"Let us not dwell on the former Emperor Diocletian," Valeria suggested. "Let us view a lesson on the world about us."

She tuned to a current news program showing the state of the world and the progress made in the great regeneration program. The entire experience mesmerized the emperor, who was still uncertain whether this was a dream or some potent magic. He was astute enough to realize a great gap existed between his knowledge of the current world and the rather simple one he once ruled. He was drawn to these educational programs with an insatiable desire to leap from his ignorant past into an age of enlightenment. Diocletian sensed immediately that the instructors on these programs were wise and gifted beyond anyone he had ever known. He realized he had been but a rather ignorant soldier who rose to power without the mental greatness and acuity that becomes a ruler. He knew that though the Romans had beaten the Greeks on the battlefield, the Romans were inferior to the Greek civilization and could never conquer them mentally.

Diocletian's first day of his new life was quickly spent when Prisca and Valeria left to go to their respective homes. This upset him terribly, for he felt that at least his former wife Prisca should stay the night with him. However, he was too rattled to be certain of anything or to assert himself. The once great ruler had become a dependent child, trying to find his way in a world of overwhelming change.

After they left, Diocletian decided to stay up late into the night tuning in various programs, trying to figure out what had gone on after his death. He was amazed at how far the world had advanced and how totally ignorant he was. He who once ruled the great Roman Empire was not qualified to handle the simple position of street sweeper today. How demeaning for one who once held such great power to be so outclassed and outsmarted! However, he had been a soldier and one thing he could accept was discipline. He had a strong will and determined he would make extravagant efforts to meet the challenges.

The following day Diocletian arose early, as was his custom. He went into the orchard and enjoyed collecting fruit for the day with his own hands. He was used to servants doing everything, but he found tending to his own little paradise rather delightful. If the truth had been known, he often tired of servants standing around waiting to do his bidding. He found to his delight that he was actually happier without them. Life was so simple on the one hand and so complex on the other. He was grateful that he was so well provided for and that he lacked no comfort.

As Diocletian looked out of his window toward the road, he saw cars occasionally passing by. Looking up he saw a small machine ascending from a pad down the road. What strange powers men now possessed! He could hardly believe what he was seeing. He knew what power over men was, but he marveled at man's power over nature. He realized he was but a babe in a very intelligent society. It was totally humbling.

Learn the Truth—Christ Is Now in Control!

Soon Prisca arrived as bright as the morning's radiance. "Did you sleep well last night, Diocletian?"

"Yes, when I finally got to bed. I was so engrossed with all the new learning tools last night that I could not let go. Never have I learned so much at one time and felt so absolutely ignorant at the same time. I don't know if I can ever catch up, but I have to start somewhere."

"Don't worry. With perfect food and a better mind, you will be amazed how quickly you will learn what you need to know. Naturally, it will take years to absorb so much information, and on top of this, new information is being discovered everyday. The world is on an intense, unparalleled learning curve. The day of brute force is over. No one rules but Christ now."

The name of Christ made him cringe. "Why do you bring up that name again, Prisca? You know it upsets me. I shall leave Christ alone, and I hope he will leave me alone. Isn't that fair?"

"I am sorry to upset you, Diocletian. However, you might as well learn the truth to start with. You are out of power, and Christ is in complete control of this world. The tables have turned and you apparently made a big mistake in the past."

"What if he chooses to torment me as I did his followers?"

"He has not dealt with you as you did his followers, has he? He has provided you with every comfort for life. Does that sound like torment?"

"No, of course not! But is this some cat-and-mouse game he is playing with me?"

"No!" Prisca was adamant. "He does not rule as men once ruled, with evil to violate other people's rights to life and happiness. The only thing that is going to prove difficult for you is facing most of those Christians you tortured and killed when they come back, and some have already returned."

"Why do you say 'most of those Christians' instead of 'all those Christians'?"

"Because some of those you tortured and killed are now reigning with Christ in glory. Others wait their time for awakening here on earth. You could not have made a bigger mistake. The sad thing, my dear, is you were by nature a kinder person."

"It is too late. The die is cast. I made my deal with the devil, and now who shall save me from my unparalleled cruelty toward Christians? All that effort to subdue Christianity was for naught, for right after me, Constantine accepted Christianity and prospered. I cannot undo the past. However, I am still a soldier; I will take what comes as my just due."

At this moment Valeria arrived. It lifted Diocletian's countenance to see his beautiful daughter. She gave him a little hug and a kiss on the cheek.

"My *Pater*, you look a little forlorn. You should be so happy! You are alive and well and have a bright future."

"Do I indeed? Your mother just told me that everyone I burned and destroyed in my purge against Christianity is now coming back to trouble me. I murdered them by the thousands and tens of thousands. They will all be vindicated, and I shall be the fallen emperor who now must face their angry faces without an armed guard or a single voice in my defense. I am condemned in a world ruled by Christ. How can I be happy?"

"There are two beautiful qualities about the Christian religion that you still need to learn. First, it extends forgiveness for sins and, second, it practices love."

"Oh, that's not true, and you know it! The Christians that I knew were no different than other people. As a matter of fact, some Christians were arrogant and invited martyrdom. Even as they went to the flames, they threatened eternal fire to my soldiers and me. Admittedly, some were beautiful people and my heart was pained, because I could not grant them grace without being inconsistent."

"Those humble and faithful Christians you destroyed are now living and reigning with Christ. The others you will meet and will have to make peace with. You know, not even an emperor had the right to take innocent human life. We tried to tell you this, *Pater*, but those two rulers you appointed, Maximian and Galerius, seemed to control you."

"What does it matter now? I was in charge and that makes me responsible."

Prisca said, "My dear, please remember that the Christian religion is the only religion that taught a resurrection of the dead. And here you are! So the Christian religion is proved to be correct in this regard. There is one other teaching of Christianity—forgiveness of sins through Jesus Christ. It is the only religion that taught free forgiveness of sins. If they were right on the resurrection, don't you think they might be right on the matter of forgiveness of sins?"

"Even if Christ were to forgive me, all the Christians I destroyed in my cruel purge are going to want to see me skinned alive and hung in a public square by my feet. They want me to suffer as I made them suffer. I destroyed thousands of those so-called Christians, so what will my punishment be?"

"*Mater* just told you the unique teaching of Christianity is forgiveness of sins. I know you cannot believe in such goodness, but that is true. Jesus has the power to forgive sins and already has forgiven you the monstrous deeds you perpetrated against his disciples. Just be thankful Christ is not like most of the rulers of the old world. He died to save us from our sins, and you are no exception. But that does not mean you will not have to face those you destroyed. They, too, need to learn about forgiveness, and in their cases, they will have to learn how to forgive you."

"Those I Killed May Seek My Life!"

"What is to prevent them from dragging me through the streets before they hang me or burn me? I have no army to defend me anymore."

Valeria gave a pleasant little chuckle. "Oh, *Pater*, no one is allowed to hurt another person in this whole wide world, even if they wanted to. There are angelic powers that prevent any form of violence from taking place. It just cannot happen. Christ did not bring you back to destroy you. He brought you back to life to give you an opportunity to see how you will conduct yourself when the light of truth is shining everywhere. You will no longer be an ignorant pagan emperor serving demon gods that really were no gods at all. Just the same, you will have to make peace with those you put to death by unrighteous edicts."

"Let us have breakfast and talk about something else for now. Shall we all sit around the table and enjoy the bounties that Christ has provided for us today?" Prisca asked.

"That sounds good to me! As I started to say when you first arrived this morning, I stayed up late last night trying to learn as much as I could. I am totally amazed. I am afraid I am going to have to sit there and learn forever to catch up."

"You will have plenty of time to catch up," Valeria assured him. "I hope you won't mind *Mater* and me offering a prayer of thanks before we eat."

"Well, yes, I do mind, but what does it matter? I have no country or flag or even a god. I am a man without authority of any kind. We Romans were credited with having over three thousand gods, and not one of them ever did a thing for me except to exploit my ignorance. One insight I learned last night was that reason should be a guiding influence in life. When religion speaks to my reason, I shall be listening. Until then, pray all you want, but I shall not join in."

They both bowed in silent prayer while Diocletian sipped his tea.

"Lev Aron Is Not Welcome!"

"I am not about to become a Christian," he grumbled under his breath.

"We have good news for you," Prisca announced. "Next week, a man by the name of Lev Aron is coming to visit you. He is being sent by the rulers at Jerusalem to spend some time with you."

"Did I invite him?"

"No, of course not."

"Well, then, he is not welcome here!"

"He is being sent by Christ's representatives in Jerusalem."

"Why would Christ send anyone to me? I am his enemy. I must admit, I am a very ignorant enemy, but I have a track record to prove my hostility to Christ."

"Oh, *Pater*, stop being so hard of heart," Valeria chided. "This is only your second day of life, and you have much to learn. Why don't you relax and let those with knowledge and understanding speak to you? Allow them to help."

"It seems I do not have much choice. I guess I shouldn't be so foolish as to offend the ambassador of your so-called new King. I am sure he is no different than other men. He may come in regal vestments, but he will only be another man."

"He is very different from men you have dealt with," Prisca responded. "He, too, was an enemy of Christ, but now he is his ambassador. I believe you will find him the most interesting person you have ever met. By the way, he has helped many people with the blood of millions on their hands."

"*Pater*, I can hardly wait to meet him!" Valeria bubbled. "You saw those Ancients on your screen last night and witnessed the brilliant majesty in all that they said. You have to admit that you never saw people like that before. Lev Aron is very much like them. Everyone speaks well of him."

"Cancel Lev Aron's Visit!"

"Well, apparently I am not alone, but it is little comfort to know that there have been others like me. I thoroughly underestimated the will of Christians to resist interference in their religion. Rome's policy had been not to interfere with religion as long as the subjects did not want to revolt; still, I thought by putting pressure on the Christians, we would end this religious nonsense. But the more they were persecuted, the more resolute they became. Anyway, I would be grateful if Lev

Aron would mind his own affairs and not mine. I do not want to meet him. Is there any way I can cancel his visit?"

"No, *Pater*, you are no longer in charge. The Ancients must believe you need extra help, or they would not be sending Mr. Aron. You might appreciate having him around when people recognize you as the one who ordered their death."

"I did not particularly enjoy persecuting Christians. I just saw them as a threat to the Roman gods."

The conversation ended as they ate breakfast. Both Prisca and Valeria felt his discomfort. They wanted to invite him to the chapel meetings but realized it would only anger him. He was still uncertain whether this was reality or a dream.

After breakfast, Diocletian asked, "Where is my sword? I want it. I would feel more secure with it at my side."

Valeria sighed and shook her head. "You have been dead for centuries and you ask for your sword? We kept it around as long as we lived. We knew it was worth a great deal of money, but it has been lost over time."

"I Want a Sword!"

"Where can I buy another one? It doesn't have to be a sword of the same quality. I want a sword!"

"Swords went out of style centuries ago," Prisca explained patiently. "Men used much more lethal weapons than swords. Nevertheless, now there are no weapons of any kind."

They both could see he was becoming agitated, so they tried to change the subject. "We wanted to take you for a drive in a car around the countryside so you could become familiar with the land as it is now. You cannot live at home forever without venturing out. Wouldn't you like to see how wonderful everything is?"

"Yes, I would. What is a car?"

"You've seen some of them out on the road passing the house. You may think of it as a horseless carriage. It goes without horses pulling it."

"That is impossible, my child!"

"Will you go?"

"If the carriage has no horses, we will be sitting in it all day going nowhere."

"If I get a carriage that goes without horses will you go with us?"

"Yes, of course."

After Valeria left, Diocletian became very pensive. He complained, "Everything is too new. I have been removed from my home, my friends, my people, and even my sword is gone. This fancy world is very fascinating, but it's not for me! I really want to be left alone until I sort things out. My world may have been mean and vicious, but I liked it better. I will never catch up with all these people and their modern tools."

"Diocletian, you are only sulking because you are not powerful and prominent. Listen, I know it is discouraging when everything is new. It is humiliating to learn that after you left this world it excelled in all ways. You feel passed by and useless, but take heart. Billions of people have returned already and are adjusting to their new surroundings beautifully, and you will, too."

"Well, I am not everybody. Everybody doesn't have my past to live with. Most people didn't rise to power only to become a problem person needing a nurse to take them by the hand and lead them around. I really did not want to go out, but Valeria has been a good daughter and I do not want to offend her."

Soon a gleaming teal-colored car drove up, and Valeria stepped out inviting her father and mother to sit in its lush interior. Her father marveled at the vehicle and forgot his gloom. He sat in the front seat with his daughter, and Prisca sat in back. The music playing was unlike any he had ever heard, and he was enchanted. "Such music must come from the gods!"

Quietly, the electric motor caused the vehicle to go at speeds that surpassed the fastest chariots of his day. This was incredible! There he sat in complete air-conditioned comfort as they passed along the pastoral countryside with orchards and homes blending in, adding to the beauty. When he saw a huge structure, he asked, "What is that?"

Feeling Obsolete in a Complex World

"Oh, that is a factory where they make computers and television sets as you have in your home. When you learn enough, you may be called upon to contribute your services. Everybody works at least two or three hours a day. Sometimes when building for the return of their loved ones, they will spend eight or ten hours. We will take you inside sometime so you can see how these things are built. You will be amazed to see machines doing most of the work, and people overseeing production."

This began to intrigue him. How could machines work by themselves? That was not possible, he thought, but he decided to keep his thoughts to himself. He was beginning to understand he was an obsolete person living in a very complex world. He spotted a shiny metallic object rising from the ground, lifting off from a stone pad of some kind. "What is that machine?"

"Oh, that is an airplane. It is like this car, but it flies in the air instead of driving on the ground. When Lev Aron comes, he will be arriving in a flying machine something like that. Maybe he will even give you a ride in it."

"How can a chariot rise straight up into the air like that?"

"Down the road there is a factory where they make those aircraft. As they become more plentiful, they will replace cars. However, right now most aircraft are used in going to countries with few highways. That way, we don't have to build many roads anymore, just small ones for local communities. We have huge aircraft that cross the oceans in hours and carry enormous loads. Some day you may visit other nations. Oh, *Pater!*" Valeria effervesced. "Life is so beautiful now! There are no more wars or fighting, no more sweat and labor, and no more sickness or dying. Love is everywhere!"

"I cannot believe what I am seeing! See that big machine there? It is moving earth, making a hole in the ground. A team of twelve horses could not move earth that way! What is it doing? This is too much for me!"

"It is digging a hole so they can lay the foundation for a new home. That same machine was used to prepare the foundation for your house. Everything is done efficiently, and we have learned to harness all the sciences to serve mankind."

"How do you know so much? Your instructors told me you were a slow learner. Now you seem to know everything."

Discouragement Setting In

"Well, since we returned to life, we all are more and more intelligent because of eating from the trees of life. As you know, they use perfect teachers and the best teaching methods, so that anyone can learn and retain what they learn. You will, too."

"It is very discouraging to awaken to life as a dullard. To think that children know about all these modern things that are mysteries to me is depressing."

"Now, dear, do not fret so. You are experiencing what most people do when returning to life in a changed world. You are discouraged because you are a very competitive person. Remember, competition does not exist in hearts filled with love. Our happiness comes from the knowledge that Christ has given us our life again and all things necessary for our blessing and happiness."

"There you go again with that name. Christ does this and Christ does that! That name happens to be the source of my present unhappiness. I tried to make that name disappear from the earth. If ever a man failed in his mission, it was me."

"*Pater*, perhaps Lev Aron will be a help to you. Yes, Christ has prevailed and you didn't, and that is wonderful because he is kind and good. Wonderful for you as well as everyone else."

"You make me out to be an ogre, child. I was always good to my friends and my soldiers. I never intended to become as ruthless as I was. It was the arrogance and insolence of some of those Christians that aroused my temper, and I then felt driven to destroy them. On a few occasions, I noticed some very devout and humble Christians who seemed noble and pure. I did regret how I treated them. These must have been true disciples of Christ."

"Yes, they were. However, don't fret about these, because they are now reigning with Christ. Probably one of them has personal supervision over you now. I know that may not sound comforting to you, but that is because you never knew anyone who ruled with love in his heart. You had your virtues in your day, but loving your enemies wasn't one of them."

The car had circled many miles and they soon returned home again.

Unfortunately, the week was rather unsuccessful in bringing Diocletian to a happy and accepting frame of mind. While he seemed to get enormous satisfaction out of learning and enjoyed his gracious lifestyle, he was distraught about his former bitter persecution of Christians. It was this that troubled him, as he recalled the countless thousands he had condemned to the flames or to other hideous deaths. Now they were the winners, and he, the loser.

A Desperate Act

This was not a physical depression, because he had never felt better at any time. Occasionally, his mind was flooded with happiness at the beauty and wonder he was experiencing. More often, he brooded about being a vanquished foe. Even though he was being kindly treated, it bothered him that Christ and his faithful disciples were in power. He dreaded the day when he would actually meet some of those he had killed and tortured. Would they look upon him in contempt and meditate how they might avenge themselves? Having been spared defeat on the battlefield in his former life, he was not prepared to find Christ on the throne with his followers and himself the defeated one.

Diocletian had thought about taking his life from the moment he asked for his sword. He had looked at the knives in the kitchen, but none seemed suitable for this purpose. Finally, he found a sturdy rope in a garden shed and decided to use that. Knowing that Lev Aron was coming the next morning, Diocletian decided to take his life the night before.

After Prisca and Valeria left for the night, he took the rope out of the shed and made a noose at one end. Then taking a bench out into the moonlit night, he found a sturdy branch on the biggest tree he could find. He stood on the bench with the noose over his neck and threw the other end over the branch and proceeded to tie the rope to it. His plan was to secure the rope to the branch and then kick the bench away. As he was about to make the first loop, his hands became paralyzed! At first he thought this was a passing cramp. But his hands were hanging limply at his side. He could not tie the rope to the limb and he could not take the noose off of his neck. His feet worked well enough, so he stepped off the bench and the rope fell off the limb, trailing behind him. Now Diocletian couldn't even hide what he had tried to do.

Angry and frustrated, he felt foolish sitting there through the night with a rope around his neck. He knew it was useless to go to bed. He could not even lift the covers. Everyone would know of his folly. Why had his hands become paralyzed? Oddly enough, he felt pleased that he hadn't succeeded in hanging himself. It was cowardice on his part and he knew it!

As Diocletian sat there through the night, he found himself praying. He didn't know to whom to pray, but he lifted his voice hoping that some deity or supernatural power would hear him.

"Dear God, look at me from heaven. You brought me back to life and now will not let me return from whence I came. I am a beaten man. I am a mere man. I cannot resist your supreme power. If I must live, I will live. I tried to end my life and you prevented me from doing so. I have a rope of shame about my neck. If I cannot do as I please, I will try to repair the life I must now live. I am humbled, I am pained, but strangely, I am glad to be alive. If it was you who paralyzed my arms, I promise I will not try to end my life again."

Strangely, he felt a measure of peace, and, moving to a lawn chair, he nodded off to sleep. He awakened to hear Prisca come through the door.

"Dear God, what have you tried to do?" She stood there shaking in disbelief. "Are you all right?" she asked.

"Yes, please take this silly rope off my neck. I can't say that I am all right, because I cannot move my two arms. I lost use of them last night. I could not even get into bed so I fell asleep here."

"You tried to hang yourself and the spirit powers prevented you from doing so. This is only temporary. We will call the Ancients' office and you must tell exactly what you tried to do. They will check with Christ to see if what you say is true. If so, you will be healed within the hour. I am going to dial the telephone and someone from their office will listen to you. I will hold it to your ear, and you must tell who you are and what you did that caused your arms to be paralyzed. Do you understand what you must do?"

"Yes, I feel foolish. Whatever that instrument does, use it. I want my arms to work again!"

"This is called a telephone, and we use it to speak and listen to people far away. I will dial the main office. This being your first offence, you will probably be healed shortly."

"Shalom, how can I help you?"

"I am Diocletian, the former Roman Emperor. I am suffering from both of my arms being paralyzed."

"One moment, I will connect you with the first Ancient Worthy available."

Within a minute's time another voice spoke. "Shalom, this is Abel. How may I assist you?"

"I am Diocletian. I decided to hang myself and placed a rope around my neck. When I tried to tie the other end of the rope to the large branch of a tree, my arms became paralyzed. I am calling to have my arms healed."

"Why would you do something as foolish as this?"

"I do not wish to be ungrateful for the kindnesses I have received, but I guess I don't have the courage to face the tens of thousands of Christians I once committed to the flames or other horrible deaths.

Since I was unconscious in the grave, why can I not return to that state?"

"That seems to be an honest answer, although a foolish one. I will confirm the veracity of your statement. If you told me the whole truth, I will know shortly. Do not hang up, I shall return with an answer in a moment." Then, "Yes, you told the truth, Diocletian. You will be healed upon the condition that you promise not to try something as cowardly as that again."

"I promise not to try this ever again. I thank the powers that prevented me from destroying my life, because actually since I have been spared, I am happy to be alive. I guess I was unwilling to own up to my past, but somehow I must do so."

"You shall be healed within the hour, Diocletian. I believe we have sent Lev Aron to visit you. Please receive him as a messenger from God. You must realize that you were wallowing in self-pity when you tried to take your life, which cannot be allowed. Neither can anyone else take your life. However, you are now on a long probation period. If you do not make a proper effort at overcoming your sins and weaknesses, you will not have to take your life, for Christ will order your death—the second death from which there will be no return to life. Shalom."

Abel spoke with great authority. Diocletian realized the power of the throne of Christ was behind every word that Abel had spoken. Yet the Ancient Worthy spoke graciously. Diocletian was oddly comforted by the assurance that no one could take his life, since he had tried to take his own life and failed. Suddenly, life was more precious to him than ever before.

He knew Lev Aron was supposed to arrive this morning. As soon as he felt a tingle in his arms, Diocletian knew feeling was returning. How thankful he was! One accepts all the bodily functions without full appreciation of them until some ability is lost; suddenly that becomes the most important thing in the world. He wanted to bathe and be ready to meet his guest. After talking to Abel, he was almost looking forward to meeting Lev Aron. Strange how things changed overnight.

Valeria arrived and immediately spotted the rope with the noose lying on the floor. *"Pater,* you didn't try to do what I am thinking, did you?"

"Yes, I did try to use that rope, but I wasn't successful, as you can see."

"Oh, how could you? Don't you know that we love you? We are so happy to have you back to life—why would you even think of doing such a thing? You have everything you need for a happy life. What does it matter that you aren't in power any more? You stepped down from being emperor by your own choice and were happy to return to ordinary life in former days. What made you so unhappy?"

"How can I explain it? All that matters is that I didn't succeed, and now my arms are healed. Rest assured, I will not try anything like this again, Valeria. Will you please take this rope and put it in the storage shed? I don't want Lev Aron to see it."

No sooner had Diocletian bathed than they heard a quiet hum outside.

Lev Aron Arrives

They hurried outside as soon as they heard the vibration. To wondering eyes, a shiny blue craft set down in the center of their pad without so much as a bump. After shutting down the engine, Lev emerged smiling warmly to greet them.

"Shalom! I am Lev Aron. This is such a pleasure to meet all of you."

"We are pleased to have you with us, Mr. Aron. I am Diocletian, and this is my former wife, Prisca, and our daughter, Valeria. I hope you will join us for breakfast as we have not eaten yet."

"That's welcome news to a traveler. Yes, I would be delighted to eat with you and your lovely family."

Valeria responded, "Mr. Aron, I know you must have lived for many years on the fruit of paradise, because you seem to be very near human perfection. We see this in the Ancients on television. Without anyone ever saying it, one can observe they are perfect. Their manner, speech, and dignity are almost overwhelming."

"Oh, please don't compare me with those marvelous people. They stand head and shoulders above me, mentally and spiritually. We are blessed to have such righteous managers over earth's affairs. Never before have we had perfect wisdom, justice and power on the throne. Please, I mean no personal offense to you, Diocletian. We know our old world was tainted with human imperfection. Even when rulers wanted to do better, they couldn't."

Soon they were seated around the breakfast table. A sense of unease settled upon them when it came time to thank the Lord for the food. Diocletian had never done so, and Prisca and Valeria did not feel free to invite their guest to offer thanks. However, Lev seized the moment saying, "I always offer thanks before I eat, so please excuse me for a few moments while I pray."

Diocletian was not offended, even though he felt a bit of reproof in his not offering a prayer of thanksgiving. After Lev finished his silent prayer, Diocletian said, "Please bear with me, Lev. I am a pagan who had many gods, too numerous to mention. If we pagans paused to offer thanks before eating, we might spend several hours thanking all our deities and then wonder which one we had offended by not mentioning him. I must admit, having one God is certainly more efficient. You know, having thousands of gods is actually like having no god at all. One cannot satisfy two masters, much less thousands of them."

"That was exactly what Jesus taught. He said, 'No man can serve two masters.' I don't know how you managed with so many gods. It must have been quite confusing."

Patronizing Gods in Hope of Material Gain

"Really, the truth of the matter is we did not serve any god very well. We only thought about the god of war when going to battle, or the goddess of fertility when we wanted children. We patronized the gods when we wanted something from them, but to worship God as you do was foreign to us."

"Well, I've learned something about pagan habits. I hope your past experiences with these so-called gods has been enough, and that you're prepared to accept one God and His only begotten Son as the present authorities. I know it is difficult to leave behind a whole way of life and enter a new realm ruled by a singular God.

"May I tell you about my experience upon returning to life?" Lev continued. "But first, may I have another cup of tea and another piece of fruit? I must be extra hungry from my trip here."

Prisca interjected, "Please save room for some breakfast cake that I made."

"Thank you! I never pass up the extra delicacies that make a superb meal even better. Anyway, I was a Jew who never accepted Christ. We Jews have a history of being persecuted. Back in Egypt we were slaves. We were persecuted for not accepting pagan gods, and then we were persecuted for not accepting Christ. Persecution made us a disciplined people. The only way we survived was through extra discipline and resourcefulness. We never could be at ease anywhere. There was always someone determined to convert us."

"Well, at least I didn't single out Jews for persecution. I was too busy persecuting Christians," Diocletian commented.

"I thank you, on behalf of my forefathers. However, the whole world turned against the Jews in the Battle of Armageddon. The nations of earth assembled a massive army intending to wrest Jerusalem away from the Jews. This was supposed to be the final solution in dealing with us. I died on the first day of battle defending my nation and people. The next day, the Lord God Almighty fought for His people Israel, and the entire army sent against us was destroyed. Thousands of soldiers died, and from that day the banner of righteousness began to unfurl over the world. From that day onward, the nations learned who God was and accepted His Son to mediate between God and man. You have not lived long enough to know all this yet, but everyone learns very fast now."

"Your People Were Slaves?"

"You say your people were slaves in Egypt, Lev?"

"Yes, and it was a harsh slavery."

"Well, my father and mother were slaves so I can sympathize with slaves. We had many in the Roman Empire. It brought the Romans a comfortable way of life, and no one likes to give up the advantages they have. I always resented slavery in the back of my mind."

"We have that much in common. I am pleased to know that. How did you manage to become emperor of the empire from such a humble background?"

"Well, I despised being a slave in my youth, but when I grew up, I found they would accept me in the army and grant me citizen's rights. I was a strong man and made a good soldier. I resolved to break free from the bondage my parents were under. I heard what you said about Jews being disciplined. You are right. When people are persecuted, they must always be alert. It was my tireless discipline and effort to excel that distinguished me from others. Ultimately, I rose through the ranks. Becoming emperor came about by a chain of circumstances over which I had no control. I happened to be in the right place at the right time, that is all."

"You have a remarkable past! Coming from slave parents to emperor of the Roman Empire is quite a success story. Do you sometimes wish you had not been so successful? Did you incur liabilities as emperor that at times you wished you did not have?"

"Mr. Aron, you certainly ask penetrating questions. The answer is, yes. If I knew then that I would live again with the same people that I put to death, I am certain the history of my reign would have been quite different. However, then I sat on an imperial throne. I did not always listen to my heart, but instead I played power politics. Paganism had been the religion of the empire for centuries, and Christians seemed bent on converting the empire to their way of doing things. I, unfortunately, had subordinate rulers, who, while loyal to me, were more like savages than statesmen. Under their constant demands that we eliminate the Christians, I capitulated. No, I don't blame them, for I was responsible. If I could live those days over again, I think I might have done differently. I suffered sleepless nights when persecuting Christians, and even more so now that I must ultimately face those who suffered at my hands."

Learn to Avoid Repeat Mistakes

"Take heart," Lev encouraged. "You have some work to do, but with humility and perseverance, you can get it done."

Prisca joined in saying, "Let us go into the living room. We will be more comfortable there."

"Sounds good to me. By the way, how about we climb into my aircraft and let me show you the earth from above. You may get a different perspective looking down for a change rather than looking up."

"Oh, that would be delightful!" Valeria exclaimed.

"Yes, I would enjoy that, too. I saw an aircraft the other day and could not believe my eyes. I was riding in a horseless chariot in solid comfort and then I looked up."

"We will make a believer out of you yet, Diocletian. Please, come aboard and I will fly you over the whole territory. As a matter of fact, why don't we take some food and have a picnic lunch in our travels."

"Oh, that sounds wonderful," Prisca said.

Soon, they were ready to go. Locking the doors, Lev started the engine. The craft lifted off the ground gently but swiftly enough for the passengers to feel themselves pressed down in their seats. As the craft banked, they looked down on Diocletian's home. Lev kept the craft flying low so they could see the terrain below. It was exhilarating to see the earth in its splendor, covered with trees, grass and flowers. They saw streams of water bubbling on their way to the seas, and people working, building homes and planting orchards. This was like a dream to Diocletian and his family. Everything they were doing and hearing was undreamed of in their previous lifetime. Never could they have imagined such grandeur.

"Look at that!" each of them cried as one sight after another caught their eye. As they passed mountainous terrain, Lev brought the craft closer to earth and circled a lovely meadow. He said, "I think we will set down there for our picnic lunch. What do you say?"

Everyone nodded in agreement. "That is perfect," Diocletian said.

Lev said, "The earth is so full of good things, we should be as happy as kings."

Diocletian answered, "Well, I was a king, and I cannot say that I was very happy then, nor now."

Lev landed the craft gently near a huge tree with a large rock by it that would serve as a picnic table. Valeria covered the rock with a cloth and set out the food they had brought. Prisca served the aromatic tea.

Lev asked Diocletian, "Would you mind if I offered a prayer of thanks to God for all of us?"

"No, not really. I am not in charge of anything anyway."

"Are you sure you don't mind?"

"Not enough to protest. I am not a believer, as you know, but I can listen like a gentleman."

"Then, I shall pray. Our Father in heaven, hallowed be thy name. We thank you that your kingdom has come to earth and that your will is gradually being done here. We thank you for life, health, beauty and this wonderful food that comes from your hand. We thank you in Jesus' name. Amen."

Touching Diocletian's shoulder, Lev said, "You see how simple it is when you have one God?"

Diocletian was silent. He felt he was being pressured to accept God and His Son, whom he had earlier rejected. About this time, an elegant buck emerged from a cluster of trees.

"Oh, if I only had my bow and some arrows. What a perfect shot! Look at the size of those antlers!"

"You would be one sorry person if you tried to shoot that buck," Lev said. "Nothing is allowed to hurt or to destroy any more. Your arm would be paralyzed for trying it. These animals have a right to live without fear of harm from anyone. Notice how tame he is. As a matter of fact, we have fruit to spare. I will give him a treat."

Lev took a piece of fruit and walked over to the buck that stood there eagerly opening his mouth for the fruit. Then Lev petted him while he munched. "They love this fruit of paradise, although it does not have the same life enhancement for animals as it does for humans." The buck followed him back hoping for another piece.

Diocletian was amazed. Never had he seen a man pet a wild buck and then have it follow him like a lamb. He said, "You mean I would have an arm paralyzed for trying to shoot a deer?"

"I'm afraid so. We are here as the caretakers of the world now. We have extensive programs in effect for controlling animal populations so that there is not an imbalance in nature. We have found and restored protein grass that animals used to eat before they became carnivorous. Animals that used to eat flesh now much prefer protein grass. It is much healthier for them, and you will notice animals no longer fear one another because they have no predators. The carnivorous qualities are lost when they eat protein grass. Men and women used to be able to train wild animals to be gentle with humans, but now little children may pet lions and bears without any fear. You see, it is easier to train animals to be gentle than to train humans to love one another." Even Diocletian smiled at that last comment.

"If I didn't see you feed and pet this wild buck, I would not believe what you are telling me. This is indeed a different society. Now I am afraid that wild animals will stand up in judgment against me. Animals usually killed for food, but we killed people mercilessly, and now I wonder, for what purpose? They are all coming back to life and some are already back. How can I justify what I did?"

You Can't Justify Former Deeds

"You really can't, my friend. What you did was cruel and ruthless, and as you say, to no purpose. We needed some form of government in those years past, but we did not need wholesale murder."

"Are you going to be my judge, Lev? I thought you might have some encouragement for me. You don't seem to understand that I was, and still am, a pagan. I was a zealous pagan and defended what I thought was right."

"I understand, Diocletian, but the sooner you acknowledge that what you did was a tragic mistake, the sooner you will be on a course to healing and forgiveness. Christianity is the only religion in the world that provides that. But you cannot be forgiven if you insist on justifying yourself. Of course, you were a pagan—that was the religion of Rome. After you left office, Christianity became the religion of Rome. Should Christians have started killing and torturing the pagans? Human life is sacred, and God never intended for anyone to take human life unless it was known that they committed murder or some such sacrilege."

"It is easy to sermonize now in a righteous world. It was not that way in my time. I was charitable with Christianity at first, but soon an arrogance emerged. That is when my subordinates became outraged and argued that Christianity had to be destroyed. Now I understand it was a wasted effort, for soon Constantine embraced Christianity. Where we killed Christians, he embraced them and gave them powerful offices in government. Our efforts turned out to be futile."

The buck, realizing he was not getting more food, wandered off and soon a black bear emerged from the woods. Everyone became uneasy. Valeria asked, "Are you sure all animals are harmless now?"

"I will go and give him a piece of fruit," Lev volunteered.

"We have plenty, but please don't risk being mauled by that creature," Valeria nervously exclaimed. "We don't know how to fly that craft home, you know. That bear might decide you would make a better meal than the piece of fruit."

"Animals are not vicious anymore. Bring me a piece of fruit. Watch this," he said as he picked up the fruit and walked over to the bear.

He offered it the fruit, which the bear took in his mouth but then held in his two paws. First he smelled it deeply and then ate it very slowly to make the flavor last. When Lev petted him, he rolled over waiting to be scratched. Lev scratched his tummy and then returned.

Prisca looked on, first with a worried look and then with pleasure. "How marvelous! I never would have believed this if I hadn't seen it."

Lev came back to get another piece of fruit. The bear followed him eagerly hoping for another treat, but minding his manners, he did not plunge toward their rock table. Valeria was so thrilled that she boldly stepped up to the bear offering it more fruit. As he duplicated his previous performance, she petted him. Bears are curious, and this one started toward the aircraft. Lev pressed a control button and closed the doors before he could get in and make some mischief. Soon, the bear wandered off toward the woods nearby.

As they were about to board the craft, they heard a faint call for help coming from the woods. They straightened up and listened carefully to hear a small boy's voice, half-crying and half-calling for help. Diocletian and Lev both ran toward the woods. There was a little child, no more than five years old. When he saw them he asked, "Please, can you help me? I am lost. I don't know how to get home."

"They shall not hurt nor destroy in all my holy mountain"
(Isaiah 11:9).

Chapter Two

Moved by the child's helplessness, Diocletian said, "We'll take you home, son. Don't worry. Would you like some hot tea and some fruit?"

"Oh, yes! Mama and Papa must be looking for me. All the trees look the same. I followed an animal trail."

As they returned to the craft, the little boy clapped his hands with excitement. "Oh, I never saw a plane up close. I would like to have a ride in this!"

"Pour him some tea and give him some fruit. The boy is thirsty and hungry and lost," Diocletian directed.

Valeria quickly poured the boy some tea and gave him a piece of fruit with a napkin.

"Thank you," the child said politely. "I'm glad you found me."

Lev said, "When he finishes his snack, we will climb aboard and head toward the other end of the forest. I will fly low and hover at times. We need all the eyes we have to look out the windows. I am sure people are looking for the child. He can't be more than a mile or two away from home. We might see his house as we circle the area slowly. So, everyone, please look for people searching for him. By the way, son, what is your name?"

"My name is Christian, but Mama and Papa and all the other family call me Chris. My whole family was just returned to life again. Mama said a landslide made us die, but I don't remember it. I did have some dreams about rocks falling on me."

Diocletian said, "I just returned to life nearly a week ago, too, Chris."

Soon they came to a clearing in a peaceful valley dotted with homes. "This must be where you came from. Chris, do you recognize which house is yours?" Lev asked.

"I think it's the one by the little stream."

Lev said, "We'll land and find out." As they landed, they found no one at home. "Does this look like your house, Chris?"

"Yes. That is my red tricycle, and there is my little duck."

They all climbed out except Lev, who remained to turn on an emergency horn that made a loud intermittent sound. A woman emerged from the woods racing toward them. She spotted Chris and ran to embrace him.

"Thank you for finding our son. We have been looking for him for over an hour. The forest is not that large, but we didn't know which way he had gone. Our neighbors are still out there, as is his father. Maybe they'll hear the horn and come home."

Before long, one by one, everyone returned—relieved to find Chris safe. His father hugged him.

"Oh, Papa!" Chris exclaimed. "I got a ride home in an airplane! We went right over the treetops."

Chris' father stepped forward, holding his hand out to Lev. "My name is Alexander and this is my former wife, Irena. How can I thank you for finding our son?"

"My name is Lev, and this is Diocletian and Prisca, his former wife, and their daughter, Valeria. Let me turn off that horn so we can hear better." Lev entered the craft, and the sound stopped to everyone's relief.

Diocletian's First Encounter

Another gentleman who just returned from searching for Chris heard Lev's introduction and stiffened suddenly. He finally walked up to confront Diocletian. "Are you, by chance, the former emperor, Diocletian?"

The sound of his voice was very troubled, but Diocletian responded, "Yes, unfortunately, I am."

The man tried to hold back his anger. "You destroyed my family and me when your generals locked the doors to our church and set it on fire. Do you know what dying by fire is like? Can you understand what it is like to see your children and your wife burning? You don't deserve to live again. I am a Christian and cannot exercise violence, but I am telling you of the inner struggle I have in facing you. You are a monster, a sadistic human being, a child of the devil, and a man most to be pitied."

Diocletian was stunned into silence. As a former emperor, no one would have dared to speak to him in this manner. Here he was, standing face to face with a man he had destroyed by a whimsical command.

The royal splendor was gone, the court was silent and the day of reckoning had arrived most painfully. He was just one lowly human being facing his gruesome and bloody past. Diocletian had dreaded such a moment as this, but this type of encounter was inevitable. How many more of such episodes would he be forced to endure?

"Sir, if I knew the truth in the days of my pride and power, I would never have done such terrible things to others."

"How does this newfound remorse of yours assuage the pain my family and I endured in that burning, shuttered church?" The man raged on. "The terror and the screaming victims piling up at the doors and the agony of death by fire with no escape—how can you understand that? Your soldiers carried out orders. They were not responsible for this hideous crime. They were *your* orders."

Red-faced and shaken, Diocletian stared at the ground. "I stand condemned. You endured pain and loss in your previous life, but now before you is a glorious pathway toward life and eternity. I am fettered now with chains I forged in my previous life and there is no peace for me. What *can* I do? I tried to hang myself and was prevented from doing so by unseen powers that paralyzed my arms. All I can tell you is that I am sorry, but that will not remove the horror you and your family have endured at my hands."

At this point, Lev interrupted. "There is no reason for anyone to be unhappy. Life is what we all have, and we have it abundantly now. Please remember, Diocletian, that death will not bring you happiness. It brings you nothing but sleep in the cold and sullen grave forever. There is no love there, no warmth, no tenderness, no joy and no pleasure of any kind. Life offers all of these and more. You have the opportunity to triumph over your past and live down your horrible treatment of others. You can give yourself to others in warm and loving devotion. As you were once a scourge to others, you may become someone who sustains and nurtures life in others. You have such a choice."

Turning to Diocletian's accuser, "We have not been introduced, but please tell me your name."

"I am Romano Magio, just recently returned to life. My wife and children will join me very shortly. I am sorry to make this scene after you assisted in helping return Chris to his parents. I have these deep feelings in my heart, and they just came tumbling out."

"Well, you have every reason to carry these feelings in your heart," Lev sympathized. "You were unjustly and cruelly taken from this world by imperial command. But, please remember, the man who issued these commands has a terrible burden in his heart. He must show to one and all that he is not the same Diocletian he once was. Can he do it? Yes, certainly, and he can do it with great humility. But if he wants to and wills to do it, only he can answer."

Romano replied, "I can see that the emperor has dug a big hole for himself, and I am certainly glad I am not in his shoes. How does anyone face people he cruelly murdered? How can he make it right?"

Diocletian listened to Lev's answer, his heart churning with contradictory emotions. "In the first place, Christ has seen fit to give

Diocletian life, and the life that has been given is with the hope that he will use it to gain everlasting life. The same is true for each of us. Christ has provided forgiveness of sins that were due to human weakness. We each have things we would rather not remember. Unfortunately, many lived on a lower plane than they needed to. Diocletian had a capacity for kindness and generosity, but the very men he rewarded with high offices pulled him down. He was not an insane savage with an insatiable lust for blood. He was a capable statesman and certainly capable of better things. Why he allowed himself to be pulled down to such savagery, only he can explain."

"Please, don't ask me to explain it," the former emperor interjected. "I know I started my reign graciously, but a dark state of mind possessed me and I changed. There was no quenching of my desire to stamp out Christianity."

"We have to remember," Lev continued, "no one can change the past or exchange the horror and pain foisted upon others with warm and tender feelings. But Christ has brought us all back to life with a fresh sheet of paper upon which we may write the things we will. Neither our past virtues nor sins will determine whether we attain everlasting life, nor will present virtues or sins. It is only if we come into harmony with Christ, righteousness, and his perfect law of love that we will gain his commendation, 'Come, ye blessed of my Father, inherit the kingdom prepared for you from the foundation of the world.'"

"I am faced with a new reality, and I am not prepared to reject or accept it yet," Diocletian asserted. "All I know now is that I am not happy about what I did. I wasn't happy when I committed these murderous acts, and I am less than happy about it now. How much better it would have been to have stayed a soldier instead of becoming emperor!"

Romano seemed satisfied at this point. He could see Diocletian had, and would continue to bear, a heavy burden as his victims returned to life. The past could not be changed, and he had to find inward strength to extend love to his fellow men. Being an emperor or a soldier had not prepared him to become a loving and kind person. On the contrary, emperors were served and obeyed without hesitation. So this was a time of beginning again. Romano's contempt had now changed to pity.

Little Chris was ignored in this intense adult confrontation. Lev realized that the events of the day had been providential. A child was returned to his anxious parents leading into Diocletian's first encounter with one of his victims. A day that started out tranquilly had become very tense and painful.

Finally, it was time to leave. They said farewell, and Chris thanked Lev for the ride in the aircraft. As they boarded the aircraft, the only two who did not shake hands were Romano and Diocletian. However, this was their first encounter and Lev knew such strong feelings were not dissipated in a moment.

The plane lifted upward and then turned back toward Diocletian's home. Everyone was very pensive on the homeward journey, each preoccupied with his own thoughts. Lev played music to soothe their minds.

When they disembarked, Diocletian thanked Lev for the day. "Today's unique experiences lifted me out of earthbound thinking. I could not have imagined a day such as this in my former life. I was obsessed with controlling everything and everyone. Suddenly I find myself asking why I was like that."

A Pawn in the Devil's Hands

"Power blinds and corrupts, Diocletian. You are not the only person who rose to power only to suffer for it later," Lev assured him.

"I still don't understand why I was so driven to destroy Christians. I am not a person who finds pleasure in seeing others suffer. Looking at my past, you would think I reveled in seeing blood flow. Is it possible that dark spiritual forces possessed my mind?"

Diocletian paused for a moment to consider this possibility. "Almost as suddenly as I became obsessed with destroying Christianity, this passion ceased. Then I stepped down to prepare the way for a new emperor who would befriend Christianity and use it in Roman politics. It is as though I was a pawn in the devil's hands. When the devil decided it was time to join forces with the Christian church, he needed another emperor. Not that I believe this, but such thoughts have been flitting through my mind."

"The devil may very well have influenced you, but in order for him to control anyone's mind it is necessary for that person to first be *willing* for it to happen. Hence, that would not absolve the guilt involved," Lev asserted. "There is little doubt that the devil was very active in much of the evil that was executed. I am glad that you are aware that such dark forces were at work. One thing certain is that the gods you worshipped were of no help to you."

"You know that the Roman Empire was a nation of many gods and goddesses. I was considered the defender of the faith in most quarters."

Lev responded, "What has become of all the gods and goddesses you offered incense to? Where are they now, Diocletian? Who is king of earth? Who has raised you from death? You know the answer. Not one of those gods had life nor could they give you life. If the truth were told, they were the creation of evil spirits that have oppressed humanity ever since the flood. But they are all gone now, and I have heard no one crying for their return."

"I admit, I haven't heard of any of these gods and goddesses being around. Even if I did, I wouldn't seek them, because I understand now that we were ignorant worshipers. But in those days, I did believe in them. The world was very superstitious, and we believed these deities had to be placated. I guess I didn't understand how controlled our thinking was."

"Whether anyone understands it or not, this is a day when only truth is spoken and truth is heard. If anyone would try to introduce any of your former gods, his speech would be taken and not returned until he learned his lesson. That Christ is reigning over the earth today is the absolute truth. Also, some of the very faithful Christians that you murdered are living and reigning with Christ. Fortunately, they are not looking to return evil for evil," Lev affirmed.

Diocletian recognized the sadness of his situation. Even he had been able to note differences among the Christians of his day. Some actually demonstrated a selfless, humble life, while others had been more self-righteous than right!

Prisca interjected, "It is time to have supper. We have had a thrilling day together for which we thank Lev. Now, please join us around the table that the Lord has provided. When I contrast how we lived before and the way we live today, how can anyone not believe that Christ is reigning over the earth? Surely the Prince of Peace is ruling."

As everyone seated themselves, Valeria continued her mother's refrain. "We have never had it so good, and I say this having been an emperor's daughter. We had servants and beautiful things, but in our home we used slaves extensively. Our comfort depended on the misery of others. We were not happy and neither were our slaves and servants. *Pater*, you have to admit we are living on a higher plane than anyone ever thought possible."

Prisca asked Lev to thank the Lord for the supper meal.

Lev turned to Diocletian, "We feel the need to thank the Lord for these blessings, so please excuse us. If you object to hearing this prayer, then we can pray privately."

"Please pray, Lev. I will not be offended." Diocletian continued to contemplate all he was learning.

After the prayer, the subject turned to the events of the day and the beauties of the trip. Valeria said, "I can't believe that Lev could feed that wild buck. Even the animal world is different now."

Diocletian added, "Today I flew around in something better than a magic carpet, with heavenly music playing and in undreamed-of comfort. Traveling before was arduous work. We rode on horses or bumpy chariots to cover a few miles. We had to prepare meals en route and find or carry water. I cannot adequately compare life as it is now with the past. I know that someone very wise and powerful is in charge of such changes. I will certainly not resist such awesome power."

Lessons in History Close the Time Gap

"Would you like to learn about what happened between now and when you last lived?" Lev suggested. "This evening, we can watch programs that will give you a view of earth's affairs up until Christ took control of the earth. You will see continuous wars, rampant disease, and never-ending poverty during the reign of evil."

"Yes, Lev, that is precisely what I need to learn. I feel that something is missing. It is unnerving to awaken to find everything different without an understanding as to why things have changed. Then you hear someone tell you 'you have been raised from the dead!' I think learning what happened all those centuries would help bring continuity to things."

When they finished their meal, Lev set up the television with history programs. He invited everyone to spend the evening learning what conditions prevailed on earth while they slept in the grave. "Perhaps you will be glad you were in the grave when you see all the terrible things that happened on earth. You will see how men used the modern advances to kill one another and how terrible wars became. With a sword, you could only kill one person at a time. With an atomic bomb, one hundred thousand people are killed at once. You will see the last great battle on earth called the battle of Armageddon. That is when I died."

As the programs began, Diocletian and his two family members became completely absorbed. Lev said, "If you will excuse me, I'll take a little walk. I need some exercise and it is such a beautiful evening. I will return in a few hours and answer any questions you may have."

Lev headed out hoping to do some meditating as he walked. He couldn't help reflect on the burden Diocletian carried. Unjustly taking human life was not something that would pass lightly. Every individual was created in God's image and God never intended earth to be a human slaughterhouse. Yet, in the course of history, men had killed and destroyed anyone standing in the way of the ends they wished to attain. People were so different. Some labored and sacrificed to help their fellow men, whereas others abused people to attain selfish goals. Now the differences were glaring. Some returned to life with joy and gladness. Others brought memories of evil that would not quickly dissolve.

*"I have spread out my hands
all the day unto a rebellious people,
Which walketh in a way that was not good,
after their own thoughts"
(Isaiah 65:2).*

Chapter Three

Lev returned from his walk to find that Prisca and Valeria had left for the evening. Diocletian was in his study learning all he could about how the world evolved after his time. When he heard Lev return, Diocletian called out to him.

"I can hardly believe how deadly wars had become, Lev. When I saw the atomic bomb explode, I realized that if this madness continued, all flesh would be destroyed. If I didn't see the scenes from those awful explosions, I would never have believed it. One man pulled the bomb release from the *Enola Gay*, and the whole population of Hiroshima was almost vaporized."

"What you saw was true and awful. Did you learn anything from watching this, Diocletian?"

"Absolutely! I learned that sooner or later the use of force becomes self-destructive."

"True. Yet, when one man kills another with a sword, or by whatever means, is it any different than one man dropping a nuclear bomb on a city and killing tens of thousands of people in a flash of fire?"

"Well, I see one difference. In war, men fight in combat. That is what war is all about. The bomb released from the *Enola Gay* killed a whole city of people who were going about life as usual."

"Yes, but even though thousands died, it did end the war. You will note that no one was taken as a slave. As a matter of fact, the victors even helped the vanquished rebuild after the war and gave them most generous terms in making peace. Would the Roman emperor have been so generous with the vanquished?"

"That's an unfair question, Lev."

"Why is it unfair?"

"We lived by the standards of the world in our time and place. We allowed the vanquished to live and serve us as slaves. Slaves did not come with packaged rights."

"I guess you should know that—your parents were slaves, weren't they?"

"Yes. That is what drove me throughout my life, Lev. I wanted to break out of slavery, and I did. I joined the army, and because I was strong and agile I became an excellent soldier. Normally, you don't become emperor unless you are an emperor's son. For me, it required some very special circumstances. I was alert and ready at each opportunity, but once I gained momentum, I was unstoppable. Lev, you don't become emperor by being considerate of others."

"So, you succeeded in getting to the top of the heap. Then what, Diocletian? Did you have to keep destroying people's lives?"

"Well, Lev, I didn't start each day saying to myself, 'I am going to hurt or destroy this person or that one.' Most of the time all I wanted was to have my will carried out. There was always someone testing the limits of authority and power. Authority had to be visible to the world. That is what people respected the most—power."

Lev Reminds Diocletian — Meanness Is Out

"Diocletian, you were capable of better things, and you demonstrated that on occasions in your life. Now you are called upon to be kind, generous and loving. If you want to live and enjoy life, you are going to have to change into a godly human being, one who loves people, willingly making sacrifices for others."

"Excuse me! You're speaking down to me, Lev, and I don't like it!"

"I am sorry that my words seem so harsh, Diocletian, but you must start being a kind and loving person." Lev moved to sit next to Diocletian and put a brotherly arm around his shoulder. "You said you were motivated by wanting to distance yourself from slavery. You succeeded, but you became a slave to sin. Your master was the devil, and you served him well."

Diocletian shrugged indignantly.

"I don't have to take your insults, Lev! I have my dignity and honor, and you are not going to tell me what I must do. I don't have to do anything! I am free to say 'yes' or 'no' to the powers that be. They can do what I did to those that said 'no' to me. They can kill me if they wish—I'm not afraid to die. I am, after all, a soldier. I have faced death in battle. I didn't tremble before the enemy. I fought like a man and prevailed." Diocletian's old personality glared out from his eyes.

Diocletian's Insolence Is Punished

Lev spoke quietly. "Well, I am surprised that you still have your voice. You are being very insolent, and that is usually punished."

Diocletian tried to speak, but his voice was lost and he turned pale. He motioned with his hands that his voice had been silenced.

"You know what you have to do to regain your voice, don't you?" The frustrated man nodded "yes." Standing up, he turned toward his bedroom, slamming the door behind him. Lev could see he was facing a very strong-willed person. Unfortunately, Diocletian's former success and power were counterproductive to his best interests now.

Lev spent a long evening in the study of God's Word and prayer, trying to see how he might be the most helpful in this situation. He had dealt with enough people to understand human nature and pride. He realized that being emperor in one world and now only a man like others was very difficult for Diocletian to accept. Going up the ladder of success was a lot easier than sitting down at the bottom. Yet the bottom was where the most valuable lessons were to be learned.

The next morning Lev rose early to attend the chapel meeting. He found Diocletian sitting at the breakfast table. Lev could see he was in a depressed mood. Lev told him that he was going to a chapel meeting and would be back in a short while. With that he said, "Shalom," and left.

Lev used the aircraft because the meeting was several miles away. He knew that Prisca and Valeria could contact the Ancients, but they would be disappointed that Diocletian had gotten himself into trouble again.

Arriving at the chapel, Lev found it well attended. When his aircraft landed, it attracted attention, because such aircraft were still scarce in populated countries having many roads. The undeveloped countries received most of these crafts because they eliminated the need for a heavy network of roads. Not only was this ecologically desirable, but it was also the most economical.

Lev was greeted by one of the chapel members. "My name is Joseph. Welcome to our gathering. The services will be starting in a few minutes."

"Thank you. My name is Lev Aron, and I am visiting the area and in need of some spiritual food."

After the services, Lev met many people. When he mentioned his name, a few people recognized it and were excited to meet him. Though no one knew the purpose of his visit, they sensed it was more than just pleasure. Lev did nothing to satisfy their curiosity, but rather he spent time fellowshipping about the topic the chaplain had covered. He kept it short though, because he wanted to get back to talk with Prisca and Valeria. He knew Diocletian could stubbornly refuse to seek assistance to recover his voice.

Prisca and Valeria were very upset, as Lev had anticipated. "He'll be all right. All you have to do is call the Ancients and tell them exactly what happened. Chances are they will have him healed soon."

Prisca frantically replied, "You didn't know this, but he already had both arms paralyzed when he tried to hang himself. Now, he apparently misbehaved and lost his voice. Did he become insolent with you, Lev?"

"Well, yes, he did lose his temper. I was very direct with him. However, everyone is going to have to learn civility and righteousness. I am sorry to hear that he tried to hang himself. That is very rare. Most people with problems enjoy life enough not to be eager to end it. He seemed quite happy during the day on our fly-around, but our discussion turned in another direction in the evening, and that distressed him. Is he still brooding in his room?"

"He was at the kitchen table when we arrived. When he didn't speak to greet us, we sensed he was in trouble. When we tried to get him to talk, he went sulking into his room. He seems very discouraged."

"I'm sure he is. All the things that brought him success before won't work anymore. That would be discouraging. He is going to have to work very hard at adjusting his attitude. Still, he can be very determined, and that can be an asset when used in the right way.

"I have to visit a factory for awhile now. You will probably be able to persuade him to call the Ancients. He can write out what happened, and you may read it for him. That is all you have to do, and I think he will be well again."

Diocletian Learns about True Power

Lev returned in time for lunch and was glad to see Diocletian out of his bedroom, looking dismayed and still unable to speak. He obviously wanted to talk, but without asking to have his voice restored. Lev finally said to him, "Would you like me to contact the Ancients and see if someone there will restore your voice? You are suffering needlessly."

Diocletian sat passively for a while. Finally, he wrote on a piece of paper, "You call and tell them what happened. Let's call from my bedroom. I don't want Prisca and Valeria to hear."

Diocletian motioned Lev toward his bedroom and Lev followed him. Diocletian then shut the door and Lev phoned on his behalf. They used two phones so he could listen. Soon they were speaking with Abel.

"Shalom. How may I help you?"

Lev explained he was speaking on behalf of Diocletian who had lost his voice the previous night. Lev said, "Maybe I was partly to blame for being rather direct with him. However, he became exasperated and lost his voice. My name is Lev Aron, and as you know, I have been sent here to assist Diocletian." Lev then explained some of the main points of their discussion.

Abel then asked, "Is this true, Diocletian? Tap once if it is true and twice if it is not."

Diocletian tapped once. "Very well. This is your second offense. You must take better control of yourself, but because you were under a lot of distress, your voice will be restored within the hour. Shalom."

The previous emperor now learned a little about true power. Never had *he* been able to be fully aware of what was taking place everywhere and then administer appropriate and immediate punishment. Twice he found spiritual forces intervened when he overstepped himself. Diocletian was like a chastened child realizing that he was being held accountable for his actions. His former position and power meant nothing anymore. He must conduct himself properly or accept punishment. On the other hand, the punishments were very mild and measured to correct, but not injure or discourage. He also realized that Lev's remarks to him prior to his outburst were valid, and he should have heeded them instead of becoming belligerent.

Lev opened the door and returned to be with Prisca and Valeria. He said, "Diocletian will be made well within the hour, so very soon you will be hearing from him again. The Lord is merciful and gracious, and all His chastisements are calculated to make proper corrections as needed. By the way, have you been to the chapel meetings? Perhaps tomorrow you would like to join me?"

Valeria said, "I have been meaning to go. I guess I was just timid about going to a new place. I know I seem very outgoing, but meeting new people has always been hard for me."

"After you go a few times, you will feel comfortable with them. You will find Christians who are eager to praise the Lord and learn His Word. Isn't that what you want to do?"

"Yes, certainly. I never believed much in all the deities we had in the Roman catalog of gods. There was no love or warmth in any of them. It seemed these gods were always upset about something and acted like spoiled children—just like the men who invented them. When Christians told me about the God of love who sent His Son to suffer and die for us, I was drawn to Him immediately."

"If you and your mother wish to come with me tomorrow, that would make me very happy!"

Diocletian Apologizes

At that moment Diocletian regained his voice saying, "I have my voice again! I am sorry, Lev, that I was so nasty. Emperors did not have to control their tempers, only other people around them. I have been thoroughly chastised and I apologize."

Lev was surprised and delighted that Diocletian's first response was words of remorse. "Your apology is accepted, Diocletian. I fear I might have been too direct with you. Sometimes when we know the truth, we feel obligated to stress it. It used to be that by making things fuzzy, one could justify things that were not right. Well, that doesn't work anymore. Anyway, I just invited your wife and daughter to go to the chapel with me tomorrow. You wouldn't want to join us, would you?"

"Please, Lev, I still need to get oriented to my new life. I'm afraid I don't know my right hand from my left, and I'm not ready to make decisions regarding any religion. I am certainly aware of who is in power—that's one thing I learned and respect. Maybe I'll be ready to come with you someday, but not tomorrow. Thank you anyway."

"By the way, Diocletian, I have news for you. The two men you appointed rulers, Galerius and Maximian, who were better murderers than rulers, are coming back within a few days. I hope you will not let them lead you around by the nose again. They were a terrible influence before, and they need a lot of good examples around them to show them the right way to live."

Diocletian's eyes suddenly brightened. "Really, are they coming back to life? That is so hard to believe! I am just getting used to the idea of my return to life, and now you mention the return of men that served me well in the Roman Empire. I know they had a hatred of Christians, but otherwise they were decent men. Perhaps I can help them get oriented."

"They will have others to lend a hand. Possibly the Ancients will send counselors like me to help them adjust to a righteous world. They will need strong guidance to clear their heads from all of the ignorance and superstition that controlled them before."

"Lev, I am sorry to differ with you. You come on too strong. For men who have been rulers, it's not easy to take your attacks. I think I could be more understanding of the changes that they must make."

"Maybe that was your trouble in the first place—you were too understanding with these cutthroats. You know you had the power to rein them in, but you lost control. You unleashed two mad dogs against Christians. Not only did it hurt the Christians, but it also hurt Galerius and Maximian. The only difference is that the Christians' hurting is past, but theirs is about to begin. They will carry a heavy burden. You didn't help them in the right way before. What makes you think you can help them now?"

"Lev, you know how to corner me even before I start. Why do you have to rub it in?"

"I am trying to be helpful, even though you may not appreciate that. However, Diocletian, you must remember that these two men influenced you in savage ways against Christians. Doesn't it seem like senseless folly now?"

"You're judging my actions by hindsight, Lev. Why didn't those Christians tell me about everyone returning to life? I wouldn't have believed it, of course, but at least they would have told me the truth."

Lev continued, "I didn't tell you about Galerius and Maximian for you to rush over to see them when they return. You will have time enough to meet them. Meanwhile, would you like to visit a factory to see how things are made and how this world operates?"

Visiting a Factory

Prisca said, "Does that invitation include Valeria and me?"

"Of course it does. One day soon you will probably be donating time there helping to produce things we need. You will have to study a great deal to catch up, but soon you will be able to handle things. When you are ready, we will leave."

Soon they lifted off. This was thrilling even to Lev and much more to those who had no idea how it worked. Flying was so majestic! Man had always envied birds, and now they could fly in great comfort and speed. Travel time had been reduced to only hours, whereas before it had taken nearly a year to encircle the earth.

Within minutes Lev set the craft down on a pad outside a large factory building. Lev explained, "Here is where computers and screens for visual display are made. This is the key to accessing the information that is growing by leaps and bounds. In your era, most people could neither read nor write. Now everybody knows or will know how to do so very quickly. Once they learn, information can be exchanged endlessly. Every day you will be learning—the process will never end. The more you learn, the greater will be your desire and the more there will be to learn. God has created a very complex world. The greatest knowledge of all will be in trying to understand our God, who embodies all wisdom and knowledge. The more we examine small things, the more complicated we find them to be. The more we examine the heavens, the more profound and fathomless they become. The God of the universe is not a god of stone that knows nothing and is lifeless. He is a God that knows everything and by whom all living things exist."

When they entered the impressive building, a lady who worked there greeted them. "Shalom. May I show you around or help you in any way?"

"Yes, you certainly may. My name is Lev Aron, and this is Diocletian, Prisca, his former wife, and their daughter, Valeria. I brought them here to show them how things work in our society and would appreciate it if someone would give them a tour of your facility."

"Are you the Lev Aron we have heard so much about?"

"Well, yes, that is my name. I have been around longer than most people in this regeneration process. While someone takes my guests around, I would like to speak with those in your research department. My brother Jacob Aron has some advanced designs coming down the line, and I would like to prepare your people for the changes."

"Yes, who doesn't know Jacob Aron in the computer world and in so many other scientific fields? He was the person that figured out how to make antimatter, and I believe you built the first factory to make it. Oh my! If we knew you were coming, we would have made arrangements to give you a royal welcome. Pardon me, I'll make some calls to alert our staff that you are here."

Suddenly, Diocletian and his family realized that Lev was someone of importance and accomplishment.

Diocletian said, "I knew you were somehow connected with this world, Lev, but I didn't know that you were held in such high esteem."

"If you had been around as long as I have in this new way of doing things, people might remember you in a different way than history records. You have plenty of time to learn, Diocletian. If your heart keeps ahead of your brain, you will be amazed how people will remember the good you contribute to this world."

Soon they saw a group of people hurrying down the hall to greet them. "Shalom, Lev! Why didn't you tell us you were coming? This is such an honor for us. My name is Sylvester Magar, and this is Patricia Dasenka, who is volunteering to help us get some new processes in motion. This is Frank Kolett, who is a great brain resource here."

Introductions were made and Lev continued. "These friends of mine have recently returned to life, and I would like someone to show them how things are done. Meanwhile, I'll be in the area and may have some spare time to spend with you regarding the upcoming new advances. Before I left Israel, I spent several weeks at the laboratory. My brother Jacob asked me to prepare you for what is coming. As a matter of fact, he said the blueprints and working models are being sent to you this week. So, let me find out what equipment you have, and maybe I can help expedite things."

Everyone was so eager to learn what Lev was going to show them that they almost forgot about his guests. He reminded their hosts that he wished to have the family taken on a tour, and they could all meet back for lunch.

When the day was spent and they were ready to return home, everyone was excited. For Diocletian and his family, some of the mystery surrounding modern technology was unveiled. While they understood little of what they had seen, they realized that these modern tools were man-conceived and man-made. They recognized that the human mind had been unleashed from the darkness of the past and that with thought and discipline, great achievements were possible. Even though this was but one corner of science, suddenly they appreciated the potential of the unfettered mind.

Fortunately, this day had been without confrontation. While many probably knew the name "Diocletian" was an odious name in history, no one realized that the "Emperor Diocletian" was standing next to them in regular clothing. This was a relief for Lev, too. He knew the day of reconciliation for the former emperor would come, and he was pleased that it was forestalled so the poor man could have more time to reconcile his own confusion.

As they flew home the music played softly, and everyone seemed to be deep in thought. Diocletian thanked Lev for taking him to see the factory. He realized he was getting an education in modern science that was beyond his fondest dreams.

"Lev, it kind of takes my breath away to see a world operating with superb intelligence. The day of raw power and savage confrontation has ended, and men must live by different standards."

"You are right! I'm so glad you've caught the vision of how things get done today, Diocletian. We exercise our brains more than our muscles. The results are glorious. However, until we had a righteous government, this same science was used to destroy men and nations. The world was on the verge of destroying itself! When the Christian religion ascended to ruling authority in the earth, Christian leaders punished kings and nations who would not convert to their religious rule the same way you had persecuted them. Other religions were afflicted with the same evil propensities. Men used religion, politics, schooling systems, armies and navies, all bent on controlling others before they had learned to control themselves."

"What you are telling me is that science without discipline of righteousness became self-destructive. Is that right?"

"Exactly! Today, righteousness and character must precede everything else. All power in heaven and earth are invested in Christ, and he, in turn, employs those who lived by the same standards that he lived by. That is what makes our world so different. We still have a residue of sin left in the human race, and more of it comes back with people returning from the grave every day. However, those at the top are absolutely pure and righteous. When the wicked ruled and were empowered, the people mourned. When the righteous are in power, the people rejoice. That is why there are so many rejoicing today."

Diocletian was not prepared for Lev's dissertation. Not that he could find fault with it, but it sounded too lily-white to be believable. He voiced his doubts saying he had only obliged those who wanted to be martyred.

"Well," Lev went on, "There were some obsessed with the idea of becoming martyrs, but most people were not of that temperament. I'm afraid when you look into the eyes of your victims, your explanations will sound pretty hollow."

"What do you propose I do? I tried to kill myself and was prevented from doing so."

"God has no pleasure in the death of anyone. However, you were given your life. Only this time, you are required to learn righteousness.

It is going to take a lot of courage to face those you destroyed, and it will require humility to ask for their forgiveness. It is going to take love in your heart to demonstrate that you have become a kind human being and not the monster you once were."

About this time they were landing. As they disembarked, Prisca thanked Lev and said, "Rest awhile and we will have some hot tea and a delightful evening meal."

After supper, both Prisca and Valeria left for their respective homes.

Owning Up to Former Actions

"Now you see that God's ways are equal, Diocletian. You were free to do anything you wanted to without paying the penalty immediately for what you did. The truth of the matter is that every sin and trespass must be brought into account. The good side to this is that owning up to your sins and living them down provides a tremendous opportunity to build character."

"I'm not interested in building character," Diocletian retorted stubbornly. "I just wish I could make all my past stay in the grave with me. At least, though, I believed that death would close everything down. There were not going to be any more chapters to my life. We all vaguely believed in some kind of afterlife. But this was a way to deny the power that death had over us. I saw a lot of dead men in my lifetime. Most of them were young and powerful soldiers killed on the battlefield. We had to tell those men left behind that their comrades had gone somewhere better, Lev."

"I know that, Diocletian. I was a soldier and I died fighting. It takes a certain type of bravery to face death. Men could be trained to be good soldiers in a short while and didn't require much in the way of a good character. In fact, the meaner they were, the more willing they were to take other men down in battle. Many men who had soft hearts died in battle because they couldn't thrust their opponent through."

"I wouldn't know about that kind of heart. Now that you mention it, you are probably right. I saw men hesitate to deal the deathblow. I thought they were too tired or too slow. It never occurred to me that they did not have the heart of a killer. Perhaps I lost my ability to show compassion. Killing became my path to power. I just dismissed those I killed as victims of war. That was all there was to it."

"You will be given a long period of time to overcome your unwillingness to change, but you must meet all your victims sooner or later. As hard as it may be to believe it, the truth is, if you will to be reconciled with those you injured, it will be possible to do so. The rewards for changing your mind are tremendous. All the glory of the Roman Empire does not compare with gaining everlasting life."

Almost as if he hadn't heard a word Lev said, Diocletian asked, "By the way, Lev, when did you say Galerius and Maximian will be returning? Maybe misery likes company, but I am looking forward to meeting them."

"Your partners really did not understand you. If my memory serves me correctly, Galerius is coming back early next week, I believe on Monday. Maximian is coming back in two weeks. I don't think that you should consort with them, but you are free to do what you will. They were a bad influence on you before, and sleeping in the grave has not changed them."

"I'm not worried about their influence on me. You know I was the emperor and they ruled by my permission. If anything, maybe I will be a good influence on them. At least I know that what we did was wrong. That is going to be hard for them to accept. I may be able to convince them of this."

"You are your own man, Diocletian, but it has been my experience that people who return from the grave with an enormous amount of blood on their hands make the best progress when keeping away from their former cohorts."

"Please, do not worry about me, Lev. I know what I am doing."

"I am here only to help you get on the right path for healing and reconciliation. Anyway, I am returning to my own studies now. Have a good night."

*"Who both will bring to light the hidden things of darkness,
And will make manifest the counsels of the heart"
(1 Corinthians 4:5).*

Chapter Four

The next morning Lev rose early, happy that Prisca and Valeria were coming with him to the chapel service. After a drink of fruit juice, they climbed into the aircraft, lifted off, and soon landed on one of the chapel pads. They were early, and this gave Lev the opportunity of meeting other worshipers and introducing Prisca and Valeria.

After they returned from the chapel, Lev suggested another factory visit. "Why don't we visit a different factory not far from here? By the way, Diocletian, you'd better be studying how to build houses, because you will have the privilege of building your father's home. He is scheduled to come back to life in about three months. They planted the trees last year and soon they will dig to lay the foundation. Have you done any building before?"

"Only a little bit, helping my father when I was a boy. Yes, I will do everything possible to receive my father back to life. He was a good man. He may not be too happy with me though, when he learns about how many people I killed. He had many opportunities to run away and probably would have not been caught, but he wanted to be with my mother and me. He did not deserve to be a slave. I guess no one deserves that kind of treatment."

"I will show you the programs you need to watch." Lev soon tuned in a program that showed how a home similar to the one Diocletian lived in was built.

"That's great! I will be watching that program every waking moment."

"Let's climb aboard my aircraft, and we will visit a factory that builds the components for our homes. Actually, much of the work is done in the factory, and it is amazing how well they build these components and how easily a house is made. If you have enough help, you can have your father's house ready for his return in less than a month. You know, every three months we have another generation returning to life."

Lev was glad to see Diocletian with a positive attitude in this area, at least. Apparently he loved his father and mother. Their owner was a decent fellow and treated them well by a slave's standards. He allowed them to marry and never sold them.

Soon they arrived at a sizeable factory. Large aircraft would lift the various parts of a house, placing them in a container and taking them to the site to be assembled. Diocletian was amazed to see one such aircraft lift a house and carry it away, as a giant bird with prey in its claws. When they entered the factory, no one seemed to notice them. Everyone was busy, but finally someone stopped to ask if he could help.

"Yes, I am Lev Aron, and I have three guests that wish to see your operation."

"Well, several people are missing today so we are shorthanded. They are receiving their family members to life, so we don't have people to spare to give you a guided tour. If you wish, you are welcome to walk around and observe on your own."

"Thank you! We will do that."

Watching Homes Being Fabricated

"By the way, sir, are you the Lev Aron that we have heard so much about?"

"Yes, you may have heard of me. I returned to life ahead of most people, so I have had many experiences since I was made alive again."

They spent the morning watching the automated equipment at work, flawlessly turning out precision-made walls with the electrical and plumbing elements contained perfectly within them. Within a couple of hours, they had seen the whole process and were amazed how machines did most of the work without human hands.

They left quietly before lunchtime. Diocletian was almost speechless. Finally he said, "I can't believe my eyes! Those houses were being put together like magic! No sweat or heavy labor. Nothing like the slave pits where men used to work from dawn until dark cutting stone or mining salt. I see what human intelligence has accomplished, and I am very impressed. I couldn't understand the computers, but I could appreciate the houses, because all the features in my house were being made right before my eyes—amazing beyond words!"

After they returned home, Prisca and Valeria left and Diocletian slipped away to his study.

When Lev invited him to go to the chapel with him the following day, Diocletian said he would rather spend the day studying. He said he needed time to be alone.

"Very well, then, I'll go by myself. My time here is running out."

When Diocletian heard that, he said, "I don't want to sound ungrateful, Lev. I learned a lot from you about the way this world runs. However, I'm sure there must be other people who need your help. Don't hold back on my account. Before you leave for the morning, though, please show me how to use what you call the telephone. That seems so wonderful to be able to talk to anyone you want by pressing a few buttons."

"That is very easy. All you need to do is to use your computer to find the names of people, and it gives you their number. Of course, you have to select the country and the area you want first, and then follow the names in alphabetical order. Here, let me call this up on your screen. Say you want to call Prisca. You select the country, like so, and then the area. There is her name and number. That's all there is to it."

"Well, that is certainly clever. I should have no problem using it. Thank you. You can be very helpful at times."

"And annoying at others, right?"

"I didn't say that. You do know how to lecture me, I must admit. I suppose I need a lot of correction. You're a decent fellow, though."

Just then the phone rang. Lev answered it saying, "Shalom."

A Phone Call from a Victim

"Is this the home of Diocletian, the former emperor?"

"Yes. Who may I say is calling?"

"He may not remember my name. Just tell him someone from the past has come to life again and wishes to speak to him."

Diocletian was eager to try out the phone, so he quickly picked it up. "What is it you wish to speak to me about?"

"I am a man who died in a church when you ordered all the entrances and exits closed and then had it set afire. My wife and I and my three children perished in the blaze."

Diocletian was stunned. He didn't know how to answer the caller. The inevitable was happening. He could hang up, but that wouldn't fix anything.

"I'm sorry. I don't know what to say. I have someone here that might be able to help you better than I. Hold on a minute and I will put him on."

With trembling hands he turned the phone over to Lev. "Here — you handle this. I don't know what to tell this man."

"Shalom. This is Lev Aron. Diocletian needs to think this matter through. Perhaps I can help. Are you by chance one of his victims?"

"Yes, my former wife, my three children and I all died in a locked church that he ordered burned. I have been alive now for a few days, and I saw Diocletian's name on the list of those already returned to life. He owes me some explanation, don't you think?"

"Certainly he does. Right at the moment, though, he's not prepared to answer. He has been dreading these confrontations, but he has not matured enough to deal with them yet. I can tell you one thing, though. If he knew everyone was returning to life, he would never have done what he did."

"That's like telling me that if a murderer knew he would be caught, he wouldn't have committed the murder."

"Well, you're right about that. You need to know that Diocletian didn't start out to destroy Christians. He tended to be tolerant in the early years of his power. It might help you to remember the Roman Empire was pagan, and there was persecution at various stages against Christians simply because they didn't conform to paganism. I know that doesn't justify what happened during those ten years of unprecedented violence against Christianity."

"Well, that's what I want this murderer to address. He will never know the horror of being burned to death and watching his own flesh and blood die in unimaginable agony. Is he some inhuman monster without conscience or feelings?" Lev could hear the quivering emotion in the man's voice.

"Give me your name. I have your number here. I'll write it down for him and ask him to call you back. He should have something to say to you."

"My name is Peter Francesco."

Lev took the man's name and number and said he would try to get Diocletian to return his call.

"You have every justification for being distraught with the one responsible for the horrible death of your family. For your own sake, though, I will pray that you find forgiveness in your heart as soon as he is ready to ask for it. Shalom."

When Lev hung up the telephone, Diocletian asked, "Why did you have to tell him that?"

"You forget, this man is a Christian. He is not calling for vengeance. He is calling for an explanation and, even more importantly, a sincere and heartfelt apology. He has a heart full of pain and sorrow and hopes to make some sense out of what happened to him and his family, added to the confusion of waking here on earth. You should be thinking of how you can address his heartache and the pain of the countless thousands that will be looking for answers from you."

"I *have* no answer. I wish I did! If there were some magical way I could relieve their pain, I would be glad to do so. How am I going to face so many victims? If they had gone to heaven as they said they would, I wouldn't have to face them now. You tell me, Lev, that some of them did have a spiritual resurrection."

Lev nodded.

"Well, I'm glad for that. I won't have to explain anything to them."

"You're missing the point, Diocletian. No one can justify wanton destruction of human life. If you imagine you'll find some reasonable explanation, you will never find it."

Worldly Sorrow and Godly Sorrow

"There are two kinds of sorrow. First, there is worldly sorrow that brings death. I think you have such sorrow now. That is why you often wish you were dead and didn't have to face your victims. The other is godly sorrow that brings repentance and a renewed heart that wishes to live down an evil past. That is what Peter Francesco is looking for. All your victims will be looking for godly sorrow on your part. No other answer will heal their pain."

"I am afraid, then, that I only have worldly sorrow and not even a good worldly sorrow. I think my pain is because I have been caught," Diocletian responded with ironic honesty.

"You will have plenty of time to change that. Once you stop thinking about yourself and start thinking about others, you will be surprised at how quickly your heart will change. Here, I have written down the name and number of the man waiting to hear from you."

It was getting late, so Diocletian returned to his studies, and Lev retired to his room to review the day and pray.

Godly Sorrow

The next morning Lev left early for the chapel since Diocletian was not yet stirring. By the time Prisca arrived, she saw Diocletian sitting in the garden. She made herself a cup of tea and went out to sit with him. Diocletian looked up at her with tears in his eyes.

"I had a rough night, Prisca. I couldn't sleep. I realize that I have been on the wrong side all along. Now I have to face all these people I murdered. What can I tell them? How can I fix this? How can I ask for forgiveness? When I tried to take my life, I wanted a way of escape from the mess I had made of my life. Now I know there is no escape. I must somehow find the courage to say, 'I am sorry. I was wrong.' What can I do to make it right?"

Prisca, though still new to the regeneration herself, had years of forbearance from her former life from which to draw. She couldn't help but respond with a degree of compassion to the crushed sound in his voice.

"Well, I am glad you are beginning to see what must be done. You have to make the name 'Diocletian' cease being a name of terror and instead be one of a repentant, trying to do what he can now to make things right. I have always been distressed knowing that you killed so many Christians. You know how I tried to discourage you from such bitter persecution, but you were drunk with power and would not listen. At least now perhaps your head is clearing, and you realize you have to make a tremendous effort to be reconciled to those you injured."

"I realize that there would be no point in Christ restoring me to life if my former life was the only basis for my judgment. I have been given a clean slate to write the things I will. Will you help me write something better on it?"

"Gracious! Those are the most sincere words I have ever heard you say. If you mean them sincerely, I'm prepared to help you. The hurt you caused won't go away in a day, but if you are confessing the harm you caused, that is what is important."

"I *do* mean what I said. I realize I have been a fool. If I had only listened to you instead of Galerius and Maximian, I wouldn't be in such dire straits today. I don't know how I am ever going to be able to explain everything to all those Christians returning to life, but I have to try. I am going to begin by calling Peter Francesco."

Prisca kissed him on the forehead and gave him a hug before she left.

A Call for Reconciliation

Not wanting to delay, Diocletian pulled out the phone number Lev had written down for him. This was the most difficult thing he had ever had to do. He knew the day was past when imperial power could shelter him. He knew that nothing he could say would take away the pain and anguish others had experienced from being burned alive. Now it all seemed so useless. Why should he have cared if they worshipped Christ? He had been a pagan with thousands of gods and, in reality, worshipped none of them. How could he? How could anyone worship thousands of gods?

He dialed the strange tool called the telephone almost in disbelief that he could speak to Peter. On the third ring he heard, "Shalom. This is Peter Francesco."

"Shalom. This is Diocletian. I am calling to tell you how very sorry I am for the pain and loss I caused you that day I ordered the place burned down with everyone in it. It was too cruel to contemplate. Nothing I can say will take away your horrid memories of seeing your children and wife consumed in that awful fire. All I can say is, I am guilty. If my death would satisfy you as some kind of repayment, I am here to say I gladly offer myself in repayment."

"It is too easy just to say you are sorry. If you think repeating words lightly will bring peace to my heart, you are mistaken."

A Quiet Answer

"What can I do to satisfy your anger with me, Peter? Christ didn't allow me to take my life as some kind of repayment for my sins. I can't think of anything else to do but to say I now truly have godly sorrow in my heart. I can't even offer to be your slave, because slavery isn't permitted. If you wish me to work for you, I offer my services. Tell me, what can I do to bring peace between us?"

There was an unusually long pause. Peter was clearly taken back by what he was hearing and he had no reply. "I longed to confront you, and now here you are and I don't know what to say. I can't say, 'I will never forgive you.' I am a Christian; Christ has forgiven my sins. How can I refuse your request for forgiveness? Yet it sounds too glib, too easy for you to mouth these words. Did Mr. Aron teach you what to say?"

"No, Peter. I've been very hard on Lev Aron. I tried to dismiss most of what he said to me, but when a man speaks the truth, after awhile it starts to sink in."

"I cannot believe that a leopard like you could change your spots. This can't be the Diocletian I knew, a man without a heart and without a conscience."

"Yes, I am speaking to you and asking your forgiveness, if you find it in your heart to do so. If not, tell me what to do. If you were in my place, what would you do?"

Another long pause followed. Peter was now at a loss to know what to say. He didn't want to grant forgiveness, and he couldn't think what to suggest that would help him forgive. Finally, in total frustration he said, "I have to think about this. Can I call you back? I guess the last thing in the world I want to do is grant you forgiveness. Yet, how can I refuse?"

"Please call me back when you sort this out. If you think of something you want me to do to prove my sincerity, I will try to do it. I know it sounds ridiculous that a man like me, who wrought such pain and havoc to so many, should be forgiven. However, if Christ has forgiven me and has given me my life to live over again, what can I do but accept it? Shalom. Please call me again. I want to lay my sin against you and your family at the foot of his cross. I want your permission to do so."

The day had passed so quickly that Diocletian failed to have lunch. He had stepped out from his past, and for the first time he was trying to do what was right. He was trying to understand the events of the day when Lev returned.

The Best Day So Far

"So how did it go today, Diocletian?" Lev asked in his usual cheerful voice.

"I feel that I have been beaten up all over, but, in fact, this has been the best day since I returned to life."

"Did you call Peter, by chance?"

"How did you guess?"

"That would be a very hard thing to do and would indicate considerable victory on your part to even try. Tell me, how did it go?"

"I apologized, Lev, with godly sorrow. Did you hear what I said?"

Lev's grin almost split his face in two. "That is the best thing I have ever heard you say; tell me more."

"He was so stunned by my call, that he couldn't accept my apology, and yet he knew if I was sincere he would have to let go of his own anger. He didn't want to do that, but he said he had to think about it awhile and then call me back."

"Well, congratulations on your first victory over the old Diocletian!"

Lev wrapped his arms around the repentant man in a big bear hug. "That is the best news I have heard all day. I didn't think a word I said to you ever sank in. The Lord is to be praised. Let us have a celebration dinner."

"Yes, by all means. I didn't have lunch because of everything that happened today. It was like the house fell in on me, but I think it helped clear my head, Lev. I can no longer dismiss the pain and harm I caused. I am genuinely sorry, not that I have been caught, but that I did such evil things to people. It is still a nightmare to find myself in this position, but the only thing I can do is try to live as nobly as I can."

After dinner Lev said, "I was contacted by the Ancients, and they told me I shall be leaving you shortly. I will have a little time at home to be with some members of my family and wait for a new assignment."

"Lev, I can genuinely say I will be sorry to see you leave. I learned as much from the way you deal with people as from your firm clarity in pointing to the right way."

"Thank you. I must say, Diocletian, it gladdens my heart that you made a good turnaround. Fortunately, you will be dealing with people who were serious about Christianity, so they should be more generous and forgiving than others."

Diocletian laughed out loud from sheer joy and relief. "I am a vanquished emperor who decided to yield to the new King, who is more kind and generous than any ruler I have ever seen."

"You have made the right decision, Diocletian. You will never regret it. How about coming to the chapel meeting tomorrow and start learning how your new King suffered and died before ascending to the throne on high?"

"And I turned myself to behold wisdom, and madness"
(Ecclesiastes 2:12).

Chapter Five

When Lev met Rebekah at the airport, he was flushed with a feeling of finishing what appeared to be a very successful mission. He was grateful that the Lord had prospered his visit with Diocletian. Rebekah, too, was all aglow having completed her great challenge of turning the Sahara Desert into a flourishing habitation for millions of people returning to life.

Lev and Rebekah were the dearest of friends, so time spent together was very precious. They hugged one another delightedly, looking forward to sharing experiences and blessings. Having once been husband and wife, their bond was all the closer, because they had shared history from their former lives.

"Oh, Lev, I missed you so much! Every time I spoke to the Ancients I asked them when we would both be home again. And now, here we are at last!"

"I felt the same way, Rebekah. My assignment ended sooner than I thought it would, because the Lord overruled matters so that Diocletian stopped his belligerence and turned onto the right path. What a surprise! I thought I was getting nowhere, and then his whole attitude changed. I'm so glad to be home again!"

"Shall we go to my house first? I have a meal prepared for us. I have a few days before I start my visit with a distant relative. I have an aunt who is returning to life and needs someone to build her home and be with her. There were other volunteers, but I wanted to be with Isha Obadiah for a very special reason."

"What is it, may I ask?"

"Well, it was a hidden secret in our family that Isha was mentally ill. They treated people rather cruelly back then because they had no means to help those with mental problems other than to confine them to some attic room. I understand she was not violent but totally irrational, so they could not let her out in the community. I want to share her experiences through those awful years. What was it like not being able to function normally and to be locked up? It seems if one was not mad to begin with, that treatment would drive you insane. Anyway, I have two days before I have to start building her home."

"May I help you? I'd like very much to learn about Isha. That would be a new chapter for me, and I really would like to understand her past life to learn about pain caused by mental illness. There have been so many with this experience."

Rebekah set the aircraft down on her pad, and they stepped out into the evening air, fragrant with the smell of the gorgeous flowers and blossoms that seemed to be everywhere. Lev felt like he was walking on holy ground being home again. He wanted to call the Ancients and ask for the privilege of working with Rebekah on Isha's return to life. It would be great to be a team together on a project, and this would be an area with which he had no experience. He felt a keen desire to learn from Isha what her life was like when her mind continually malfunctioned.

"Oh, that would be great, Lev. I think this will be a learning experience for both of us. I have thought about Isha and the thousands like her who suffered mental illness in the past. The whole family suffered with her, especially because there was such a great stigma associated with mental illness. Whole families had to endure ostracism when one member was afflicted. It was bad enough having someone irrational in the home screaming or rocking incessantly. Mental illness was as unwelcome as the plague. I understand that Isha's parents were marvelous people. They cared for her and really dedicated their lives to make her life tolerable."

"That's so good to hear. I understand some people were beaten and abused terribly because of a lack of understanding. At least Isha had love and kindness to make her life bearable. Say, is it time to eat yet?"

A Home-Fixed Meal

Rebekah laughed. "You always did have a good appetite, Lev. I don't think you will be disappointed."

"Wonderful! I'm starved!"

Rebekah's kitchen was decorated to reflect the beauty of her character. She had chosen soft woodsy shades of brown with candles creating relaxation and peacefulness. The whole house smelled of freshly baked goods and tea. There was a wonderful fruit salad and a host of vegetables that would satisfy royalty. They spent the evening catching up on all the news about family members and their personal experiences. The evening passed so quickly that they lost track of the time, and soon the clock was striking midnight.

"I better head home, Rebekah. I want to get up in time for the chapel services. I haven't even been home yet. I hope there is room for me there! I never know who might be using the house while I'm away."

"Don't worry, Lev. No one is there now — you will have your home all to yourself. I'll take you home."

He kissed her saying, "Thanks for the offer, but I want to walk home. It's such a lovely evening, and I need the exercise. Besides, it will give me time to reflect on past mercies and future plans. Shalom, Rebekah."

The following morning after the chapel services, Lev contacted the Ancients about working with Rebekah for the return of Isha. They were pleased to grant his request. The more he thought of it, the more Lev was drawn to Isha's case. The suffering caused by a family member with such a handicap endured a lifetime. The sick person would require care beyond the years that one normally spends raising a child, with the added burden of outsiders' ridicule or curiosity. The important thing was that her return would find her sane and renewed. She would have total recall of her experiences and, therefore, would be a study of extreme interest. The happiness accompanying her return would create even greater excitement.

Lev called Rebekah to tell her the good news and asked where he might report for work that day.

"Oh, how exciting! Meet me at my house and we'll fly there together. It's too far to walk, but we can fly there in minutes. Better yet, I'll pick you up. I am so excited and really amazed at my happiness about Isha's return. I am twice blessed to have you as my co-worker, Lev."

A Life and Mind to Be Restored

"You know, Rebekah, I have been thinking the same thing. I am really excited about this project. We want to make Isha's return as bright and happy as we can. Let's make this reawakening really special. I can't wait to enjoy her pleasure when her life is restored along with full mental soundness. At last, her parents will be rewarded for their faithfulness in caring for her and keeping her with love and tenderness. They were real heroes, and I want to roll out the red carpet for them when they return."

"I'll be early. Make an extra pot of tea for me, Lev."

"Will do."

Soon her aircraft hovered over his pad, landing easily. They sat down at the breakfast table anticipating the day's adventure.

"Have they laid the foundation for Isha's home yet?"

"Yes, Lev—I called them a few days ago and had the heavy equipment dig for the foundation, and the next day they laid the footing."

"I can hardly wait until Isha returns. Can we be there when she returns or are other family members on the list before us?"

"We will have plenty of workers, so this will be a breeze. There is no end of willing volunteers to help build her home, but the list is shorter for those wishing to be present at her return. The Ancients will decide that."

"Okay. Whatever the Ancients decide will be best. We are certainly blessed with such leadership."

"No One Has Slipped Through the Cracks"

"Yes, when you stop to think of the billions of people who have died and returned to life, it is truly amazing that no one has slipped through the cracks. No one has returned without adequate provisions or without helping hands being outstretched to them."

"You know what, Rebekah?"

"What?"

"I have been thinking about joy. When a baby comes into the world, he doesn't know what joy is. He must learn it—first in small ways, and then as the child matures, in greater ways. And we are learning joy on a daily basis. Every morning I awaken astonished at my own happiness and the joys that keep unfolding. There doesn't seem to be a limit to joy once we get rid of pride and selfishness."

"Hmmm." Rebekah mused. "I never thought of joy as being something we learn. You're right. In that event, our happiness should continue to grow forever. Well, we'd better be going."

"Give me a minute to change into my working clothes."

Soon they were headed for the site. A cooling breeze was blowing while the sun's rays kissed the earth with its life-giving blessings. It was hard to believe that once this was the Negev desert. Everything was lush and green with little streams flowing like shimmering silver ribbons decorating pillows of lawns, orchards, and woodlands. Soon Rebekah descended to a little pad that was waiting for a house to appear.

"Would you believe that we have several million people living in this area now which was once a hostile desert?"

"By the way, how did you make out on the Sahara project? I know you stayed there longer than I did. It was such a thrill to have people filling up that once enormous wasteland of sand and see it blossoming like a rose!"

"Yes, especially the people who once lived in the desert by the few oasis regions that enabled them to sustain life there. They were overwhelmed when the rains came and protein grass started growing everywhere. Trees and bushes grew and blossomed, streams and ponds began to flow and the sand seemed to turn green overnight. It has turned into the Sahara Paradise now, and with all the vegetation, even the temperatures have moderated. It no longer has the burning heat of day and cold nights. It was like a dream working there, Lev. Seeing streams of homeless and migrant people return to life in beautiful surroundings with every temporal necessity provided was a joyful experience. My old mind and heart would never have been able to hold it all. It was what you were talking about earlier—they were all learning joy on a scale they never imagined possible."

"Absolutely!" Lev replied exuberantly. "I found the same thing among those returning to life. There were few attitude problems among them. When people who had nothing suddenly have everything, they are so overwhelmed. Still, when people who had everything come back and find they no longer have vast estates and power over others, they don't have the contrast to make them as happy. In time, however, the leveling process of society will be complete. The high places will be brought low and the low places shall be exalted. That is happening on such a magnificent scale, it takes my breath away."

"If we sit here talking all day, we will get nothing done. So we better join all those workers and see what we can do." Rebekah jumped out of the craft, ready for a day of exhilarating work.

Everyone seemed so busy working that they scarcely paid attention to the aircraft landing on the pad. Lev spoke to one of the men, introducing himself. "Welcome to our happy throng. If you are here to work, we can still use an extra hand or two." The man seemed delighted to have more help.

Kinfolk Meet

"This is my former wife, Rebekah. She is related to Isha through a long line of descendants," Lev continued.

"Pleased to meet you Ma'am. My name is Noah Obadiah. I am Isha's brother, just recently returned to life. If you have been around awhile, we could use some experienced help here. I am kind of new as are most of the workers, and we are green with all the electrical work. Lev, I heard you are up on all the sciences, so you can help us with that. Rebekah, since you are from the Obadiah family, you must have a green thumb. Why don't you take care of the lawn and the atrium plantings? We need someone with an artistic eye to lay things out. I'm an Obadiah, but somehow I didn't inherit a talent in gardening."

"Noah, you could not have given me a better assignment. I love working with plants. I don't know how you can be of the Obadiah family and not be a horticulturist! Well, I'll forgive you for your shortcoming, but I hope this regenerating process will soon cultivate your 'green thumb'," Rebekah teased.

Noah laughed good-naturedly. "I'd like nothing better."

"We both have a special interest in seeing Isha return to life," Lev asserted. "We learned that she suffered with mental illness. We are so excited to see her return to life with a sound mind in the new body Christ shall give her. What a deliverance that will be for her and for your whole family!"

"If you are excited, imagine how I feel. I am her brother, and everyday of my life my heart ached for my poor sister imprisoned with a mind that didn't function. I knew in my heart she tried to act normally and longed to be whole, but she would fade in and out of reality. When she was a child it wasn't so bad, but when she became a grown woman, she had to be denied a normal existence because her actions were beyond her control. Anyway, I am pushing this project hoping for her early return. Thanks for joining us.

"Lev, you follow me. We already have the foundation in. The house has been delivered in sections. Perhaps you can manage this operation putting it all together because most of us have a general idea of how it works, but it will save time and energy if we have someone with a lot of experience directing things. First we had to learn to read, and after that we tried to learn how to build. So you can see, we are still inexperienced about how these modern houses go together. Back in our day, houses were essentially bare rooms with a few windows and doors. Now, they are a work of art with every scientific wonder functioning in them. Even kings could not have imagined how comfortable they could be in a house like I live in.

"Come on, Rebekah, I'll show you the area that needs your attention. Over there you will see a lot of potted plants that need to be arranged. The trees from Eden are already growing wonderfully, but this area is where the planting will begin. After the main house structure is up, the land will be leveled and you may begin planting. Meanwhile, you can identify the plants and draw a layout of how you want them."

"I'm on my way, Noah. Thank you."

The days passed swiftly, and the excitement about Isha's imminent return continued to build. Lev had called the Ancients and confirmed the date for her appearance. Everything was ready on the appointed day. It was determined that Isha's brother would be there alone to greet her. She knew him, and this would give her assurance to have someone familiar at her side. Rebekah and Lev would be allowed to come after Noah had spent time with his sister.

Noah arose early awaiting the return of his sister. Rebekah had filled the house with flowers and laid out everything so beautifully that there would be no cause for fear or anxiety. Beauty tended to awaken the senses peacefully.

Isha Returns to Life

I lay quietly after I awakened. I knew something was strangely different. When I opened my eyes, I expected to see the small attic room I had spent my whole life in, but this room was bright and spacious with flowers and several pieces of pretty furniture. There were big windows with light softly filtered through white lace curtains.

It was all so lovely. I'd never had such a beautiful dream. I usually had terrifying nightmares that made going to sleep at night something I fought as hard as I could. Often I awoke screaming several times every night. Many times during the day I fell asleep from sheer exhaustion. But here I was, opening my eyes, feeling refreshed and at peace. I'd never had that experience before.

I began to wonder where I was. How did I get here? Was I going to have to go back to my small gloomy room with its one shuttered window and hard bed? I felt a sense of panic at the strangeness of it all. The beauty was enchanting. Never had I seen such a delightful room. Even the smell was an aroma of life. When I rose, I realized my usual clothing was gone, but there on my bed were new garments laid out for me. There was a beautiful rose-colored blouse with a floral skirt that fit me as if someone had taken my measurements and custom-made them. Never had I been dressed so nicely. I felt like a queen—not that I knew anything about queens. My mind had been too muddled to be aware of the world outside my dingy room.

I walked about the room examining the furniture. There were two wooden chests with drawers full of more pretty clothes. Above one was a mirror. Who was that lovely girl in it? She resembled my mother. When I put my hand up to my lustrous, wavy black hair, I saw it was me!

There was a soft-cushioned chair with a little pink pillow in its corner. Beside the chair, bright yellow flowers stood in a crystal vase on a small table, which also held a black book. I couldn't read, so I had no idea what it was.

Being alone was something I was used to, but in this place I was a bit uneasy. I longed to see my brother. Where was Noah? If I could only find him, he could tell me where I was and why everything was so different. I slowly walked toward the shiny wooden door, wondering if it was locked. I never went out of a room alone, except when I was raving and forced my way past whoever had opened it. I remembered when my neighbor, Erna, had run after me, taken me by the hand, and invited me into her house for some cookies and milk. That worked to quiet me and then after I had eaten my fill, I was ready to go back to my small room. I vividly remembered Erna. My mind seemed to be working in a way I was unaccustomed to. I felt in complete control of myself. There were no urges to scream, dark moods or sullen withdrawals. What had happened to me? I was afraid to open the door fearing the dream would end, and on the other side of this door would be my old room.

I turned from the door to look out the window to see an unspeakably beautiful garden. Was this heaven? I felt my arm, and it was real. How could I explain my presence here if someone should find me? Amidst all this confusion, I was absolutely amazed that my mind was so clear and my reasoning was strangely coherent. Yet, in spite of everything being new and unexplainable, I had no urge to scream and did not feel depressed.

Isha and Noah Embrace

Noah heard Isha's footsteps because he was listening intently for the first sign of activity. He knew this new environment would be troubling to her, so he called her name, saying, "Isha? It is I, Noah. Are you all right? Do you need my help?"

Isha's heart seemed to stop. That was Noah's voice. She recognized it. Still, instead of opening the door, she paused. Her mind was racing, as was her heart. What if she opened this door and found her old room again? She didn't want to go there ever again. She felt free of it somehow, but trembled at the thought of returning. At last her curiosity overcame her fears, and she opened the door a crack to see Noah standing. She ran into his open arms.

"Isha, Isha, Isha! You are back again!" Noah said as he embraced her. "You are so lovely! I have been waiting for you!"

"Oh, Noah, I'm so frightened. Where am I? How did we both get here? What happened to my room? Please don't send me back there!"

"Oh, Isha, you are never going back to that room of yours. This gorgeous home is all yours. You are now rich and have everything that you ever dreamed of having. Most of all, my sister, you are well and beautiful. You are going to be so happy now. Take my hand, Isha, let me show you your splendid home."

"No, let me sit down first. I feel so strange. Noah, I have never felt this way before. My mind is clear for the first time, and yet I feel this is all a dream. Are you really Noah, my brother? Something has happened to me and I don't know what. Tell me, why is everything so strangely different and yet so wonderful?"

"Oh, my dear sister, I am your very own brother. Something strange *has* happened to you. It also happened to me. I know exactly how you feel. Just a few months ago I was raised from the dead like you have been today. I felt exactly as you do now. Be at peace, my sister. You will have those feelings for a few days and then you will be convinced this is not a dream. You see, you died and have been raised from the dead many centuries later, even as I. Rest where you are and let me give you something to drink. I promise you that the little room you lived in does not exist anymore."

"I feel so different. All the dark thoughts that possessed me are gone. I feel so good I should be jumping with joy, but how can I believe all this is real? I don't seem to be mad and yet I must be. Everything is so confusing."

"Isha, be at peace. Here, have some tea. Be careful, it is hot."

"It smells so good. I never had tea like this before." Upon tasting it, she said, "Noah, this is just what I need. Thank you."

"As soon as you feel strong enough, come with me to the kitchen table. We will have a breakfast like you have never tasted before."

"Why does everything have to be so new? I will be glad to have the bread we always ate that I dipped in olive oil. That was good enough for me."

"Yes, that was good, but what we have now is much better. You will be eating perfect food for the first time from the Garden of Eden."

"I remember Momma telling me about Adam and Eve being in a wonderful Garden of Eden. Now that you mention it, my mind can clearly recall those memories. I can't believe I remember that."

The Past Recalled

"Well, we all come to life with total recall of the past. You will remember what you have forgotten because Christ has given you back every thought and memory that you ever had."

"Who is Christ?"

"He is the new ruler of this world. That is all you need to know now. See this fruit, Isha? Just taste it. I think you will like it better than bread dipped in olive oil."

She reached for it, smelling its vital fragrance. "My how lovely. It is too nice to bite into."

"Go ahead; eat it anyway. You'll love it."

"Oh, my! Never have I eaten anything so good. This cannot be real."

"Well, I know the newness is too much to comprehend at once. In a few days, this will be as natural as everything was before."

"I don't want to go back to what was before. Please don't take me back there."

"Isha, no one will ever take you from here and from these wonderful new things. They are real, and they all come as Christ's gifts to you."

"I can't bear to think about that small room. Why was I punished by being locked in that little room? Why was my mind so tormented? What did I do to deserve that?"

"Isha, you had an illness in your mind. Some people suffered as you did, and others suffered in other ways. I understand that all this suffering resulted from sin and it is ended now. Christ has ended the reign of sin and death and the things that went with it. He is now in the process of healing the world of illness, pain and suffering. Maybe we will understand it better later. There must be some purpose served. Maybe we had to learn what sin was about. Now we are beginning to see how costly sin was. But at any rate, you are well now, and we are going to be happy and healthy forever."

Isha's Little Room

"Noah, I can't trust my thinking. This is too beautiful for me. Beautiful things were always for other people. Forgive me, I am so uncertain about everything."

"Trust me, Isha, your anxiety is only temporary. Soon you will realize this life is very real, and no one will send you back to those awful days of your past. You know Momma and Papa loved you. I loved you. We had to lock you in that room to keep you from harm. You were not able to function as other people. However, now you are whole and your mind is no longer tormented. You are free and well and may go about as you please. And you are also very beautiful. Did you notice how lovely you look now?"

"I looked in the mirror and could hardly recognize myself. I feel like a little child in a grown woman's body. I was so tormented. I do know that Mamma and Papa loved me. They always were so kind. That is what made life bearable."

"They couldn't heal you, but they could love you, and that is what they did. Soon they will be coming back, and this time you will be able to help build a house for them and love them in return as they loved you. We will all be so happy when they return. How proud they will be of you! I can hardly wait. Remember how sad you were when Papa died? You wanted to go to his funeral and Momma could not let you. You cried and screamed. Well, now you will be there when he returns to life. You will be able to return to him some of the love he showed you. We all suffered with you, Isha. You were not alone in that room. In our hearts, we were there with you every day. Momma and Papa were so sad because they could not heal you or even understand what was wrong. They devoted their lives to taking care of you and now you can return the favor."

"I knew I was different from everybody else. My mind was never at peace. I had panic and fears that would explode in my mind, and I couldn't turn them off. Then I would become frightened, depressed, and angry."

"I am glad to assure you over and over again that you will never, ever go back to that place in your mind, nor that dreary little room. There is no need for you to be there. Your mind is now whole and you are able to behave as all people do. You are fully in charge of yourself. Before we couldn't let you out of the house for fear that you might be injured. You didn't know it, but there were some evil people who could have harmed you. You were too innocent to go about freely."

"How can that be true? Erna found me outside and she gave me milk and cookies. She was good to me."

"Yes, Erna was a very dear neighbor. If everyone were as good as she was, we would not have had to worry so much. You didn't even know that animals and snakes could harm you. You were very sheltered from the evils that were in the world. Momma and Papa kept you from all harm and wicked people. Now it is so different. No one *can* harm you now, neither man nor beast, so you may walk about freely without fear."

"Why is it so different now?"

"Because Christ rules the world in righteousness now. He does not allow harm to come to anyone anymore. He employs spiritual forces that prevent harm before it can occur. People learn this quickly and behave themselves. We are so blessed now, Isha."

"I don't understand all that you are telling me, Noah. I am only a child in understanding. I couldn't read or write. I didn't learn how to make my living. My meals and clothing were supplied, and that is how I lived. Momma and Papa worked to care for me and when they died, you took care of me."

"Tell me what you remember as your last thoughts."

"Well," the girl started slowly, "I know that I was sick. I couldn't eat or keep food in my stomach. I had a fever and chills and a lot of pain. I remember you putting a cold wet cloth on my brow, Noah. That felt so good until I got the chills. Then you would put blankets on me. Soon the room began to fade away and you seemed so far away. My breathing was so painful and then the pain stopped. That is all I remember."

Death Ended Your Pain

"That's when you died, Isha, and went to sleep for many centuries. Just today Jesus called you back to life. He did more than bring you back to life. He has given you a new body and healed your mind so that you will never have those dark and frightening emotions rolling over you. You are now functioning as all healthy people do. Soon you will be getting an education better than queens ever had. Your greatest joys will be in learning. Your mind will be able to exchange information with everyone else. There is an ocean of knowledge waiting for you to swim in. I have been alive for only a few months, but I've already learned to read and write, and so many things are opening up to me. I have to pinch myself to realize that I can now understand so many things I knew nothing about before."

"I can't learn, Noah."

"Oh, you will now. Within a week you will be reading simple words. Your mind is now bright and eager to learn. There are no limits—everything is open to you. Time will pass quickly. The hours and days will speed by and you will not know where they went. You will quickly know the glory and honor of life that you never knew before."

"You make me sound like some princess. I am only a wretched person people couldn't even stand to look at. I do wish what you are saying was true, Noah."

"Isha, you will soon feel like royalty under Christ's new government on earth."

"Noah, you always tried to make me feel good. You have been so kind. Are you sure I am not that crazy woman that no one wanted to know?"

"You are both intelligent and beautiful now, Isha. Soon you will not only be lovely, but you will be educated and you will have the opportunity to explore all your talents. I am telling you the truth, for that is the only language spoken now."

"Anyway, this was the best breakfast I have ever had. I cannot believe what is happening to me now."

"Come with me, Isha. I want to show you your house and garden and the orchard that grows that delicious fruit you enjoyed so much. There are trees that bear fruit every month so you will never be hungry again. And we make tea from the leaves of those trees."

Although he showed her the features of her house explaining how everything worked, it was more a mystery afterwards than before. Light that came with a touch of a button? Water by the turn of a handle? Rooms for each purpose in daily life? She knew there was an enormous amount of intelligence demonstrated everywhere. She absolutely loved walking through the garden so beautifully laid out by Rebekah. The aroma of the trees, the colors of the flowers, and the songs of birds all filled her senses.

Having shown her the wonders of her new home, Noah took her into her study—an absolutely astonishing experience! When he turned on the computer screen and it lit up with people speaking to her, she was startled.

"Where did these people come from and how did they enter the house?"

"Don't be frightened, Isha. This is what is called television. These people are in Jerusalem, but airwaves carry their images, and this machine collects those airwaves and makes these pictures for us; it also carries the sound waves the same way. Here is a button; you can turn them off whenever you want. Try it."

Carefully, she touched the button and the screen fell dark and the sound ended.

"Now touch it again and it will come back on. See?"

Isha was absolutely enthralled at this, trying it several times to satisfy her curiosity.

"These are the Ancient Worthies in Jerusalem who do much of the teaching and instructing now. They are perfect, so we have magnificent teachers who make learning so easy you hardly have to try."

Learning to Read and Write

"The first thing I want to learn is to read and write. Can they help me?"

"Can they help you!" Noah exclaimed, "They taught me to read simple words within a week, and now I can read simple books. Within a year, I hope to be able to graduate to technical studies. I just love it. I spend my evenings studying now, and I don't know where the time goes. I have to force myself to turn off the programs so I can get some sleep. Suddenly, I no longer feel like an ignorant peasant. I can learn anything I want to, and I want to learn so much. You'll find it to be the same way."

Noah brought up a program that taught reading and writing. Soon Isha was watching and being pulled into the program almost unconsciously. It had a unique way of teaching the alphabet and the assigned verbal sounds. Soon Isha was repeating and memorizing words effortlessly. When Noah called her for lunch, he had to stop the program before she would come.

Visitors Are Coming Next Week

At lunchtime Noah told her they would have visitors next week.

"Rebekah Obadiah Aron and her former husband, Lev, are going to be with us. You don't know her, because she was born many centuries later than you. She is, however, a part of our family, and she wanted to meet you. She and her former husband have been newly alive longer than most people. After dying in the battle against Jerusalem, Lev returned to life in the earlier years of the regeneration, and Rebekah lived through Armageddon without experiencing death. So they have had many years of growth in knowledge. It is a great honor to have them visit us, and you'll enjoy their visit."

"Well, I must study very hard before they come. You know, Noah, I have never entertained anyone before in my life. I hope they will understand my lack of social skills."

"I am not much better in social matters than you are. We were poor and never had guests at our house."

"You mean our parents couldn't invite people to our house because of me, don't you?"

"Well, yes, I think that is partly correct, but additionally our parents had to care for you as well as provide for our living. There wasn't a lot of time for social activities. Momma was so devoted to you. She knew you had handicaps, and she wanted to give you extra love to make up for it. Papa was the same way. He was such a good man. He never complained. He was always so cheerful. You remember him, don't you, Isha?"

"Oh yes, I do, and I am so excited knowing they will both be back again. They will be so proud of me. I want to be their princess now, one that is able to pay them back in some small way for the great love they gave to me."

"Rebekah will show you how to dress and to make yourself even more lovely. She knows the social graces and will teach you everything you need to know. Lev is her former husband, and I understand he is very learned and very wise. You will be seeing people much nearer to perfection than we are."

"Perhaps they will think of us as ignorant peasants. That will certainly be true of me, but not for long, I promise you. I intend to make up for my lost years."

The week passed quickly and Isha counted the days, trying to prepare to receive their two new guests—her first company in her own home. She was so excited!

Lev and Rebekah Arrive

On the day appointed for their arrival, the brother and sister were sitting in the garden waiting for their guests. Isha had never seen an aircraft, and when she saw it drop out of the sky onto the landing pad, she was absolutely astonished.

"I can't believe what I am seeing," she said.

"Me neither," Noah gasped. "Now be sure to do what I told you. Welcome them into your home and invite them in for breakfast—don't just stand there staring at them."

"I'll try, Noah. I will try not to stare, but I don't think I can help it."

Sure enough, as Rebekah and Lev exited the aircraft, Isha stood speechless staring at the two extraordinary people.

Noah poked her, "Remember what I told you."

Isha spoke stiffly. "Welcome to my humble home. Please come in for breakfast with us."

Lev greeted them with hearty handshakes and a warm smile. "This is such a pleasure meeting you, Isha. We have been so excited looking forward to this visit. We do hope it is convenient for you to have us."

Before anyone could answer, Rebekah said, "I hope Noah told you that I am from the Obadiah family, so that makes us related. It is such a privilege to meet you. When I learned you were returning to life, I begged the Ancient Worthies to let us visit you, and they gave us permission as long as it was all right with you. So thank you for having us. We have known a lot of people who have returned to life, but none more exciting to meet than you, my dear Isha. Let me give you a hug."

Noah stood in awe of the aircraft, saying, "You couldn't give us a ride in that after breakfast, could you? I am sorry to be so bold, but I can hardly help myself. I often wanted to see the world from way up high."

"Of course, right after breakfast I'll take you around to see the whole territory from above. You will find it very thrilling, but Rebekah and I are more thrilled about seeing you folks. Everybody has a different story to tell, and we want to learn about Isha."

"Why would you want to learn about me? I guess I behaved very badly, and so I could not be let out to meet other people."

Isolation Ended

"That is all the more reason we need to learn about you, Isha. You suffered in a life that kept you apart from the world. Now you can be where you want to be, and that is what we want to hear about," Rebekah said.

"But first, let's have some breakfast," Isha said, being a better hostess than she realized. "This past week I have learned to read a little bit, and already the world is starting to open to me. I can't explain how happy I am now; especially since I know I'm not going back to the ugly room I lived in all my previous life."

Lev added, "Once you learn to read, Isha, you can learn the thinking of other people. No one can isolate you because the whole world is open to you. You will find you were not alone. Millions of people suffered as you did in locked rooms with a mind that couldn't find rest."

The conversation stopped for a moment. Noah was a little embarrassed, because they had not been praying before eating as their Momma and Papa had. But sensing the quiet pause as a call for prayer, he asked Lev to thank the Lord. Isha had started pouring the tea without realizing she should wait until the prayer was offered. She had not been capable of prayer in her former life. Now that she was capable of it, she had not yet learned how to pray, or the reason for it.

Lev waited until the tea was poured and then asked everyone to bow his or her head for prayer. After the prayer, Isha asked about why they bowed their heads. She was so innocent, but Noah was embarrassed.

Lev gently explained, "Isha, that is how people pray. Bowing our heads shows our humility, and closing our eyes shuts out distractions as we pray to our heavenly Father. We thank Him for our food and blessings. We not only need to *feel* thankful, but we should express these feelings to God."

"Oh, dear," Isha said dismally. "I'm afraid I have offended God by not praying. I did not know. However, in my heart now I am very happy and thankful that my mind is at peace and I am no longer tormented by thoughts that I cannot turn off. Back then, I could not change my thoughts for days and weeks. It was maddening to have them repeating over and over again without a break. I would scream, hoping that something would happen to change them and give me peace. Only when I slept could I escape from those thoughts that imprisoned me, and then I would be awakened by hideous nightmares."

At Home with Love

"You were blessed to have such a good family who loved you and cared for you," Rebekah affirmed. "So many people with mental problems were treated cruelly. They were beaten, starved, and kept in total confinement or in prison. Instead of receiving love and understanding for their condition, it was as though they deserved punishment. They were helpless victims of body chemistry gone wrong. In later years, we began to understand mental illness and treated people more kindly. Sometimes with proper medication people were able to live normal lives. However, now the Great Physician has completely healed you, and you will go on to a beautiful and happy life. Hopefully, your long years of suffering will make you appreciate even more your blessings now."

"Oh, I do, I do! My first few days of life I kept asking Noah not to send me back to my old room again. Now at last, I know that I am free of that and all the horrible thoughts I endured there. I could sing for joy!"

"Well, Isha, maybe tomorrow we will take you to the chapel service with us," Lev suggested. "You can sing along with other people who are thankful to be alive again under such wonderful conditions."

"Oh, that would be wonderful, Lev. I want to go out and talk to people. I want to have friends and sing and laugh. Oh! I'm so, so happy!"

Lev smiled appreciatively. "After we eat, we will fly over the houses and treetops, over the mountains and lakes and rivers. You will see the good earth as God sees it from above. You will see how majestic this earth is, in a way you never saw it before."

Touching the Clouds

"I used to watch the birds from my window, and I wished I could fly away and be as free as they were. Can we go up and touch the clouds?"

"Yes, we can do that," Lev promised.

"Before we go, however, I brought along a wonderful resurrection cake. We must all have a piece. Everybody loves this cake and I am sure you will, Isha. I made it especially in your honor," Rebekah said as she took it out of the refrigerator where she'd placed it upon arriving.

"My that looks so good. I want a big piece."

"That is not polite, Isha. You should never ask for a big piece," Noah chided.

"But, that is what I want," Isha replied with confusion. "Why shouldn't I ask for a big piece?"

"Because that is considered poor manners." Poor Noah didn't know how to instruct his sister without causing everyone embarrassment.

Rebekah interceded, "Never mind, Isha, you shall have a big piece. This is your cake and we want you to enjoy it. You will catch up. I think you're going to be the happiest person around."

Isha dived into the cake with relish, not waiting for others to be served. "Oh, this is so good. I cannot believe it. Maybe I can have a second piece?"

Noah winced. "Please, Isha, you must learn to be a lady now. Anyway, your eyes were always bigger than your stomach."

"Don't worry about that now, Noah," Rebekah rejoined. "Isha has plenty of time to learn the social graces. She is speaking the truth of her feelings, and we love that kind of innocence. Sometimes people get kind of stuffy with all this correctness. If she wants a second piece, she shall have it."

Lev interrupted saying, "But it is better not to eat too much before your first aircraft ride, Isha. It will make your stomach tingle a little even if I fly very slowly."

"Yes, this cake is very filling, but it is so delicious. I'll save my second piece until later."

They eagerly boarded the aircraft. Lev made sure Isha had the best seat so she could see everything. He turned the power on, and soon the craft lifted gracefully going higher and higher while Isha giggled with glee.

"Oh, my! My house looks so small from up here."

Soon they were speeding away; first circling the local area and then Lev headed toward the Mediterranean Sea. They followed the coastline for a bit as Isha watched little boats down below. Noah was just as excited, as this was his first flight as well. Lev asked, "Would you like to see the headquarters of the world, the city of the Great King?"

The "Beloved City"

"Yes," Isha shouted as Lev turned the craft eastward. They noticed the terrain rising quickly as they headed toward Jerusalem. The "Beloved City" soon came into view. It was on a hilltop—a city that could not be hidden, the light of the whole world.

"Maybe we could set the craft down, and if we are lucky, perhaps one of the Ancients will be walking by. Would you like to meet some of those people who are your teachers on the screen every day?"

A shiver went up both Noah's and Isha's spines. "That would be so wonderful! They speak so clearly that even I can understand every word."

As Lev landed the craft on a pad among other aircraft, he noticed a beautiful woman walking toward one of the parked aircraft. "Why, that looks like Sarah! I am sure that it is."

He opened the door and hurried toward her, saying, "Shalom, Sarah! Can you spare a minute?"

She paused and approached Lev smiling. "Yes, Lev, by all means. It is so good to see you! And who might your friends be?"

"Well, you know Rebekah, but this is Isha Obadiah, recently returned to life, and her brother, Noah. They are Rebekah's ancestors and your secret admirers."

"The praise all belongs to our King. I would invite you to dinner, but I was on my way to an appointment."

Socializing With Isha

"Don't apologize—seeing you made our day. Isha is just learning to read and write, and you are one of her favorite instructors. So this is great that we met you."

Isha added, "Yes, Sarah, forgive me for staring, but you are even more lovely than on the screen."

"Well, thank you, but beauty is what has come from God. What God looks at is the heart. It is more important to have a holy character."

Isha said, "I don't know very much about character. I lived in a little room most of my life and couldn't learn like other people. I did have a very loving family, so I know what goodness and kindness are."

"Well, my dear, then you are not far from the Kingdom of God. Try to be like your parents, and you will find yourself running with joy up the 'highway of holiness.' Sometimes people with previous handicaps fare better than others who had none. You see, you did not learn to do evil and spend your energy trying to justify the evil. That is a great advantage."

"What is evil, Sarah?"

"Evil is anything that people do that makes other people unhappy or sad."

"Oh, I never wanted to make anyone unhappy or sad. My unhappiness and sadness was not anyone's fault—I just couldn't think clearly. I was tormented with all kinds of thoughts that wouldn't leave my head. Since I returned to life it is very different now. My mind is clear, and I am learning to read and write and am able to remember so many things. It is wonderful to be free from dark thoughts that made me scream at times."

"Oh, dear one, Christ will make your life pleasant now. For every past day of sadness, you will have never ending joy every day from now on forever, if you trust and obey."

"That means I shall never have to go back to that little room again, doesn't it?"

"Yes, my dear," Sarah said as she gave Isha a little hug.

Turning to Lev she said, "Your next assignment will be to visit Nero when he returns to life next year. Until then, you will have some time to yourself. Nero is one of those rare people whose character, I think, has never had a good side. There is no sin he hasn't committed and no vice of which he was not guilty, so you will need an extraordinary amount of patience and wisdom trying to help him. We are all hoping you will accept this assignment."

"Well, you can tell the other Ancients I will go if they think I am suitable for the task. I cannot say that I will enjoy confronting such a man. However, let's hope that he isn't totally depraved. Perhaps there is some good quality that can be appealed to, and all we have to do is to find it."

Sarah Wishes to See Isha Again

"I must be going, Lev." Turning to Isha, Sarah gave her another hug. "My dear child, perhaps when all the dead are raised, you can come and spend some time with me. I would love to have you visit and we could get acquainted. You have such a very special past. Your sufferings may make you more beautiful now. Rebekah, remember to bring Isha to be with me in the future. Shalom to you all."

As she turned to leave, she kissed Isha on the cheek, saying, "I love you, my dear."

Isha was thrilled as tears ran down her cheek. The warmth of Sarah's love exceeded her physical beauty. Isha could feel it even as she felt her parents' love and that of her brother. She could understand love, and it was so sweet.

Rebekah said, "Well, you have quite an assignment, Lev. From what I read of Nero, he was a man without virtue and had a heart of stone."

"Who was Nero?" Noah asked.

"He was a ruler of Rome who was known for cruelty and sinfulness," Lev explained.

"If he was that bad, why would anyone try to help him?" Noah queried.

"Everyone is to receive one full and fair opportunity to turn their life around and learn to live in righteousness, if at all possible. The Ancients will not leave a stone unturned in trying to help people toward that goal."

Rebekah said, "We better get back in our craft and head home. Every time I meet one of these Ancients I get goose bumps. They are so very holy. Yet, when the work of God is completed, everyone on earth will be of similar beauty. What a tremendous task lies before the human race, to be washed and cleansed of all the sinfulness that clings to us from six thousand years of human depravity."

Soon they were flying back to Isha's home. She was so stimulated by the day's experiences that she would repeat occasionally, "I can't believe how happy I am!"

As they landed they all felt that the day had been perfect—it could not have been better!

They knew that Isha was well on her way to the happiness that was opening up to her on a daily basis. The darkness of her past was now to be replaced by beauty and light.

"For God shall bring every work into judgment,
With every secret thing whether it be good, or whether it be evil"
(Ecclesiastes 12:14).

Chapter Six

Lev spent his free time learning about Nero. He wasn't looking forward to this assignment. Looking for Nero's good qualities was like looking for a needle in a haystack. Things were more relaxed now since the regeneration projects became easier as the clock turned backward. The vast majority of people had lived after the time of Christ, so numbers returning were gradually becoming smaller with more and more capable people prepared to receive the diminishing numbers from the grave.

Lev had spent nearly a year at his own home learning at an accelerated rate as each day passed. Researching Nero's life was painful, full of the vileness of sin at its worst. He looked long and hard to find some shred of virtue in this man and could find none. It was hard to conceive how a man so lacking in character had been granted power and imperial authority. Nothing was sacred and no one was precious to him, not even his own mother whom he had murdered.

Lev waited to be called to his assignment. The date for Nero's return had been already announced. This was the man who had condemned both the Apostles Paul and Peter to death. However, spilling innocent blood was a very common occurrence under his malevolent rule. Envisioning him as an innocent baby who had become a skilled practitioner of evil strained the mind. Apparently, Nero had no fear of God, and as long as he held power, he had no fear of man. At first his two counselors Burrus and Seneca gave his rule credibility and propriety, and under their guidance the first years of his rule went well.

Alas, the man who lived by murder and mayhem could not retain his hold on power. Ultimately, he overplayed his hand and the Senate condemned Nero to be flogged to death. When word reached him of such a humiliating end that was normally meted out to common criminals, he committed suicide, avoiding death at the hands of the Roman authorities. He never lost his self esteem, for his last words were, "What an artist the world loses in me."

Nero Awakens

I awakened realizing the pain of the sword that pierced my body was gone. I felt about for the sword thinking that someone had pulled it out while I was unconscious. If I had to withdraw it now, the pain would be worse than when I thrust it into my body. Mercifully, someone had withdrawn it, and I felt relieved. But not for long, because if I had survived this ordeal I knew what awaited me. I envisioned being flogged to death as a common criminal with scornful people looking on, saying, "Is that the great Nero?"

Oddly, I could not feel the wound either. I moved very slowly with my eyes closed hoping no one would observe my movement. I was sure that a Roman guard would be standing nearby. I found myself breathing easily and without the searing pain caused by the self-inflicted wound. I reasoned I must have been lying unconscious for a very long time to be healed. How could this be? I knew I had aimed the sword at a place certain to bring death, but somehow cruel fate made me fail in my attempt to end my life. Now it would be even worse. They had obviously allowed me to heal so that they could watch me suffer as they scourged me to death. I kept my breathing as slow as I could in the hope no one would notice I had awakened. Fearing that the Roman Senate would be looking for me to have me flogged to death made me tremble. What right did the Senate have to condemn me to death as a common criminal? Was I not still the Emperor of Rome?

Finally, I risked opening my eyes just a crack to see what the situation was that I found myself in. To my amazement no one seemed to be around. The room I was in was not as ornate as I was accustomed to, but it was sunny and beautiful. This certainly could not be a Roman dungeon. Perhaps a guard was standing outside the door. I rose as quietly as I could, trying not to make a sound. I could not believe how good I felt. I examined my body and couldn't even find the scar where my wound had been. My oversized stomach was gone and never before had I possessed such a handsome physique. I stood taller, and my skin was without those blotches I had been accustomed to.

Though it was neither my clothing, nor anything with which I was familiar, I quietly dressed. It was very practical and fit perfectly. Interesting! Perhaps someone understood my importance and custom made unique clothing fit for an emperor! There were odd shoes as well, but I preferred being barefoot. Entering a smaller room, I was amazed to see what my eyes had never seen before. This was not a Roman bath at all! I saw metal handles. I turned one and, to my surprise, water came out! I quickly turned it back. Above a very unusual basin was a mirror. I could see my image quite clearly. I marveled at how grand I was. But what was this? I had some decayed teeth, but now when I smiled, all my teeth were whole and sparkled brightly. This was indeed very strange.

Where was I? Why did I look so good? What had happened to my blotches and why were my teeth so beautiful? My mind began to race. Perhaps I should escape and hide until I could assess the situation. Looking out the window, I thought my best chance was to head through the orchard to a small forest. Perhaps I had better go back and get those shoes. Quietly returning to the bedside, I noticed how really superb the craftsmanship was. They fit perfectly and felt extremely comfortable. I turned around and knocked over a small vase that thumped on the floor. It didn't break, but I feared the sound would signal a guard that I was up. My mind raced. What should I do? I was about to head back to the smaller room to open the window and escape, when I heard a male voice call, "Nero, are you awake?"

Standing there paralyzed, not knowing whether to run toward the
window or to answer the voice speaking to me, I reasoned that if this
were a Roman soldier he would not have inquired if I were awake, but
would have stormed in instantly at the sound of the vase hitting the
floor. Maybe this was my faithful secretary, but I didn't recognize the
voice. Anyway, whoever it was, he was not in authority. I would take
my chances on what lay beyond the door.

Nero Meets Publius

Opening it slowly, he saw a handsome young man standing there
with a friendly smile.

"Be at peace, Nero, you are in no danger and need not worry. I am
here to welcome you. My name is Publius, and I am a volunteer to
help you adjust to your new life."

Nero's eyes narrowed. "You might prove to be useful to me. Tell
me where I am and how I came to be here!"

"You are outside what used to be the city of Rome, but it does not
exist as it once did. As far as you can see are homes and orchards, all
beautifully vibrant. How you came to be here is rather complex, and if
I tell you, you might not understand."

Nero was insulted! "I am an intelligent man. Do not be impudent
with me, young man. I have a short temper. Tell me, I demand! How
did I arrive here?"

The man smiled generously. "Nero, if you want my help, you had
better adjust your attitude. The first thing you need to know is that you
are no longer an emperor. You are no longer in charge of anyone or
anything except yourself, and you are not doing a good job of it."

Nero felt rage building within him, but he realized he had been
in dire straits when he tried to take his life, so he backed off and
tried to be civil. After all, he might find this man useful in providing
information; so until he'd assessed the situation, Nero decided to
modify his demeanor.

"Well, Publius, no offense. I *am* a man of authority and I can be overbearing at times. I would be grateful for any information you can provide."

"Perhaps you would like some breakfast while we talk?"

"Ah, yes, that would be very good. I would like some fresh bread, olives, eggs and ham. A glass of wine would be welcomed, too, but it must be excellent wine. I am used to the very best."

"I am sorry; no one eats that way anymore. We have much better food than that."

"I am not interested in what you call better food. Fetch me what I requested. That is what I am used to eating, and that is what I want. If you do not have fresh bread or these other foods, why don't you scurry to the market and buy some? I can wait, but hereafter I would like these laid in store ahead of time. I can understand that you did not anticipate what I like to eat."

"Well, Nero, I am not scurrying anywhere. If you want to fetch the food you requested you may do so yourself, but you may have a very long walk to find such a market."

"Are you being insolent, young man?" Modified demeanor was going to be more difficult than he had first thought with this arrogant individual.

"No. You need to know that I am not your servant, but I am here to help you as your friend."

Nero had all he could to control his anger. If he did not have such a strange feeling of insecurity, he might have had a fit of rage. However, everything seemed so unfamiliar, at times he was unsure of everything. He really needed this man who seemed to possess the knowledge he so desperately wanted. With great effort he subdued his rage and spoke more gently.

"Publius, you seem like a good Roman. I shall take care not to offend you. In that you indicate that the food I desire is not available, perhaps I shall try to eat what you do have."

"Very good. You will be very glad to eat what I am about to serve you. You have never eaten anything so delectable before. Please be seated while I pour you some tea."

Nero followed him to a strange area, brightly lit and gleaming with oak cabinets, another basin with little handles, and other unusual containers and fixtures. He sat at the white, tile-topped table while Publius brought out a large bowl of remarkable looking fruit. Then he poured some tea, which had a delightful aroma he had never smelled before.

"My, that tea does smell good. Is it from the Far East?"

"No, actually it is from the trees in your yard. Not only is it delicious, but also it is very good for you. Try some fruit, Nero. Once you eat this, you will never want bread and olives or eggs and ham again."

Nero found his mouth watering with the aroma of the tea and the fragrance of the fruit. As he ate the fruit, it was obvious that he savored every bite. But rather than praise it, he only said, "Where am I?"

"As I told you, we are located outside what was once the city of Rome. It is going to take a little more explaining, and even when I get done, you might have trouble believing what I tell you. Please relax and I will tell you everything gradually." Publius folded his hands. "Please excuse me. I always thank my Lord before I eat."

Publius bowed his head in silent prayer while Nero became agitated again. When he lifted his head, Nero said, "You are not one of those Christians, are you?"

"Actually, I am. This is going to be very difficult for you to accept, but Christ is the new Emperor of earth. Perhaps you will learn to pray soon as well."

Nero's face was flushed as if he were going to burst a blood vessel.

"Are you saying this to taunt me, young man? Perhaps you don't know, but I dealt with the vile scourge of Christians in a very direct manner. The Christ that I heard about was crucified in Jerusalem, and the world is better off without him. A Roman centurion proclaimed him dead, his enemies knew he was dead and secured his tomb, his friends believed he was dead and asked for his body. Now what are you talking about, young man?"

"You apparently don't believe his disciples' testimony that Christ arose from the dead, do you?"

"Of course, not. No Roman officials were apprised of his resurrection to life. Come on, young man, do not spoil my day with nonsense."

"We speak only the truth and Christ *is* the Emperor of earth. I understand that this upsets you, but part of answering all your questions is to tell you that the people you persecuted, the followers of Christ, are now reigning with him."

What Happened to Rome?

Nero sat there silently, growing pale. This man *must* be taunting him. He had a feeling of great uneasiness. Nothing seemed to be real, and very likely what this man was telling him was not real either. Nothing was making any sense. If they were near Rome, what happened to that great city? Looking out the window toward a road passing by his house, he saw a vehicle moving by itself without horses. Publius saw him stare at the vehicle as though he had seen a ghost.

"That is an automobile, Nero. We don't use horses for travel anymore."

"Tell me I am not mad. Am I mad? I don't know what to believe. Either this is all a dream or I am completely mad!" He was frantic.

"Calm down, Nero. You are not mad. The world is different from the one you lived in."

Hoping to divert Nero's attention for a moment, Publius asked, "Did you like the fruit you ate?"

"Yes, yes, I actually did. I have never tasted better food. It seems to please my stomach, not like the food I ate before. That tea was very good; pour me another cup. It seems to soothe my nerves."

"Surely, have another cup," Publius said as he poured it out. "By the way, I have some fruit juices in the refrigerator which I would like to offer you as well."

"Everything is so good." He swallowed the cold nectar. "How do you keep it cold?"

"This box is called a refrigerator, and it keeps everything cold and fresh. This is a stove that makes food hot." He turned on a gas burner and it lit a blue flame. Then he turned it off. "See? It works almost like magic. You will enjoy how convenient everything is. By the way, Nero, you will have to serve yourself when I leave. You have no more servants."

Nero's frown was deep. "You know I am royalty. Surely, someone has overlooked my rank. There must be an oversight."

"It is no oversight. Your days of having servants are gone. In fact, you will have to learn to serve other people. The new way of greatness is through service."

"Are you trying to be insolent? You mean I am now a servant and must wait on other people? What an outrageous indignity! Emperors must be served. I am royalty, I tell you. I must be heard."

"Raise your voice all you want; rant and rave, or weep bitterly if you so desire. You have a very mean and ruthless past. You do not deserve the good treatment you are getting, so be very careful before some serious punishments are inflicted upon you. By all standards you are being treated far better than you deserve."

Nero dropped his head into his two hands. "I don't know how I failed to kill myself. I felt I was dying and here I am well and healthy, but I must be completely mad. Nothing makes sense."

"Come with me, Nero. Let us walk around a little. It will clear your head. You will not be able to understand everything all at once. Gradually, everything will seem real again. You see this lovely house you are in? It is yours now and as long as you live. Let me show you that grove of trees you see out of that window. It is also yours and will supply you with all the delicious fruit you will ever want."

Nero felt better walking about, and the fragrance of the orchards awakened his senses. Everything was resplendent. Reaching up his hand, he picked a luscious ripe fruit and ate it right there. Having tasted it, the desire for this fruit would never leave him. Never was he so satisfied with anything he had ever eaten before.

"This is incredible. Where did you find such trees as these?"

"These are trees from the Garden of Eden. This is the kind of food Adam and Eve ate. Christ preserved the seeds from these trees, and when the Ancient Worthies, noble and faithful men and women who served God before Jesus lived, were brought back to life, they brought these seeds with them. Since then, these seeds have been planted, and now trees are growing all over the earth supplying us with perfect food and the best tea."

"It sounds like a wild story, but I think I must be mad, I really do. Why do I feel so strange? Why does this all seem like a dream to me?"

A Good Job of Killing Yourself

"If you find this any comfort, you did a good job in killing yourself. You did not bungle your suicide."

"Oh please, do not be ridiculous. I cannot have killed myself. I am standing here. Look at me. I am real, not an apparition. Obviously, I did not die."

"I see you are here all right. You were very dead though, Nero, and you have just returned to life this morning. Did you look in the mirror by chance? What did you see?"

"Well, yes, I was surprised to find myself looking better than I ever remember. My teeth are all here and not crooked either. My skin doesn't have blotches. I loathed those blotches and, yes, I am glad to have them gone. It is very strange and I cannot explain it, but I do not believe I was dead. How could I be here if I died? If I am not already mad, talking to you I soon shall be. Please, I am in no mood for jesting. Can't you see I am a troubled man needing something firm that I can believe in?"

"You are used to making your own truth, which is why I am having trouble convincing you of reality. The truth is that you died and have

been dead for almost 2,000 years. You were raised today by the power
of Christ. That is the whole truth. By the way, none of those three
thousand Roman gods have returned. They were only a figment of
your imagination, and the world is better off without them. Christ has
been merciful to you, who showed no mercy to his followers. You had
best accept what I am telling you, because truth is the only language
spoken now."

"Publius, you have a good Roman name. Why have you decided
to become my mentor? Have you no better thing to do? I would prefer
someone I know to be with me, someone whom I could trust."

"Only your secretary was with you at the end, and he is not with
you now. You forget that you had no friends. You had people who
feared you and obeyed you because they had to, but as soon as they
sensed you were failing in power, they deserted you like a sinking
ship. Let's face it, Nero, who could love you? Who could abide with
your deceit and treachery? You destroyed everyone who befriended
you. If you could have loved someone else instead of yourself, you
might have a loyal friend now."

Nero growled, "Fortunate for you that I do not have soldiers at my
command at the moment. I am not used to such insolence, but as long
as you are here, tell me why Christ should raise me from the dead,
pretending for a moment that what you say is true."

"I will not trouble you very long. My task was to get you acquainted
with living conditions and some of the new features of your home. As
soon as I have accomplished this, I shall be gone. When I leave, a
man by the name of Lev Aron will visit you. He is a Jew and an avid
servant of Christ. You will be well advised to be on your best behavior.
I find my patience tried with your arrogance and belligerence. You
are no longer emperor, Nero. It was because no one could abide in
your perversity that they all turned against you. You were forced to
take your life by your own hand to escape the painful and humiliating
death by flogging. It is imperative that you learn from all of this. Your
arrogance and treachery brought your downfall. Now it is necessary to
behave in a more humble manner."

"How do you know such details of my life?"

"Much is known about you. Unfortunately, somewhere you lost your humanity when you succeeded in securing power. Having power without a shred of decency or integrity was a bad combination. The devil seems to have been your master. Anyway, Christ brought you to life to give you an opportunity to live down your sins and reform your life. You have another chance at life. So gratitude is in order. Until now, you have been your own worst enemy, so maybe at this time better counsels will prevail in beginning over again."

"I know I was in a terrible situation when I tried to take my life."

"You succeeded very well in your endeavor, I hasten to remind you. You were dead. Christ has raised you to life again. That is the truth. It may take a few days to convince you that this life is very real and not a dream or hallucination."

"I have no reason to believe anything you are telling me about being dead. I know I tried to take my life, but apparently I was not successful. Anyway, I am very confused. Why should I believe you? I don't know you. Are there no servants or slaves about that I know?"

Nero Stiffens at Hearing of His Mother, Brother and Wife

"I understand your uncertainty and frustration, but we all experience this when we return to life. Most people return to loving family members, and this makes it easier to adjust. But when you have no one you know, it's very difficult. Of course, *you* know what you did to your mother and brother and also to your wife. I think you are more comfortable with me than you would be with them."

Nero sat silently listening to his last comment. He knew he had murdered them and wondered if Publius somehow knew this. He decided to change the subject. "You know, I am an artist. If you have some paint and brushes, I would like to relax and try to find my sanity in my art."

"I am afraid we don't have such things here, but perhaps I should take you for a stroll through your estate and show you all the marvels you have never seen before."

"Yes, a walk would suit me. Perhaps it will clear my head. I cannot explain it. I feel quite well, better than I have felt in a long while. Yet I keep thinking I am dreaming or some such thing."

Publius arose and motioned him to follow. He first took Nero through the garden and into the fragrant orchard. After that, he showed him the garden that was full of flowers and the vegetable garden.

"The vegetables taste good, and they provide some variation to our diets. We do a little baking, too, but for the most part all we need is this fruit and tea that comes from the leaves of these trees."

Publius began showing Nero the modern features of his home. Finally, he warned Nero, saying, "You are not going to believe this, but I am going to turn on your television to show you the kind of world you live in now."

As the screen lit on the wall, Nero was frightened.

"Be calm, this is what modern science has enabled us to do. You are seeing people in Jerusalem. These pictures are sent by airwaves, picked up here and focused on this screen. Let me show you what we have on Nero and tell me what you think about the records they have on you."

Soon Nero saw a history of his life being portrayed with amazing accuracy. As he saw his past for the first time as an observer, he was astonished and frightened.

"Was I really that bad? Perhaps we can turn this off for now. How about something that will tell me where I am and why I am here."

"Yes, I can show you a satellite view of our area. You might recognize some of the rivers and mountains of Italy. Perhaps when Lev Aron comes, he will take you for a ride in his airborne chariot, and you can see your town from flying over the rooftops. See, this is where we are, and here is your home as seen from satellite images, which are pictures taken from high up in the sky."

A Satellite View of Earth

Nero was absolutely breathless. "What else can this tell us?"

"Anything you really want to know or learn. We don't go to school anymore, because all the schooling we need is here. You can learn history, science, geography, languages, and every bit of information men have accumulated through the years. Once you learn to use it, you will find it totally absorbing. This is the information age and learning is non-stop. You lived in a time of ignorance and superstition with false gods and a penchant for evil on a very large scale."

Nero found it fascinating when the initial shock of technology wore off. "I am sure that I am dreaming now. Who could believe such a thing?"

"Perhaps we will turn on some music for awhile, and it may soothe your nerves." Soon the room was filled with heavenly music that he had never heard before. The melodies were absolutely superb, and hearing the instruments playing the various parts of music awakened his artistic mind.

"I have never heard such incredible music before. It is a tonic to my troubled mind. Continue playing it."

Nero settled back and became calm, infatuated with music that seemed to come from nowhere but filled the room. He said, "I could listen to this forever."

"Enjoy it now, but we are too busy to sit around and enjoy music all the time. Once you get adjusted to your new life, there will be work for you to do. You will need to build a home for your mother and father, and when that is done there will be others."

"What? I have never soiled my hands with work. Surely, you cannot imply that I must submit to manual labor? My mother is dead and so is my father, and they do not need homes. I am royalty. Do not forget that. We have slaves to do manual work."

"There are no slaves anywhere in this whole world. Yes, you will have to become a common laborer, because you are only a common human being. Cheer up! It's not that bad. You might even enjoy it. Too bad you didn't have to labor before. It might have saved you from getting into all the trouble you did."

Publius noticed Nero stiffen when he mentioned his father, because it reminded him of his mother. The very thought of her return to life posed a grave problem for him. The last thing he wanted was for her to return. This was absolutely unacceptable to him.

"Don't I have any say about who returns? This seems outrageous to me. This could place me in a very uncomfortable position. I can always claim my innocence in her death. However, things would certainly be more peaceful if she didn't return. She has not returned, by chance, has she?"

"She will return soon. Yes, I fully agree that things would be more peaceful for you if they remained in the grave. That is true in so many cases, Nero. However, Christ has pledged that '*all* that are in the graves shall hear his voice, and shall come forth' (John 5:28, 29). I am afraid your peace shall be disturbed, like it or not."

"I cannot believe the way things are developing. It is bad enough I arrive in this world confused and dethroned. I am without power or recognition of any kind. A common Roman citizen is telling me what little I know. This is all outrageous! Is there no consideration for my rank and position? People died for insubordination in my time, but now it seems there is no law to protect my status. Where can I lodge my complaint? How did I get into this intolerable situation?"

"I am sorry, Nero. You forget that your sovereignty ended when the Senate condemned you to be flogged to death as a common criminal. The judgment they concluded against you was long overdue and well deserved, don't you think? You surely must believe that justice finally caught up with you. If it didn't catch up then, it has now."

Nero's anger could be seen in his face. "I should have you flogged for such insubordination!"

"I am sure you would, except you no longer have any authority. You are without power or a shred of influence. I know you find that galling, but we are all on the same level now. You had your day of power and misused it. Who would give you power in this righteous world now?"

"I will have you know my early years as emperor were very good for the Roman people. They were some of the best years. Why am I talking to you about this anyway? Who are you that I should have to defend myself from your accusations and insinuations?"

My Service to You Will End Soon

"*Pax*, Nero. I shall not trouble you much longer. My job is to get you acquainted with your modern way of life, and then I shall be gone. Lev Aron will be here in a couple of days, and perhaps you will find him more charming. So I am going to stick to my assignment of teaching you about the facilities in your home and how you can enjoy a very happy and peaceful life as far as your natural surroundings are concerned."

"Good. You obviously have exceeded your authority by sitting in judgment of my regal reign."

"Very well, Nero. I shall fulfill my charge in the few days left, and then you will be visited by someone who serves the present King."

"And who might that King be?"

"I have told you before. Christ is reigning over the earth. He reigns over every nation, people and tongue. There is no place that his righteous power is not felt."

"I will have to accept your word for that. I am so out of touch with things as they are. However, I know how to use that box to open up knowledge. If you don't mind, I shall spend my time learning and may need some help to learn how everything works. I am quick to learn what I want to know."

"Be not deceived; God is not mocked:
For whatsoever a man soweth, that shall he also reap"
(Galatians 6:7).

Chapter Seven

The sound of Lev's aircraft was heard in Nero's room. He had slept late, as was his custom, and was still in his nightclothes. Nero was not eager to meet Lev, but it seemed his wishes were never considered, and he was becoming used to being told his agenda. Throwing on his robe, Nero opened the door to see the beautiful aircraft setting down with great precision on his pad. He watched in utter amazement. He had seen horseless carriages moving about, but this was unbelievable except that his eyes were forcing him to believe the impossible. How could a machine be made to fly? How ignorant he was in this new society!

Lev opened the door to his aircraft as soon as the engine stopped. The handsome man with regal carriage instantly commanded Nero's respect.

"Shalom. I'm Lev Aron," he said, extending his hand. "Sorry to impose on you this way, but you need someone to be with you now that Publius has left. I am sure we will make out well together."

Nero extended his hand hesitatingly. "Why is it that no one ever consults me? I am simply told you are going to be here and that is that. I am a man used to running things and voicing my wishes. Apparently, they are now being totally ignored."

"Well, Nero, you need a lot more help than you realize. I have been around under this new arrangement for many years, so you might find me a very valuable aid. Don't take it personally. This is the way things are done—quickly, efficiently, and with no mistakes. Just bear with me for a season and things will be fine."

"In that I have no choice, welcome to my abode. I haven't had breakfast yet, so if you would like, you may join me."

"Sounds great to me. Perhaps after breakfast I could give you a ride in my craft. I hear you won a chariot race. You will find this chariot more secure. You can't fall out of it."

"I won that race, I'll have you know, fair and square. I did somehow manage to fall out of the chariot, but fortunately my horses stopped, and I was able to get on again and win the race. Anyway, how do you know all these things?"

"I read a little about you before I came. Did it ever occur to you that no one wished to win by defeating the Emperor of Rome? Anyway, you saw your noble competitor in that race rein in your horses to stop them. Did it occur to you that he did not have to do that?"

"Do you make a practice of humiliating your host at the outset?"

"Sorry, Nero. Truth is very important to us today; don't be offended so easily. Anyway, getting a true perspective on things is not what we call humiliation. Anything that helps us understand a situation is very needful, since self-deception is gone. Everything is properly labeled as right or wrong, good or bad. You will become used to it after a bit. Thank you for your offer of breakfast; I shall eagerly accept your kind invitation. I left very early this morning and only had some tea."

"Well, follow me," Nero said less than graciously as he turned toward his home.

"You have a beautiful place. Does it meet with your artistic tastes?"

"I must confess it is very beautiful, and the artist who laid out the garden and the designs of this home was very gifted."

"Well, I guess Publius didn't tell you that he worked to build your home for you with about a half dozen others, but he was the design artist for your garden. He did not even tell you what he had done for you. I hope you treated him with respect and not contempt."

All Are Common Citizens

"Well, his artistic abilities are not what distressed me. Publius had a sharp tongue for a common citizen."

"We are all common citizens now. The highest power in the earth today is Christ, who rules in earth's atmosphere. He is a mighty spirit being with unlimited power and wisdom. That should interest you. Whatever power you once held was very limited and tentative, and if you possessed wisdom, very little of it appears in your history."

"You also seem to possess a very sharp tongue. Doesn't anyone have respect for royalty anymore?"

"Royalty was an illusion of yesteryear. The earth always needed to have rulers of some sort, but royal blood was no different than any other blood. Anyway, let's talk about things that might be helpful to both of us."

Nero felt a little humiliated having to serve his guest. He always had servants to do such work, so it seemed demeaning.

"I hope you enjoy this breakfast. It is the first time I have ever served breakfast. At least everything is simple. I would not be able to cook anything. Though, since eating this diet, I have never felt better or more fulfilled. Do you feel the vitality in this food pulsing through your veins like I do?"

"Yes, this is perfect food and will ultimately restore your body to perfection. What a difference it makes! If your armies had had food such as this, they probably would not have deserted you. They would have been happy or at least happier in your service."

"How do you know they deserted me?"

"Why else would you have taken your life?"

"You seem to know everything that happened. Can you tell me why my sleep in death was disturbed? To awaken divested of all authority and influence is difficult to accept. You know, I did not ask to be here."

"No, but you did not ask to be born in the first place, and you didn't seem to mind that. So why do you mind your rebirth?"

"I'll have to think about that."

"Would you like to go for a ride after breakfast?"

"Yes, I would. If I didn't see it, I wouldn't believe it was possible. However, so many things that seem impossible are happening that I don't doubt anything anymore. Could I secure one of those aircraft? Somewhere I must have enormous riches hidden away. I know I left this world very rich."

"Nothing is secured with money anymore. In time, everyone will have a craft such as this, but for now these are used in lands without roads and bridges. That way we do not need to waste a lot of land for highways. When things level off, the great highways will be removed with only small roads between communities being preserved. Aircraft will provide most travel. Right now they're in limited supply, and so your desire for one must wait."

"How come you have such a craft then? Are you better than the rest of us?"

"I happen to have helped to make this kind of aircraft, so the King graciously rewarded me with one for my services."

"You mean you had the knowledge to make something such as this?"

"I had a lot of help, but, yes, I had much to do with this aircraft and the power source that it uses."

That suddenly quieted Nero. He unexpectedly realized the intelligence of the person with whom he was speaking. He couldn't avoid feeling his inferiority in such a brilliant world.

Nero Fearful of His First Flight

Nero, while eager to fly, at the same time exhibited some fear about leaving the good earth. He said, "Are you sure this vehicle is safe? What would happen if we rise hundreds of feet above the earth and the power source should fail?"

"I am afraid we would die. This craft is quite heavy, and it would fall back to earth. However, we have never had a failure in our power source that resulted in a free fall. Your fear is logical, but not justified. This aircraft has a one hundred percent safety record. If, indeed, something should cause our power source to fail, the spiritual force that is at work in our midst would prevent an accident that would result in our death or injury. You have a double safeguard. Please rest assured about your safety. Christ did not bring us to life to have malfunctioning equipment end it."

"Well, I have been a cautious man, especially regarding my life. I am not convinced of what you are telling me so understand my hesitancy."

"That is no problem, Nero. I helped make this craft, and when I first flew it I was a bit nervous. It is not like the early days of science when aircraft did fall out of the sky. We have better science and more sustainable power. We could fly around the world several times with all the energy possessed in this craft."

Having said this, Lev closed the door and powered the engine causing the craft to rise vertically. After they reached a proper altitude, Lev headed toward the western sea. Soon the outline of water came into sight giving a panoramic view that Nero had never experienced. His eye caught the beauty of earth with water lapping at its shores. "I wish I could paint this scene," he said.

Lev turned on some extraordinary music that Nero loved instantly. "Oh, I could listen to that forever," he said as he tried to hum the tune.

"Forever is a long time. Enjoy it now, for eternity may not be yours if you don't manifest progress in showing love for God and your fellow man."

"Are you some kind of preacher sent to make a proselyte Christian of me?"

"No, but I can tell you 'every knee is going to bow' before his throne. You don't have to bow, but you don't have to live either."

"That kind of talk infuriates me! If Christ will leave me alone, I will leave him alone. That's fair, isn't it?" Nero uttered his customary growl.

"How did you handle murderers when you ruled Rome?"

"If they were citizens, we beheaded them. If they were not citizens, we usually crucified them or threw them to the lions. Why do you ask?"

No License to Murder

"You are a murderer, that is why. Do you think because you were an emperor that you had the liberty to murder innocent people?"

The ex-emperor refused to answer.

"Christ returned you to life to face yourself and all of your evil deeds, but not with a view to condemning you to some awful fate," Lev continued when he didn't get a reply. "He wants to see you change your heart condition so that you might live."

"You tell Christ that I was happy sleeping in the grave."

"You didn't hear beautiful music in the grave, did you?"

"No."

"You said you could listen to this music forever. It is good hearing such music; it lifts you up and makes your heart rejoice."

"Yes, but it doesn't solve my problems. I loved being in power, but I find myself now without any authority whatever."

"Really? You have a lot of authority over yourself. Isn't that the place to start exercising it? When you learn to rule self properly, perhaps you might be trusted to deal with other people. You obviously didn't learn to discipline yourself. Whatever evil caught your fancy, you felt free to do."

"The gods endowed me with unlimited authority, so why shouldn't I use it as I pleased?"

"You know your gods had as much life and power as you did while sleeping in the grave. The gods of Rome were imaginary, and no one believes such nonsense anymore. You lived in a dark time of ignorance and superstition, when demons created false gods so ignorant people such as you could fantasize about them."

"I burned Christians for telling me such things. Now that I am without power, I have to endure such insults."

"You mentioned how you wished you could draw the majestic scenes below. You seem to enjoy life despite your complaint that you were not asked whether or not you wanted to leave the grave."

"I Knew How to Live"

"Lev, I am a connoisseur of the good things in life. I had the finest food, the best wines, and beautiful women. I knew how to gratify every craving. Nothing was forbidden—I had the power to do whatever my heart desired. That was the kind of life I enjoyed."

"Then why did you kill yourself?"

"Because my army deserted me and my power was terminated. There was little alternative for me. I had a choice of dying by my own hand or being flogged to death as a criminal."

"You had to end your own life because you lost the respect of those associated with you. Everyone knew that you were interested in your own pleasure and cared for no one but yourself. You destroyed the last vestige of respect you held. How did you manage to do that?"

"How would I know?"

"Don't you think it was your responsibility to understand what was happening under your watch?"

"Obviously, too many people were unhappy with me. I can safely conclude that. It is not that I starved my soldiers, or that I didn't provide adequate wages for them. Perhaps I should have kept in better touch with my base of support. I was an artist, not a warrior. I thought as long as they were provided for that they would remain loyal. I was obviously wrong."

"A man who would murder his mother and brother, then beat his pregnant wife to death, is not going to retain anyone's respect. There were nobler and more gifted men who would forego their own immediate pleasure for the good and well-being of the nation. Perhaps you lacked that ability. Do you think they may have deserted you because they perceived you were an abuser of men and not a true leader?"

"How would I know? Anyway why should I be talking to you about these matters? I don't know you, and that chapter in my life is closed. Why even discuss it? If there was a chance for me to regain my throne, I would be willing to hear about that!"

"No, Nero, your throne is long gone and will never be restored to you or anyone else. Reminding you who is King now only makes you unhappy."

"I have already been told that Christ is reigning. That infuriates me! It seems that all my devotion to the gods of Rome did nothing to help my cause. However, I am not about to join with Christ, unless he might need me to occupy a throne somewhere."

"There is a small throne he might assign you to. That one is to rule yourself and be responsible for your actions."

"You are being rather trite. I need more inspiration than that."

"Anyway, there will be no demands for your services from Christ's throne. I hope you will be learning to build homes, because you have a mother and father who are coming back to life. They will need provisions, and you are responsible for taking care of their needs."

"Can I forego this so-called privilege?"

"If you refuse, others will do it, but you will injure yourself greatly by refusing."

"Haven't I already injured myself greatly?"

"You must realize that you have. All the people you murdered and deceived will be coming back soon if they are not already alive. Did you realize this?"

"Now that you mention it, I find that very disturbing. I took my life because I wanted to end it all, and now someone is determined to bring me back to life only to put my feet to the fire. Why couldn't I just remain dead?"

"That is an option you may choose after you have lived for a century or so. However, first you will be forced to face all those you abused while in power. You have a lot of company, Nero. There are people who did worse than you and on an even grander scale. The fact is, you can be reconciled to all your victims, but it will take discipline and virtue to live down your sins. However, it can be done."

Not Willing to Eat Humble Pie

"Thanks for the encouragement, but I am Nero. I do not humble myself to beg for forgiveness from anyone."

"Apparently all these wonderful sights and heavenly music are not enough to make you choose life."

"I will take the splendid sights and heavenly music whenever I can, but I will not stoop before lowly Christians."

As they returned from their flight and were landing again on Nero's pad, he thanked Lev for the ride and the music. "I did enjoy that, even though our conversation did not appeal to my sensitive nature."

"I am sorry that it was disagreeable to you, Nero, but perhaps you will need to develop a better character in order to meet your present responsibilities. Christ is very patient, so there is time. If not today, there will always be tomorrow, or next week, or next month, or next year."

"Do not speak down to me! I hope you realize that in the day of my power I had men put to death for even thinking what you speak. You do not seem to know how to address royalty."

As they had lunch together, Nero was rather belligerent. "Why don't you take your aircraft and fly away? I really don't need you here. If this is my house, why can't I decide who enters it?"

"Oh, I would be glad to leave. I didn't request this assignment. The Ancients asked me to come, and that is the only reason I am here. They are the people in authority under Christ, and I take my orders from them. I think you would be well advised to keep me around, since I can be a great help to you. Without receiving some guidance for awhile, you might get yourself into trouble. Christ demands that all people will learn righteousness, and you might need some guidance along the way. For you, I represent the awesome powers that are in control of this world, so you should tread lightly in dismissing the ambassador they sent you as a favor."

"All right. Stay on if you must. I may need your services—I realize I don't know much about this present life. However, I do not need your lectures and your manner of speaking down to me."

"You must not be so sensitive, Nero. I cannot in good faith strengthen your weaknesses. I speak the truth at all times, so one thing you need to know right away is that instant punishment will await you when you try to lie or deceive."

"I don't frighten easily. I am a long way from Jerusalem."

Lev just smiled and nodded his head. "All right, don't say I didn't warn you. You are closer to Jerusalem than you could ever imagine."

Nero then went to concentrate on some learning sessions, and Lev retreated to his room to find some peace and spiritual refreshment. Later that afternoon the doorbell rang. Lev asked, "Do you want me to answer that?"

"Yes, but if anyone asks for me, I am not home."

"But you are home, Nero, and that is what I will tell them."

"I never had such impudent people with me. Don't you understand that I do not want to see anyone?"

"Well, they might insist on seeing you, and I will not lie for you."

An Angry Man Appears

Lev opened the door to a man who seemed enraged. "Are you Nero?"

"No, my name is Lev Aron. What can I do for you?"

"I am looking for Nero. My information is that he lives in this house."

"Yes, indeed he does. Shall I call him for you?"

"No, just take me to his room."

"What is your name, that I may tell him who is calling for him?"

"My name is Julian Mostroni, but he won't remember me though I remember him very well. I could never forget him. If he doesn't come here, I will tear down his door."

"Please, sir, calm down. Be seated, please, while I ask him to come out to meet you."

"I will not sit down. Tell him I will only wait a minute for him to appear, or I will come in after him."

Lev opened the door to Nero's room to find him cowering by a window. "Don't try to get out the window. Come out to meet your guest. I guarantee no harm will come to you. Trust me."

Nero seemed very pale, but he agreed to meet the visitor. "You promised me no harm will come to me. I am taking your word for it."

Nero entered the parlor, not in his usual regal manner. Slouching into the room, he met the man glowering at him. "That's him! Hello, Nero. You don't remember me, but I was a victim you burned to death along with my family. I am here to repay your kindness." He stepped forward into a place to prevent Nero's escape. "Don't try to run away. I have been waiting a long time for this moment. See these two hands. Look at them very closely, because I am going to strangle you with them."

Lev knew what was going to happen, so he took a seat so he could watch.

Nero shouted, "Aren't you going to defend me? You promised no harm would come to me—you traitor!"

Nero tried to escape, but Julian was faster and reached both hands out grabbing his throat to strangle him, only to find his arms paralyzed and soon hanging limply by his side.

Nero, seeing his assailant's predicament, took the opportunity to swing at him with all his strength, hoping to floor him with one blow, only to have his own arm paralyzed also.

Both men stood there helplessly, staring at one another in shock.

Lev sat there peacefully. "Are you both ready to listen to reason? Violence is not permitted. You have both been punished by a spiritual police force. I hope you learned your lesson. Now, be seated while I talk to you."

"Julian, I know you are angry and you have every right to be so. This man is guilty of destroying you and your family unjustly, and that was a heinous crime. Christ administers justice, so you must *never* take justice into your own hands. Nero will have to confront thousands of people he murdered and abused in the day of his power. Because he murdered thousands, if everyone coming back to life wanted to kill him, how could they each do it? No, Christ will administer justice so that Nero receives just punishment. He is starting to pay for his crimes even now. Your task, Julian, is not to punish anyone, but to struggle to be reconciled to this man who caused your death and that of your family."

Lev continued, "What he did was evil. Will he pay for it? Yes, to the extent of his culpability. However, many of his sins and yours may be attributed to inherited human weakness, and only Christ knows that perfectly. The main work for men is to be reconciled to one another. That is not going to be easy or done overnight. It will take a lot of growth in character for reconciliation to take place. Nero is going to have to learn true godly sorrow for what he did, and you, Julian, must learn forgiveness and compassion. You can do it if you sincerely wish to. If you harbor anger and a grudge in your heart, it will eat as a canker and be very detrimental to you."

Julian's frustration was so great he fought angry tears. He shouted, "I can never be reconciled to this monster. I *hate* him. I *despise* him. I *loathe* him, and I only regret my hands failed me the very moment I was about to fulfill my heart's desire. I wanted to squeeze the life out of him so badly. This man does not deserve to live."

Nero sat there pale and frightened. He was a coward and felt relieved that his assailant was helpless now. Still, he was most uncomfortable facing the sins of his past. It had been easy to condemn men and their families to horrible deaths without even an ounce of compassion. Now his past was returning, and his peers were judging him for his deeds. His victim was sitting there before him loathing him with a fiery passion so hot he could feel it.

Requesting Julian's Removal

"Can you remove this creature from my house, Lev? I don't need the likes of him around," Nero sneered.

"Not so fast, Nero. It is very important to listen to this man's story and learn about the suffering you caused him and his family. He died through the agony you forced him to endure. The least you can do is appreciate the enormity of your crime and feel some of his pain. So be quiet and listen to this man. You need to hear his tragic story and remember it forever."

Lev spoke with such authority that Nero became silent. Never before was he one to listen, but with his arm limply hanging by his side, he knew and felt powers unseen. He was momentarily frightened and humbled.

"Now, Julian, tell us how and why Nero had you put to death."

"Well, everyone knows that this demon, Nero, wanted to rebuild parts of Rome. Some of the city was old and run down. The Senate refused his request. So Nero ordered his servants to set fire to the city, and the fire soon got out of hand. A large part of the city was consumed in the blaze. The Senate was angry, and they suspected Nero was guilty of this crime. However, this sly liar claimed that Christians had set the fire and then ordered them rounded up and tied together with pitch poured on them. He rode by that evening in his splendid chariot while his servants lit us with flames. He drove by while men, women and children screamed in the flames. My family was not even Christian, but we had been friendly to several Christian families. They were nice people, and when they were rounding them up, I protested and the soldiers grabbed us. I had no idea what was to happen. I thought we would be jailed for a few days or even beaten, but I was horrified at the turn of events. It was unbearable. It was doubly unbearable to watch my wife and children consumed in the flames. I could not understand the cruelty and the injustice of all this. Rome was supposed to have a legal system, but Nero was above the law."

"So, Nero, what do you have to say to Julian?"

"I don't normally explain my actions to anyone, much less to some gangsters who lived in Rome. I didn't set the fire."

No sooner had he said this then he lost his speech and momentarily had trouble breathing. He tried to clear his throat, but his voice was gone. His arrogant manner suddenly turned into childish tears running down his cheeks.

Lev said, "I am afraid you lied and lost your voice. If you think that because you did not set the fire personally that you can say you were not responsible for it, you are very wrong. You set the fire, Nero; you gave the orders, didn't you?"

He nodded sheepishly.

"So you had all these innocent people burned and destroyed to cover your own mischievous conduct. What kind of a man were you?"

Julian shouted, "He is no part of the human race. I only wish I could squeeze out his life. He is a monster, a liar and a murderer by his own confession."

"Calm down, Julian," Lev commanded. "Nero is now in Christ's court. Be assured that he will receive appropriate consequences for his crimes. Justice belongs to Christ, not to you or me. You have to believe that in order to have your own peace of mind. No one is getting away with anything, and we *all* need Christ's mercy, so settle down. You have to accept Christ's sovereignty in this matter."

Nero seemed most uncomfortable with his right arm hanging limply by his side and feeling his voice box in a vice.

Lev, seeing the distress of both men, decided to explain how they could get relief. He continued, "Obviously, you are very new in this world, and you don't know instant punishment is meted out to anyone violating Christ's laws. Since you are both new and ignorant, I will call headquarters and secure one of the Ancients to speak to you. Now listen. You must tell them exactly what has happened. You must tell only the truth and not try to justify any actions. If you do tell the truth without trying to justify yourself, you will probably be healed within the hour. However, if you do not, your punishment will last longer. I will have to talk for you, Nero, but you will tap on the phone once indicating 'yes' or two taps indicating 'no.'"

Deborah Hears the Report of Their Punishments

Lev reached Deborah, one of the judges in the Old Testament, who spoke with grace and authority to both men. Speaking to such a distinguished woman immediately subdued them, and they behaved almost like obedient children. In less than an hour both were healed, and with that, Julian thanked Lev and departed very meekly. His whole demeanor had changed, and the experience was a good lesson for him. With Nero, it only made him meek until he had gained his voice and the use of his arm; then his old arrogance returned.

That evening, Lev showed Nero a program giving instructions on building homes. "You better start learning how to work on your first project. Your wife, Poppaea Sabina, who was with your child when she died, is returning to life, and you will be able to share your home with her, *if* she chooses to live with you. If she will not live with you, the house that you build might then be for Poppaea. If she chooses to live with you for the sake of the child, then the home will be for your mother."

"Wait a minute, am I some common laborer? This is insanity. Slaves should be building the houses. What became of my riches? I could use them to pay workers to do the building for me."

"You entered the world originally with nothing, and you left it with nothing. Christ has freely given you all that you now possess. You have no slaves and there are no laborers who work for money. There *is* no money. Work is done out of love and concern for others. Failing in this, it is done out of decency and out of our obligations to progenitors and those near us. Your trouble started when you had people around you who did not criticize your excesses. A true friend wouldn't do that, but is one who will not strengthen your weaknesses. Instead, he would lovingly point them out to you. Your counselors, Burrus and Seneca, graced your early reign with reason and wisdom. With their passing, those who surrounded you encouraged your every vice and weakness, which only helped bring on your demise."

"Indeed, Burrus and Seneca made my early years very successful. Rome probably had the best government they ever had during the years of their strong influences. They were good men and served Rome well. However, I am not a laborer. It is so demeaning to ask a man who served as the emperor of Rome to build houses. Anyway, I am not eager to meet either Poppaea or my mother. You mentioned that volunteers might be found for building for my father. I should be grateful for such a service."

"I am one of the volunteers. I have built many homes already, and I deem it a privilege and an honor to serve my brothers and sisters of the human race in this way. What is so humbling about doing honest work?"

"Truthfully, I am not a handy man," Nero said with a sniff of superiority. "I am more of an artist, and perhaps my skills could be employed in producing paintings. They would sell very well, I'm sure."

"Nero, at some point you must face reality. Any painting of yours would have no takers in today's society. Furthermore, there is no money to buy anything with. Homes are what people need as they return to life. Every human being must be amply provided with food, clothing, and a lovely, self-sufficient new home. It's time for you to take some responsibility. You lived off the sweat and labor of others too long. It's time for you to sweat and labor for others."

Not Eager to Work

"The very thought of work makes me ill. What would the citizens of Rome think, seeing me as a common laborer?"

"That you had gained your sanity."

Nero snorted. "It's embarrassing for me. You seem to know everything, so you know I was responsible for Poppaea's death."

"Yes, I know that, and you are responsible for many others. It is a bit awkward now isn't it?"

"That's why I should have been left in the grave."

"You forgot how to be a kind and loving human being. People are so happy today. All the goodness they did in their former life comes back to bless them doubly. They are being daily received into open arms with thankfulness and joy. Every former deed of love and kindness returns as a sweet odor. Thank the Lord, most were wholesome people who cared for their own and for their fellow men."

"That's no comfort to me. Sometimes I looked at the common people who seemed to be so happy, and I could never understand it. They laughed and danced and rejoiced in the smallest things of life. I envied their happiness. I had everything, yet I had nothing. I didn't have a true friend who loved me, but I guess I never really loved anyone but myself."

"Now you are beginning to see the light. The secret of life, or you might say the mystery of life, is love. Our capacity for happiness grows as our love for our fellow men grows. You were a victim of a shriveled heart bent on self-gratification. Did it bring you happiness?"

"It brought me pleasure."

"That's a good distinction. But that which gives pleasure for the moment disappears and leaves you empty.

If Only Love and Kindness Had Been Sown

"As emperor, you had abundant resources to bless people with love and kindness. Yet you tried to squeeze out pleasure for yourself, and you ended your life a forsaken and hated person. Whose fault was it then?"

"You know, you are a likeable fellow, Lev, when you're not judging me. Why don't you discuss your own faults?"

"I can do that. My faults were in failing to love more than I did and to give more than I did. I'm trying to make up for it now by doing double duty. No, I didn't betray my friends or kill those I loved. I did kill when I was a soldier, but all to no purpose. I was doing what I was trained to do, but I deeply regret having killed any man now."

"So you were no angel? I am glad you had some faults. It makes me feel better."

"Well, I'm not here to make you feel good about yourself. You really don't have much in your past that should make you feel good. It would be much better if you could feel some genuine sorrow for your past."

"I know I would be much more comfortable if I didn't have a lot of people seeking to kill me, I can tell you that, Lev."

Lev sighed. "All you're interested in is your own comfort. When are you going to begin to take responsibility for the past?" Lev entreated. "You have to live down what you did. You are going to have to demonstrate you are sorry and show the kind of life that proves your new heart condition. You will not change unless you decide to. It is going to require action and will on your part. Why can't you see this?"

"Because the man you are describing is not me, that's why. I am still Nero, remember? I have not changed since I have awakened. And I have no plans to."

"Well, I am glad you like Nero, because no one else does. Anyway, you had your first contact with one of your victims today. You learned something of Christ's power—and that you are now a subject and no longer an emperor. You are being given precious time and experiences to live down your evil past. You can do it, but you must first want to do it, and the actions will follow."

"Why can't you understand what I'm telling you? I am Nero! You want to turn me inside out and make me into a 'Lev Aron.'"

"You have not been given another opportunity at life so you can continue on your nefarious course. That will not be permitted. What happened when you tried to lie?"

"I must say, someone has tremendous power. I cannot deny that."

"Well, are you going to help in building a home?"

"I suppose I could do that if I had to, but how can I face Poppaea or my mother?

"You are going to have to face them, whether you build or don't build. They will return to life. Poppaea might feel better about you if she thought that you did build for her in the event she chooses not to live with you. Remember, you are not the first murderer who had to face his victims. It is something you will have to do, like it or not."

A Weak Consent to Build

"All right, all right. I shall start learning about building. Has someone built my mother, Agrippina, a house already?"

"That depends. If Poppaea decides to live with you, then her house will be your mother's. She will return as one angry woman, though."

"I couldn't build my mother a house," remarked Nero.

"She would be afraid to live in any house that you built, Nero," Lev chuckled with a touch of irony.

"Better is a poor and a wise child than an old and foolish king,
Who will no more be admonished"
(Ecclesiastes 4:13).

Chapter Eight

Nero soon got over his discomfort at being a laborer. Actually, it gave him a feeling of worth to be doing something constructive. Lev could see that it wasn't the work that troubled him, but the realization that he would have to face his wife again. Nero had come home in a surly mood late one evening after drinking, and she had criticized him. He never dreamed he would become so violent with her, but as she continued to carry on about his lack of responsibility, he remembered becoming unusually angry. After all, he was the emperor of Rome and he need not endure being demeaned by his wife. In his rage he kicked her as hard as he could, knocking her to the floor.

How could he have done this? He hadn't intended to hurt her. She was great with child. He immediately felt so mean and ugly. She was so beautiful, how could he have killed her? It seemed so unreal. He did have affection for her. Killing others never bothered him; but she was his wife and was expecting his child and only heir soon. What had possessed him? He tried to say he was sorry, but he was speaking to the silent dead. Her wet pale face was indelibly etched on his mind. How could Nero face her?

Lev had gotten additional volunteers, so the work went quickly and easily. Soon there was a house, orchard, and garden nearly ready to receive another human being back to life. As the construction continued, Nero became fascinated with all the technical features of modern building. Self-sufficiency intrigued him. He warmed to the idea of not having servants standing around. Everyone was completely independent.

He also found physical exercise invigorating, and working with such a man of distinction as Lev added glamour to the work. His only procrastination was caused by the thought of Poppaea's return—*that* was maddening. That was one death that he actually felt bad about. Other deaths had made him uncomfortable. There was certain uneasiness and nagging of conscience when he had inflicted death on others. He had also drunk more heavily when he had sentenced people to death.

Nero Desires to Escape Confrontation

When the day of Poppaea's return to life arrived, Nero wished he could find a good bottle of vintage wine before having to face her, but none was to be had. He thought that Lev could provide him with wine with all his influence, but he was told to drink grape juice, which was the same thing without alcohol.

Lev finally countered Nero's pleading. "No one will strengthen your weakness. If you had not been drunk when you came home that night, you probably would have behaved differently. And now you want me to help you get drunk so you can face the wife you murdered. The answer is no, absolutely not!"

"I don't know how I am going to face her in the morning. I still see her pale, lifeless face in my mind as though I was standing there. You know, I did have feelings for her. She was not just anybody; Poppaea was my wife, and a very good wife to me. How can I explain my actions to her? She will loathe me, and my presence will only make her fearful and upset. I just cannot face her."

"Gather your strength, Nero. You will have to make your peace with her sooner or later. You did not have to be a man to kill her, but you will have to be one to receive her back to life. Any wild, insane savage could have murdered her, but it takes humility and grace to acknowledge what you did with godly sorrow. You do feel sorry, sorrier than you admit, so why not be truthful with her? No, you cannot undo the ugliness of that moment, but you can stand tall by confessing your remorse and seeking her forgiveness. Poppaea will be coming back with the unborn child, so you will soon have a newborn. Some day both of you will also have back Claudia Augusta, your four-month-old daughter who died of illness. This should make you happy."

"I don't think I have ever been what they call 'happy.' I was sated with the excesses of this world, drunk in my power lust, but never really happy. People bowed to my wishes, but in their hearts they hated me. I was constantly fearful that someone would poison me or stab me to replace me on the throne. After all, that's how I got to the throne; my mother poisoned her husband, my stepfather Claudius, so I could ascend. Later I feared my mother would poison me so my brother could replace me. Murder for power was common. Outwardly, Rome looked secure, but within we were insecure and on edge."

"Poppaea is returning tomorrow morning, and you must be there to receive her. She will not realize that she died, so she will just think the doctors healed her. She was mercifully unconscious during most of your beating, so she will not know how deadly the wounds that you inflicted on her were. Just speak gently to her, and maybe your first meeting will not go too badly. Do not argue with her; speak only gentle and loving words. I will come in the afternoon. I need to know if she is willing to stay with you, so that when the child is born, you may be a father to it. It is desired that you both live in your house. If she is willing, then your mother will have the house we just built. Until she returns, I will live there."

"You make it sound so easy, but I shudder to think of my meeting with her. However, if I must, I will somehow try to undo some of the damage I inflicted upon her."

"By the way, didn't she love dogs, especially that gentle poodle she had with her most of the time? I can get a dog similar to that, if you think it would help make her feel comfortable."

"Yes! Yes, please do! That is a great idea! Of course, it won't be Fifi, but perhaps she will not know the difference immediately."

Lev Secures Another "Fifi"

"I will secure the dog this evening. I will be back to take you and the dog to the house. Put her in the room where Poppaea will awaken and wait until she comes out. Give her time to get adjusted to life; don't intrude into her room. She needs some time to be alone and collect her thoughts. She may even scream, but that will only be an impulse from her last moments of life. She will return perfectly well and will need no immediate attention from you. The fact that she will still have her child will be very reassuring to her."

In the morning Nero was ready to go with Lev and take his new Fifi. They all climbed aboard and in minutes were at the home they had just built. They arrived about an hour before Poppaea was due to return. Nero put Fifi into her room and made some tea, both for her as well as to steady his own nerves. He found himself in a cold sweat and dreading to face the events of this day. Never, even in his most extreme dreams, did he ever envision an event such as was about to take place.

Lev had left for a chapel meeting and promised to return in the afternoon. Nero realized he had come to depend on Lev more than he ever thought possible. He seemed to have all the answers and always knew what to do. It was Lev's sincerity and genuineness that made him trustworthy. Nero had had many servants; some he could trust more than others. But for the first time, someone treated him as a true friend. It was good to have a friend.

Nero found himself pacing up and down the living room, occasionally stopping to sip some tea. The tea actually calmed his nerves, but still the dull feeling of guilt—or was it shame?—pervaded his thoughts. When the clock struck, he only imagined what was happening in the other room. Having Poppaea return to life was such an awesome experience. He felt the excitement of such a momentous event. The gods he had served were nothing more than dead statues of stone, but what awesome powers were being demonstrated in that next room!

Soon he heard Fifi bark and Poppaea speaking to her. He could tell there was some activity in that room, but he obeyed Lev's instructions to give her time to become somewhat oriented to life again. A long fifteen minutes passed and still the door remained closed. He was dreading when it would open, when he must face Poppaea again. Soon, the door opened a crack and he called out to her, "Is that you, Poppaea?"

The door closed immediately. "Please come out my dear. You are safe. I will never harm you again." Another ten minutes passed, and he feared she would not come out. However, she opened the door a crack again, saying, "Nero, I am coming out, but why don't you leave me alone? I have lost all trust that I ever had in you. You are nothing but a savage animal!"

"Yes, you are right. I hate myself for what I did and am so thankful to see you well again and still carrying our child. Please, have no fear. I promise I will be on my best behavior. Anyway, I have a lot of pleasant surprises for you. Please, come and have some breakfast. Smell this wonderful tea; you have never tasted anything like it. It is just wonderful!"

"Oh, don't try to talk to me sweetly, you ogre. Have you forgotten how you beat me? I thought I was going to die. How could you do that seeing my delicate condition?"

"I was drunk, but I have not touched wine for over a month."

"You mean I was unconscious that long? I guess my child and I are lucky to be alive. But the child was due in just another few weeks, how could a month have passed?"

"Come, Poppaea, have some tea; it will calm your nerves and make you feel tranquil again."

"It does smell good, but promise to stay away from me. Don't touch me!"

Nero Tries to Be a Gentleman

"Very well, I will not touch you. I promise. I am so glad to see you, my dear. I am so sorry. How can I make it up to you? You know I have not touched alcohol and probably never will again. I have made some changes in my life. Please taste the tea; you have never tasted anything like it."

She stood by the table and picked up a cup. After taking her first sip, her eyes brightened. "This is delicious! Where did you get it? With tea like this, I can see why you quit drinking wine. Does this come from India?"

"No, everybody grows it now. It is just some new tea that came along and has become an instant success. It's good for you, too! How about a nice breakfast?"

"I am hungry! I have to eat for two, you know. Why are we in such an unusual house? I don't remember anything like this before. I don't even think this is Fifi. Something seems so strange about everything. I don't know how to describe it. If I didn't see you, I would think that I was in heaven. Where are we? By the way, even you look taller, thinner, and more handsome than I remember. I just have the strangest feeling, like this is a dream or something. Even when I looked in the mirror, I have beautiful straight teeth, and I can see things so clearly! I feel taller and stronger. I feel wonderful, especially considering what I have been through; and yet everything seems unreal. Am I dreaming this?"

"No, no, my dear, you just have been sleeping for a long while. Everything will gradually become clear to you."

"Why wasn't my child born then?"

"I can't exactly explain that. I honestly don't know about such things. Maybe the answer is that you did die and have been raised from the dead this very morning."

"Oh, don't be silly! This is no time for bad jokes."

"Well, I have another surprise for you. Have some fruit. This is our main breakfast meal. It is the most delicious fruit you have ever tasted."

She sat down, still apprehensive about his mood. "I don't mind fruit for dessert, but don't you have some bread and olives, and some eggs and ham or something like that? I am really hungry!"

"Well, that is almost what I said when I was given this fruit for breakfast. Once you eat it, you will never ask for bread or olives, or for eggs or the like. It is the most delicious fruit. It will satisfy your hunger and make you feel so good when you eat it. Your system will crave this fruit."

"Well, it does smell good. If that's all you have, I guess that's what I'll have to eat."

Her eyes opened wide upon tasting the fruit of Paradise. "Oh, I have never tasted anything like this before! It is absolutely delicious! Where does it come from?"

"Right from your backyard. You have a whole grove of trees that bear fruit the year around. This is our main diet now."

"That cannot be true! We never had trees that bore fruit all year around. Anyway, I never tasted fruit like this before. Something very strange is going on. What are you hiding from me?"

"I can't explain it all, but as soon as you finish your breakfast, I will show you the trees where this fruit came from. You will believe me then, I hope."

"I don't mean to doubt you. However, everything is so—so strange. Where is our palace? Where are all the servants? What has happened?"

"If I told you we all died and have been raised to life under new conditions, would you believe it?"

Death Does Not Seem a Plausible Explanation

"Oh, don't be silly! We are both very much alive! What is the matter with you? Why are you talking such nonsense? There is no odor of wine on your breath, but so much of what you are saying makes no sense at all. Please do not lie to me! I already feel disoriented. I need to hear things that make sense, and that I can believe."

"I know exactly how you feel, my dear. I would not tell you anything that is not true. I don't know how to convince you of this, but we both have died and have come to life again. Remember all the Christians I destroyed? Well, Christ is King of this whole world now."

"Nero!" She yelled, almost angrily. "You are speaking utter nonsense! I am not a child to believe such wild stories. Now, tell me the truth!"

"I know that what I am telling you sounds wild and unbelievable. I felt exactly as you did when I inquired about our servants and palace. When I was told they were all long gone, I responded just as you did. However, be patient with me because I am telling you the truth."

"I think I need some fresh air. Please excuse me while I step outside. My head is spinning around."

"Please, let me show you the orchard outside." They walked through the most beautiful garden with not a blemished plant or weed to be seen. When they came to the fragrant orchard and Poppaea saw the fruit, she knew at least some of what Nero was saying was true.

She remarked, "I have never seen such gorgeous trees. This seems to be the very same fruit I ate. There is something very strange about all of this. Why is our house so small and yet so beautiful? Everything in it is magnificent. I could almost believe that I died and went to heaven, but I would never expect to find *you* there."

"Was I that bad?"

"You did so many awful things! You persecuted the Christians and blamed them for what you yourself did. You were horrid!"

"I never told you this, but a man by the name of Paul stood before my judgment throne twice. He embodied every virtue. Jews had charged him with heresy, but when I saw him the first time, I knew he stood for everything I didn't. He was a follower of Christ and preached about the resurrection of the dead. He spoke with such authority and wisdom that I was enamored with him. I have never forgotten that man. He was absolutely brilliant and spoke with such authority, one might think he was on the throne and I was in the audience. I could see he was a good man, of rare virtue who had a charisma about him that was electrifying. He was the most impressive man I ever met."

"So you had him killed?"

"No, not the first time. I knew that it was out of envy that the Jews had charged him falsely so I set him free."

"The *second* time! What happened?"

"Well, I hate to admit this, but when Paul appeared before me the second time he was rather emaciated, but he still had that fascinating charisma. He spoke about the resurrection of the dead that time, too. It was so strange. Here I was, sitting on the throne embodying every vice, and this man standing before me stood for every virtue. I blamed the Christians for the fire that I set, so I had to condemn him to death because he was a Christian. However, he was a Roman citizen, for which I was glad, because he would die a rather painless death—by beheading."

"Oh, Nero! You knew Paul was a good man and innocent of any crime, and yet you condemned him to death? How *could* you?"

"I was a victim of my own lie. I couldn't kill other Christians and let him go free."

"Well, if this is a resurrection of the dead, he will be back soon, won't he?"

"I am going to have to ask Lev about Paul. He will know the facts about him. He seems to know everything else."

Lev Will Know the Answer

"Who is this 'Lev'? My head is swimming now! Please, no more strange stories and people."

Fifi followed them into the orchard and, finally, Poppaea said, "This is not Fifi! It is a nice dog, but *not* my Fifi. What is going on here? If I am not crazy, you are driving me crazy!"

"No, no, my dear. I know everything is strange because it is different. After a few days, you will feel more at home. It takes awhile to get adjusted."

"Adjusted to what? You are driving me mad, Nero! Why must everything be different? What happened to our beautiful palace? Where are all the servants? You don't expect me to clean and wash and take care of everything by myself, do you?"

"I have been doing everything myself, and look at me. I am just fine. Let me show you how easy life is now. We don't need servants standing around getting in the way and eavesdropping on our conversations in their annoying manner."

Going back to the house, he showed Poppaea the modern washing machine. He threw in some towels and clothing that were waiting to be washed and pressed a button and the machine started to wash the clothing.

"There, you see? In twenty minutes they will be washed, and then they will be dried. In hardly any time, they will be fresh and clean."

"How does all this work?"

"I don't know how, I just know that it works."

Then Nero showed her the bathroom.

"Remember how servants had to heat water and pour your bath? Look at this!" He turned a metal handle and out came hot water. Then he turned another handle and out came cold water. "Like magic, isn't it? We don't need servants. And here is the shower. They call it a shower because it is just like rain, only it is warm, and you can bathe in complete privacy without your maidservants."

She stood there wide-eyed and spellbound. "I can't believe what I am seeing. It is very wonderful, but how can it be?"

"Well, let me tell you this! Houses are cooled in the summer and heated in the winter automatically. Everything runs by itself. When you want light, you touch this switch, and behold, there is light. If you want to turn it off, touch it again!"

"Is this some kind of magic?"

"It looks like it, but I helped build the house and I know that it is called 'electricity.' Everything runs on a hidden powerful force. Let me show you the computer television."

Like an excited child, Nero tried to show his former wife everything all at once. Going into the parlor, he touched a button, and a screen became alive with people. Poppaea jumped back, startled. "How did these people get in here instantly?"

"They are not in here. That is only a picture carried by airwaves. You will use this television to get education at home. Everything you want to know can be learned quickly and easily this way. Learning is easy now. I will show you more about it in the evening. Now do you believe you are living in a different time? When I told you we both died and have come back to life, I was telling you the truth."

"Maybe I will get used to this, but right now I am more frightened by all of it. How can my world have changed so much overnight? One day I am living in a palace, and the next day I am living in a house of magic. I am eating different food, our servants have vanished and everything is making me feel that this is a dream. It cannot be real!"

"You Did Die!"

"My dear Poppaea, you did die, and I also died! I found it as hard to believe when I awakened as you now find it. Nearly two thousand years have passed and we are living in a time when knowledge is greatly increased. Mankind has learned to harness science to do many things. I know it seems like magic, but it is man's creative ingenuity that has made these things. When we lived, most people were ignorant and superstitious. Few people were educated and governments suppressed the spread of knowledge. Now everyone is being educated—there is no limit to learning. As knowledge pours in, it is shared generously with everyone. People may easily learn whatever they wish to know. We have wonderful teachers that make subjects easy to learn without much effort. I love learning this modern way, and you can't believe how the time flies. If you don't watch the clock, you can easily spend the whole night learning. The amazing thing is that we remember things clearly."

"If I died, then our baby died. I know the baby is alive and well within me. Perhaps in a few weeks it shall be born. I looked forward to having that child. When you turned so violently against me, I was sure the child would die. How could you do that to me? Most men loved their own children, but you could not even do that."

"I was intoxicated with power as well as wine; nothing was denied me. Men lived or died by my word, and to be truthful, I didn't care if they died. I could condemn people to death and then turn around and sing songs or write poetry. I was absolutely disconnected from the pain and suffering I caused others. I was never sensitive to other people's feelings. However, when you died, Poppaea, I still remember your pale face wet with tears. I felt remorse for the first time. I could not believe you were dead. You were so silent and beautiful. I was drunk at the time and arrived home with a terrible headache, and when you shouted at me, I lost my mind. I am truly sorry, my dear."

"You killed me and now you are sorry! What kind of man are you?"

"What else can I tell you? What I did was very wrong. I stood over you in disbelief. I spoke to you, but you did not answer me. I could not believe you were dead. I kept thinking that you would awaken. I became sober too late. No, I was not the husband I should have been to you, and you have every right to be angry. I did have feelings for you, and I still do. I have not touched you or kissed you since you returned to life. I know I must earn your love and respect, and I know I don't deserve it."

Can Nero Be Sorry?

Poppaea was astounded. "I never heard you say you were sorry about anything before. *You* were always the emperor who had a right to do whatever he wanted because it was in your power. How does it feel being a human being without special privileges and power?" She felt somewhat triumphant at his downfall.

"At first it was very hard. Although, I must tell you, I lost my throne before I died. The Senate knew my soldiers had deserted me, and they sentenced me to be flogged to death as a common criminal. When word of my fate reached me, I seized the opportunity to die by my own hand before they apprehended me. I killed you, and later I killed myself. I remembered how, when I wanted somebody out of the way, I would send a messenger to advise him to take his own life before I did. It never failed. Everyone I advised to take his or her life did so. Strange the same fate should come to me. You know, Poppaea, I died with no friends. I learned to love no one and no one loved me. When I left this world, I was bitter, and I still am. I did not want to come back. I still resent being here, even though life at times is very sweet."

"At least you paid for your sins with your own life. You know, I, too, was dazzled with the glamour of being queen of the empire, even though I knew you weren't faithful to me, just as you betrayed your former wife. I knew you were a man of passion, but I wanted the power and luxury of the imperial palace. I soon learned that I had everything and that I really had nothing. Our marriage was hardly made in heaven. I had hoped this child that I was bearing would somehow help our relationship. When you attacked me in such a violent manner, I realized our marriage meant nothing to you—and the baby meant nothing to you. You only lived to fulfill your passions." There was a definite tone of bitterness in her voice.

"But you did mean something to me, Poppaea. I realized too late that I deeply regretted what I did in my drunken rage. I knew I had lost my way. I had no values, no virtue, no loyalty and no shame. I could see disdain in people's eyes, even while they bowed before me. It never occurred to me to change. I thought my power and privilege would last forever. I clung to power to the very last minute, and when the moment of truth came, I grudgingly took my life. Death saved me from the pain and humiliation of being flogged to death and kept me out of the hands of those who hated me."

"So that is how you left this world. Was your death painful, Nero?"

"Yes, there was searing pain. Suddenly I was conscious of death. It was so easy to watch those Christians burn, screaming and writhing in pain, yet I did not feel any serious guilt about what I had done to them. When it was me that was feeling pain, it was different. It seemed wrong for me to have to die." Shaking his head, hardly believing what he was about to say, he remarked, "Oddly, I tried to think that I had been a good ruler for the people."

Death Wasn't Bad

Poppaea paused for a moment, thinking about what Nero said. "In some ways I am glad that I missed out on the closing days of your life. Death wasn't bad. It was the process of dying that involved suffering. Being dead was like it was before we were born. I felt nothing, knew nothing, and did not exist. I can see that with your background, all the people you destroyed will become a problem for you now."

"I know. I was already confronted by one of them."

"What happened?"

"He tried to strangle me with his bare hands. I was saved because his hands became paralyzed the same instant he grabbed my throat, and then they hung limply at his side. I tried to floor him once he was paralyzed, but my arm then became paralyzed. I was glad for the spiritual protection, but I was shocked when my own violence was punished. Because it was our first offense, we were both healed soon thereafter."

"Not to change the subject, but I am going to need a midwife before long. Do you know where we can find one?"

"No, but I know someone who will know. Lev Aron is coming this afternoon, and he seems to know everything. He has been living under these new conditions for many years, and he is extremely intelligent."

"Why is he visiting us?"

"Well, the Ancients, who are the human agents for the King, thought I would need extra help, so they asked Lev to be with me while I got adjusted to this new method of life. He may come for lunch, but I have picked plenty of fruit and have a lot of little extras, so he will be well taken care of. You know, it is so easy to entertain now. Our meals grow on trees or in the garden. Everything is done quickly and easily."

Lev's Aircraft Sets Down

Just before lunchtime, Nero heard a small aircraft outside. He called Poppaea to the window to watch her first aircraft set down on the pad outside their home.

"What is that? That *cannot* be real!"

"That is what I thought at first, but it is real! Soon you will see a real person, Lev Aron, stepping out of that aircraft."

Sure enough, the door of the craft opened and out stepped the most handsome man Poppaea had ever seen.

Nero and Poppaea both rushed out to meet him. "Shalom! I am Lev Aron and it is such a pleasure to meet you."

"I am happy to meet you, Mr. Aron."

"Welcome back to life, Poppaea. You will find it much better than anything you experienced before. It is a little strange at first, but in a few days you will find yourself very much at home here. Do you like your new surroundings?"

"Yes, I think I do. This house is not as big and luxurious as our palace, yet everything is like magic here. We have push-button servants instead of people. At first I was disappointed, but each passing hour I like it more."

"That's what we like to hear! There is no going back to the past with all its inequities and injustices. You say you missed your servants at first, but be assured, your servants are all glad to be free, and they live just as well as you do, in some ways better."

"How could it be better?"

"Because they are rejoicing to be delivered from the bondage in which they were held. Those in power abused them, but now they are independent and eager to create a world of happiness for themselves. They don't have too much baggage of evil brought with them in their return to life. Their lives were very simple, and their privileges were very few. They are like canaries let out of a cage."

"Oh, Lev!" Nero said. "You make it sound like our servants were abused. I will have you know they were very well fed and taken care of."

"Would you have been willing to trade places with any one of them?"

"Of course not! Emperors were not common laborers. You never held such a position, so you would not understand."

"More likely, I understand the injustice and inequity of the past only too well. When God made the world, He made man to be lord over the animal world, not over his fellow men. Each man is an emperor in his own right and should not bow his knee before another man. I bow only to my God and to His dear Son, who now rules the world. However, every man and woman is my equal, so I look down at no one."

Poppaea said, "I like that. Who is it that now rules the world?"

"Jesus Christ has ushered in a reign of righteousness such as earth has never known. No one is allowed to hurt another in this whole wide world. Ask Nero what happened when he tried to hurt another person."

"Nero already told me about that incident. Christ must be very powerful to enforce his laws uniformly over the entire earth."

"It is the same Jesus Christ whom Pilot had crucified. It is the same Christ that Christians followed and whom your husband had burned with fire."

Nero had a new idea. "If he was so powerful, why didn't he stop us from doing what we did?"

"Because evil was permitted and allowed to take its course so that everyone could look back and know what the reign of sin and evil was like. It is quite an education to look back at how men conducted themselves with unbridled evil and without compassion. However, that is true history. Now evil is not permitted anywhere at any time. Christ allowed his followers to demonstrate their loyalty to him under the reign of evil. Now they are reigning with him in glory."

Poppaea interjected, "Please excuse us for letting you stand out here, Lev. Come in and have lunch with us. Nero prepared our lunch, so please come in."

"Thank you! I think I am ready for some nourishment. Is this a first for you, preparing food for lunch?"

"Poppaea, do you have to announce my servitude?"

Lev smiled, "I am glad she did, Nero, as that is the only way to gain true greatness. This is a humble start, but true greatness can only be attained through serving others. That is how Christ became exalted to the right hand of power. His life on earth was a legend of service."

Christ Not Appreciated

Nero rolled his eyes. "Oh, not again! Please, no sermons—especially about Christ. You keep forgetting we Romans had our own gods and goddesses. Things went very well with our nation under them. Looking back, I think it is the Christians who brought about the ruin of our empire."

"Shall we pause to eat?" Poppaea interrupted.

Lev asked, "Do you mind if I offer a prayer of thanks before I eat?"

Nero said with disgust, "Does it matter what I think? Go ahead, offer your prayer, but don't include me in it."

"You are being rude!" Poppaea said, addressing Nero.

After a short silence with his head bowed, Lev lifted his head and said, "Don't worry, I'm not easily offended. I never eat without giving thanks to God, and in time you will learn to do the same."

Nero was very uneasy, making Poppaea nervous as well. Lev, sensing the situation, tried to diffuse it with some small talk.

"You know, Poppaea, you have a choice of where you will live. Couples who have children are encouraged to live together until the children are grown so that every child may benefit from having two parents. If you live with Nero in his house, this house will be given to Agrippina. That way she may return to life in about a month, giving you a chance to have your child."

"Oh, does that mean my mother-in-law is coming back? How long will it forestall her return if I stay here?"

"Not very long, perhaps two months. She will be coming back regardless of what you decide, but if you live as you should with Nero, it will speed things up a little. The main reason is to benefit your child.

That should be your primary consideration. Are you prepared to do what is right?"

"That is really a hard question. You know how I died, don't you? I don't want to go through that again."

"Yes, I know the unpleasant details, Poppaea. You need not relate them. You need have no fear of it happening again. You will not be living with the emperor anymore. You know that, too, don't you? He is just a man with a short temper when drunk, and we don't provide anything that will make him drunk these days.

So you have no reason to fear. Every child needs two parents. That is what God intended. Perhaps if you discipline the child, he or she will not grow up to be another Nero."

Nero uttered one of his little growls. "There you go again, Lev. You are making me out to be the worst man that ever lived."

"Sorry, Nero—I don't mean to put you down. You do have a bad track record is all that I meant to say. That is not to imply that other men placed in the same situation might have performed as badly or even worse. Being placed in almost unconditional power with very little virtue to guide you was a sad combination. Perhaps your *misfortune* was to have become emperor. Had you been an artist or musician, that might have saved you from being in the difficult position you are in today."

"I did enjoy being emperor," Nero acknowledged. "I imagined my name would go down in history as the artistic emperor who could sing, paint and still rule well. Fickle supporters were my undoing. I was betrayed and left to fall before my enemies. I shall never forgive such betrayal."

"Maybe your soldiers and supporters deserted you because you had become a disgrace to the empire. Anyway, you will be able to talk to them about why they deserted you. You might as well get used to having everything come out into the open."

"I can't say that I like that idea. I think it was better when people feared what might happen should their loose tongues be overheard."

"Do you think you will be getting everything you like these days?"

After a long pause, Nero said, "Lev, you are relentless. You know I am dethroned and out of power, and you are showing me no respect whatever. You would not have lasted long in my court in the days of my power. We had a way of dealing with insubordination."

"I know you find it galling to be out of power and having to endure people such as me. However, Nero, please remember, greater powers are now on the throne and they, too, have a way of dealing with insubordination."

The Throne Is Occupied by Another

Nero blushed. He was trying to control his temper. He was being forced to face the awful truth that his days of power were over. The emperor was now being reduced to the bleak realization of his present status. "All right, all right. I know I have been dethroned and will not very likely find another throne to sit on. I can sit and listen to you, but I don't have to like it."

"That is why I am here. My task is to encourage you to take your present opportunities and make the most of them. You have a rich and rewarding life ahead of you, more fulfilling than the grandest days you spent on a shaky throne."

"It is easy for you to say, Lev. You are rubbing elbows with the elite ruling powers today. You are on the upside of things, and I am about as low as I can get."

"Oh, stop feeling sorry for yourself, Nero. That will get you nowhere. Your past is over and done with. You must live in the present and bend to the powers that be or be broken."

Poppaea listened intently to their conversation. She realized Lev was speaking with great authority and very simple logic.

"Nero, Lev is right. I knew you did many evil things, but wives had nothing to say, and when I finally did say something, it cost me my life."

"Now you've joined with the enemy. Here you are giving him comfort and deserting me. Isn't there anyone in this world on my side?"

"Only the devil, and he is in the pit where he can't help you," Lev replied matter-of-factly.

"I could use a bolt of lightning from one of my gods, Thor. However, even he has deserted me, too. I never imagined in my previous life that I would face the situation I am in today. Why wasn't it known that we would have to account for our deeds?"

"Let's get back to a subject more to your liking. If Poppaea decides to live with you, then your mother will be returning to life very soon. I hope you love your mother enough to welcome her return."

Nero swallowed hard. "My mother will poison me the first chance she gets, or even something worse."

"Wasn't she the one who made it possible for you to ascend to the throne? You enjoyed being an emperor. The least you could do is be grateful to your mother for preparing the way for you to sit upon her husband's throne."

"You don't know my mother. Her husband did not make her a co-regent, so she poisoned him. This did open the way for me to sit on the throne. However, she wanted to be a co-regent with me, and I couldn't stand having my mother stealing my regal power."

"So, that entitled you to kill her?"

"No, but I tried to move her away out of reach from the throne. However, she was a very determined person. She began to groom my brother for emperorship. I suspected that she would poison me as she did her husband, and I was afraid of her. She was bent on being in power."

"So how did you take care of the threat from your brother?"

"Oh, you know the answer—I poisoned him. That took care of matters momentarily."

"So why did you have to kill your mother?"

"I didn't really want to do it. I tried to divert her ambitions for power, but it was to no avail. She was determined to share my power in some way. So, I had a special room built for her in which the ceiling would collapse. But she was like a cat with nine lives. She survived, half suspecting my hand in the matter. Then I had a boat made especially for her to take a nice cruise on. It was made so that when it got out into the high seas, it would fall apart and sink. Well, the boat fell apart too close to shore, and my mother managed to swim ashore. All my efforts to end her life in what would seem an accidental way did not succeed."

"So, what was your next plan?"

The Last Resort Was Poison

"At last, I had her poisoned. Mind you, I didn't want to do that, but my mother was an aggressive woman. She was too much like me. She was too ambitious and we could not coexist. I refused to share power with my mother."

"Do you suppose that what you did was wrong? How many men would poison their own mother?"

"You don't know my mother. If she were your mother, you might have poisoned her, too."

Poppaea said, "Let's change the subject for a minute. I shall need a midwife very soon. Do you know where to find me one, Lev?"

"Yes, no problem. I know a lady who used to be a doctor who lives not far from here. She will be glad to attend your birthing. Here, let me give you her number. Better yet, I will call her myself and prepare her for your request. If she cannot attend to you, there are others. Don't worry. You will have someone with you. However, with perfect food we don't have birthing problems anymore."

Lev reached for his phone, saying, "Excuse me one minute, and I will make contact for you." He found the former doctor, Angelina.

Shortly he hung up, saying, "You may have Angelina as your doctor if your baby comes in two weeks."

"I am due in that time frame. That is a big relief. Thank you."

"Just have Nero call her the very first sign you need her. She has her own aircraft and can be here in ten minutes. I gave her your landing pad number, so you should be set. Actually, I gave her Nero's landing pad, because I am thinking you will be there. However, if you remain here, you will have to call her and give her the pad number at this house. By the way, you haven't indicated what your intentions are. Will you be moving in with Nero, as I am hoping?"

"I have not decided that yet. I cannot forgive and forget his brutal behavior so quickly. I know he was drunk at the time, but still I get the chills thinking of that night. I know he cannot get drunk now and he cannot harm me. But a woman needs to be loved—not assaulted."

Nero turned to her, genuine sadness on his face. "You know I am sorry for what happened. I can only wish that you would join me. Should you decide to do so, Poppaea, I promise you better treatment. I have come down from my lofty throne. Please remember, I was not only drunk with wine, but also with power. Both forms of intoxication made me do things I should never have done. When I kicked you, you fell backwards, smashing your head against the corner of a table. I think that is what caused your death. I am truly sorry. Please forgive me, Poppaea."

"I shall be willing to live with you on a trial basis for two weeks. If you treat me properly, I shall then stay with you for the child's sake. You have caused enough death in your former life, and it is time you help nurture life and realize how precious one life can be."

Lev then said, "Good! That's a wise decision, Poppaea. If at the end of two weeks you are satisfied to live with Nero, then we shall arrange for the return of his mother and brother."

Nero scowled as Lev announced plans for the return of his family members.

"I don't know how I am going to handle my mother and brother. I hope she cannot get her hands on any poison. My mother can be as vicious as I was. She was an ambitious woman."

"Let's wait and see how it all plays out," Lev suggested.

"Honor thy father and thy mother"
(Exodus 20:12).

Chapter Nine

Poppaea and Nero seemed to get along very well. A son was born to them named Augustus, and in their home void of royal pomp and pageantry, he brought true joy and meaning to life. Nero found himself attached to the child in a way he never believed possible. Finally accepting the loss of power and exaltation, a new, more meaningful concept of life flashed occasionally before the eyes of his understanding. Yet, there was still a great deal to overcome.

As the day approached for his mother's return, Nero found himself in great anxiety. He knew his mother had suspected his attempts on her life, and she probably knew that it was he who poisoned her and his brother, Britannicus. This would not be a warm and loving mother-son reunion. Killing one's mother had been an odious thing to do, but he had known of no other way to thwart her ambitions for sharing his imperial power. He owed Agrippina his rise to the throne, but none of that had seemed important to him in his lust for power.

Nero had wanted to rule without her interference, so he tried to send her to live outside the palace. He had hoped this would quell her ambitions, but she was driven by a similar desire for power as he. He knew she had kept Britannicus in reserve so she could manipulate his rise to power, as he had been more amenable to give her co-regency than Nero was. If she had poisoned Claudius, his stepfather, in order to groom Nero for the throne, she would probably do the same with Britannicus. Nero had it all figured out. When it had come to his quest for power, he never left a stone unturned.

The day of Agrippina's return finally arrived. Nero wanted to meet her alone, without Poppaea or his new son. He felt she might try to be violent with him. It was shameful to have to admit what he did, but in today's climate, truth was inevitable, so he knew he could not cover up his deadly attempts on his mother's life.

Nero paced back and forth, occasionally sipping some tea, hoping it would soothe his frayed nerves. He found himself breaking out in a cold sweat. He really had no love for his mother, and he believed she didn't really love him. Somehow he believed she saw him as a means to get to the imperial throne, and being in her likeness, he had felt the same about her.

As the time for her return to life neared, he felt the urge to run away. He did not want to face his mother, and he found his knees became weak under him with his stomach tied in a knot. He had never imagined such a day as this.

The clock struck the hour for the moment of her return. He waited outside her room in a tormented state of mind. He was wishing the door would never open, but he knew everything ran like clockwork in this new arrangement. There would be no slipups and no deferred returns once the hour was appointed. He had all he could do to restrain himself from running out of the house. He would have to face his mother, and this was that awful moment.

He watched the door slowly open. Then it slammed shut. She had seen him and decided she was not going to face her murderer.

"Mother, come out! Have no fear! I have been waiting for you."

The door opened a crack again. It stayed that way for a minute while she decided whether to step through. Finally, the door swung open and she stepped out, her face stony with anger. He could feel her anger penetrate his very bones. He feared she would soon start throwing things, as she had been known to do.

"You wretched and miserable creature! The gods gave me a beast for a son! Why don't you get out of my sight? I loathe you! I did everything to bring you to the throne, and you poisoned me to show your gratitude."

"Mother, please! Do you feel well now?"

The Poison Was Not Strong Enough

"Yes, I do!" Her lovely features appeared ugly with contempt. "You are so inept! You could not even make the poison strong enough to kill me, so now you must face my wrath. I will make you pay for this you wretched, ungrateful son."

"Now, Mother, please try to control your temper. All is well that ends well, and here you are robust and in excellent health."

"Something is very strange. I could have sworn that I was dying. Yet, as you say, I am quite well. Am I dreaming this? Did you find some doctor to save my life after all?"

"Oh, let's not talk about such things right now, Mother. Come, sit down at the table here and have some very good tea, something you have never tasted before."

"I will not taste anything that you pour for me!"

"Look, I will drink from the same container. Watch me pour this and drink it. That way you will be sure that I intend this for your good health, Mother."

She watched him very carefully while he poured and drank the tea. "Very well. My nerves are shattered. By the way, what am I doing in this building? It is beautiful, but it is utterly strange, like some fairyland house. I didn't die and go to heaven, did I?"

"No, no, Mother. You and I are not the kind of people who would be received up there. You are here in the outskirts of Rome. We built this house for you especially, and you will be delighted with it once you learn of its many features. Now, please help yourself to some fruit. That will be another surprise for you. Never have you ever eaten anything so good and refreshing."

"It does look very good, but don't you have something more substantial for breakfast?"

"Before you say another word, try it. Some things have changed around here and this is the kind of food we eat. There is a long story about it, but for now, let's just call it the fruit of paradise. Please, just try it."

She seemed disappointed at such a simple meal, but it did smell wonderful and she could feel her mouth watering as she reached for the fruit. Biting into it, her eyes widened. "Where did you get this?" she demanded.

"It grows in the orchard in your own yard. I told you many things are different now."

"Where are all the servants? What has become of the palace? If you think this house is going to interfere with my desire for co-regency, you are wrong, Nero. It may be pleasant, but I am a regal lady and I expect better than this."

The Throne Is Occupied

"Now, let's take one step at a time, Mother. Just be thankful that you are alive and well and don't start scheming again."

"I was sure you poisoned me, Nero. I guess I was wrong. I must confess I feel very good, better than I remember in a long while. Yet, there is something strange about all of this. Something is not quite right. This seems more like a dream than reality. I can't explain it; my head is clear, but I am confused and very uncertain."

"Mother, just be thankful that you are well. Have some more tea. It will help your nerves."

"How about some good wine? You know I like wine with my meals."

"Since we have this exceedingly good tea, wine has fallen out of use. Unfermented grape juice is all we drink now. I have some of that if you wish."

"That is a poor substitute for wine, but if that is all you have, I will have some. However, I want to see you drink from the same vessel with me."

"Certainly, Mother."

"There is something different about you, Nero, now that I think about it. You look a little different, better than I ever remember. There is something very strange about everything. I have the feeling that I must be mad or dreaming. Something is not right, and you do not seem to be as nasty as usual."

"Be grateful then, my dear Mother, if I am not my usual nasty self. Maybe we are too much alike to be at peace with one another."

"Is that the reason you do not want me in your palace?"

"Mother, forget about the palace. We are not in imperial clothing are we? I am trying to tell you, things have changed. If I had a throne, I would be glad to grant you co-regency."

"You mean you have been dethroned during my illness?"

"Something like that, although it is a long story. Just accept the thought that the regal days have disappeared."

"You are lying to me! I made you emperor and now, you ungrateful scoundrel, you will not suffer your own mother a place in the palace."

"Mother, look at me very carefully. I do not have a throne of any kind anymore. I am out of power."

"No! You are a deceitful man and most unappreciative to your mother!"

No Imperial Palace

"Yes, I have told many lies in my life. But this once you must believe I am telling you the truth. I have lost my imperial throne. That is the whole truth of the matter."

"Do you mean that in the short while of my illness you managed to get yourself thrown from the palace? You can't be serious. No one could take you away from that throne alive."

"I am not dead, and I do not have that throne anymore. That is the simple truth!"

"Please, Son, I am very insecure since my illness. Do not try to confuse me. Now that you are here, there are some things I must talk to you about. You did try to kill me by having the ceiling collapse on me while I was sleeping, did you not?"

"Now, Mother, this is no time to discuss such things. No matter what I say, you would not believe me."

"All right, if you will not answer me on this matter, then how about the cruise you sent me on? I was told that boat was built to fall apart on the open sea. Fortunately, it fell apart close enough to shore so I could swim and reach it. How do you explain that, Son?"

"Mother, can't we talk about something pleasant?"

"What is there pleasant to talk about?"

"Well, you are a grandmother of a new baby named Augustus. He is a beautiful child that Poppaea gave birth to."

"I didn't know she was with child. I couldn't have been ill that long. What is going on? I am absolutely frustrated. Nero, something strange is going on. I demand to know what it is!"

"Mother, Poppaea and Augustus will be visiting us in the afternoon, so please, let us make this a happy family gathering."

"I know that I am upset inside because something is not right, and I do not know what it is. I know I feel very good, but I am very insecure. Having a devious son does not make me feel comfortable."

"Let's walk about your new house and let me show you its wonderful features. You must also see the orchards where this fruit of paradise grows."

"Don't try to sell me on this home! I know it looks beautiful, but if you built it, maybe the roof will fall in on me."

"No, it is very sturdy. Besides, I had help, so the work was overseen."

"All right. A walk may do me good. I have all these feelings pent up in me, and perhaps I am taking it all out on you."

"That is more like it, Mother. Come with me and let me show you the magic world that you live in now. Don't be frightened, but everything is very different now."

Nero showed the various rooms to his mother. "See this switch? Go ahead and push it." When she did, the light came on in the room. "Now push it again." She did, and the light went out.

"Is this some kind of witchcraft?"

"No, Mother! I will tell you of these new and marvelous things about your house. Instead of having servants to light lamps, you just press a button and you have light."

Taking her to the laundry room, he showed her a washing machine.

A Machine Washes Clothes by Itself

She jumped back as the machine seemed to come alive with water filling it, beginning the washing process. "When the clothes are clean, it will ring a buzzer and begin drying the clothing. You see, you don't need servants to wash your clothes. You do not need them standing around in the way all the time."

"This is making my head spin. I cannot believe what I am seeing."

Continuing into the bathroom, he showed her the hot and cold running water and the shower. It all startled her, making her forget her pent-up anger.

"I keep getting the feeling that this is a dream. I felt so good this morning, but now I think I am mad."

"It is going to take getting used to, Mother. Now come with me outside. You will find nothing magic here—just beautiful trees and luscious fruit and a garden growing without weeds. Everything looks perfect. If I had an easel, I would like to start painting some of these scenes. Have you ever seen anything more perfect?"

"Son, when you start being good to your mother, I know something is wrong. You are not capable of being good."

"Mother, I am going to try to make up to you for everything that I ever did wrong to you, real or imagined."

Agrippina snorted derisively. "I wish I could believe that!"

"I am trying so hard to be on my best behavior, and you refuse to treat me in a civil manner. I want us to end our warfare. Poppaea is coming with Augustus and for their sakes, please be kind and friendly. Let us behave like a normal mother and son. Do you suppose that is possible just once?"

"All right—I guess I am too stressed. Son, everything is very beautiful even though it is all very strange, and you do not seem to be telling me everything. Some pieces of this puzzle are missing. I shall try to relax a little. I think I need a little more of that tea."

Poppaea and Augustus Visit

Poppaea arrived at Agrippina's home with little Augustus in a lovely baby carriage. It was a longer walk than she had expected, and she arrived a little weary. However, she entered her mother-in-law's home with a cheerful attitude, showing warmth and love. Agrippina was quite excited to see little Augustus, who was sleeping soundly.

"Oh, what a lovely child—the name suits him perfectly. We will someday have him on the throne of Rome, I am sure."

Nero just rolled his eyes, not wishing to contradict his mother. Poppaea knew that her mother-in-law was still out of touch with reality, so she let the statement pass without comment. She knew Agrippina was a designing woman with intemperate ambition, so for the moment there was no use in trying to correct her designs.

Nero said, "Perhaps we should let him grow up first, and then let him decide on the course he wishes to take."

"Oh, come now, Son. He is royalty! He shall be tutored to the calling to which those with royal blood must rise."

"Mother, I was dethroned—I have no regal standing. But now we have everything for a full and happy life. A great and powerful regent not only rules Rome, but also the whole world."

"How could you have lost the kingdom, Nero? You probably were too busy singing and painting to protect your crown. I should have placed your brother on the throne. Britannicus would not have fiddled away the throne. At least if you had allowed me co-regency, I would not have let the kingdom slip from our hands. Do you realize all that I did to secure the throne for you and now you tell me you lost it? This is absolutely dreadful news! Nero, you were just like your father!" The former queen's ire was rising.

"Mother, I have not told you everything yet."

"Ah, I knew you were hiding something from me. What more terrible news do you have for me?"

"I did not tell you everything because you would not believe it, even as you will not believe it when I tell you now. So for once in my life, I am going to tell you the truth. I did poison you and you did die. You have been raised from the dead this very day, and that explains your feelings of insecurity and the consciousness of a time lapse that is unexplainable. Not only did you die, but also Poppaea died and I died. We all have been raised to life."

His mother's face hardened even more. "Oh, Nero, no wonder you lost the kingdom. You are completely insane! I know you tried to kill me several times, but I am very alive now. Please do not tell me stupid lies."

"I know it sounds far fetched and ridiculous, but it is the truth no less."

A Man Named Paul

"A man by the name of Paul stood before me twice in my court of judgment." Nero continued, refusing to be upset by her lack of understanding. "The first time I released him, but the second time I condemned him to be beheaded. He was a man of sterling character and impeccable righteousness. He preached to me twice about the resurrection of the dead at the last day. Did I believe him? No. But I should have, because everything he said has happened. I had him beheaded because I was raging against Christians. That was the biggest mistake of my life. I knew instantly that he was head and shoulders above other men, even though he was short in stature, for he spoke with power and logic that no one could refute. Pilot ordered Jesus Christ crucified, and I ordered Christ's disciple, Paul, beheaded. Guess who is enthroned in Jerusalem over the whole world now, Mother?"

Agrippina laughed at what she supposed was an idiotic joke. "I suppose you are going to say Christ, with Paul his co-regent."

"Exactly! Christ *is* reigning over the world along with Paul and thousands of Christians. The gods of mythology whom we worshipped were no gods at all. We were on the wrong side. Oh, how can I make this clear to you? Nothing will stop his universal kingdom from overspreading the earth."

Agrippina sat stunned. She was hearing the unthinkable and half believed, for once, that Nero was speaking the truth, even though what he said was incomprehensible to her. Nero was usually shifty eyed when speaking, because he was up to no good. This time he looked right at his mother and spoke deliberately, with conviction.

Poppaea at last joined the conversation, saying, "Mother, Nero is telling you the truth. We all did die and have been returned to life. I died with Augustus within me, and I awakened to life with him living still within me. He was born soon after. I felt very insecure on returning to life, and the first few days I thought I was dreaming at times. However, this is the whole truth. We were dead for centuries and have been awakened to life. That is why the world is so different. I looked for the palace as you did. That is as long gone as the Roman Empire."

Living—Not Dead

"Has everyone lost his mind? If we died, how is it we are living? I tell you, I am alive. How could the great empire of Rome be gone? I simply will not hear this nonsense."

"Calm down, Mother. I enjoyed having power and riches and the privilege of indulging myself however and whenever I wanted. That day is long gone and both you and I sadly are out of power."

"Why are you such a weakling? For Augustus' sake we must find a way to the throne again. I will not hear this weak-kneed surrender to, of all places, Jerusalem. We ruled Jerusalem before, and we can do it again."

"Ambition and power control your every thought. You will *never* relent. You cannot accept the truth. Sorry, Mother, but you are your own worst enemy."

Augustus stirred and started crying. It was sweet to hear the innocent cry of the child in contrast to Agrippina's relentless tirade against her son for losing the empire.

Poppaea picked up the baby from his little bed and the crying stopped. The miracle of seeing a pure and innocent child was not lost on anyone. Nero smiled at his precious offspring. The focus of his world was changing from the glories of Rome to the awesome presence of this new human being. Agrippina at first showed displeasure at the child's cry, but soon she, too, was smiling at the little bundle.

She said, "He does look a little like you, Nero. I only hope he will not grow up to be a failure. With a name like Augustus, he is bound to amount to something."

"Oh, let him be a little baby so he can enjoy the little things in life without a competitive spirit. Unfortunately, all I was taught was that power and riches are life's only goals. That is how I lived and that is how I died."

"By the way, Nero, how did you die?"

He looked straight into her eyes. "Remember how you taught me to deal with my enemies? You taught me to send them a notice that it might be in their best interest to commit suicide. I did that many times, and it always worked. It wasn't messy that way. No one knew that I sent my enemies a message, so their death seemed like inner defeat instead of something I precipitated. Then my turn came. My soldiers deserted me, and when the Senate knew my power base was gone, they sent word that I was to be flogged to death as a common criminal. I am much too sensitive a man to endure that kind of treatment, so I committed suicide. It was the easiest way out for me under the circumstances."

"Was it very painful?" she asked, more out of curiosity than compassion.

"It was much more painful than I ever thought possible. However, it didn't last long because I soon lost consciousness. I did not have any poison, so I had to use a knife. In some ways, Mother, you were more blessed leaving the world when you did. Things started deteriorating in the kingdom. Rome lost a great statesman, artist, and musician with my passing. Such are the fortunes of life, Mother."

"Oh, don't justify your hateful treatment of your mother."

"I tried sending you off into residences in the countryside, but you would not stay there."

"So that justifies your poisoning me?"

"I had to do something to remove you from seeking power. If you had been a normal mother, you could have lived in the royal palace and received the admiration of the citizens of Rome. Unfortunately, I never learned to respect human life. You taught me the rules by which I lived. When you wanted to make me emperor, you poisoned your husband Claudius. That is how I solved my problems, too. I followed in your footsteps, Mother."

"I never taught you to poison me! You are not worthy to be my son!"

Poppaea sat with Augustus who was all smiles and happy. Nero was glad that Augustus' smiles changed the subject, because his mother was becoming more hostile by the minute.

"Well, he is a beautiful child, I must say," Agrippina exclaimed. "Let me hold the little fellow for a moment."

"Of course, Mother. Be careful, he just ate and he may bubble up a little."

"You know, I, too, was a mother. I know about such things. Just give me a little towel and I'll handle whatever happens. Maybe Augustus will learn to love his grandmother, because her son does not."

As little Augustus turned his charms on her, smiling and giggling, Agrippina left her tirade against her son. The magic of life was casting its spell upon her, at least for the moment. This innocent child was a little out of place in a viper's nest. As she cradled him in her arms, she said, "My little Augustus, we lost the kingdom, but maybe you will live in a happier world where people do not poison one another."

Poppaea said, "Yes, Mother, it will be a happier world. Life with love is better than a thousand thrones in a pit of snakes. You and Nero were both consumed with a passion for power, and in the end power turned into an elusive bubble that burst as you tried to grasp it. What do you have from those few years spent on the throne? Nothing. Even worse, it made you insensitive to virtues that men and women of character maintained at all cost."

"Don't you preach to me, girl! I am too distracted to know whether I am coming or going. All I know is that Augustus is a beautiful child. We need not burden him with our troubles."

Nero took this turn in the conversation to say, "Perhaps we should have some lunch. I think we all need some of that tea. After lunch I still have many things to show you, Mother. Our food has changed, our housing has changed, our way of living has changed, and the biggest change is in education. I want to show you how you will be schooled from now on. We have perfect teachers who only teach the truth, and they teach so well that it is impossible not to retain the knowledge. All subjects are at our fingertips day or night. To exist in this world, you need to have a continuing education. Learning is almost automatic because the food we eat keeps our minds so bright."

"I am curious to know what in the world you are talking about."

"I can't explain it, but after lunch I will show you some of the modern miracles. They may frighten you at first, but have no fear; it is all a part of this modern age."

Lev Aron Is to Visit Us

Poppaea said, "You forgot to mention that Lev is going to visit us this afternoon. He is someone very special, and I think you will be very pleased to meet him. You have never met anyone like him before."

"Who is Lev, and why should I be excited about meeting him?"

Nero answered, "He is someone well connected to the authorities in Jerusalem. If you like powerful people, you will like Lev."

That piqued her interest. "Is he some politician who calls extravagant attention to himself?"

"No, Mother!" Poppaea said. "He is handsome, kind, generous, and extremely helpful. He is brilliant to a fault, so don't think you can influence him."

"I know men. They are all alike. What you describe is a thin veneer but underneath is a scheming and manipulating power broker who knows how to make you feel good while he puts a ring in your nose to lead you around. Obviously, he has already deceived you and probably my son as well," the jaded woman accused.

"No, Mother Agrippina. He has neither weaknesses nor vices and cannot be manipulated in any way. He speaks the truth with gentleness and conviction. The political world you revolved in has not prepared you to meet Lev Aron."

"I am surprised that you both have been deceived by this smooth operator."

"Mother, you have not even seen him and already you have declared him the enemy. I treated him in the most uncivil way I am capable of, but never did I succeed in putting him down or winning in any discussion. He is intelligent, and neither you nor I can match wits with him. At the same time, he is gentle and understanding, but he does not rest until he has made his points abundantly clear. I met some men like him while I sat in judgment; one was Paul and the other Peter. I sentenced them both to death knowing full well they were men of virtue and nobler than I in every way. They frightened me with their virtue."

"Oh, Nero, you were bewitched. Men are all alike. Maybe he deceived you, but he will find me a more formidable quarry. For once, Nero, let me do the talking. You never were a deep thinker. I should have waited for your brother to take the throne. He would not have frittered away the kingdom while singing and quoting poetry."

Agrippina's acid tongue managed to spoil an enjoyable lunch. When they heard Lev's aircraft setting down, Agrippina turned a little frightened at the noise. "Don't worry, Mother, that is Lev's aircraft landing on your pad."

Please, Meet My Dear Mother

"If it is mine, tell him to get off of it! How dare he invite himself?" As she looked out the window, the shiny blue craft was descending from heaven. Suddenly her tone changed. "This must be one of the gods; I hope he didn't hear my conversation." Fear blanched her face. "What kind of person possesses such powers to descend from heaven itself?"

"Come, Mother," Nero said. "This is your home, so you must come out to greet him."

Agrippina quailed as she followed him, "Nero, if you know him, introduce me as your *dear* mother."

No sooner had the plane landed than the engines were turned off, and out jumped the most handsome man she had ever seen. He was very unlike the staid politicians she had known who were self-centered, egotistical, and basically mean-tempered.

Lev rushed over to meet them with a broad winning smile, giving Nero a hearty handshake while also greeting Poppaea warmly. He then turned his full attention upon Agrippina.

"Nero, is this your mother?"

"Yes, Lev; please meet my *dear* mother."

"Agrippina, you returned to life this very morning. Is that correct? At least those are the arrangements I made for your return. I hope your little family of four had a happy time together. You know, Agrippina, it is always hard the first few days of finding yourself alive again, but soon that will pass. Well, I have been looking forward to meeting you. Your son does favor you in appearance."

Nero said, "Do come in, Lev. We just finished lunch but we have plenty left. May we fix you a little tea and some fruit?"

"Yes, thank you. And oh, here is little Augustus. What a beautiful child! What a wonderful time for him to be living. No more sickness, pain or suffering, no more poverty or insecurity. What a glorious future is his! Life will certainly be different for him than for babies born in the last age. I am so happy to find you with your little gift from heaven."

Lev continued, "How does it feel to be the grandmother of such a beautiful grandson?"

"Of course, he is absolutely delightful! He is of a royal line, you know!" Agrippina said haughtily.

"That might have distinguished him above other children in your time, but now only wisdom and virtue will distinguish him above others. It is not what we inherit in the way of a title that distinguishes a person today. Only those who demonstrate their love for their fellow men will be in line for eternal life."

Agrippina said in disgust, "Love for fellow men? As soon as you turn your back on them, they will stab you. What kind of world do you come from? You apparently never sat on a throne and do not know that people keep trying to find your weakness so they can wrest the throne from you."

Poppaea asked Lev to be seated, poured him some tea and invited him to sit with them. Lev excused himself to offer a humble prayer without any pretense or shame.

"Well, this looks good for a hungry traveler. Perhaps someone could join me in a cup of tea and make me feel more at home!"

Both Agrippina and Nero joined him.

Lev paused and said, "You may think that I don't understand your history, but I think I do, Agrippina. I read the history of your time before coming to be with Nero. My heart went out to you. It seems that in trying to gain the whole world you lost your guiding virtues and then you lost your ill-gotten power and glory. Was it heartbreaking to strive so hard and ruthlessly to ascend to such power as you attained, only to find your few minutes of glory were over?"

Agrippina sat there in a long and troubled silence. She had no acid reply. The question Lev raised had an obvious answer, but she dared not admit it. In her heart she knew that in her drive for power she had lost the sweet taste of life.

Nero Remembers the Sweet Taste of Power

Nero, though, seemed ready to answer. "Power is sweet even if it is only for a few moments. I loved power and I miss it now. Nothing was denied me, nor did I need to deny myself. Every pleasure was for my taking. There were no limits and no painful self-denials."

"You are probably right, Nero. Yes, I suppose it was exhilarating riding the winds of fortune. It was a great ride. Then what happened? Was it just as exhilarating coming down?"

"I can answer that," Agrippina finally admitted. "It was very bitter. Even more bitter was it for me to find that it was not the common people that brought me down. It was my very own son for whom I had made every sacrifice to place on the throne."

Though his words were strong, Lev's voice was very gentle. "If you lived in a snake pit, why should you be surprised that you were bitten?"

"Well, I understand that snakes do not usually bite their own kind."

Lev knew when to change the subject. He had made his point and now backed off gently, offering his usual ride in the aircraft. The awe-inspiring views usually gave newcomers to life a greater perspective of their circumstances.

But Agrippina replied, "Not on your life! You want to lift us up and then bring us down with a thud, is that it?"

"No, no, Agrippina. I assure you this craft is very safe. However, if it frightens you, how about taking a walk down the road a short distance to a little meadow that I saw as I was flying here? There are many sheep, goats, cows, and horses grazing there. If you don't like walking, we can fly low so you will not be frightened. The horses there were magnificent creatures."

Nero said, "I love horses. You know I won some chariot races."

"How remarkable, especially since you fell out of the chariot and still won the race. I think the horses I saw on my flight here are quite tame; maybe we could ride them bare back. Nero, what do you say?"

"That sounds good to me."

Agrippina said, "That is not for me. I will stay home with Poppaea and Augustus and get acquainted with my grandson."

"Germanicus" Goes Horseback Riding

"Very well then, Nero, let's go and I will try to find those beautiful horses. It would be good if we could at least find two bridles. You don't know if your neighbors might have any?"

Poppaea said, "Yes, the neighbor in the third house down the road occasionally rides with his son. You might borrow bridles from him for the day. He is very friendly and even came over to give me a hand on occasion while building this house."

"Great! Come on, Nero. Let's call on the neighbor."

Soon they were meeting with the neighbor. "Shalom. I'm Lev Aron. I have a favor to ask of you. We want to do some horseback riding on the horses we've seen today. Could you loan us a couple of bridles?"

"They are probably the same horses that we were riding. They are gentle and you will enjoy them. They roam freely, and occasionally they come this way. Take some fruit with you, and they will come running to you. Let me get the bridles I keep around here."

He returned with two in hand. "Here they are. Enjoy the ride. These bridles are all I have, so please bring them back when you're done. And by the way, Germanicus, has your mother returned to life yet?"

"Yes, she did this morning, thank you."

Lev raised his eyebrows at the name 'Germanicus.' He knew that was a part of Nero's name—Nero Claudius Caesar Augustus Germanicus. So that is how Nero hid his odious name! That was the unrecognizable part of his title.

"Well, thank you," Lev said cheerily. "That solves our problem. Hope we can return the favor sometime."

Before long they were circling over the meadow where Lev had seen the horses, but he could not see them now. Lev circled a little wider and found them on the other side of a small river and landed not far from them. They walked toward the horses who were watching them curiously. When Lev held out some fruit that he knew they loved, they came trotting over. He petted them gently for a short while and then put the bridles on.

"There, we're all set to go. Can I give you a lift getting on this horse, Germanicus?" Lev teased.

"No, I don't need it," Nero said, taking a little running start hoping to mount on top the horse. However, the horse was too high and he landed on the ground, unhurt except for his pride.

"Here, let me help you," Lev said, cupping his hands together for Nero to put his foot in to mount his steed.

"I'll walk my horse over to that log. It's high enough to mount this horse without stirrups."

Soon they were riding about enjoying the meadows and trees, crossing small streams and taking various paths. Several hours had passed, and finally they decided to return to their craft. Nero wanted to take a shortcut that crossed a small river. When he kicked his heels into the side of the horse it galloped toward the river. At the last minute it stopped abruptly, causing Nero to go flying over the top of its head into the middle of the stream. Fortunately for Nero, the water was about four feet deep and he wasn't hurt. He came up sputtering from the water in an ugly mood. Even though he tried to suppress it, Lev couldn't help laughing.

"Better go to the other side," Lev offered. "I'll help you mount again, unless you prefer walking the rest of the way."

"I am not getting on that beast again! If I had my sword I'd use it."

"I'm afraid not, Nero. Remember, there is instant punishment for people who lose control of their tempers. If you would rather sit down, I will go to the aircraft and pick you up here while we leave the horses free to roam about."

"That sounds good to me. I'll sit on that stump and wait for your return."

At the aircraft, Lev found some people looking at it and wondering what had happened to the occupants.

Lev greeted them saying, "We just went horseback riding and left the craft here. I hope it hasn't inconvenienced you."

Curious About the Aircraft

"No, we were just curious. We saw the craft hovering about and decided to follow it because it looked like it was going to land. You know, there aren't many of these aircraft around here."

"I am sent out on many different assignments, so I've been given one to make my work easier."

"Does it take long to learn to fly it?" a perky young girl asked.

"Not really, but you do have to learn about the various features of the craft. I happened to work on building it, so that part was easy."

"You mean you helped build this?" her friend queried.

"Not this particular model, but the original one was a part of my assignment."

"Who are you?" a third girl inquired.

"I am Lev Aron. I am sorry not to have time to get better acquainted with you, but my friend is waiting for me to pick him up."

Lev boarded the craft, instructing his visitors to stand clear as it started its ascent. He found Nero, who looked about as happy as a wet hen, waiting on a rock.

"Climb aboard. I'll turn up the heat to warm you a bit and maybe it will help dry those clothes of yours."

"The heat does feel good. You know we have to go to my house. I can't let Mother see me this way. Besides, I don't have any clothes at her place."

"As you wish, Germanicus," Lev smiled.

As they approached Nero's home, Lev spotted a group of people walking toward it. He waved to them as they passed over and landed while they were a short distance away. Nero hurried out of the craft to get into the house to change clothes.

Lev shut down the engine while he waited for Nero to return. Meanwhile the people arrived. They had seen Nero enter the house and came up to Lev's craft.

Angry Visitors

"We are looking for Nero. Is this the correct address?"

"Yes, you are at the right place. Is there anything I can do for you?"

"Yes, you could supply us with some tar and feathers. We would like to use them on him."

Lev could see the anger in their faces. "He should be coming out soon. He will probably think you are admiring my craft, so if you wait here, you will be able to meet him. I hope you are not here to take justice into your own hands."

"If we did, we would have to take turns strangling him."

"You know what will happen if you try to do that, don't you?"

"Yes, we know we would be punished and that we can't fulfill our hearts' wishes in killing him, but we intend to confront him and let him know we are victims of his evil past."

"I hope you're not trying to challenge Christ. If Christ brought him to life, are you sure you wish to question his wisdom or authority in so doing?"

"Who are you, anyway?"

"I am Lev Aron. I have been sent here by the Ancients to help Nero straighten out his life. Please do not bring harm to yourselves by unwise confrontation with Nero. You are free to state your case against him, but you are not free to hurt him. Is that clear?"

"I know," the man said in a frustrated tone. "I've been paralyzed already. However, in my former life, I wouldn't have hesitated to kill him if given the chance."

"Tell him that if you wish. Here he comes. Remember, no violence."

Nero came along thinking the crowd was admiring the craft. However, he no sooner reached them than the people surrounded him, shouting angry words and waving their fists into the air. When Nero tried to pass them and enter the craft, they formed a wall around him.

"Every dog has his day and yours has arrived, Nero. You are a loathsome creature, and we want you to know what we suffered at your hands. We would like to return your wicked deeds and let you feel what it is like to burn with fire."

Poor Nero turned pale and trembled. Lev felt sorry for him, but he also understood the feelings of those who reminded Nero of his evil deeds. As the crowd shouted in anger, Nero stood silently for about ten minutes until the crowd wearied itself and finally decided to leave.

"They were pretty upset with you, Nero. I hope you won't forget this experience. I am afraid your sins are coming to face you."

"As long as they can't touch me, I guess I am safe. These people would sacrifice their life to kill me if they could."

"Did it occur to you that these people are not so excited about killing other people? What did you do to deserve this kind of hatred?"

Being the Center of Attention

"I don't remember these people or most people who suffered under my rule. That should prove that I didn't have a personal vendetta against anyone. They were just pawns used for political expediency.

I was surrounded with people falling all over me for favors. I had no friends, but I was the center of attention. That's what I liked."

"Well, you seem to be the center of attention again, and I suspect you don't like it."

"This is different. They hate me without fear."

"Could it be that your servants or those falling all over you for favors hated you, but knew they couldn't reveal their feelings?"

"Yes, that is possible—even probable. However, what did it matter? I was in power, and they had to cower before me. Oh, that I had such power now. These sniveling creatures would be on their hands and knees, begging for mercy."

"Nero, can I tell you something that you need to know?"

"I'd rather you wouldn't, but you will anyway, so you might as well say it now as wait for some crafty moment to interject it."

"As long as you are not prepared to admit your crimes against humanity, you will continue to justify yourself and continue your wishful thinking. That will get you absolutely nowhere. You are still mired in the past. These people don't hate you without a cause. You perpetrated a terrible evil by cruelly taking their lives and the lives of their loved ones. It is what you have *done* that they hate. The only way to change this is to show them that you have godly sorrow and you, too, hate what you did to them."

"If you think I am going to get on my knees and beg for mercy, you are wrong. Emperors don't do such things."

Who Started the Fire That Burned Rome?

"There are many emperors who tried to rule justly and mercifully. The people loved them. Why do you suppose you are hated?"

"You should ask them, not me. I didn't hate them personally."

"Are you sure that you don't know why they hate you?"

"All right. I did accuse Christians falsely of starting the fire that nearly destroyed Rome. This was the reason I started persecuting them."

"Wasn't it your duty to thoroughly investigate and apprehend the real guilty party or parties?"

"I didn't need to do that."

"Why not?"

"Because I had ordered the fire started, that's why."

"So then you accused them falsely and executed innocent people, and you still cannot figure out why people hate you?"

"Well, the Senate was angry with me. They suspected I started the fire because I wanted the city rebuilt for my glory. I had to find someone to blame, so I blamed the Christians. There was nothing personal about it."

"When are you going to accept responsibility for what you did? These are questions you need to answer. Your very life will depend on it."

Nero changed the subject. "Don't you think we should be heading to my mother's house? They will wonder what happened to us."

"You're right. We have been gone unusually long." Lev started the engine and soon they were landing at Agrippina's pad.

Poppaea ran out to meet them. "Why are you so late? We have been worried about you."

Lev replied, "I should have called, but we ran into a few delays that we didn't count on."

Agrippina's sharp tongue was waiting for Nero. She said, "I knew you should not have gone horseback riding. Now, you're probably going to tell me that you fell off the horse and you had to call Jerusalem to get healed or some such fool thing."

"Mother, please. I did have a very hard day. What I need is a large bottle of wine to make me forget it, but I'll settle for some tea."

Poppaea said, "You were lucky to be away from here today. No sooner had you left than a crowd of angry people came here looking for you, Nero. I have never seen such angry people. They thought we were lying when I said you weren't here. We told them to search the house to satisfy them that we told the truth. When they didn't find you, they left but promised to be back. So you better stay away from home for awhile. I really think they were angry enough to try to kill you, Nero."

"Fortunately, they can't touch me," Nero exclaimed. "Isn't that true, Lev?"

"Yes, but they can hold up a mirror for you to look into and see yourself for what you are. They are rendering a valuable service, even if you don't see it that way yet. You have to confess your sins before any forgiveness will take place."

Agrippina was listening to this very carefully. Like Nero, though, she was not ready to confess anything or admit to her failings. "Lev, who made you a judge over my son?"

Lev raised his eyebrows with this brazen remark. "Nobody. I am not the one angrily screaming at him, am I?"

"No, but you are justifying vicious crowds, siding with them against us," Nero exclaimed.

"You admitted that you set Rome on fire and when it got out of hand and nearly burned down the whole city, you blamed Christians for doing this. That started you on the road to unjustly persecuting Christians who were innocent. Was that right or wrong?"

"I can't say it was right, yet it was the only course I could take to save my crown, so it was best for me."

"Oh, so it was you who started the fire, Nero!" Agrippina reacted immediately. "I heard that rumor, but I never believed it. I'm afraid I gave the nation a fool for an emperor."

Nero was absolutely exasperated with his mother's tirade against him. "Lev, could you take me to my house? I'll leave Poppaea and Augustus here for the night. I need to find a quiet corner to get some peace. I fear for my sanity."

"Yes, I can do that. It might give you time to think things through. Let's have our supper, and then I will take you to your house. You have had a very hard day, I agree. However, things will not get better for you until you accept responsibility for all that you have done wrong and then show godly sorrow. If there were another way to smooth this out for you, I would surely tell you. However, this is the only way — it is the way of truth and righteousness."

More Troubled Than Angry

Nero was more troubled than angry. He could find no relief, and his peace and tranquility were marred. He would be happy if people left him alone, just as he wanted to leave them alone. He had too many people that he had murdered and tortured, too many people that he had dealt with deceitfully.

Lev took Nero back to his home without saying a word to him. They left little Augustus and Poppaea with Agrippina for the night. Upon arrival, Nero went to his room and shut the door. He did not even thank Lev for bringing him home.

The next morning, Lev left to take in a chapel meeting and then to visit one of the high-tech factories. When he returned at the end of the day, he found Nero rather anxious. He said, "Where have you been? I have been looking for you all day! Aren't you supposed to be with me to help me?"

"Yes, that was a part of my assignment. However, I don't know if I can help you at all. You don't seem willing to hear anything I have to say."

"I was worried all day that those people who were here yesterday would return again today, or another batch of people would learn that I am alive again and would be seeking my life. I need you around. They respect you but not me."

"Have you thought about giving some answers that would temper their anger? I mean truthful answers. You know you can't lie now without being punished."

"Yes, and the only answer I could give them is what you suggested, and that is not in my vocabulary yet."

"What is that?"

"That I am sorry with a godly sorrow."

"Are you?"

"No. I am sorry that I don't have the power to chase them away and tell them not to bother me."

Still the Old Nero

"Then you haven't changed. You are still the old Nero who murdered, lied, and abused people."

"I can't bring myself down to grovel for forgiveness."

"Well, you have the power to choose. If you choose to be your old self, that is what you will be. I can't change you. Only you can change yourself. Do you want to?"

"I would want to if there were a magic wand to suddenly make me into the new Nero. However, I am still the old Nero. I still have a battle-axe for a mother. There is no place for me in this world, as I see it."

"You have time. I'll tell you a secret. You will catch more flies with honey than with vinegar. Shall we visit your son and Poppaea this evening? Perhaps give her a phone call and ask what she needs so we can bring it."

"Yes, a good idea. We must not let little Augustus be deprived. I will do that." He quickly phoned and received a list of things Poppaea needed.

They arrived with a warm reception, even from Agrippina who said, "We missed you both today. I even think little Augustus was looking for you."

For the first time, Lev saw Nero actually take his son into his arms and express fatherly love toward him. The baby was a charming child.

Poppaea said, "You arrived in the nick of time with the diapers. I am so glad you brought the other items, because I had only expected to be here for the day originally."

Agrippina admitted, "Nero, you have a delightful wife and a son who will make us all proud. I enjoyed bonding with the boy. I never realized being a grandmother was more fun than being a mother. Whenever he was hungry and cried, I gave him to Poppaea. This was one of the happiest days I can remember."

Nero Almost Speechless

Nero was almost speechless with the kind and encouraging words coming from his mother. The best part was she was speaking the truth—she did enjoy little Augustus. As a matter of fact, so was he, finding pleasure in someone other than himself. Yesterday had been a total disaster, but today a little ray of sunshine had broken through. Remembering Lev's words about catching more flies with honey than with vinegar, Nero decided to do it.

"Mother, I think little Augustus likes you. He always smiles when you look at him. That is wonderful, because love is the only thing you can give away freely and still have more to give."

"Why, that is beautiful, Nero. You should put that in some kind of poetry."

Lev seized the moment saying, "The Ancients are giving a report on the regeneration this evening. We are close to completing the work for people who died after Christ's birth. While this only takes in the last two thousand years, it by far includes most of the people who have ever lived. Going back before Christ, the regeneration will accelerate rapidly. From Adam to Christ involved much fewer than a hundred generations that spanned four thousand years. Shall we tune in to this progress report? In fact, I heard from former King David, and he was pleased and relieved that the work is finally rounding the corner."

Soon they all were seated in the comfortable upholstered chairs, waiting for the program to begin. There was an aura about these Ancients that commanded attention and respect. Agrippina, who usually would have some caustic remarks to make about everything, paid close attention to the whole program. It was fascinating, and the reasons given for the remarkable accomplishments were the untiring sacrifices that were being made to implement the enormous task of providing for all returning to life.

The Ancients reported that no effort had been wasted on anything destructive or that did not contribute to the common good and well-being both of men and animals. Somehow, everyone was participating, so the process was running smoothly and gaining momentum daily. There was an equitable distribution of the world's wealth; there were no homeless, no indigent, no sick or handicapped people, and above all, no violence of any kind. The program closed, saying, "Such are the conditions that prevail, because Christ is in sovereign control. Of the increase of his Kingdom and of peace there shall be no end."

That they were subjects of a very benign sovereign caused this little audience, especially Nero and Agrippina, to come to grips with a new reality. They realized the authority with which the Ancients spoke and actually felt no resentment. It also helped close a chapter on old Roman history.

Lev realized it was the first break in the seemingly endless resentment expressed in this household. True, it was only a moment of civility, but a very welcome one. Lev knew that his time with the family was coming to a close. John the Baptist had called him, requesting he take on another assignment shortly. It was a visit to Annas, the High Priest who helped gain Jesus' death. John wanted Lev to visit Annas after he adjusted to life again and his new circumstances.

The remaining time spent with Nero and Agrippina still generated some vexation. Both knew what they needed to do, however, they seemed imprisoned without the sinful pleasures of uninhibited vice. They had not learned to love and to give. Would they be willing to change and put away the old stony heart for a heart of flesh? Only they could decide this matter. Facing the endless number of their victims would only become more painful unless there was true godly sorrow for what they did, and until they expressed it sincerely. They were sorry to see Lev go and even said so. Lev left them with certain knowledge of what they must do if they wished to live in a world filled with righteousness and love.

"Ye shall see Abraham, and Isaac,
and Jacob, and all the prophets,
In the kingdom of God, and you yourselves thrust out"
(Luke 13:28).

Chapter Ten

When John the Baptist first approached Lev about spending time with Annas, the High Priest of Israel and the man probably most responsible for Christ's death, he was chilled by such a thought. Lev knew that men who used religion in nefarious ways were the most difficult to reach and the most hardhearted. Religion, which was supposed to be man's noblest quest for God, had often turned into a savage quest for power and self-exaltation. Strangely, the vilest of history was written in the name of religion.

In checking on the short account about Annas in the Bible, Lev learned only the basic facts. He was the first to interrogate Jesus the night before his death and had badly handled the case. After he had Jesus arrested, Annas found himself in the embarrassing situation of not having given a specific charge. Since this had not been properly done, Annas had interrogated Jesus, hoping that by cross-examining him, he would come up with some charge. However, Jesus was much too knowledgeable for Annas and accused him of false arrest (John 18:20, 21). Annas knew he had bungled matters and knew that Jesus should have been charged with a crime before the arrest. After all, the Sanhedrin was composed of legalists.

Annas sent Jesus to Caiaphas, the High Priest, probably admonishing him to find charges against Jesus, if need be, from false witnesses.

However, the second trial that was before Caiaphas fared no better. Not only was it an illegal nighttime meeting, but they could not even get their false witnesses to agree on anything. Under Jewish Law they needed at least two witnesses with testimony that agreed. This failed.

"Christ, the Son of the Blessed"

Lev noted that in the second illegal religious night trial, they asked Jesus, "Are you the Christ, the Son of the Blessed?" (Mark 14:61, 62). That was when Jesus gave the fateful answer—"I am." He admitted to this truth in an illegal trial and that was the testimony they used against him in the third legal trial of the whole Sanhedrin at daybreak. Their blood lust was running high at this point, and they turned him over to the civil authorities, asking the Roman government to execute him. However, oddly enough, they did not have any clear charge against Jesus when he was brought to Pilate.

They had never found Pilate to be merciful in any previous case they brought before him, so they thought that saying Jesus was a malefactor would be sufficient for Pilate to grant their wish. However, Pilate was very reticent to condemn Jesus. Wishing to rid himself of the case, he sent Jesus to Herod. Herod, who apparently was still chafing about having been tricked into killing John the Baptist, was also unwilling to condemn Jesus, sending him back to Pilate.

Pilate, after repeatedly declaring, "I find no fault in him," finally washed his hands of the execution and granted the Jews their wish— that Jesus be crucified. In this last civil trial, the religious leaders finally admitted the reason they sought Jesus' death. They said, "We have a law, and by that law he ought to die, because he has made himself the Son of God" (John 19:7). Lev mused on this charge remembering that the religious leaders had said of themselves, "We have one Father, even God" (John 8:41).

The Two Reasons Why Jesus Was Crucified Were Both True

As Lev studied the case against Jesus, he realized that the two accusations against Jesus were both true. He *was* "the Son of the

Blessed" and he *was* "the King of the Jews." The religious leaders had rejected Jesus as the "Son of God" and as their "King." This was going to make his visit with Annas most interesting. Having been a Jew and sympathetic with Judaism, Lev was saddened to read of these three religious trials and three civil trials that had resulted in Jesus' death.

Lev knew his meeting with Annas at some point would involve discussing the world's greatest trial. Obviously, Annas would find his position very uncomfortable as he bore grave responsibility for the death of the only holy and righteous man that had ever lived since Adam. Lev had dealt with many brutal men who cruelly took human life without an ounce of compassion, yet this case involved a religious zealot who claimed to be serving God while seeking to kill God's Son. He wondered if he could really be of any meaningful help in this case. How wrong can one be and still turn his life around?

Lev's visit with Annas was to take place about two weeks after he had time to adjust to life again. Annas did not have a loving relationship with his family, and if the history Lev read was true, one of Annas' own sons revealed the place where he was hiding from the rabble that was seeking his life. Things had not gone well for Annas after Jesus' death. How much did he regret about his former life?

Lev decided to fly his own aircraft to Jerusalem. He had never felt more insecure about meeting anyone. Lev did not want his loyalty to Christ to cause him to be short with Annas. Just as Paul and Nero came from opposite poles of light and darkness, so likewise there was a contrast in the holiness of Jesus with the depravity of Annas. Now Christ was enthroned in glory along with Paul and all the other body members, and righteousness and truth were enthroned. Those who had served Satan were also returned to life, but their leader was chained in the abyss. It was not the best of times for those who had sold themselves into evil.

The Awakening of Annas

I awakened in the still morning air, thankful that the howling mob had finally left me. I hesitated to open my eyes for fear someone would be watching for any signs of life. There was little doubt they wanted me dead. My pain was gone, and I wondered if perhaps I had died and awakened in some spiritual state, but I could feel my heart beating. Somehow I must have survived the hail of rocks, the kicks, and the assaults. Anger was surging up within me in place of my fear. I remembered some of the leaders of that mob, and I would have sweet revenge.

I opened my eyes ever so slightly so no one could recognize my conscious state, but no one was standing over me. So I opened my eyes wide to find myself alone in a lovely room that was like nothing I had ever seen before. I began feeling my body and found smooth skin where bruises and lacerations should have been, and gratefully found no pain whatsoever. Perhaps I had been unconscious for many days; I knew I must have been, for I could not have healed so completely in less time. Who saved me from that mob? Did the Roman army intervene on my behalf? That was the most likely possibility, since they didn't like rioting. Why was I in this place?

I had never seen a room such as this. It was not big or pretentious, but it was inviting; and the bed I rested in was soft with richly colored linens. As I began to move my hands and feet again, I was amazed that they were not even stiff or sore. Even my rheumatism was gone! The time of rest had served me well indeed. I was pleased at the ease with which I arose. Someone had removed my bloodstained garments. I was sure the arm with which I covered my head had been broken by the impact of a rock. The same was true when a rock struck my shin and seemed to shatter it causing me to fall to the ground. I remember the crowd kicking me and mercifully a large stone must have struck my head rendering me unconscious.

Why didn't they finish me off? Yes, those hated Roman soldiers probably intervened. Surely divine providence intervened on my behalf. After all, I was the High Priest of Israel, which was the highest spiritual office. I never felt better, and my body was youthful and strong again. I spotted some clothing, not the vestments I was accustomed to, *but I found they fit me well even though I felt slightly uncomfortable without my traditional garb.*

As I quietly walked about the room, I admired the furnishings and the décor. There were rich, deep blue draperies at the window matching the coverings on the bed. I walked across some soft fabric. Never had I seen carpets that went from one wall to the other seamlessly. I tested a sturdy chair made of wood, and I was surprised at the movement the rounded runners at the base of its legs allowed. It had a fluffy cushion that matched the other fabrics in the room.

Entering a small room, I was amazed at the beautiful facilities there. Automatically I reached for a metal handle and turned it to find water coming out. Moving it back, the water stopped. I did it several times and realized that was the way it was designed to operate. It was remarkable! Never had I seen anything like this. There was a crystal clear mirror above the basin. Imagine my surprise to find myself clean-shaven! What kind of indignity was intended? However, I did admire my handsome face and was amazed at my youthful look and beautiful white teeth. Although not particularly unpleasant, all was very unreal, more like a dream.

The birds were chirping in the trees and everything seemed so peaceful outside the window. Where was I? Was I out of danger? My thoughts became very troubled. I remembered the conditions in Jerusalem had become wild and intolerable. Had the Roman army quelled it? Having no king but Caesar must have paid off. All kinds of thoughts were racing through my head. What should I do? Perhaps I should open the door to my room and find my rescuer. I had stored gold and silver in many places, so I would reward my benefactor generously.

Opening the door a crack, I strained to see if anyone was looking.

Malchus, Servant of the Priesthood

Happily for Annas, he spied a servant of the priesthood, Malchus, whom he immediately recognized. He opened the door widely, stepping out with a youthful spring to his walk. Annas went over to him and greeted him as an old friend, but Malchus seemed unresponsive to his friendliness. Annas knew he had never treated his servants civilly.

"Malchus, how good to see you!"

"I can't say that it is mutual, Annas. I am here because I volunteered to be here for your return. None of your children or your wife wanted to be with you, so it was left to me to assist you."

"What? Ungrateful children! 'Honor thy father and mother.' I brought them up in the fear of the Lord and see how they behave now — wretched, ungrateful children. I shall deal with them. How did we get into this place? Where are we? How did I escape that bloodthirsty mob? What has happened?"

The Danger Is Past

"You can be at peace, Annas. You are no longer in danger. Perhaps some tea will settle your anxieties. Come into the kitchen, and I will begin to explain things to you over some tea and fruit."

"What kind of house is this? It does not resemble anything I have ever seen. Is this real?"

Malchus poured the aromatic tea that immediately aroused his senses.

"That smells absolutely delightful. Even tea is different. Where is the bread, olive oil and wine I am accustomed to?"

"There are answers to all your questions, but first offer your thanks for this food set before you."

He was accustomed to long prayers on every occasion and this was no exception. Upon lifting his head, he tasted the tea and his eyes widened with pleasure. "Ah! This is very good, indeed. You have been a good servant, Malchus. I am sorry that I haven't treated you better. Are you sure there is no bread in this house?"

"Things have changed, Annas. Try the fruit and you will never ask for bread again."

Annas bit into it. Again, his eyes brightened and the complaint disappeared from his lips. "This is extraordinary. Where on earth did you find it? Something very strange is going on. The last thing I remember is trying to defend myself from the rocks and kicks of that mob. How did you manage to find me and nurse me back to health?"

"No, Annas, all that I found was your poor broken and bloodied body that they threw on your doorstep. I did not nurse you back to health. I buried you. No one could have survived the treatment you received. You were dead."

"What kind of talk is this? I am very much alive. Please do not add to my confusion. I have awakened and everything is different."

"You did die and I did bury you. Jesus Christ has raised you from the dead this very morning."

Annas turned pale and then red with resentment. "I do not want that name mentioned in my presence ever again. He was a deceiver, and we justly put him to death. Now is that clear? I do not want to hear that name 'Jesus' again. I have suffered enough already because of him, and the mere mention of his name enrages me."

Malchus continued giving information in a matter-of-fact tone.

"As you wish—nonetheless, you were dead and you have been brought to life by 'someone.' Who that may be that gave you life again I will not mention. You are in the unfortunate position of finding yourself out of office, out of power and having no money or influence. Things have changed, and not all the changes will be to your liking. However, you are well provided for. This is your home and everything you need to live is comfortably provided for you. You will never want for food, clothing, or shelter. Your home is abundantly warmed and cooled as you wish it to be, and the property you live on makes you self-sufficient in food. Abraham, Isaac and Jacob are sitting in Jerusalem and in charge of affairs in Israel and the whole world. That is some of the good news."

Annas Remembers His Riches

"What happened to all my money? Did my children find it and waste it in riotous living? You know I was very rich. Surely, some of that money is still there for me."

"No, money is not used anymore. Love, not money, controls the world in which we live today. Therefore, it is a very happy world without war or strife. Even if you found the caches of money you squirreled away, it would buy you nothing. The Sanhedrin is long gone. Our temple has been completely destroyed with not one stone standing on another. You lost all your power and influence when the mobs killed you. You do have your life again, but it is a very simple life without the power and influence you once enjoyed. You may be disappointed to hear all your fortune has been lost. But rejoice! You are alive, well and secure."

"You cannot be saying that our sacred and beloved temple is no longer here! I hope you are telling me this to taunt me, cruel as that might be. I do not know what to believe. What you are telling me sounds like a nightmare. It cannot be true. Why do you torment me when I am so insecure? Everything you have said only confuses me more. What are you hiding from me?"

Malchus' heart couldn't remain hardened in view of Annas' pitiful state. "Only the truth is spoken now. You did die and I buried your broken body. You have come to life this morning. Did you look in the mirror? What did you see? Did you see the old and decrepit Annas? No, you saw a younger, strong, and vital person, didn't you? All your teeth were there, and all your hair turned dark again. You were raised from the dead. Many centuries have passed. That is the truth."

Dropping his head into his hands, Annas groaned, "This cannot be true. I know I am different in some ways and even you look younger than I remember. I have the gnawing feeling that there is a missing element in my life."

"Just be glad there is no angry crowd standing outside. You are at peace, and it will take several days to get over the oddness you feel. We all experience this when we return to life."

A Severed Ear Restored

"Malchus, was it true you had your ear cut off and then had it healed again?" Annas remembered hearing a rumor to that effect.

"Yes, of course it is true, but back then you would not hear my testimony. You were too strong-willed to listen to anybody."

"Mind your manners, Malchus. Remember to whom you are speaking. I still carry the title of High Priest even though I left the office some years ago."

"Forget about your office and title. You are plain Annas as I am plain Malchus. I am no longer your servant, and you have no special privileges anymore. I am here out of the kindness of my heart. I now serve the Lord Jesus Christ."

Annas stood abruptly, almost overturning the table, turning red with rage. "What did I just tell you? You must not use that name in my presence! For that matter, you can no longer be my servant if you have changed your loyalty! You are a most ungrateful person. We paid you well, and you had special privileges. This is how you repay me? I do not need the services of a traitor. You may leave."

Malchus didn't make a move to go. "I agreed to stay with you and get you adjusted to life as we now live it. I cannot leave. You are totally unprepared for life now unless someone teaches you all about the new living conditions. So please, be calm. I am no longer interested in your opinions. I must tell you that you erred grievously in some matters, and the sooner you accept responsibility for what you did, the better."

Not knowing what else to do, Annas sat down again, trembling. "Well, Malchus, you have me in a very powerless position. I still do not know where I am and why I am here. You are even strange. I thought I could rely on you. I see you have developed an evil eye toward me. What have I done to you to make you so belligerent?"

Equals

"What have you done? Your wife chose not to be here. Your sons were asked to receive you and they refused. There were no volunteers to be with you. When I was asked, I could not say 'no' out of loyalty to…well, you know who. I am not here to be abused by you. I had enough of that in our previous life together. Now I am your equal."

Suddenly Annas realized he must not antagonize Malchus. He needed him desperately. He was too confused and uncertain to make any decisions or even to care for himself in this complicated new living arrangement.

"All right, Malchus, I will forget about my status. Let us be friends. I do need you, at least for awhile. I have got to find some answers or I will have to conclude that I am insane."

"Very well, Annas. I have to speak plainly to you; and when I do, please do not think that I am being arrogant or rude."

Poor Annas knew that he was guilty of this and had justified it because he had held the exalted office of High Priest. He bit his tongue and endured being humbled. This was a terrible blow to his pride and prestige, but he felt like a lost child. What else could he do?

"Malchus, do you know if there are any other former priests or members of the Sanhedrin that I can contact? I need to talk to some of my peers to find out how they are surviving under these difficult conditions."

"Well, Caiaphas lives in Judea somewhere. I can look up his phone number and let you talk to him."

"What is a phone?"

Pulling out his hand-held phone from his pocket, he said, "This is what it looks like. I will dial him for you until you learn modern numbers, and it will ring Caiaphas' phone and you can talk to him right from where you are seated."

"I can scarcely believe that! Show me!"

Soon there was a voice speaking, "Shalom. This is Caiaphas."

"Yes, Shalom, this is Malchus. Annas has returned to life and wishes to speak to you."

"What does he want of me? Tell him that I cannot help him."

"No, wait, please! He says he needs to speak to you."

"All right, put him on."

"Shalom, Caiaphas. Is this really you?"

"Yes, of course it is. What is it that you want from me?"

"I need to find my sanity, so I wanted to speak to someone I know. I have awakened to a nightmare and perhaps you can help clear my mind. Is it true that our temple is destroyed and our offices as High Priests have ceased to exist?"

"Yes, of course, it's true. Didn't Malchus tell you that?"

The Priesthood Is Out of Business

"Yes, yes, he did. But how can I accept such a statement? Our beautiful temple was forty-six years in building, and you say it is gone as though it means nothing to you anymore."

"I am afraid that it was only stone and timber. It is all gone—no use lamenting about it."

"Is there no place in your heart left for our beautiful temple?"

"Annas, it is all over with. You cannot re-create the past. It is gone, whether we like it or not. The Aaronic Priesthood is gone too. We are out of business."

"You are being very short with me, Caiaphas. I am not used to being treated that way."

"I have every reason to be short with you, Annas. You led us down the wrong pathway."

"How can you say that, Caiaphas? We adhered to the very letter of the Law of Moses. How could that be wrong?"

"How could it not be wrong? The Law of Moses promised that we would be blessed in basket and in store if we kept the precepts of that Law. How were we blessed? We held power and privilege for a short season and then lost everything. How did you die? An enraged multitude killed you when your own son revealed the place you were hiding. We had neither love nor respect. All the money you amassed by practicing fraud in the temple services did not save you, did it, Annas? How wrong could we be and still think we were right?"

"Take heed lest you speak blasphemy, Caiaphas. We were good men. We prayed and fasted. We worried about keeping the Law in great detail."

"Yes, and we devoured widows' houses and laid great burdens on the people and would not as much as lift a little finger to lighten their load. Yes, we made long prayers in the streets to be seen of men, but God would not listen to our prayers. We were proud, we were cruel, and we were stubborn. We reaped a bitter harvest."

"Was not Jeremiah thrown into a pit for speaking the Word of the Lord? Was not Isaiah sawn asunder for preaching the same? How was our end different from these men of God?"

"Jeremiah and Isaiah are both ruling princes in the earth now, along with a host of faithful men and women to whom God has seen fit to give a 'better resurrection.' We are not included in that honorable listing, Annas. We are not ruling in Jerusalem, but we have been cast out of power and are odious in the eyes of the people. Look on your television and there you will see the ancient and venerable men and women whom God has honored. They are in control of the whole earth—and where are we?"

"Surely, there must be some misunderstanding, Caiaphas. We were great and honorable men. How could we be looked upon otherwise?"

"The whole nation of Israel instantly received these Ancient Worthies when they returned to life. Who has received you, Annas, and who has received me? Even our own families did not choose to be with us when we returned. Where is your wife and where are your sons? Have any of them embraced you? The only one who condescended to be with you was Malchus, an abused servant. What does this tell you?"

"I have an ungrateful wife and disobedient children, that is what it tells me."

"The money that we stole corrupted our families. This ill-gotten wealth rotted our own hearts as well as theirs. Do not be so blind, Annas!"

"Well, I can see you are ungrateful for the privileges I bestowed upon you, Caiaphas. Instead of appreciating the power of office I conferred upon you, there is only contempt for me."

Ill-Gotten Gain

"All that you conferred upon me has eaten like a canker into my heart, Annas. The High Priest of God was to be blessed and honored. I was not blessed and I was not honored. I was feared, but never loved. Moses told us to 'love the Lord thy God with all thine heart, and with all thy soul, and with all thy might' (Deuteronomy 6:5). That is what all the holy men and women of God did. We loved money, power, and privilege. Most of all we loved ourselves. Now it is all revealed and we are cast out of power, odious in the eyes of our fellow men."

"Who has made you my judge, Caiaphas, you proud and cantankerous son-in-law? I have never been so indignantly treated, even by the savages who took my life. Please do not bother to speak to me again until you apologize."

Annas handed Malchus the phone with trembling hands. He had looked for some solace and comfort from his former priest appointee and was only derided. Malchus heard at least half of the conversation and felt some pity for Annas who was learning, to his great sorrow, that his present situation found him without friend or contact.

"Is it true, Malchus, that Abraham, Isaac and Jacob are seated in power in Jerusalem?"

"Yes, I shall show you that as soon as I can get around to it. You have many things to learn, and that is what I am here to do. I must teach you what you need to know before Lev Aron arrives."

"Who is Lev Aron, may I ask?"

"Well, the Ancients, knowing some people are going to have special problems, send out a wise and gifted counselor to help make the adjustments needed in this new way of living. There is no longer any deceit or corruption permitted. No violence is allowed. This government is righteous within and without. It is difficult for those who once were in power and practiced evil to learn it all. That is why Lev is coming. You will find him extremely helpful and a man of great character."

"Thank you, but *I* did not invite him. Is he free to intrude himself on me?"

"He is coming under the direction of the highest authority in Jerusalem, so, yes, I think you had better receive him graciously. He is a charming man, and even all the people he has visited speak well of him. You will, too, once you meet him. He is being sent here for your good."

"I respect the Ancients, and if they arranged for this man to visit me I shall at least try to be civil, if I am able."

"Good. Let me show you your facilities and how comfortable you have it now. You will not miss your servants standing around. Everything is done so that all the daily needs of life are easily provided for with only the slightest of effort."

With this, Malchus showed Annas all the features of his estate, finishing with the computerized television. When he turned it on, Annas jumped up, saying, "Where did these people come from? Surely this is sorcery!"

"No, you will soon learn that this is done through modern science." Malchus explained the working of modern electronics, as well as the ease and benefits of modern education.

Respect for the Ancients

As Annas watched, he could not help but notice the commanding authority and brilliant way the Ancients conducted their presentations.

Malchus explained, "I am going to call up information about the day in which you lived. Now listen carefully that you may have a correct view of your own conduct."

John the Baptist was the speaker. This startled Annas. "I heard that John the Baptist was murdered by Herod? What is he doing here?"

"He was among the first raised to life with a 'better resurrection,' as the Bible calls it. He is with the Ancient Worthies ruling in Jerusalem. Better listen carefully."

Annas quieted down as he heard the powerful voice of John explaining the era in which he lived. He described the hypocrisy of the religious leaders and how, instead of repenting, they multiplied their sins until they had crucified their Messiah.

"Turn this off. I cannot bear this kind of message. In the first place, it is not true. It was Pilate who ordered Jesus to be put to death."

"How many times did Pilate say, 'I find no fault in this man'?"

"Too many times, to be sure. He was frightened by his wife and was afraid to do his duty. She had some dreams regarding Jesus and urged Pilate to have nothing to do with that man. At last he did the right thing and ordered Jesus to be crucified."

"When he washed his hands of this whole unfortunate circumstance, what did you and the mobs of murderers with you cry?"

Annas listened but remained silent, unwilling to repeat what he had said.

"You remember very clearly what you said. Why are you ashamed to repeat it now?"

"Have you, a mere servant, now become some kind of lawyer and judge?"

"You aren't so quick to shout now what you did once with the crowd, 'His blood be on us, and on our children' (Matthew 27:25). Why does this displease you now? Are you still so sure of your righteousness?"

Liked Sleeping Better

"This morning it was pleasant to find myself alive. Now, with a friend like you, I think I liked sleeping in death better. Malchus, you have become my accuser and my enemy. Have you no fear of God?"

"I am sorry you find my words strong, Annas. However, you obviously must know that you made some dreadful mistakes, and it is going to be painful for you until you acknowledge that you killed the Son of God."

"No, we sought the death of him who *claimed* to be the Son of God. He was surely an imposter. He could not have been the Son of the Blessed. We told this imposter to come down from the cross, and we would believe him. Why didn't he demonstrate to us that he was the Son of the Blessed if, indeed, he was?"

A certain reverence came over Malchus as he responded to Annas' defiant questions. "Because it was prophesied of him that he would die for our sins. If he came down from the cross, none of us would be alive again. We would all still be sleeping in the grave."

"That would be better, I am sure. No one would be deriding me now."

Malchus knew their conversation was going nowhere, so he suggested they take a walk through the peaceful community. "Let us go for a walk. Perhaps we will both feel less frustrated enjoying the beauties of this world."

"That sounds like a good suggestion. My head is swimming, and I feel confused and very insecure."

"Well, that is a better feeling than a gang throwing stones at you, isn't it?"

"Yes, that was a painful and bitter moment for me. There was no escape and no mercy."

"Why should you be looking for mercy? You know you were not compassionate or merciful with others."

Annas didn't respond.

Isaiah's Prophecy Fulfilled

They walked silently for awhile, until they came upon a lamb, a wolf, a leopard, a kid, a lion, and a calf all lying down together. Annas froze as he saw a little child walk up to the animals without any fear.

He was about to shout to the child to stop and retreat, when the child sat down by the lion and petted his mane. Annas instantly recalled the prophecy of Isaiah that had described such a scene as this (Isaiah 11:6), but he could not believe his eyes. As they both stood silently, the child arose and the phenomenal company of animals followed the child as he walked off into a field.

"Surely," exclaimed Annas, "this is the day Isaiah spoke of. I cannot believe my eyes. I read this passage so many times, but I never believed I should see it fulfilled. Without a doubt the earth has changed. I am feeling faint. My knees are weak and unsteady suddenly. Did we actually see this or was it a vision? Those animals were real and so was the child. Shall we return home?"

"Yes, these animals never were peaceful with each other before and never would a child survive doing what we just saw. We shall return home."

"Without any doubt, God is in this place!" exclaimed Annas.

A long silence followed as the two men drank tea together. Finally, Annas broke the silence, "I know Isaiah prophesied of this time, and we have seen his very words fulfilled. What shall we do? You saw it, too, so there were two witnesses to this event."

"Yes, Annas, I witnessed it also."

"Is it possible we are both mad? Can we both be seeing visions at the same time? This makes me feel weak and fearful. Pour me more tea, please."

Malchus noticed a different tone in Annas' voice. Instead of his usual arrogant and harsh mannerism, he was subdued and his tone of voice gentler, though shaky.

Annas excused himself saying, "Forgive me while I retreat to my room. I need quietness to reflect on the events of today."

Time for Serious Reflection

Annas skipped lunch and appeared at the supper hour. The conversation changed from the constant confrontation that had been going on before, to a very quiet time at the supper table.

"You did say that Abraham, Isaac, and Jacob were now ruling in Jerusalem, didn't you? Is it they who are in authority now?"

"They are only under the authority of the ruling Messiah. You asked me not to mention his name, Annas, but you surely must realize we no longer have Caesar as our king."

"I am, therefore, in great difficulty, am I not, Malchus? The very one I could not rest until we had crucified is now in power. Woe is me! It would have been better for me to remain sleeping in the grave. Why was I wakened? This is a dark day for me. I am very troubled."

"My task is to teach you about modern ways of life, Annas. When Lev Aron comes, perhaps he can help you adjust to your distressing situation. I sense your feelings, and I would not want to be in your place. It seems you erred grievously and there is no way to undo what has happened."

"What troubles me is that Judas, Jesus' own disciple, came to us wishing to betray his leader. This seemed positive proof that this man Jesus was an imposter, not the real Messiah. Why would one of his own disciples sell his leader for thirty pieces of silver? This convinced us that his scheme of pretending to be something that he was not was falling apart, and his own disciples were abandoning him. Even one of his leading disciples denied with cursing being associated with the man. This helped convince us that he was a false messiah and, therefore, we were justified in having him put to death."

"Maybe Lev Aron will be able to satisfy your inquiries. Do not ask me about the past. The task I volunteered for was to acquaint you with present-day conditions so you could live an independent life."

During the next two weeks, both men avoided discussing the topic.

"Woe unto you, scribes and Pharisees, hypocrites!
For ye pay tithe of mint and anise and cummin,
And have omitted the weightier matters of the law,
Judgment, mercy, and faith"
(Matthew 23:23).

Chapter Eleven

When Annas heard Lev's aircraft landing, he became agitated. He had never seen anything so astonishing. He was apprehensive of bitter confrontation while trying to justify himself.

Annas told Malchus to greet Lev, while Annas remained inside. Malchus greeted Lev warmly, partly because he knew it meant he could now leave, and partly because he had heard so many wonderful things about him. Lev was not offended by Annas' lack of enthusiasm. He took the opportunity to question Malchus.

"Malchus, it is such a pleasure to meet you. It is as though you stepped out of a page of history. All we know of you from the biblical account is that you were a servant of the High Priest, and that Peter cut off your ear and Jesus healed it. Tell me, after Jesus healed you, did you feel that his arrest was proper?"

Miracle Convinces Malchus

"Of course not! That miracle could not have been by anything less than the power of God in response to Jesus' request. However, I was not in charge of the mob, but merely went because my masters sent me. I was in shock to lose my ear and even in greater shock to have it healed. All the pain and blood disappeared as though nothing had happened. I saw my ear on the ground, and when Jesus picked it up, I thought he might show it to the crowd to slow down the arrest. To my great surprise, he quickly put it back so that those who were not watching would not have known what happened. I knew then and there that he was a man imbued with God's Spirit and power."

"Thank you for volunteering to be with Annas. That was very kind of you. The Ancients send greetings along with their thanks. How has Annas fared since his return?"

"Annas is in great distress to learn he is out of power and office. I knew him before, and of course I feel his present pain. He was a man without a shred of kindness or mercy in his former life, but he finds he needs much mercy now."

Time slipped by as they talked. Annas, whose plan was to make Lev wait to meet him, was fuming inside. If Lev had come to see him, why was he wasting time talking to Malchus? The longer they talked the more irritated he became. When he was just about to explode with anger, Malchus and Lev came in.

"What took you so long to bring our guest into my house, Malchus?" he demanded.

"Shalom, Annas! My name is Lev Aron, and I'm very pleased to meet you. I am sorry if I delayed Malchus. I am a student of biblical history and meeting Malchus is such an extraordinary event that I took the opportunity to ask him a few questions. You and I will be together for awhile, so we will have plenty of time to get acquainted."

Lev's genuineness settled Annas down. "Welcome to my humble home. I hope you will be comfortable here during your stay. I am not exactly sure of the purpose of your visit, but hospitality has always been a priestly grace. I hear that you are connected with those who are governing from Jerusalem."

"Not really. I'm nothing more than a servant of the King. I go where I am sent. For whatever reason, they feel I have done more good than harm in my visits, so I guess that is why they keep me on. They are very kind to overlook my shortcomings and failings, and I hope you will be so kind as well."

Malchus Eager to Leave

"My, you are disarming, indeed! I can see you are a hard person to dislike."

Malchus interrupted, "Now that you are here, Lev, I shall be on my way. I left a project building houses for my parents that I really need to get back to. So I shall say Shalom to you, Annas, and to you, Lev."

"Can I give you a lift?" Lev asked. "You might like a ride in the aircraft."

"Yes, thank you, Lev. I don't mind the walk. It is only three or four miles from here, but I would really enjoy a ride in your flying machine."

"Why don't you come along, Annas?" Lev invited.

"No, thank you. If the Lord wanted us to fly, he would have given us wings."

"It would be very hard sleeping with wings," Lev smiled, "and they would get in the way much of the time. Meanwhile, Malchus, if you are packed, let's be on our way. I will enjoy a few more minutes with you."

Lev turned toward the former priest. "Excuse me, Annas. I will be gone less than an hour. I intend to show Malchus the countryside from the air. It is quite breathtaking from up there, you know."

Annas was disturbed by the attention Lev was showering on Malchus. When Lev returned, he found his host a little hostile.

"I thought you were sent to visit me."

"Yes, indeed, I was. But I couldn't let this good man walk with his luggage."

Annas made no response, but he was obviously annoyed.

"Well, now that you have seen a bit of this modern world, how does it compare with the past?" Perhaps ignoring Annas' mood would allow him to get over it, while saving face.

"I had fine food to eat in the past, and I eat very well now. I had priestly garments of distinction, and now I wear these nice but odd clothes. I lived in a spacious palace with servants, and here I am comfortable but must serve myself. I would prefer the past if I had a choice, but now that I am here I am learning to make do."

"That's an admirable spirit!" Lev's practice was to encourage any positive effort. "Change is inevitable even though it is sometimes hard to accept. You lost some things and gained some things. When you add them up you will find, in all probability, that you have gained more."

Former Days Were Better

"I don't believe that one bit," Annas huffed. "I was rich and powerful. I was respected and feared. I held a very high office among the Lord's anointed priests. Now, I have no prestige. Am I supposed to rejoice in that? I find it impossible."

Lev seated himself on the sofa in the living room. "One great advantage is that you are not in the position to make the mistakes you made before. Having power and authority without the discipline of righteousness and mercy can bring one to ruin."

"You are judging me! I never was, nor am I now, a criminal! I defended the rights of the Jewish priesthood!"

"Who was threatening your rights?" Lev asked calmly, gesturing for Annas to join him on the sofa.

Annas ignored the gesture. "Now you want me to burst into a tirade against that lowly Nazarene!" he shouted. But he thought better of his tone and sat down. "No, I shall not do that. We left him alone for nearly three and a half years, so as you see, we were not against the good works that he did."

"What caused you to desperately seek his life when you did?"

"You know that only the priesthood of Israel was permitted to make atonement for sins. Yet this man implied *he* could forgive sins without using the Jewish altars appointed by God. This was not acceptable to us who were entrusted with keeping the Law of Moses."

"What happened to your Jewish altars? The temple was twice destroyed and rebuilt, but you lost the Ark of the Covenant when Solomon's temple was destroyed. So your services were limited and crippled without the Ark of the Covenant." Lev maintained an even tone while continuing to probe the logic of Annas' statements.

"True, and we did realize our loss. However, we still kept those services that could be performed without the Ark. People who sinned were to come and offer appointed sacrifices. We were not prepared for a blasphemer to lay aside the Jewish Law and grant forgiveness on his own."

"What happened to your sacrifices and to your temple?"

"I understand the temple was destroyed and the priesthood scattered."

"Were you prepared for that?"

"How could we envision such a great evil befalling us?"

"What was to become of forgiveness of sins?"

"I cannot answer that, Lev. We followed the Law of Moses as far as we could. Do you fault us for doing that?"

"The Lord is the Righteous Judge." Lev leaned toward Annas earnestly. "Whatever happened, it is clear the Lord did not choose to continue the Aaronic Priesthood forever."

"Yes, so it seems. However, I always knew I was in the lineage of Aaron. I am amazed to find that it means nothing now." Annas seemed genuinely perplexed.

The Aaronic Priesthood Was to Be Replaced

Lev tried to explain. "The Aaronic Priesthood was kept until the greater sacrifice for sin was made—a once-for-all sacrifice that could forever take away sin. Isn't that better than the continual animal sacrifices that had to be repeated because they were never effective? Oddly enough, by your own hand you offered up Christ who has become the satisfaction for your sins and for the sins of the whole world. Should not the law have taught you the futility of offering sacrifices that could never take away sin?"

Annas crossed his arms and sat farther back on the oversized chair he had chosen. "I cannot answer that. All I know is we zealously followed the Law of Moses." He suddenly stood. "Now, I have delayed offering you hospitality. You must be hungry, thirsty, and tired from your trip here. If you will excuse me, I shall make tea and serve you supper."

"Thank you. Yes, I think I could use some refreshment. I saw vegetables on my way in, perhaps we could add a few cooked vegetables to the menu tonight for supper."

"I don't know how to prepare them, but if you know how, I do enjoy them now and again."

Lev went out to pick up the vegetables. A neighbor waved to him and asked if he owned the aircraft.

"Well, they let me use it, for which I am grateful."

"Are you the guest of Annas?"

"Yes."

"I hope you can turn him into a civilized member of the community."

"I can only answer for myself. If there is anything I can do for you, please let me know."

"How about a ride in your aircraft?"

"That can be arranged. Why not? Only not today—I'm quite tired. Yes, you shall have a ride."

"Thank you! I will hold you to it."

Lev returned eager to prepare the vegetables the way he liked them. When all was ready, they sat down to a sumptuous meal. Annas thanked the Lord and Lev added under his breath, "In Jesus name."

"I must say, you are a better cook than Malchus," Annas complimented grudgingly.

"Thank you. Someday I will have to make you a cake. I do a little baking too. By the way, would you like to meet your family members?"

"No, they do not wish to see me, so I will not disturb them. Nobody likes a man who is down."

"You don't look down to me. You are well provided for and have an abundant life here. You have all the services you need. I would never have been comfortable with servants. I love to work and love to learn. Have you found yourself being pulled into the learning cycle?"

Learning Is Easy to Absorb Now

"Yes, actually I have now that you mention it. Time passes so quickly while learning that I find myself losing sleep to get in extra study. I find it quite overwhelming, this ocean of knowledge along all lines."

They talked into the evening along the lines of their respective studies until finally Lev excused himself and retired to his room, weary from his long day.

The next morning Lev rose early while Annas was still sleeping, as he wished to take in a chapel meeting before breakfast. When Lev arrived home he found Annas finishing his breakfast.

"I am sorry I started to eat without you. When I awakened I found you were gone, but your aircraft was still here. I had no idea what had become of you."

"I always go to chapel meetings wherever I go. You might find it a joyful experience to worship God with all your neighbors."

"How can a Jewish priest go to a Christian chapel? They would run me out as the one responsible for Jesus' death."

"Oh, that's not true, Annas. Anyone who wishes to worship God is always welcome in the house of God."

"That is easy for you to say, Lev. You are connected with the powers that be, but I am on the outside. The worst part is that I have enemies who hate me without number. One by one they will return to taunt and mock me."

"Is it possible that you did things that invited this kind of contempt?" Lev asked softly as he sat down to eat.

"I lived by the letter of the Law of Moses. This should cause people to respect me. But I know they won't and instead will impute evil to me."

"Nobody will hate you for being a kind and compassionate person. Are you sure your conduct did not invite reproach?"

"The law required rigorous efforts to keep things right. That would not always make me the nicest person." Annas' face looked as if it were carved of stone.

"Are you sure you did not break the law while professing to keep it?"

"That is insulting!"

"I simply asked the question. I have only a perfunctory knowledge of a few things recorded in the Bible about your dealings, and even there you don't seem very compassionate."

"That was written by my enemies. What else would you expect?"

"Anyway, I am flying off to visit one of the factories here. You're invited to join me and see how things are done if you are interested. We will be back by early afternoon."

"No, thank you. I have no time for worldly frivolities. I am a man of prayer and devotion."

"Well, as soon as you get educated, you will be called upon to build houses for your parents and for others and also to devote time to the general good of mankind."

"You do not understand! The Priesthood of Israel was kept from menial labor so that they could serve the Lord in his temple. Who is changing the rules?"

Aaronic Priesthood Had an End

"Certainly not me! The Aaronic Priesthood served its purpose in a given time. If the Aaronic Priesthood was to be forever, why did God create a higher Priesthood after the order of Melchizedec? That was to be a Priesthood without an end of days. Didn't that imply the Aaronic Priesthood would come to an end? In fact, it did. The Aaronic Priesthood became extinct after the destruction of Jerusalem along with its temple."

"What you are telling me is that my status as priest is ended, and I must report as a common laborer. Is that correct?"

Lev smiled. "Annas, no laborer is common. It is an honor to serve in any capacity to help in the great regeneration program. Bringing all to life again is a breathtaking project, but that part is being done for us. What we have to do is build homes and plant orchards to care for people when they return. It is joyful work, and I might add, ennobling as well."

"I prefer to leave such work to others," Annas retorted haughtily. "We had servants to do all that work for us."

"Weren't the Priests servants of the people in spiritual matters? Making sacrifices on behalf of the people to atone for their sins — wasn't that a service?"

Clearly, Annas was not prepared to adjust to his new situation and was bitter at his lot.

Lev excused himself and prepared to leave to visit an electronics factory twenty miles away. "I'll be back in the afternoon. This is only a short visit to see if I can be of any help while I am here."

"I thought you were here to be with me."

"I am. That doesn't mean I have to be with you every moment of the day."

"Well, have a good visit. I shall be here when you return."

Lev visited a high tech factory that made computers. He was warmly welcomed even though it was a surprise visit. Several were familiar with his name, and a few confused him with his brother Jake.

He found their operation on top of every advance and working to improve things daily. No help was needed, so he decided it would just be a social call. As he was preparing to leave, the temporary manager spoke to him on the side. "Lev, if you have time to spare, we do have two people here who are very gifted and brilliant but seem to have a very competitive spirit. These two can only criticize each other's contributions. So while we are on top of things technically, we are having a bit of trouble with relationships."

"I am not having much success where I am now. If I get a chance, I will come and spend a day here. Meanwhile, encourage them to go to the chapel meetings. They may benefit from some higher wisdom."

"Thank you! I do hope you will return. Shalom."

Lev returned to Annas' house just as he was sitting down to eat, so he joined him. "Well, did you accomplish anything this morning?"

"No, the factory is running smoothly. The manager did ask me to come back to help resolve some personnel conflicts. People reconciling with each other is taking more time than it should." Lev continued, "You know what I saw on the way back from the factory in a field near your house?"

"How would I know?"

Isaiah's Prophecy Fulfilled

"Well, I'll tell you. I saw a lion, a lamb, a wolf, and a leopard along with a bear all resting together in a field along the way. This was a perfect picture of the peaceable Kingdom."

"No, it wasn't. To fulfill Isaiah's prophecy it needed a little child leading them. That is what Malchus and I saw before you came. It was beautiful even though at first I was about to cry out to the child fearing for his safety. But the little fellow just marched up to the lion and petted it. When he left, all the animals got up and followed the child. I could not believe my eyes."

"At least you know you are in the Kingdom of peace. Even the animals feed on protein grass and no longer eat one another. Animals have not been regenerated so we don't have savage animals coming back. However, the humans do bring back an enormous amount of evil and sometimes savage memories."

A thought came to Lev. "Annas, would you have enough faith to pet the lion?"

"Are you serious? Of course not."

"Then you don't believe you are in the peaceable Kingdom, do you? Come with me. I'm going to find the animals and see if I can pet the lion and the leopard. Are you game to come along?"

A Test of Faith

"I'll come along, although I think you are doing a foolish thing. I would hate to see you torn by the lion or leopard. What are you trying to prove?"

"Annas, if they were dangerous animals, do you think the community could allow them to roam freely in this area? What I am trying to impress upon you is that you are living in the day that Isaiah prophesied about. It is here now. We live in the day, for the night is past and the 'sun of righteousness' has risen."

"I will go with you. Just don't ask me to pet these wild creatures. With my luck, they would let you pet them and eat me."

"Let's go before they get up to feed."

Lev hurried back to the field where he had seen the animals with Annas trying to keep up. "There, see, they are still resting. I want you to know I have never petted a lion or a leopard before, but because of my faith in the Scriptures, I am not afraid."

"I hope they are not too hungry. You might appear a more delicious meal than protein grass."

Lev was confident the animals would be friendly. He walked slowly and gently toward the odd company of animals. The lamb came running to him, and Lev paused to pick it up and stroke under its chin. The other animals watched without moving. He proceeded up to the lion and stood before it. Putting down the absolutely fearless lamb, he reached to stroke the lion's mane. The animal stretched like the big cat that he was and began to purr. The leopard wanting attention rubbed Lev's leg, and he petted it too. He couldn't help laughing with delight. After a few minutes of this he returned, saying, "Now it is your turn."

"Not on your life. I am thankful they did not follow you, otherwise I would be running."

They walked home with Annas nervously looking back to be sure the animals didn't follow them. He said, "I am afraid to walk about freely now, for fear that a lion or leopard might return to their former habits."

"That will not happen. The world is not spinning out of control anymore. There is nothing that can hurt or destroy in this kingdom. You know that, don't you?"

"Oh, that's what you keep saying! My life could be tolerable if I were not such an object of scorn to so many people."

"The way to remedy that is to become a loving and caring human being. People will forgive the past if they see your heart of stone has become a heart of flesh."

Not as Ugly as I Am Made Out to Be

"I can't believe I'm as bad as I am made out to be."

"Well, why wouldn't your own family help prepare for your return?"

"Ungrateful children! I was not blessed with a loyal family. Am I to blame for this also?"

"What about your former wife?"

"I do not understand her attitude. My former wife was well cared for and lived in comparative luxury. We had servants to do all the work. Many women would have been glad for the advantages she enjoyed."

"Yes, but some people who shared hard times together did so successfully when they loved one another. Now their love is blossoming forth and bearing fruit unto life eternal. Without love, life is very unfulfilling. Wealth and status are not substitutes for love. Character, character, character! That is what we all need. I mean, a godlike character."

Annas looked at Lev, his face the picture of perplexity. "I was looked up to as a pillar of the priesthood. I was no mean person."

"How many of your fellow priests are with you now praising you?"

"None."

"People in power are always surrounded by those seeking some favors and privileges. You misjudged their praise. Did any of your fellow priests love you?"

"From the looks of things, apparently not."

"Did you love your fellow priests?"

There followed a long and troubled silence.

"I cannot answer that. Anyway, why should I bare my inner being before you?"

Was Love the Governing Principle?

"I'm sorry, Annas. I am not trying judge you, but in your heart you should know whether you operated out of love for others, or whether you were driven by a love of self, power and prestige."

"What does it matter anyway? I lost the respect of my people and was killed by a mob. Now I learn my own son helped the mob find me."

"The first requirement of each of us now is to know what is in our heart. Before we did outrageously evil things and called them good. We could kill, speak evil of others, abuse others and say, 'The Lord is glorified.' But now, truth must be everywhere all the time—and that includes truth about our own heart condition."

After a brief pause, Lev continued. "As long as we are talking, I would like to question you about the three religious trials conducted in securing Jesus' condemnation. In the Bible we have a view given by his followers. I want your view. Are you willing?"

The World's Greatest Trial

"Yes, just once will I give my version of events. You may proceed with your questions."

"Very well. When you had Jesus arrested, he was brought to you first. The most significant thing about this to me is that you had Jesus arrested without a charge. Was that the proper legal procedure?"

"We had not perfected our case against the man. He was a threat. We needed a charge that would justify our asking for the death penalty. We could have had him arrested for overturning the tables of the moneychangers at the temple. Pilate would have gladly arrested him for that, but he would have only given Jesus a light prison sentence. We were careful not to charge him with any good work that he may have done, even if it was done inappropriately on the Sabbath Day."

"So you did not have a clear charge! Even when he stood in your court, you cross-examined him trying to find a charge. Wasn't that a false arrest?"

"Technically, you are right. However, this man was very wily. We perceived his little charade was unraveling when one of his disciples came to us seeking money to betray him. We were facing the Passover and our window of opportunity to put this deceiver out of the way was very short."

First Religious Trial before Annas

"The first trial you conducted was illegal, was it not? It was at night in the first place. In the second place, one man was never to be the judge and jury, was he?"

"This man Jesus could not be arrested during the day. The crowds adored him—we had to operate at night."

"Yes, but you were a legalist, a follower of the letter of the Law and here you were breaking the Law."

"We made an exception because we had to. If we had waited until morning, the crowds of his followers would have gotten wind of it, and there would have been a riot. We needed to get the Roman government to execute him. The people feared the Romans and would not riot against them."

"Jesus knew you were violating the Law in arresting him without a charge and he said so. He mentioned that he had spoken in the temple and synagogues openly, and if you had something to charge him with, you should have collected your evidence there."

"All right! We should have had a charge. But we did not have much time. When Judas came to us seeking money, we were convinced that shortly his following would disintegrate. The very evening of his arrest another one of his disciples denied knowing him. That only strengthened our resolve. The other disciples all fled, except for John. What kind of loyal followers were they?"

"They proved *very* loyal subsequently. Not only so, but they succeeded in spreading the message of Christ throughout the whole world. Jesus wanted his disciples to flee, lest you collect them and sentence them all to death as well. It seems your bloodlust was running quite high at that time."

"I admit that all our efforts to halt their preaching failed."

"Yes, and Judas was replaced by Paul, who became the most powerful and eloquent preacher of the Christian faith. So you certainly misread events, believing your actions would end the Christian faith and teachings."

"Yes, that is true. Little did we realize making Jesus a martyr would only prosper his cause."

The Second Illegal Religious Trial

Lev continued with his questions. "I'm concerned with the second illegal trial held at night before the Sanhedrin. You could not get witnesses to agree in their testimony. You were not to have trials by night, especially one that involved a life and death judgment. You still could not level a charge against Jesus. It seems in desperation you asked him, 'Art thou the Christ, the Son of the Blessed?' It was then that Jesus said, 'I am' (Mark 14:61, 62). That was the answer that you used to condemn him. Yet, if he was the Son of the Blessed, how else could he answer, but 'I am'? What troubles me is why you would consider this blasphemy when from among your own members it was said, 'We have one Father, even God' (John 8:41). Why was it all right for those of your persuasion to claim God as your Father and you accused Jesus of blasphemy for admitting the same thing?"

Annas snickered. "You are a clever lawyer, Lev. With you as the examiner, I am sure our case would have sunk beneath the waves. However, we did not believe Jesus' testimony to be true, so it was labeled 'blasphemy.' It looks now as if we were wrong. You have hindsight and are judging us for making the wrong conclusion without the benefit of hindsight."

"Still it was all illegal in the first place. You had no right by your own code of law to prosecute anyone at night."

"You must remember, this man had a huge following, and we could not do this any other way. Although we did have the trial, we waited until daybreak for a legal one, and that is when we convicted him."

Third Religious Trial

"Yes, but in the third trial Jesus did not answer the same way. When you inquired, 'Art thou the Son of God?' he did not say, 'I am.' Rather he said, 'Ye say that I am' (Luke 22:70). He obviously was referring to his admission, and you could not use testimony gathered in an illegal trial. You needed his affirmation of this matter in the legal trial, and you did not have it. For doctors of the law to have twisted things so badly seems tragic."

"We wanted it to be a nice, neat case. However, Jesus was much too clever for us to succeed against him by strictly due process."

"Is that a justification for violating your own rules and your own interpretation of law?"

"Looking backward, I can say 'no.' However, we were concerned about losing our place and our authority by this person that seemed a rebel out to destroy the institution that Moses had ordained. You must understand, we saw him as a real threat. We were convinced of the legitimacy of our office and did not wish to have him replace us."

"Whatever your fears, was there any justification for abusing the judicial system as you did?"

"Again, our problem was a complex one. It was easy for us to conclude this man ought to die. How to have him killed was the problem. We dared not order his death and execute him by our law. The people would have risen in his defense. He had too many people that he had healed and helped. The crowds would have stoned us if we ourselves put him to death. Our biggest hurdle was to get the Roman authorities to crucify him."

First Civil Trial before Pilate

"Of course, I understand that. When Pilate asked what you charged him with, you said, 'If he were not a malefactor, we would not have delivered him up unto thee' (John 18:30). That was a strange indictment. Malefactors must do something in violation of the law, but you did not say that you had judged him worthy of death because of 'blasphemy.'"

"That would have meant nothing to Pilate. He was not interested in defending our religious concerns. He was a Roman pagan. He might have put Jesus in prison for a season, but we were not interested in that. We wanted him dead, and we knew Pilate was the only one who could carry out the death sentence without creating a riot. The people feared the Roman power, and they would not risk the severe treatment the Romans meted out for rioting of any kind."

"So that is when you lied to secure your demands. Did you not then say, 'We found this fellow perverting the nation, and forbidding to give tribute to Caesar, saying that he himself is Christ a King' (Luke 23:2)?"

"Yes, that is the record."

"Was it true?"

"We did not have documentation or witnesses who could agree to this."

"Are you admitting then, that your charges were false and unsubstantiated?"

"Those were massive generalizations on our part; yes, I admit that."

"Certainly, it was not true that he perverted the nation or that he forbade anyone from paying taxes to Caesar. In fact, he said, 'render unto Caesar the things that are Caesar's.'"

"Well, we had to have something to catch Pilate's attention. We had no *proof* that he perverted the nation or that he forbade people from paying taxes to Caesar. However, he did enter Jerusalem as King of the Jews."

"Then casting around for a charge, you finally mentioned his ride into Jerusalem as King."

"Yes."

"So trying to connect that with the idea that he had tried to dissuade people from paying taxes was an outright lie, was it not?"

"Well, yes, but we were desperate for a conviction with something that would concern Rome."

"Your arguments certainly did not cause Pilate to rush to judgment. It is clearly written that he saw it was out of 'envy' that you delivered Jesus to him."

"Pilate's reticence to convict our prisoner was very frustrating. It seemed like our case was lost. We knew Pilate. Normally he was ruthless. In nearly all cases we had brought to him previously, he was eager to mete out punishment much worse than we imagined. We thought that all we had to do was bring Jesus before him, and he would sign the death warrant. We were totally unprepared for his rejection of our petition."

"So when Pilate ended the first civil trial without a conviction, you were in a frenzy; is that correct?"

Second Civil Trial before Herod

"Yes. We figured Herod would not be eager to seek a death sentence for our prisoner. He had already killed John the Baptist and was uncomfortable about that. He knew the people were very displeased with him already. It would have taken more courage than he possessed to order Jesus' death."

"Did you see your case sinking when Herod gladly received Jesus, wanting to see some of his miracles?"

"Fortunately, Jesus would not perform for Herod. Had he done so, Herod would have freed him. We were at our wit's end. Three religious trials and two civil trials—and we were no closer to our objective. We were in desperation going back for the last civil trial before Pilate."

Third Civil Trial before Pilate

"Yes, and that is when you finally admitted your real reason for wanting him dead, is it not? You said what you did not have the courage to say at the outset, 'We have a law, and by our law he ought to die, because he made himself the Son of God' (John 19:7)."

"Yes, but to our dismay Pilate became fearful when we told him that. He was afraid that this man might have been the Son of God, and then he tried to release Jesus."

"So up to this point your whole case seemed dead in Pilate's hands, is that right?"

"Yes, we were at the end of our rope, so to speak."

Lev drove home his point. "You did an abominable thing, then, did you not? You said, 'If thou let this man go, thou art not Caesar's friend: whosoever maketh himself a king speaketh against Caesar.' Then you cried, 'We have no king but Caesar' (John 19:12, 15)."

"Looking back, it does look like a mob-hanging rather than a decision handed down by a proper trial and judgment. Perhaps it would have been better for us if we had failed completely. However, we were not willing to see our prisoner go free."

"Yes, your lot might be less difficult than it is now. Are you prepared to admit that the only reason you had to resort to such unconscionable methods to secure his death was that, in fact, you were putting to death an innocent man? The only holy, harmless man, who was separate from sinners, and you could not endure a true holy man in your midst."

Annas was incredulous. "Are you are asking me to issue my own death warrant?"

"No, obviously you have been raised to life again for some good purpose." Having brought out the whole truth, Lev softened his approach. "You have your life to live again. Are you going to make the same mistakes?"

Easy to Say We Erred

"It is easy for you to say we erred grievously. The end we sought seemed to justify the means. I know now that it does not. Given a choice of knowing what I know now, I would not have done what I did."

"You could not kill a holy and just man in any proper court of law. You are admitting that you had to resort to lies and half-truths and false claims of loyalty to Caesar. Your hearts were full of evil intent, and when that happened, evil actions followed very easily."

"If you are trying to get me to say, 'I made a mistake,' you have succeeded."

"No, it is obvious you made a grievous mistake." Annas' mentor tried to reach his heart. "What I have not heard from you is that your heart is filled with godly sorrow."

"You want me to crawl before the world and say, 'I am the worst criminal that ever lived.' Is that what you want?"

"How would it remedy your case? You obviously have to admit massive irregularities in a trial that should never have happened."

"Then why are you tormenting me?"

"Because only you can change the present. A public confession followed by a demonstration of godly sorrow is necessary for the healing to begin. You have already accepted the responsibility for what happened, saying 'His blood be upon us, and on our children' (Matthew 27:25). If you accepted that responsibility then, it is only right that you should confess your mistake with godly sorrow now."

Enough Already!

"Haven't we suffered enough? From what I learned of history, my people endured never-ending persecution and hatred. Isn't that enough already?"

"Yes, your people suffered unjustly. Attacking you for the past now would be a grievous error. Annas, nothing I said was meant to berate you. My only reason for being here is to help the healing process begin. Unless you admit the problem, you will not fix it. Anyone can see you made mistakes of the head in the past, but only you can admit to the far more serious mistakes of the heart. If you do, then only you can correct them and live them down."

"I shall have to think about this, Lev. You have made your point. It might be easier for me to seek the ultimate release of returning to the grave."

Lev realized he had gone as far as he could go with Annas. No amount of pressure from the outside would make a difference. Annas saw himself out of power, out of favor with men, and even out of favor with God. The way back was long and difficult, and he did not know if he had the desire to change or the strength to persevere in the work to be done if once he did change.

Lev could see his work was largely finished here. Annas knew what he had to do, and only he could will to do it.

"David wrote a letter to Joab, and sent it by the hand of Uriah.
And he wrote in the letter, saying,
Set ye Uriah in the forefront of the hottest battle,
And retire ye from him, that he may be smitten, and die"
(2 Samuel 11:14, 15).

Chapter Twelve

During his long respite at home in Israel from his assignments, Lev reveled in his studies and in spending time with his loved ones. He actually thought perhaps his assignments would be over, since the work of receiving people back to life was moving swiftly toward its close. The earth was close to being comfortably full and the number returning to life was systematically getting smaller and smaller.

The wealth of the world was great now that none of its resources were wasted on war or foolishness of any kind. Years of living under righteousness were yielding the return of human happiness and mental maturity. Character was growing exponentially in the world, and people were not being dragged down by evil anywhere. Still, occasionally problems emerged among some of those returning. The victims of murders posed an enormous problem to the murderers and were a cause of intense drama. There were deep feelings of anger that needed to be dealt with on the one hand, along with guilt and shame on the other.

Uriah the Hittite Is Coming Back

Lev received a phone call one evening from Jerusalem. "Shalom. This is Lev Aron and how may I be of service to you?"

"Shalom, Lev. This is David, formerly King David. I am facing a problem and I have thought of you often as the person I would like to help me."

"Thank you for your confidence, David. You know I am at your service any hour of the day or night. What could be so heavy on your mind?"

"Uriah the Hittite. He was a man I murdered, as you know. You know the whole story of how I took his wife Bathsheba, and subsequently I had Uriah, her husband, murdered."

"Yes, I know that. Everyone who has read the Bible does. I also know that God punished you with a punishment worse than death, at least so it seems to me. I would rather have died than to have gone through what you went through. Anyway, how can I help you? I know God has forgiven you and you have paid for your sin. That should end all discussion."

"Yes, God has forgiven me. Therefore, though I carry pain in my heart, it is not the pain of unforgiven sin or guilt. God has forgiven me, but Uriah, whom I murdered, has not forgiven me. I must face him and apologize to him. However, I need someone to prepare for his return to life, to build his home and provide for his every need. There are many people I could call on to do this, but I am asking you, because I would like you to be the one to explain his death to him. You must tell him why I murdered one of my most trusted soldiers. He risked his life daily on the battlefield as my loyal servant, and this is how I repaid him."

"I will be glad to be with him and try to smooth the anguished wrath of this poor man when he learns the truth."

"That is precisely what I need. I cannot send Bathsheba to be with him because of her relationship with me, but more particularly, she, in God's providence, is the great-great-grandmother of our Lord Jesus. You know that is incredible that we both sinned and after being punished, we were still permitted the great honor of being progenitors of our Lord through our son, Nathan, down to Mary, the mother of

Jesus. Bathsheba and I actually had four sons—Shimea, Shobab, Nathan, and Solomon (1 Chronicles 3:5)."

Uriah Must Know That King David Was Punished

"Of course," David continued, "you know how severely I was punished, but you must tell Uriah this because Solomon followed me as king of Israel. Nathan, the least esteemed of my sons, seems to have been special, for God marked him to carry on the lineage that would lead to Mary and to Christ. I want you to make Uriah understand that Divine providence moved in our relationship even though it started out immorally. Let him know that I was punished severely by God and no further punishment will be acceptable coming from him. When Uriah becomes familiar with the wonderful history that followed my relationship with Bathsheba and understands our bitter punishment, I shall visit him personally to be reconciled with him."

"You will have my prayers in that meeting. I know Uriah was a mighty man of war and valor. I will try to have him in a peaceful frame of mind before you meet. He will have every reason to be angry with you when he learns the facts. I will try to let his anger take its course, while I try to educate him on how the Lord overruled this for a great triumph in continuing the genealogy that leads to the Messiah. I hope that will soften his anger toward you. He will have to know that God has judged you worthy to be a Prince at Jerusalem in serving Christ. It will be a triumph of God's grace when you are reconciled with each other."

"I see you understand your mission, Lev. I am personally indebted to you for your service, and I know that if anyone can deal with Uriah's initial anger when he learns the truth, it is you, Lev. You have served faithfully. May God prosper your new assignment."

"When do you want me to leave?"

"The planting has all been done on his site and the building will start in one week. I request that you help supervise the building of his house. Just ask for whatever assistance you may need. Since he had no children, you will be the one to greet him and tenderly deal with him as you break the news of how and why he died. Carefully educate him with the absolute truth. Do not minimize my sin or fail to make known my deepest sorrow for what I did. I will also tell him of my grief in sinning against him and the Lord when I seek his forgiveness."

"I'll do my best to be a minister of reconciliation, David. You have been such a noble inspiration of untiring devotion in carrying out this regeneration program. It brings me great joy to be able to serve you in some small way. Thank you for the privilege of service."

"May God's grace sustain you, Lev. Uriah will be living in your general area on the outskirts of Beersheba. I will send the necessary information to you later. I will need the grace and strength from Christ to apologize for his murder. Thank you, again. Shalom."

Lev was so excited with his new assignment that he slept only fitfully the rest of the night. He had dealt with many of the world's worst murderers and barbarous people, but this was a very different case. Uriah was a good man and a very dedicated person. Oddly, David also was a very good man, a man after God's own heart, except in a weak moment he broke three of God's commandments. He coveted his neighbor's wife, he committed adultery with his neighbor's wife, and he killed his neighbor. For this indiscretion, he was punished bitterly, yet God's mercy continued to follow the house of David.

In the morning he called Rebekah to tell her about his next assignment.

"Better you than me, Lev. I don't know how you will deal with his anger when he learns the truth of why he died."

"I worry about that too, Rebekah. I put myself in Uriah's place, and I know I would be uncontrollably furious. Perhaps the Lord will help modify his anger in some way. He really was a wonderful man. He served King David faithfully and this was how he was repaid!"

"Who said life was fair in the old world? It never was. The important thing, Lev, is that the Lord makes it fair in the end. Uriah lost his life and will have it again more abundantly than he ever dreamed possible. He missed having a family with his wife, but a soldier goes out every day on the battlefield not knowing if he will return. If he understands what David went through, perhaps he won't want to place any further burden upon him. I think you are the very best choice for this task, I really do, Lev."

"Thanks for your encouragement. I don't feel nearly that confident. However, it is the same with every assignment. I always feel inadequate."

"Well, I hope it won't take long. It has been wonderful having time together again now that all the work has leveled off. Please keep in touch. Shalom."

Lev Touches Down at Uriah's Pad

When Lev touched down on Uriah's aircraft pad, there were about a dozen people there to greet him and express an eagerness to help, especially because this was a service request for former King David. They gathered around greeting Lev joyfully. "We are here as volunteers. We don't want you doing all the work. Just tell us what to do."

After the introductions, Lev agreed. "I like to work, too, and with so many hands it will be light work. I see you have the foundation dug and poured. Tomorrow the housing components will arrive, and we can begin putting everything in order. Today we will work on the garden. I see some of the work is already done, but I had Rebekah draw some layouts. We want it to be especially beautiful, even though Uriah was probably not the artistic type. As a matter of fact, Rebekah loaded my aircraft with flowers and plants, and here is the layout to go with the house. Want to help me unload? Then we can start planting and arranging."

The work went along swiftly and easily. It was the easiest house on which Lev had ever worked. There was so much eager help that it was done several days ahead of schedule.

The morning of Uriah's return to life had come, and Lev found himself with mixed emotions waiting to greet this mighty man of valor. He had been nervous, wondering how to handle it all. He figured former King David was probably having fitful nights, too. For that matter, there was little doubt that Bathsheba, too, was nervous in anticipation of her former husband's awakening.

Uriah Returns to Life

I awakened with a start. My instincts as a warrior still were alive. I remembered being surrounded by enemy soldiers. I knew my fellow soldiers had deserted me at the front, and now it was too late to retreat. I decided if I were going down, I would take as many of the enemy down with me as I could. For a few minutes my sword brought its deadly message to four of the enemies who confronted me, but being outflanked I could not protect my back. I fought furiously, but to no avail. At last I felt the thrust of cold steel. The pain paralyzed my movement for a second, and in that moment I felt several swords thrusting me through. It all happened quickly, but the pain was unbearable. I had watched men die whom I had thrust through many times, but it was different being the victim. I felt my sword fall from my hand and my knees buckling. I didn't want to die before my enemies but felt my body fall to the ground. I was glad I was dying so quickly. They could not taunt or torture me. Everything blurred as my eyes closed, and only faintly did I hear the laughter of my enemies and felt them kicking me. War was brutal.

Swords punctured my lungs, and as I fell to the ground the little air that was in my lungs was knocked out. I remembered the terrifying inability to breathe. Mercifully, I lost consciousness at the same time.

*Suddenly I found myself breathing easily and without pain. As I lay here now, I cannot believe my **enemies** nursed me to health again. Even if it were possible, those savages were not capable of such kindness. Perhaps they had left my fallen remains and my fellow soldiers had returned to rescue me. Yes, that must be what happened.*

I opened my eyes slowly, not knowing what to expect. To my amazement, I was in a strange and very beautiful room. This was not an army camp! Never had I experienced anything so pleasing to the senses. I could hear birds singing outside the windows. Slowly I moved my hands to feel if my wounds were healed. To my amazement, not only were there no wounds, but there were no scars! How could this be? I had feared someone might be standing guard over me, but I was alone in a royal bed more comfortable than I imagined could ever exist. Could King David have brought me to his own palace to be healed? I was a soldier unaccustomed to comfort, but it felt wonderful!

I found clothing, but it was different than any I had ever seen. It, too, was very, very comfortable. Quickly I dressed. All the disciplines of a soldier still controlled me. I was totally alert and listened for the faintest movement outside of my door. I searched in vain for my sword. Without it, I felt a vulnerability that troubled me. With that sword I could give a good account of myself anywhere. Why this strange clothing? The room had beautiful flowers and their fragrance filled the room. My warrior instincts seemed out of harmony with the luxuries that surrounded me.

Everything was peaceful. Where was I? Although I had never been in the private quarters of the palace, I could not imagine that it looked like this. The workmanship of the furnishings was beyond anything in all of Israel. How did I get here? Who had nursed me back to health? All of these questions flooded my mind. I had been a warrior and every nerve was on high alert. I did not know if I should open the door to find guards or the kindness of friends waiting for me. It was too quiet to be an army camp. It was too lovely to be anything but a woman's chamber. Could Bathsheba be waiting outside?

Uriah Emerges

Slowly he opened the door a crack, prepared for whatever might be. Fortunately, he saw no guards. Throwing the door wide open, he found a handsome fair-headed man sitting in a sunny room. The man rose up smiling and greeted him with a warm, "Shalom."

"My name is Lev Aron. I am here to serve you and take care of your every need. Did you find everything comfortable?"

"My name is Uriah, a soldier in the service of the nation of Israel. What am I doing here and how did I get here? How did you manage to fix me up from all my wounds? Where is my sword?"

Lev could see Uriah was a man of extraordinary strength, agility, and great efficiency. All it took was a glance to see he had been a mighty man of valor. Enemy soldiers coming face to face with him would despair at meeting such a fierce warrior. His eye movements were quick, and he was taking note of every detail as he stood ready for action.

"Be at ease, Uriah. You are in no danger. You have no enemies. There is no war anywhere, so you can relax from your soldier's disciplines. I will explain everything to you, but first will you join me in breakfast? I have some tea already made. Will you please be seated? You are in no danger whatever. Perhaps we can talk."

Lev led him into a room that was beyond Uriah's comprehension. It was encircled with exquisitely crafted wooden cupboards. The floor, instead of being packed dirt, was tiled white with a red pattern. The white walls gleamed. Here and there were small pictures with scriptures on them, each more beautifully decorated than the next.

Lev indicated that he was to sit at a highly polished table which contained plates filled with delectable fruits.

Lev could see Uriah was still apprehensive and couldn't relax. Everything was too strange, and he could see Uriah felt the huge gap between his last condition and the present one. The smell of the tea was pleasing, and Lev invited him to partake freely.

Uriah sat down rigidly in the chair across from Lev. As he sipped the tea, it warmed his insides.

"This is absolutely delicious! Everything is so strange. I am sitting wondering whether I am hallucinating!"

"No, you are not, Uriah. Relax! I know you have been through a very difficult time. Please try some of the fruit. You have never eaten anything like this before, but you will find it absolutely delightful."

"This is delicious. Am I in some kind of heavenly home?"

"No, you are in your very own home. This is where you now live."

"What country am I in?"

Armies Are Gone

"You are in Israel. You were a valiant soldier. This home has been provided for you, but you are no longer in the army. As a matter of fact, there are no more armies in the whole world. Your sword is gone, and you will never have to lift up any sword against your fellow man again."

"Are you a poet out of touch with reality?"

"No, I was once a soldier just as you were. Only we didn't fight with swords; we developed better killing weapons than swords. I will show you later how we fought our wars. The world has changed since you fought and died on the battlefield."

"What are you saying? I am very much alive! Do not jest with me! I do not mean to be discourteous, but I am very tense—everything is so strange. Oddly it is all very beautiful, but still I do not know you. Where is my wife, Bathsheba? What are you doing here?"

"There is so much to explain to you. But let me start with the first thing. I told you that you were killed on the battlefield, and that is the truth."

"Then how do you explain my being here? Don't I look alive and well? What kind of a fool do you take me to be?"

"Wait a moment. Did you feel any wounds on your body when you awakened?"

"No and I thought that was strange, because I felt the places where I had been pierced. But, no, there were no wounds and not even any scars."

"You are probably a few inches taller, and you never felt as healthy before, have you?"

"No, I cannot recall that I have, except for an oddness that I cannot describe."

"Did you notice *all* the scars are gone? And the one finger you lost in your first battle? It is back on your hand."

"Yes, now that you mention it, that is true. How do you know so much about me?"

"You happen to be a very important person in history, Uriah. I cannot explain that to you yet, but it turns out that history does record a part of your life. That is how I know about you."

"I Am Angry"

"Anyway, I am angry! My first feelings upon awakening were strange and uncertain. At first I thought the enemy captured me. However, this did not look like an enemy camp and no one was guarding me. I was sent up to the heat of the battle. I had been there before. But this time, the soldiers who were supposed to protect my flank abandoned me. When I realized they had left me all alone, it was too late to retreat. It was not like the team of soldiers I fought with to desert me this way. I become very angry thinking about it. It almost looked like I was set up to die. Of course, I find it hard to believe they were the kind of men to do this to me. I did have a little quarrel with one of the men that morning. It was nothing more than soldiers that are under a lot of tension. You go out to battlefield each day not knowing if you will return. I had no reason to feel that my fellows plotted my death. Yet, it almost seems so. I have never been deserted up at the front before. This was very strange. On many occasions the bravery of my fellows saved my life. So I do not know who to be angry with."

"At least you are accepting the fact that you did die."

"I am not sure of anything or anyone at this moment. I do not know you. I do not even know why I am confiding my feelings to you. I am a private person and I will get to the bottom of this. If I find that someone betrayed me, I have not lost my skills. I was not a victorious soldier without good reason. I swear I will kill whoever did it. I passed Joab, our captain, that morning and he didn't even greet me. He usually had encouraging words to men going up to the heat of battle. If he ordered my death, I will get him if is the last thing I do."

"Uriah, this is a different time. I must tell you that any act of violence on your part will be immediately punished. If you lift your hand against anyone to hurt him, your arm will be paralyzed. I speak from experience. I tried to swing at an old enemy of mine to flatten him, and my arm hung at my side."

"It looks fine to me now. Don't try to intimidate me."

"It is my duty to tell you the truth."

"I feel confused. Everything about me is bizarre. All I know is that I was left to die up at the front. Somebody wanted me dead."

Violence Is Not Permitted

"Let me remind you again, no violence of any kind is permitted today. I know you were a soldier and a very good one at that. However, we do not have soldiers anymore. Christ, the Messiah, rules the world, and consequently the whole world is at peace. You died and were raised to life again this very day. Try to believe me because I am a man who only speaks the truth. I, too, died and was raised to life. Most of mankind has been raised to life. Later I will prove it to you but for now, just try to believe me."

"Very well, but where is everyone I know? Where is Bathsheba? Where are my fellow soldiers?"

"I don't know who you knew and whether they are alive at this moment. We could find that out on a name-by-name basis. However, I can tell you Bathsheba is alive."

"Then why isn't she with me here?"

"She married again and had four children. However, marriages all end at death, so she is no longer your wife or anyone else's. You will see her again at some point, but for now, just try to accept that she is not your wife. My former wife is living, and I know her and we are the best of friends, but we live separately."

"I cannot believe that! I suppose as a soldier I was not the best husband for her, but I loved her and she knew that I was fighting for her nation."

Lev knew that this was enough information for the moment, so he said, "Perhaps I should show you around your house and garden. You know this is all yours, and you are now very rich. It will be hard for you to grasp, but thousands of years have passed since you lived."

Lev started with the kitchen, since Uriah would only have known about a cooking fire in his former life. He was astonished at the stove that gave heat by turning a knob and could be turned off the same way. Also, the refrigerator that made ice, something he had rarely seen during Israeli winters. Then Lev showed Uriah the heating and cooling facility that ran on water that was broken down to hydrogen and oxygen from which a new energy called electricity was made. Electricity made everything run by invisible energy.

Lev illustrated electricity by turning on a switch creating instant light and then turning it off. "You see, you don't need to light lamps anymore or make fires to cook with. It is very different, but you will get used to this easy way of life." Lev purposely wanted to let Uriah's angry emotions drain a bit as well as his anxieties. Lev still did not know how he was going to break the whole truth to him. This was such a messy situation that no matter how he handled it, Uriah would be furious. His plan was to slowly drop pieces of information, giving him time to adjust to the bitter truth.

Uriah was fascinated with the light switch and asked if he could try it. When told to do so, he kept turning the light on and off like a child. "Are you sure this is not some witchcraft?"

"No, we don't have any witchcraft now. Only truth is spoken."

Lev then took Uriah on a tour of his garden and orchard, explaining to him the fruit from the trees of Eden. Uriah took it all in with great interest, but he finally had to ask Lev the questions bothering him.

"This is all very interesting, but can you tell me if General Joab is alive? I somehow have the feeling that he gave the order for the men to leave me up at front in the heat of battle. I know the men I had as partners, and I know they would not have betrayed me by leaving me unguarded in the heat of battle. Something is very unsavory about my death, and I want to get to the bottom of it. He might have some answers for me. Can I locate him?"

"In time you will probably meet him. Remember, you cannot take justice into your own hands anymore. You will be punished with paralysis if you try."

"I don't know what to believe. You may be right; I would not mind dying to get even with the one responsible for my death. I stood in danger on the battlefield and I was prepared to die there. But I didn't just die, I tell you, I was murdered."

"Allowing that you were, you have your life back now in better form than before. You are rich and self-sufficient. Is the past so important? Everybody died sooner or later, so if you died prematurely, perhaps you were spared a lot of heartache and tragedy."

"I have a keen sense of justice. If Joab had a grudge against me, why didn't he face me like a man? Why did he have to have others do the dirty work for him? I don't mind having died; it is being betrayed that eats in my heart like a canker."

"I assure you that you will soon have answers to all your questions. You are still too disoriented to take everything in. In time all the pieces will fit together. I know you are still seething in anger, and you have every right to feel that way. However, anger needs to be handled differently now. Justice is the Lord's, and He renders justice far better than you or I could ever hope to do. One thing I will tell you, though. Your suspicions of being murdered are correct."

"Ah, so you *do* know more than you are telling me. Just tell me what happened."

"Uriah, I am here as your benefactor. I helped build this house for you. There is a special reason why the whole truth must come to you slowly. You must realize that God's Law ruled Israel. When that Law was broken, God's justice overruled so that the one who ordered your death was punished far more than you could ever do. God will not allow that person to be punished twice."

Uriah Becomes Violent

Uriah turned red with anger. "Stop stalling! Tell me what you know or I will use my bare hands on you to get the truth! I was left surrounded by enemies because someone with authority gave those orders. Before I died, I vowed that I would kill the one who betrayed me."

"I will tell you when I think you are ready for that information— not before."

"I'll be the judge of that! I am ready right now! Tell me or else..."

"I am warning you not to try to use physical force on me. You will know the truth when you become civil enough to receive it."

Uriah stood up trembling with rage. "I have nothing against you. I do not wish to hurt you, but you are going to tell me who betrayed me."

Lev remained calm, sitting relaxed in his chair anticipating what was to take place.

As Uriah lunged to grab Lev's throat, his arms fell helplessly at his side. His anger instantly turned to shocked distress.

"I warned you not to try to use violence. Now you have lost the use of both your hands. However, the Ancients will hear your case, and if you tell the truth, they will restore both your hands to you almost immediately," Lev assured Uriah.

"Dear God, is there no justice in this world? Why am I paralyzed for trying to find the truth?"

"It is *because* there is a God of justice that you have lost the use of your arms. I told you full punishment was given to the one who ordered your death. Can you believe that?"

"I don't know what to believe or who to believe. If you had told me the truth, I would not be paralyzed. I am being punished for trying to learn who my murderer was. Is that fair? I have a right to know."

"Yes, and you will know the whole truth. Nothing will be withheld from you. However, you have to learn to be civilized first. The days of warfare are ended. You cannot take justice into your own hands. Christ the Messiah is ruling the earth, and you have just had a demonstration of his enormous power. You will have another demonstration of his power when he heals your paralyzed arms and returns them to full strength."

Healing Requested

Lev picked up the phone. "See this little device in my hand? It is called a telephone. I can use it to communicate with Jerusalem and one of the Ancients will listen to your case. If you tell them the whole truth, without trying to justify yourself, you will probably be restored to health within the hour. Whenever you calm down enough, I can talk to someone who will help you."

Uriah sat there helplessly. Lev could see he was a determined person who was driven to know the truth. His resentment was not going to fade easily. However, being almost helpless without his two arms, it didn't take long for his desire for healing to become greater than his resentment.

"All right. You did tell me I could not resort to violence. Why didn't Christ prevent me from being betrayed if he has so much power?"

"Because he was not ruling over the earth then, but he is now. You have many things to learn and one of the most important is that Christ is in complete control. He will see that every sin will be fairly punished, so never try to take justice into your own hands again. Are you ready for me to call the Ancients to get someone to heal you?"

"All right. I am useless this way. If I must ask to be healed, I will do so."

Uriah was soon speaking to righteous Abel. "Why did you try to choke Lev?"

"I wanted the truth about who murdered me. He knows, but he refused to tell me. I swore that I would kill the man who betrayed me and caused my death."

"Well, you do have reason to be angry. However, justice has been served in your case, so you must promise never to execute it yourself. Do you understand?"

"Yes, but I swore vengeance."

"Any oath you took in your former life is not valid now. God has punished the one who betrayed you far more righteously and effectively than you could ever hope to do."

The authority with which Abel spoke was powerful, and Uriah sensed he was talking to someone in a high position.

"You must understand that Lev has been sent to help you adjust to your new life. He certainly did not deserve to be assaulted by you. You must apologize to him for what you tried to do and listen to instructions. He is a man serving the King, and his reason for delaying the truth until you are able enough to receive it is valid."

"I understand."

"Apologize to Lev right now if you want your arms restored to you."

Turning to Lev, Uriah said, "I am sorry, Lev. I never had any malice toward you."

Hearing Uriah's apology, Abel continued, "Very well, then, Uriah. I understand you have anger in your heart. You must exercise yourself to accept that God has imposed a just punishment for what happened to you, and that you must never try to settle the score your way."

Uriah was still confused. "It seems I am being hurt twice. I am betrayed into the hands of the enemies, and now I am punished for trying to learn the truth."

"No, you aren't being punished for trying to learn the truth. You are being punished for being violent. We have all had to learn basic principles before we fully understand everything."

"Very well, if I must wait, I will wait."

"Good, Uriah. This is your first act of violence in your new life, and I hope it is your last. Because you have grounds for being angry, you will be restored to full vigor momentarily. Do not feed your anger. You must accept that God has delivered a punishment worse than death to the one who ordered your betrayal."

"Yes, but I cannot get rid of all the feelings of anger in my chest."

"They will abate with the passing of time. You must learn to live and forgive in this life. Shalom."

Uriah seemed to have calmed down during his exchange with Abel. While still upset, his burning anger was subdued and he became civil again. He said, "Lev, I am sorry that I went after you the way I did."

"Your apology is accepted. I understand exactly how you feel and to some extent your anger is justified, even though violence is not."

"This way of life is very mystifying to me. I cannot comprehend what great powers must be in the hands of those who rule the world if nothing goes unnoticed and every evil deed is punished instantly. That is certainly better than innocent men dying on the battlefield often not even knowing what the war they are fighting is about."

The Evils of War

"War was one of the great evils, previously," Lev agreed. "Millions died on the battlefield, and looking back it is almost impossible to know why. It seems when one generation learned the horrors of war, a new generation came along willing to repeat the same mistakes. Those are not permitted now, and soon people will learn righteousness. God will cause every sin to receive a just punishment whether in the previous life or in the present. No one is getting away with anything. Now righteousness is the absolute standard for everyone."

"I suppose that is better. If I had not experienced that judgment and punishment, I could not believe what you are telling me. Now I know that what you say is true."

"Uriah, I promised you the whole truth on what happened, but I want you to subdue some of your anger and hostility before I tell you. What I will tell you is going to be very painful, but again I remind you, punishment has been served and your death has been avenged. When you learn the terrible punishment that resulted, you will agree that God is a righteous Judge."

Several days passed, and Uriah seemed to be more tranquil and began enjoying life under the new conditions. He was enthralled with the learning possibilities of computerized television and delighted in the various studies. Lev purposely skirted the Bible, lest he read about the cause of his death in the open pages of the Book. Uriah had lived a very Spartan life as a soldier and was a disciplined person. The comfortable lifestyle was becoming easy to appreciate.

It was a new experience to find his mind so challenged. He used to train endlessly to keep his full physical strength so he could succeed on the battlefield. Now the new battlefield was in the mind, and Uriah was starting to respond to this new front. Oddly, a whole new way of life began to excite him.

Uriah Learns the Truth

Uriah seemed to flourish in his new environment, and he no longer pestered Lev about who was responsible for his death; so the time had come for him to learn the truth.

Early one morning, Lev said, "Uriah, I think the time has come for you to know the truth. I am going to read to you from this Bible. It will tell you the whole story better than I could do myself. It is accurate and tells exactly who ordered your death and why. Are you ready?"

"I don't know. It must be awful, because you have purposely delayed telling me. I have a bad temper so I will try to control it; I promise I will not swing at you for telling me the truth. You are only the messenger, Lev, so I am as prepared as I can be for this. After you break this news to me, please leave me to digest it. I heal better when left alone. So tell me what I have been waiting to know."

"I will read you the account that the whole world knows about, and now you will also. It is in 2 Samuel 11:1-4:

"'And it came to pass, after the year was expired, at the time when kings go forth [to battle], that David sent Joab, and his servants with him, and all Israel; and they destroyed the children of Ammon, and besieged Rabbah. But David tarried still at Jerusalem. And it came to pass at eventide, that David arose from off his bed, and walked upon the roof of the king's house: and from the roof he saw a woman washing herself; and the woman [was] very beautiful to look upon. And David sent and inquired after the woman. And [one] said, [Is] not this Bathsheba, the daughter of Eliam, the wife of Uriah the Hittite? And David sent messengers, and took her.'"

Uriah turned pale. "How could he do that to me? I guess that a soldier can't compete with attentions that a king could shower upon her." His bitterness was apparent. "So, that is why she is not here with me. She betrayed me and so did King David. Now it all makes sense to me."

"Do you want me to continue?"

"Does it get worse than this?"

"You will have to be the judge, but some of this will instantly clarify what happened when King David called you back from the front lines. Do you remember the awkward meeting he had with you?"

"How could I forget? He called me and inquired how the war was going and asked about Joab. I thought that was unusual. There were messengers providing that information almost daily. Then he sent me to my home, but I was uncomfortable going home to be with my wife while my comrades were up at the front. I slept in the servant's quarters that night. Then the next day, I ate a banquet meal with him and drank enough to get drunk. I guess he thought I would go home that night, but I could not."

"Shall I read on?"

"Yes, I can almost guess the rest, but read it to me anyway."

Lev read from 2 Samuel 11:14, 15. "And it came to pass in the morning, that David wrote a letter to Joab, and sent [it] by the hand of Uriah. And he wrote in the letter, saying, Set ye Uriah in the forefront of the hottest battle, and retire ye from him, that he may be smitten, and die."

"He stole my wife and then lets me carry my own death warrant to Joab. How vile! Dear God! Is there no justice in this world?"

Lev could see that all this was absolutely devastating to Uriah, who sat there trembling with hurt and anger. It was not necessary to read the rest of the account, for Uriah knew now why he was left to die alone on the battlefield.

"I think I'll take a walk. I will be back later and tell you how God punished David. It will assure you that there is a God of justice. He paid a price more bitter than death. You need to know for it will help heal your anger. And there is also a good side to this story."

"How can anything good come from such betrayal and wickedness? I risked my life loyally on the battlefield, while this man stole my wife and then had me killed. I thought he was noble. Please leave me alone with my thoughts for awhile." Uriah buried his head in his hands.

Painfully Wounded

Lev could see the anguish in this painfully wounded man. He was sweating profusely and having a difficult time trying to control his emotions under such duress. No man could take this kind of news calmly. As he left, Lev said, with deep compassion, "I'll be back at noon. I'm so sorry to be the bearer of such bad news. Yet, remember, you have only heard of his sins; you haven't heard how severely God punished him."

Lev felt great sadness as he walked. It probably was easier feeling the raw steel penetrate his body than to hear what Uriah had heard this morning. It was miserable reading him the facts, but this truth had to be known before the healing could begin. Not knowing the rest of the story could be maddening, but Uriah first had to deal with this triple betrayal. He had been wounded in the house of his friends and that was bitter to take.

Lev strolled around the neighborhood feeling Uriah's pain in a way he had never felt before. He had always looked at this through David's eyes but failed to realize the full anguish of Uriah. Even a mighty warrior's heart felt pain and betrayal. However, it was not the pain that could result in hardened bitterness. It was how he would deal with it that would either enable him to rise above it or to wallow in self-pity and callous hatred. Lev knew his mission here would be a complete failure unless he helped Uriah conquer his grief. Uriah had good reason for anger and hatred. Yet, there must be a place for compassion. Uriah must trust in the Lord to restore "the years that the locust hath eaten" (Joel 2:25).

Lev saw children playing and laughing while a lamb and a lion rested together watching them. He sat on a bench to rest. There was room for infinite happiness once one could rise above the affliction of the past. The world was at peace, but human hearts were still throbbing.

A ball came rolling his way, so he picked it up and rolled it back to the children. The children ended their play and a little girl came and sat down beside him. She was adorable with dark curly hair and deep blue eyes and a face that lit up when she smiled. Sitting next to him, she said, "Mister, you must be new in this neighborhood."

A Delightful Encounter

"Yes, that is true. How did you figure that out?"

"Oh, I didn't do any figuring. I just never saw you before."

"Tell me young lady, what is your name?"

"My name is Hannah, but everyone calls me Han."

"Can I call you Han?"

"Sure, I like that name. Now can you tell me your name? You look so wise sitting here thinking."

"My name is Lev Aron. I am visiting here for a while. How did you know I was thinking?"

"Oh, I don't know, but you seemed far away in your thoughts until I interrupted them."

"I am glad that you did. You seem to be so happy. Can you tell me why?"

"Yes, my daddy returned to life yesterday. I returned to life a month ago."

"How about telling me about your daddy and what he did before he died, and if you want to, about how a young girl such as you returned to life again?"

"Well, my daddy was a soldier in the army under General Joab in King David's army. He died in battle one day. Mommy said I was the 'apple of his eye.' We were all very sad to learn of his death. My mother and grandparents took good care of me after that, but one day I was playing in the field and somehow a poisonous snake bit me as I walked past a large rock. I tried to walk home, but I couldn't help falling asleep right there. They found me, I was told, but it was too late to save me. I hate snakes! I still remember how much it hurt."

"Dear Han, you have a sad story to tell, and yet you seem so very happy."

"Oh, I am happy! My daddy is back, and I am still the 'apple of his eye.' Why don't you walk me home, Sir, and I can have you meet my mommy and daddy."

"I would love to do that. Thank you. They must be wonderful people to have a lovely young daughter like you."

"Oh, they are so good and kind. Everybody loves them. When my daddy died, I felt so sad. I never knew I would see him again. It is like we have our family life to live over again. We are all so happy, and daddy doesn't have to go off to war anymore. He hugs me and kisses me like he used to."

Soon they arrived at Hannah's home. When she saw her daddy, she ran into his open arms and said, "I asked this man to walk me home so he could meet you and mommy."

"Shalom, I am Lev Aron and I could not resist your lovely daughter's invitation to meet you."

Lev Meets Abishai

"Welcome, Lev! My name is Abishai. Thank you for accompanying my daughter. You have no idea how happy I am having this little bundle of love in my arms again. When I was wounded and dying on the battlefield, I thought of my little Hannah and my dear wife. How I wanted to live! But one does not always win on the battlefield. As I died, I thought of all the soldiers I had killed and the sadness I must have brought to their families. I am so glad that war is ended forever."

"Yes, I know. I was a soldier, too. I felt the same as you when I died. Somehow I always thought it was the enemy who died, but when I lay there— well this wasn't supposed to be happening to me. However, I am glad to be back as you are."

"Come in and meet my former wife, Michal."

After a brief introduction to Hannah's family members, Lev tried to learn more about Abishai. "You say you were under General Joab. Are you the man who saved King David's life when the giant Ishbibenob was about to take the aging King David down (2 Samuel 21:16)?"

"Yes, I remember that occasion very clearly. I saw our King was too weak to deflect the giant's merciless blows. Fortunately, I dispatched my enemies quickly and arrived in time to take on the giant. By God's grace I found the strength to take this massive bulk of sheer terror down."

"By chance did you know Uriah the Hittite?"

Abishai's face dropped. "Yes, he was a brave and mighty man in King David's elite guard."

"I am so glad to make the connection. I am visiting Uriah. I had the unfortunate task of explaining to him how he died."

"Oh, my! I have had nightmares ever since we left poor Uriah without any back-up. I was a close friend of his and my orders that day were bitter. My men and I had developed a strategy for effectively thinning the enemy ranks. We could go against larger forces and easily cut them down. Often that gave us an advantage, because in getting to us they had to climb over their dead and wounded and we kept thinning their ranks. They never learned to use their larger numbers effectively against us."

Bitter Orders

"So then, Joab gave you those orders to leave Uriah, trained as a team fighter, without his team behind him?"

"I am sorry to say it, but yes, that is true. I argued with him fiercely, but he had his orders. I am sorry to say I followed my orders that day. I have regretted it ever since. We had fought numerous battles with spectacular results. Uriah thought we would stand by him as usual, but we fell back as soon as he started to engage the enemy. He fought bravely and took many men down before he was surrounded and thrust through. I have had sorrow in my heart ever since. It was a terrible thing to do to our friend and companion. I shall never forgive myself for following those evil orders."

"Neither you nor Joab were responsible. It was King David that gave the orders, and it was he that God held accountable for Uriah's death."

"I know the facts now, but I must tell Uriah how sad I have been for betraying his trust and leaving him to die without a fighting chance. How often I have prayed, 'Dear God, why was I required to be a partner to that crime?'"

"Soldiers are trained to take orders, and you were following them. I know it does not heal your conscience because you were being forced to do the dirty work for someone else."

"I hope he will be as kind as you, Lev."

"How about meeting him this afternoon? This morning I told him the truth recorded in the Bible, at least about his wife and King David. He was absolutely devastated. He wanted some time to be alone to handle his feelings, so I went for a long walk and met your daughter. I think this was providential, because I really believe he would be glad to see you, knowing the truth now. Would you come to his house this afternoon, Abishai?"

"If you think I could be some help, yes, I will come."

Lev gave Abishai the directions to Uriah's home.

When he got back, he found Uriah still utterly smitten and dejected.

Uriah asked, "Why has God brought me back only to face humiliation? I fear my heart will never heal. My wife, my King, my General, and my trusted friends have betrayed me. What is left? No one has the courage to look me in the eyes and confess. This leaves me with no one by my side."

"Poor friend that I am, I am here."

"True, but I don't know you. You are just a pawn for King David. He probably wants you to soften me up so I will pass his treachery unnoticed."

Understanding David's Punishment

"I told you earlier that King David was punished certainly more bitterly than *you* were in death. He will come to offer his heartfelt apology. God made him pay a terrible price for his sin, but still King David was forgiven and restored to God's favor. I know that is hard for you to understand, unless you know the terrible tragedies that followed him because of what he did to you."

"He obviously was not left to die deserted on the battlefield."

"No, he didn't die, but often he wished he could have died to pay for his sins. He lost his kingdom, and then his own son Absalom rebelled against him and took the nation with him. His son Absalom was slain in battle, the child he had with your wife out of wedlock died, he was faced with continual warfare, his own people rejected him and only slowly accepted him back as King. The men of Judah, his own tribesmen, were the last to bring back the King. I want you to read the story of his suffering to see if that will bring you any solace."

"I might as well learn the whole story. Give me the Bible and tell me what to read."

Lev did just that and left him alone to read of David's tragedy and sorrow and seeing his own son lead the nation into treasonous rebellion, and his enemies cursing him as he fled from the forces that sought his life. He wanted Uriah to read Nathan's story of the man who had only one little ewe lamb that he loved, and how a rich man took his only lamb to his guests, sparing his own flock (2 Samuel 12:1-22).

He hoped that Uriah would read this history before Abishai arrived. It was better to have Uriah read the story than for Lev to tell it. There was majesty in the Word that was penetrating and effective. Lev knew he would learn of David's bitter punishment, a punishment that many believed was worse than death. He would be able to read of David's pain and suffering and most of all of his repentance and sorrow.

No sooner had Uriah finished reading the account than his mood seemed to change to one of somberness. He said, "I see what you meant. God did punish him with more pain than I think I endured in dying."

Just as Lev was about to get back to King David's punishment, Abishai arrived.

He stood at the door a tall and muscular man, but a man who knew military discipline. At first Uriah didn't recognize him, but in taking closer notice he saw his former military teammate. He probably wouldn't have let him in had he not just read the history. He now knew Abishai was under orders, and fully understanding that kind of situation, he was gratified to see one face that he knew.

Abishai Enters

"Come in, my betrayer," Uriah said with no rancor in his voice.

"Oh, please don't say that Uriah! I hate myself for what I did to you! All the men were bitterly angry with Joab for the orders he gave us. And Joab was furious with King David, but you know we were soldiers who lived by taking orders."

"I know that. I don't hold you responsible. At least now I know the one who was responsible was bitterly punished. I just read the biblical account."

"Yes, I have read it many times, and it gave me solace to know that God did not let this great sin go unavenged."

"It also tempered my anger reading that."

"You know, Uriah, I have hated myself for doing what I did to you. It was terrible going up to the front with you and then falling back so you would be surrounded and killed. It was plain murder. Uriah, we fought many battles together, and we were an almost invincible team. We would never have done what we did by our own choice."

"I know that, Abishai. If I would have had orders like yours, I probably would have followed them as well, even though I would have hated it."

Tears welled up in Abishai's eyes. "I never thought you would forgive me. Sin brings its own weight of guilt and pain. Every day of my former life haunted me, seeing you surrounded by enemies while we slithered away like snakes. It was evil, and we all knew it. It was as though the devil was our commander that day."

"Well, you don't know how glad I am to see you. How often we fought shoulder to shoulder never wavering under the fiercest assaults against us. We seemed almost impregnable. We were, by God's grace, a successful band of warriors, weren't we?"

"Yes, successful in a sordid sense. It is not like the present where success comes from doing well and blessing other people. It is not easy to kill other people. I can still smell freshly-spilled blood and see the horror in the faces of men pierced by a sword. I never enjoyed killing a man, Uriah, did you?"

"No, but the heat of battle conditions you for this grim business. Truthfully, in the quiet moments of my life there was always a tragic sense about it all. In the evil world we lived in, power was the last resort to all struggles. Now it all seems so irrelevant, because we all died anyway. Why hurry people to their grave?"

Lev was pleased to hear these two warriors reliving the past and confessing some of their inward pain to each other. As a former soldier, he felt the same conflicts. The discussion was bringing Uriah out of his shell, and for the moment he was forgetting his betrayal. It was therapeutic for him to talk about the past, especially with an old comrade-in-arms. Due to their intense shared experiences, there was camaraderie among soldiers.

Lev invited Abishai to have supper with them. He replied, "I would love to, but my little girl is waiting for her daddy. She is the joy of my life. I have never been so happy before. So with your permission, gentlemen, I shall say, Shalom. I do wish you would pay me a visit, Uriah. We need more time to air our feelings." He gave Uriah a manly hug as he left, and Lev could feel the affection between the two soldiers.

Meeting Overruled by Providence

Lev felt the Lord had overruled this meeting. For the first time, Uriah had broken out of the barricades around his wounded heart.

As they ate supper together Uriah said, "Lev, reading of King David's sad life and the pain he endured made me realize that God knows how to punish His people for their sins better than we do. As much as I raged against David in my hostility, I felt his pain as God brought the bitterest of experiences to him. You know, I was angry with Abishai and my other partners without a cause. We shared a rugged life together, but there is a bond that is formed when men share common suffering and pain."

"Do you think you may be able to receive King David? You said you felt his pain, but I want you to know, it is still very alive in his heart. He wants to meet you and offer his heartfelt apology. God has forgiven him, and he has paid dearly for his sins. However, unless you forgive him from the heart, he will still experience mourning. He wants to meet you when you feel strong enough to face him."

"I suppose I can meet him. I still have mixed feelings inside. Give me another week or so to get settled into this new life. Being a soldier made me put up a brave front. Every day as I went to the battlefield, I wondered if I would return or if I would come back without an arm or a leg. It is wonderful not to have such fears anymore. I don't miss war, but I do miss my wife."

"Well, that is the good part of the story. Your wife Bathsheba became the great-great-grandmother of Mary, the mother of Jesus. It was through her son, Nathan, that the lineage of Christ emerged. It means that by marrying David, she had the son needed in the genetic selection that led to Mary and the Lord God Almighty causing Christ to be born of Mary. That is good news to you and to the entire human race, for all receive life again through him."

"Theoretically, I suppose, I should be able to rejoice at that. For now, I just miss my beautiful wife. I also suppose I was not much of a husband to her, always away on the battlefield, but I did love her. I can see that when a rich and powerful king turned his attention toward her how she quickly forgot me. I shall get over this loss. Does she wish to see me again?"

Bathsheba Could Not Be Your Wife Now

"You know even if she had not left you, she would not be your wife now, don't you?"

"Yes, I understand there is no marriage."

"So in reality, life will not be that much different now without her. She will still be your friend without being your wife. My best friend is my former wife, Rebekah. I am still amazed at how fulfilling our relationship is. It is even better now, because we don't have imperfection confusing our communication."

"Yes, but she did not prove unfaithful to you, Lev, did she?"

"That is true. But you do not know if Bathsheba had any regrets or godly sorrow for what she did. She will also see you when you are ready. Then you might learn a lot more about how things went with her."

"I suppose you are right."

The week passed swiftly, and Uriah seemed brighter and happier each day. He learned that feeding his anger was a self-destructive course, and soon he was absorbed in many other things. Life was so interesting and challenging that his old angers slowly dissolved. Lev called the former King David when he thought the moment for him to come had arrived.

King David Seeks Forgiveness

Lev hoped that he hadn't misjudged Uriah's frame of mind to be more than it really was. He was apprehensive that David's appearance would awaken deeply-felt rage. When Lev heard David's aircraft setting down on the pad outside of the house, he announced that former King David was landing.

The thought left Uriah a little shaken, but he managed to control his feelings better than Lev expected. Lev ran out to meet the former king, embraced him warmly, and invited him into the house. A flood of emotions raced through Uriah's veins as he waited inside.

David stood in the doorway, and he could see Uriah was trembling and pale. David's eyes were moist, and his voice choked as he spoke.

"Uriah, you have every reason to be angry with me and to hate me. I am still angry with myself for what I did to you. If there were one thing in this world I would change if I could undo my past, it would be that of coveting your wife and ordering your death. It was so wicked that for awhile I did not think even God would forgive me. I cannot undo the past, but I am here telling you that I feel deeply sorrowful over all I did. Hardly a day has passed when I do not grieve about it. God punished me for my sins with a punishment worse than death. Many times I envied you sleeping in the grave while I fled from my throne, pursued by my own son. My people deserted me. My kingdom was in civil war, and I was an object of scorn. I thought of taking my own life, but I knew that God wanted me to live down my sin and not faint under his chastisements. I lived through some of the darkest experiences that a man can have. Because of God's just chastisement, it is no longer guilt that I feel but a continual sorrow for what I did to you."

Uriah was surprisingly calm when he finally spoke. "Then there are two of us that carry sorrow in our hearts. I could not believe what you did to me. There I was on the battlefield fighting to uphold your throne and kingdom, and this was my reward. It *was* very wicked. However, if God punished you, and I know he did, I cannot seek a double punishment just to assuage my anger. If you had appeared when I first returned to life, I would have attempted to strangle you with my bare hands, but now I am accepting what happened to me as God's providence for my life. I am willing to leave it there. I still hurt within, but my wound will heal. At least I am neither bitter nor angry."

"Can you find it in your heart to forgive me, Uriah?"

"Yes, David, I can because I know that God punished you very severely. When I read of your punishment, I felt sorry for you. I think I had an easier time of it. Anyway, the Lord is giving me such an abundant life and every day brings joy and happiness that I never thought possible. Why should I be bitter? They say all is well that ends well, and I guess that God has brought both of us to a large place."

"Thank you, Uriah. You were a great warrior, and now you are a great man. I am in your debt now and forever. I will not be satisfied to just be forgiven, but I want you to be my friend. I won't betray your friendship the second time, I promise."

"You have my forgiveness, David, but friendship is something that is not built upon words alone. To be my friend you will have to share with me some of your life and experiences. That is how men earned friendship before, and I think that is still true."

"Yes, Uriah, you are absolutely right. However, we both now serve a King not as fallible as the one you once served. Our King is righteous altogether, and if we both serve him in truth, that will create a bond of friendship between us."

"I can accept that. I have some fresh grape juice. Let us drink a toast to friendship in serving the great King."

"I shall pour the juice if you let me join in the toast," Lev smiled with great relief.

"Before you go, David, can you arrange for me to at least see my and your former wife?" Uriah asked.

Bathsheba Desires to Meet You

"Yes, definitely. Bathsheba has returned to life for some time now and she, too, has expressed a desire to meet with you and seek your forgiveness."

Lev said, "She lives not far from here. Perhaps I can arrange to take you there in my aircraft and drop you off to spend the day with her."

"I would appreciate that. There is a void that she left in my heart. I understand the past relationships are over, but I do not like the way mine ended."

David nodded. "I am sure she doesn't either, Uriah. There is pain in her heart for betraying you. She told me that many times in our life together. When she heard of your tragic death, she was devastated. Sin always brings such heavy burdens. She didn't know that our son Nathan would carry the lineage forward to Christ. We all thought Solomon would have that honor, but we were wrong. Although Solomon had his good days, he betrayed God's trust in giving him the kingdom. Nathan was a good man, but he never seemed to be a powerful leader. Yet he had the highest honor in carrying the Davidic genealogy to Christ. So life is full of turns. I shall arrange for her to see you. Then perhaps you will visit me in Jerusalem to see how things are done in our operations there. Lev could bring you, and we shall share a day together. Things have slowed now so that I can have a day off."

"That sounds good to me, David."

David left saying, "Blessed is he whose transgression is forgiven, whose sin is covered. Blessed is the man unto whom the Lord imputeth not iniquity, and in whose spirit there is no guile" (Psalm 32:1, 2).

Bathsheba Seeks Uriah's Forgiveness

Lev arranged to take Uriah to Bathsheba's residence. After breakfast they flew off in the beautiful morning sunlight. Lev didn't take a direct route because he wanted to give Uriah a little sightseeing excursion of both the Mediterranean Sea and the Sea of Galilee. Uriah found it exhilarating and marveled at the beauty of the earth in its morning splendor.

Finally they landed at Bathsheba's pad where she was waiting for them. There was an awkward moment as Lev opened the door, and Uriah seemed reluctant to leave the aircraft. Bathsheba was a beautiful woman, but she showed the strain that this meeting produced. Lev tried to make small talk to reduce the tension, all to no avail. When Uriah finally came out, her eyes flooded with tears and she turned away running toward the house. Uriah called to her, but she did not stop.

Knowing how very private this matter was, Lev said, "I am leaving you here, Uriah, and will return for you at the end of the day. You must try to understand her pain. Bathsheba does want to see you, and she wants to repair the hurt you both feel. I can well imagine how she must feel. I cannot be much help here, because this was a very personal relationship between you both. It takes a lot of character to rise above the pain of the past and find joy in today's new relationships. Shalom."

Uriah stood weak-kneed as Lev lifted off and disappeared over the horizon. Pulling his courage together, he walked to the house and knocked on the door gently.

Bathsheba opened it smiling, having dried her tears, but Uriah could see she was very stressed. "My dear, I have wanted to see you. I didn't have a chance to say good-bye, and if I had, it would have been agonizing then to know you had left me."

"Oh, Uriah, I never thought anything would part us. I sinned against you and God, bringing about events I never imagined. However, in the Lord's tender mercy, my son was a progenitor of Christ. I also suffered through all the distress that God brought upon David. We both knew it was the price we had to pay for our sins. Sin brings its own unhappiness—shame, guilt, and degradation. You died in your honor. I lived in dishonor. People knew my history, and some looked upon me as a dishonorable temptress. King David protected me in some ways, but I heard the whispers behind my back."

"As I lay there dying, I knew someone had betrayed me. But I did not know that you were the first, although I am sure you had nothing to do with ordering my death," Uriah added quietly.

I Would Die Myself Rather Than Seek Your Death

"No, never, never, never—I would rather have died. However, once I passed over the line, things were impossible. I was with David's child. How could I greet you when you returned home? You would have known immediately. Then I worried about the child. Would God let him live, or would he die for our sins? I knew I had betrayed you. Under the law my penalty should have been death, and sometimes I felt that would have been the easiest way out of my dilemma. Yes, at times I longed for it. I had ruined your life and mine so hopelessly."

"Bathsheba, I loved you and would have taken you back even though you dishonored me. However, that was not to be. It seems I had to die for your sin and David's. But I am not bitter now. I have forgiven him and you. However, it does hurt."

"I have had continual sorrow in every thought of what I did to you. I betrayed a sacred trust, and there is no justification whatever for what I did."

"At least I know that you did not forget me," Uriah quietly interjected. "That is some comfort. When I learned what transpired, I was so angry that I wanted to kill David. I was raging, but somehow my anger is now gone. I still carry hurt in my heart, but my present blessings so greatly outweigh my former loss that there is no bitterness."

Agape Love

"We can love each other with an *agape* love, the kind of love that God and Christ have shown toward us. Friendship still can be ours and happiness can be shared with countless others. *Agape* love is not a limited love shared by two people, but an unlimited love that grows and increases without boundaries. It is love in its purest and highest form."

"You are talking to a hardened soldier. I spent my time destroying enemies, not in loving them. What you are saying is very beautiful and it appeals to me, but it is out of my reach. All I know is that I still love you, Bathsheba. I will be glad for your friendship, and if you shower me with *agape* love, maybe I will learn to appreciate it and develop a similar love. I am willing to try."

"I will not be your wife again, Uriah, and do not deserve to be. However, I can love you with an *agape* love and I fully intend to do so."

Soon Lev's aircraft was heard setting down on her pad. Uriah kissed Bathsheba on the cheek with a warm hug as he turned toward the aircraft.

"Because the creature itself also shall be delivered
From the bondage of corruption
Into the glorious liberty of the children of God"
(Romans 8:21).

Chapter Thirteen

Lev had been at home for some time without any outside assignments and was thoroughly enjoying the blessings of the reign of righteousness. He spent his time in various pursuits but mostly in research with his brother Jake. He thought his assignments were largely over and this was how life would be until finally the last human being returned to life.

The pressure of the early days to get the regeneration project under way was much greater than it was now. As the last few million returned, everyone felt they could relax. When the last few hundred thousand returned, it seemed that man's appointment with destiny had been realized. However, one last task remained; perhaps it would be better stated that two tasks remained—the return of mankind's first parents, Adam and Eve.

There was a lot of talk about their return and what a great homecoming that event would be. However, there were no known plans and no date had been announced. One morning, while Lev was eating his breakfast after having returned from morning devotions at the chapel, the phone rang. To his surprise, it was the Ancient Worthy Abel, the son of Adam and Eve, whom Cain had slain.

"Shalom, Lev, this is Abel. We are requesting your services once again."

"Shalom, Abel—I am ready to serve now and always. It is my joy and privilege to serve our King."

"Yes I know, and that is why we have freely used your services. This time my request is not for your diplomatic skills in reconciling people. Our need runs along another line. I am in charge of making preparations for my parents to return to life. However, we do not wish to make a standard house. These houses are only temporary and will last for many centuries, but we want to create more natural dwellings, much like in the Garden of Eden. It did not rain then, so they did not need a roof over their head. They enjoyed similar orchards that we all now enjoy, but their home was very open with shrubs and plants providing their shelter."

"How interesting!" Lev exclaimed. "I am not sure what my assignment might be, but anything I could do to receive our first parents would be my top priority. I suppose that would be true of most people."

"Yes, that is true. I find myself very excited anticipating this great moment in time. The penalty of death will be lifted after our first parents' return. We all know our Savior is the one who made this possible. When you think how the regeneration has effectively brought everyone back to life, it is almost too much to comprehend. The crowning moment will be when Father Adam and Mother Eve return."

"I am sure you have something specific you want me to do, and I am ready as soon as you let me know what my assignment is."

Eden Replicated

"You know how our first parents were driven out of Eden. We know its exact location, but the trees of life are not there and many changes have taken place. However, Christ has promised to open the great spring of water that fed the four rivers that led out of Eden. I have asked Rebekah's parents, the Obadiahs, to replant Eden. They may enlist all the help they need. They, however, will decide the whole garden layout. I have received some secret information from

Christ on how it actually looked. I will convey that information to the Obadiahs so they can design Eden to resemble what Adam and Eve will remember."

"That is so exciting and, might I add, brilliantly planned. What joy it will bring to their hearts to awaken in Eden with no angel and flaming sword to keep them out. I often think of how much they must have missed the fruit of paradise and longed to eat it again. There it will be, as though they had never been driven out. Whatever it is you want me to do, I am eager to do it."

"Good, that is the kind of enthusiasm we need. We are all looking forward to this. As to your assignment—there is one significant difference between the earth now and the way it was then. Do you know what it is?"

"Yes, my guess is that then it did not rain and now it does. Am I right?"

"Yes, that is so. It was easy for them to keep comfortable while living by the warm and pure body of water gushing from the earth. The temperature was almost constant night and day. They needed no shelter from the rain for there wasn't any. Now they will need some shelter. We do not want their home to be like our usual houses. It must preserve the appearance of the original garden, only now we will use plants and shrubs to make a living house. Instead of rugs, we will put thick grass that does not need mowing. The grass, shrubs and bushes will be watered by underground pipes."

"That is absolutely brilliant. Are you sure that I could add anything to this splendid plan?"

Privacy without Bricks and Mortar

"Yes, we need to have a plant house that provides privacy and comfort as well as any home today but without bricks and mortar. We need to have a means of keeping the rain off of them as well as the usual temperature controls we have in normal houses. We need bathing facilities, modern lighting and electricity just as we have today, but remember, this is a garden house. The Obadiahs are already at work planting the orchard and general garden, but they cannot plant the house until you come up with a plan," Abel paused.

"Lev, you may call on anyone for help, and it will be freely provided. This is what I am asking you to research and design—a house of the future that resembles the Garden of Eden inside. Upcoming homes will probably favor this design in the temperate zones."

"How much time do I have?"

"No more than a couple of months. We have to grow the house, so it will take more time than usual although we will use mature plants and shrubs to speed things along. Remember, this is top priority. Anyone you need should feel obligated to leave whatever he or she is doing to join this project. We want to delight our first parents—who are also my mom and dad."

"I will start calling for assistance immediately, Abel. I have never had a happier assignment; it sounds thrilling!"

"Yes! Thank you, Lev! Shalom."

Lev first called his brother, Jake, a scientist and a creative problem solver. "Hello, Jake, I've got a new assignment."

"Great, but make it short. I have a busy day ahead of me."

"Well, this is top priority. Whatever you were planning can wait. Abel just called me and authorized me to enlist anyone I needed for this new assignment. So I am recruiting you."

"You sound so serious. Is that really true?"

"Definitely! Abel is making preparations to receive Adam and Eve back to life! He is asking us to design garden houses for them. I will be at your office in about twenty minutes. I want you to collect your whole staff of problem solvers for a think-tank meeting."

"I'll do that! This will really enthuse everyone! It is more exciting than any other task I have had. Thanks for including me, Lev. I will rearrange our schedules and get a committee to engineer this new project."

"Good! I am going to call Rebekah to join us, because her parents are already working on the garden. She might have suggestions for blending horticulture into modern housing."

"That sounds great, Lev. It gives me the goose bumps to think that Adam and Eve are coming back, and we can help in providing suitable housing for them that will remind them of Eden."

"Me, too! This is the most exciting project ever. See you shortly."

Lev soon arrived with Rebekah, and as they entered the office, cheers went up. The whole staff was electrified with the news that Adam and Eve were soon returning, and they could help make a house that simulated their Eden home. As Lev stood before the group, they became silent so as not to miss a single word.

"Abel called to favor me with this project. I have decided to enlist your best efforts to engineer a shrub and plant house that will keep out the wind and rain yet appear like their original home in Eden. It must have all the utilities and amenities of our modern homes, but plants are more enduring than bricks and mortar. They do require some pruning and care, but they provide constant beauty, fresh air, and the rustic look of a beautiful garden."

Everyone listened intently as Lev outlined Abel's request. "Adam and Eve will be back in Eden, their original home. Christ has promised that the original fountain that supplied four rivers will be activated. The water that comes forth will be as clear as crystal and warm, so that it will provide natural warmth by day and night. What will be different is that then it did not rain; only a mist went up from the earth and watered plants. Now it will rain, so we need to create a roof that keeps raindrops out but lets sunlight in. Rugs will be replaced with thick grass that will be watered from underground pipes. We will be able to place some posh furniture on special platforms and may use natural stone in the kitchen and bathroom areas for flooring. I am open to suggestions on the walls, but they have to serve as regular walls for privacy and also keep winds and weather out. We will open this for discussion first—any ideas?" Lev finished.

A Consensus on the Eden Home

Many ideas were given as the group enthusiastically envisioned a home suitable for their first parents. A consensus eventually emerged. There would be an inner row of plants and shrubs and an outer row with a clear thick glass panel between the rows. Windows would be provided where gaps were left in the plants. Actual doorframes could be made for private rooms and panels would be used for room separators.

They needed special glass for the roof to keep out rain and to provide shade from the penetrating rays of the sun. One of the benefits of the regeneration was that the lost art of making flexible glass was regained, and now it was the newest trend. The flexible glass could withstand intense stress and would not readily crack under pressure. It was stain resistant and easily cleansed with a hose or rain and could be translucent or opaque.

Everyone was very excited, and the ideas bubbled forth like water from an artesian well throughout the day until there was consensus of what the Eden home would be like. Soon they had designed a garden home with all the beauties of the original Eden, yet all the comforts and conveniences of the modern age. Within days blueprints were drawn and Lev sent them to Abel for his approval.

The very next day, Abel called Lev and confirmed his delight with the plans. He even thought this would be a model for other homes more compatible with the earth and its environment. Abel expressed his appreciation and amazement at the speed with which they had conceived the plan, even though he knew the staff would not rest until they produced the very best they could envision. The plans were so thorough that none of the Ancients had any changes or additions to suggest.

Lev ordered the materials for two new houses and issued a top priority request to get the buildings underway. They already knew the exact dimensions and upon learning the location of Eden, they began to lay the homes' wiring underground, as well as the piping and plumbing. All the inner walls of plants and shrubs were planted, then the carpeting grasses. Rebekah worked with her parents to select the ideal plants for inner walls. Soon the glass walls arrived along with the roof. There was no hammering, no bricks or mortar; only plants provided walls of beauty. When the inner plants had all been placed, they put another group of plants on the outer walls so, for the most part, the glass was invisible.

The whole world wanted to see the homes of Eden on television. There was unparalleled exhilaration about the thought of their first parents returning. The Ancients promised there would be two weeks of celebration when Adam and Eve returned, for this would mark the complete return of the human race from the grave. This was the greatest and most successful project made possible only by divine wisdom and direction. Human energies from selfish and destructive habits of the past were now redirected into restoring the human family to a sane and orderly manner of life. Spiritual power had been needed to maintain a discipline that mankind could not impose upon itself.

It took over six thousand years to generate the human race, and in less than a century they would all be regenerated. Christ had called all in their graves back to life, and mankind had diligently worked to feed, house, and clothe those returning. Never had wealth been equitably divided among mankind and humans made self-sufficient with abundant provisions for life and happiness. Thus was fulfilled what had been written: "Death and hell delivered up the *dead* which were in them" (Revelation 20:13).

Lev tested the facilities in the two Eden homes and everything performed in excellent order. He endeavored to learn as much about Eden from Cain, Abel, and Seth, as well as from the other sons and daughters of their first parents. Cain and Abel were the first children and apparently picked up enough information about Eden giving them a fair knowledge of how their parents lived in those happy days. They lived near the huge fountain of water that bubbled up fresh water.

This huge fountain supplied four rivers, but they were not muddy rivers like the ones formed by rain running off the earth. The waters of Eden's rivers were as pure as crystal and the foliage along the waters was most luxuriant. Fish were clearly visible, and the animals frequented the rivers for water. The animals ate protein grass in Eden and were tame. The days were warm and the evenings were cool. They slept near the fountain that also kept them warm at night. The most they needed was a few giant leaves as a cover at night from the mists that went up from the earth.

A Pure Fountain of Water

A fountain again was bubbling up pure warm water, although the volume of water it issued now was significantly smaller. It was running off in four different streams similar to the original Eden. As Cain and Abel studied the new Eden, they were pleased that much of the flora and fauna were quite similar. The Obadiahs had shown extraordinary insight in trying to reproduce a garden that would make Adam and Eve feel that at last they had returned to their original home. How they must have longed to return to the original Eden where they were created, but no matter how great their desires were, they had been denied access to it by an angel with a flaming sword. The angel was now removed, and Adam and Eve would return to life, not in an unfinished earth, but in a garden resembling Eden.

The time for their return was announced, and on that day all work ended and the whole world waited with bated breath for their first parents to return to life. It was innate in mankind to seek their roots. When the awesome moment arrived for the original progenitors of the human race to live again in the garden which God Himself had planted eastward in Eden, it cast a spell of wonder upon all mankind.

Eve Returns

I stirred to life, conscious of a familiar smell. Was this my imagination or could it be real? As I lay there with my eyes still closed, I smelled the fragrance of the trees of life. I thought I must be dreaming. I remembered my labored breathing. Now, breathing was easy and the air was so fresh with the smell of Eden. When I opened my eyes, I saw lush foliage that looked very much like my memory of Eden. This was not the same goatskin bed. I marveled at the softness of the fiber and how comfortable this bed was. All my aches were gone, and I felt like I once had felt back in Eden when I was vibrant and beautiful. I quickly arose to find clothing laid out for me in the large room where I was. I noticed the fine material of the fabrics and how well the clothing fit. I had never known such clothing before, and they were not made of animal skins. I quickly dressed and started to look around.

I saw a small door and entered what seemed a room with a beautiful waterfall of warm water running into a lovely small pond. I noticed some handles that, when I turned them, created fountains over the pool. I didn't understand anything else in that room. This was surely a dream. It looked like Eden and smelled liked Eden, but I knew the angel with a flaming sword would never let me return there.

I looked into a reflecting metal hanging on the wall. I was so surprised to see my withered and wrinkled skin looking so smooth and beautiful! I paused to admire the clothing I wore that complemented my natural features. I felt a little disoriented, because the last I remembered I had been very weak and could not even stand, but now I felt as vigorous as when I had first been created. Everything seemed so strange. Why was I alone? Where was Adam? He had always been beside my bedside. Where were the children?

I continued my exploration and returned to the first room and saw that a door opened to another room. Again I hesitated. What was beyond this door? Why was it so quiet? Could my senses be deceiving me into thinking I smelled the fragrance of the trees of life? Would the angel with a flaming sword be on the other side of the door and drive me out again? I had this uncertain feeling never before experienced. I stood at the door trembling, not so much with fear, but with confusion at the wonder of everything about me. Everything was so beautiful and so carefully laid out that only loving and thoughtful people could have provided it. Who might they be?

I opened the door slowly, not knowing what I might find on the other side, but I was pleased to see more garden surroundings. I noticed a transparent roof above allowing the brightness of the sun to shine on me.

Cain, Abel, and Seth

Suddenly Eve saw three men. They looked liked Cain, Abel, and Seth, but that could not be. She knew Abel was dead; she and Adam had buried him.

The men smiled and came toward her. They looked like her sons, but only Abel looked as she last remembered him. He was young and strong and actually more handsome than she remembered him. This could not be, unless it was one of her grandsons that looked like Abel. Yes, that must be the answer. Without realizing it, Eve was staring at them.

Abel rushed to her side to give her a hug and kiss. "Mother, we are together again at last."

"How can I be your mother? You certainly look like Abel, but you cannot be."

Cain, also hugging and kissing her, said, "Mother, we are all your sons, and this is Abel, whom I murdered."

"Please, let me sit down. I am complimented that you call me your mother, but, Cain, you were a much older man when I last saw you, and so were you, Seth."

"We all did become old and we finally died as you did, Mother. Abel was the only one who died a young man."

"I know I was ill, but how can you speak of death and dying? I am alive. I always hoped that on my sickbed, the angel with the flaming sword would relent and let Adam in Eden again to get some of the fruit from the trees of life. I knew that would rejuvenate me. Perhaps that is what happened."

Seth, having waited to hug and kiss her, finally did so and replied, "No, Mother. That was a fond wish then, but it has been realized now. See out that window—there are the trees of life."

"They certainly do look like the trees I knew and they do smell like the original orchard in Eden, but I know we were driven out and kept away by the angel with the flaming sword. Oh, how often we longed for that fruit! Our bodies craved it, but it was forbidden to us because we had sinned. What you are saying is almost too good to be true."

The Fruit of Paradise

Cain said, "Here, Mother, let me serve you some fruit from the trees of life."

Eve's eyes widened with immense pleasure. "Yes! Yes! This is the fruit I once ate." She bit into it with gusto. Her eyes sparkled with pleasure. "This is the same fruit of Eden that the Lord planted for us. Can it be that I have returned to Eden?"

Abel poured her a cup of aromatic tea. As Eve smelled it, she gasped, "Dear Lord! This is tea made from the leaves of the trees of Eden. Oh, this is so wonderful! Where is Adam? Where are the rest of our sons and daughters?"

"Adam is returning at the same time as you in an adjoining home. As soon as he has some tea and fruit, he will be here to greet you along with your other sons and daughters. I have to tell you, Mother, you have a very large family. They would all like to be here, but with all the children and grandchildren it is not possible. You have no idea how big your family really is. Literally, the world is full of your children and grandchildren."

"Please, may I have some more fruit and tea? Oh, my! How often I dreamed of this fruit and tea as we labored in sweat and toil living off the unfinished earth. How we longed to return to Eden! Having eaten this fruit and the abundant life it provided and then losing it was a terrible tragedy. You have no idea how we longed to return. Are you sure we are in Eden?"

"Does it look like the Eden you remembered?"

"Yes, it does. Is there still that great fountain of water bubbling up from the earth forming four rivers?"

Abel answered, "Yes, it is there, but it is not as big as it once was. We will show you everything, but first we want you to relax. We know everything seems unreal and at times you wonder if you are dreaming, but you and father are the last two people to be called to life again."

"You mean that Adam died? I know he was getting old and infirm, but my mind is confused. If he died, how could he be alive?"

"The very same way I am alive again, Mother," Abel replied.

"I am very confused. I never heard of anyone coming to life again from the dead. This is very strange, indeed. Forgive me, but I am unable to grasp what you are saying. I hear your words, but I do not understand them."

Abel seemed to be in charge of the arrangements. Eve could not help but be totally enthralled with him. Not only did he look like her son, but also his words and carriage were just like the Abel she remembered. He seemed somehow superior to Cain and Seth, both in appearance and mannerism, but he reminded her of Adam before he sinned. There seemed to be a radiant perfection that one could see and almost feel. Yet, Abel was so young when he died and so very innocent. Where had he gained such an excellent stature and such manifested wisdom? She remembered Abel's former goatskin clothing, but now he was dressed in clothing she had never seen before. She remembered his boyish charms and his great devotion to God. She noticed Cain was no longer the angry young man she remembered but also seemed very mature. It was a joy to her heart to see both Cain and Abel so comfortable with each other, as though nothing had happened to their friendship.

Meanwhile, in the adjoining house...

Adam Returns

I found myself breathing easily and oh! So comfortably! I just lay there inhaling deeply and thankful that the pain was gone. As though in a dream, I smelled the fragrance of the Garden of Eden, but I quickly dismissed it. I was certain the way to Eden was still blocked by the angel with the flaming sword, but it was a pleasant memory anyway. I lay there afraid to open my eyes, for then the dream would end and I would be suffering again. My sons and daughters were very kind and seemed to be standing over me constantly wiping my fevered brow. However, I felt so good now, I had no burning fever.

I opened my eyes slowly, and was surprised that my thoughts were uninterrupted. When I looked around, it was so lovely it reminded me of Eden. How often I had tried to return to Eden, but I was always denied entrance. Could the angel with the flaming sword have relented and allowed me back in Eden and given me fruit from the trees of Eden? I could not explain nor understand my present condition.

Upon arising, I found clothing to which I was unaccustomed. To my amazement everything fit perfectly. I especially marveled at the shoes! They felt so soft and comfortable on my feet. Walking about, I thought this place was very similar to my garden home in Eden. Only I was in a contained structure with living plants, shrubs and grasses growing together. Someone had even pruned all the plants. That was my job in Eden. I admired the furniture and bed I had been in, all set on stone surfaces and surrounded with living grass. I saw myself in the most perfect reflection I had ever seen. I looked like I once remembered myself—no longer old and haggard, but strong and handsome. Surely, I must have been allowed back into Eden and permitted to eat that wonderful fruit from the trees of life. That must be why I had recovered.

Where were my sons and daughters who stood at my bedside to care for me? I remembered with sadness how Eve had died, and nothing they did seemed to remedy her situation. Why was my life extended?

I turned and saw a door that led out. I wanted to walk boldly through it, but I had a strange feeling of uncertainty. Something was so very different, and yet everything was too real to be dreaming. What other explanation could there be? I knew with certainty that the way to the Garden of Eden was blocked. No matter how I desired to enter it, never was it possible to even imagine. I smelled the wonderful fragrance from the trees of life. I knew that smell and my heart jumped for joy. This had to be the Garden of Eden, for only here did the trees of life produce fruit every month of the year.

Trying to take charge of my wild emotions, I opened the door.

Welcome Home, Father!

There, outside his door, stood his sons and daughters smiling, greeting him.

"Welcome home, Father!"

Adam found himself being hugged and kissed by his children. However, even though he recognized them, they looked younger and better than he last remembered. He felt slightly uncomfortable—there was too much that was unusual. He could not deny that these were his children, but what was different and why did he sense another dimension?

After each one personally embraced him, they led him to the kitchen area where he saw a table filled with fruit that he instantly recognized. Its fragrance and appearance were unmistakable. This was the same fruit he and Eve had once dined on daily.

"How did you ever get this food? You have no idea how often I yearned to have this fruit again. Once you have eaten this, you will not be satisfied with anything else. I never knew or even suspected that we would be driven out from the Garden of Eden. We both would surely have done differently if we had known what the consequences of our disobedience would bring."

Without pausing, Adam asked, "May I eat some? My mouth is watering in anticipation of this unexpected pleasure. Has the angel with the flaming sword left the Garden of Eden and permitted us to return?"

His eldest daughter, Miriam, said, "I guess you could say that, Father. There is a long story here. Let us all share in this bountiful fruit! Allow me to pour you some tea that you will probably remember, too." Then she asked her father to seek the blessing on the food.

Where Is My Beloved Eve?

Adam's face lit up as he ate the succulent fruit. However, soon his face saddened. "Here I am eating of the fruit of Eden again, but oh—how I miss my beloved Eve! We both hoped and prayed that one day God would allow us to return to the garden we enjoyed so much before we sinned."

Miriam replied, "As soon as you have refreshed yourself, we want to take you for a little walk, Father. We know your heart is sad when you think of Mother, but perhaps a little walk in the beautiful garden will make your heart glad again."

"I loved to walk in that garden before, but I remember how lonely I was before God gave me your mother. I was truly happy, but when God gave me Eve, you have no idea how it brightened my life. It makes me sad to think that here I am in the garden of God again and she is not here with me. It is almost like it was before she was given to me."

As soon as they had eaten, the family followed Miriam out the door. She took her father by the hand and led him along a short pathway that led to another house. She said, "Father, you have a neighbor that we would like you to meet. As a matter of fact, this neighbor is probably waiting for you."

"Who could it be? There were no other people living in Eden with us."

No one answered Adam. Miriam knocked on the door, keeping her father in front of the door while everyone waited for the door to open.

They could hear voices within, and soon Eve opened the door, exclaiming with surprised delight, "Adam!" Adam recognized her immediately and opened his arms to receive his beloved Eve. They stood there in a loving embrace, crying for joy along with all their children.

"Oh, my beloved Eve! God has also brought you back to Eden. I am so afraid this is a dream and you will vanish."

Cameras recorded this moment for the entire world to see. Their meeting was broadcast live throughout the entire earth.

Time did not seem to matter. Love had triumphed over death. Neither Adam nor Eve knew what was happening, but they knew the love they felt at that moment was real. The tragedy that had followed them was now turning to joy. Adam looked up and saw Abel, standing behind Eve. His eyes were surely deceiving him.

"Young man, you look so much like my son Abel!"

Abel stepped up to his father and threw his arms around him. With his eyes full of tears, he said, "Father it is I—your son, Abel."

"My Son—"

Adam's eyes filled with tears. He did not know how or why, but he grasped that this was Abel, whom they had buried with such poignant sorrow. Abel's voice was the voice of truth, and it was all the assurance he needed. Adam cried, "Abel, my son, my son," and embraced him for the longest while, each moment filling his heart more with unspeakable joy.

Cain stood sadly by, knowing that he had killed his brother. His eyes filled with tears, saying, "I never intended your death, Abel. When I was so angry and struck you with my staff, you fell backward hitting your head on a rock and I think that is what caused your death. I am so sorry! Never in one day of my life did I forget what I did to you and the pain I caused Father and Mother. Many times I wished I had died instead of you, my brother. Can you forgive me? Can everyone forgive me?"

Abel quietly replied, embracing Cain, "Do not feel guilt, my brother. You know I have long since forgiven you. I lost a few years of life, but God has given me an abundance associated with some of the most faithful and beautiful people that have ever lived. I speak not only of their physical beauty but the beauty and purity of their hearts. I have been in the service of the King daily, and my joy could not be greater. You did not intend my death, and therefore, God has forgiven you. Be at peace, Cain! This is a day of extraordinary gladness! Do not mention what happened again. It is all forgiven through Christ.

God has turned everything into joy through the loving-kindness of His dear Son."

Now all the sons and daughters came in to embrace Eve. One by one, they all came up to her and kissed and hugged her. Every eye was filled with tears of joy. Never in anyone's fondest dreams had they ever envisioned such a time as this.

Abel said, "Mother and Father, you are the last people in the whole world to return to life. You cannot begin to comprehend all that this means. You have no idea how large the human race has become and every human being who has ever lived has been returned to life through the power of Christ. No one has been left out or left behind. No one is homeless and no one is sick. Everyone is amply provided for with a wonderful home and with perfect food for sustenance forever. All the world's wealth is equally shared, and everyone has the potential to grow into full physical and mental perfection. There are no disadvantaged people unless they have returned to life saddled with their own willful sins. Even this damage can be repaired if they truly have godly repentance."

Most of the family was so relatively new to life that they did not fully absorb what Abel was telling them. They did not comprehend how God had condemned the whole human race in Adam's transgression or how Christ, by ransoming Adam, purchased the whole human family that was still in his loins. It was so simple, yet it had become obscured and confused. Only now was the truth beginning to be fully appreciated—"For as in Adam all die, even so in Christ shall all be made alive" (1 Corinthians 15:22).

As the tears dried, Abel took charge of the occasion.

"This must not be a time of sorrow, but of joy! We have prepared a feast of good things. A festive time of two weeks has been declared by the Ancient Worthies. There will be no work for this is a time for rejoicing and praising God. Today only our immediate family will share time with our beloved parents, but the whole world is waiting to join us in this joyous occasion. Tomorrow at the chapel meeting the television cameras will be focused on the two most important people in the human family—our Father and Mother, Adam and Eve."

Miriam added, "We have prepared all kinds of food beyond our wonderful fruit from paradise. We have a number of resurrection cakes, cookies, and all kinds of wonderful recipes. Between our meals, several individuals will share the story of his or her life. This will enable us to become acquainted with all of our brothers and sisters and their children. Then we will have both our mother and father reflect on paradise lost and how they feel with paradise restored. We want to learn a little of what they experienced in the nine hundred plus years of life not covered in the Bible. We and the whole world are eagerly waiting for their story. After Father offers thanks for this glorious day, we will follow our parents to the festive tables in the garden area."

Even in Eden, Adam and Eve had not seen such a spread of good things. When they tasted the resurrection cake, they couldn't believe how delicious it was. All the baked goods were made with flour from fruit of the trees of life, so they were indescribably delicious.

Some of the daughters first told of life's experiences, explaining how the family tree kept growing and spreading. Then several sons told of their joys, struggles, and the hard labor to make the stubborn earth yield its fruit to them. The last two to share their stories were Cain and Abel.

Cain Speaks

Cain began, "You all know the early part of my life and that I was responsible for the death of Abel. I had chosen a life of tilling the soil and working from dawn until dark most days. I desired to acknowledge God, but when my sacrifice of the fruit of the ground was not accepted, I became hurt and angry. Then when I saw that God accepted Abel's sacrifice, I could not believe how the killing of a helpless lamb would please God! I had labored so hard and long to produce my offering, and Abel just took a lamb from his flocks. I was frustrated that all my work and labor had been rejected. Little did I know that God one day would offer His own Lamb for our sins, and that is why He was pleased with Abel's offering. When you are angry you never reason clearly. Instead of trying to understand why God had accepted Abel's sacrifice and not mine, I slew my beloved brother in jealous anger.

"You cannot imagine how bitter my life became. I had not pleased God with my sacrifices of garden offerings, and I also killed the very one who had pleased God. How wrong can a man be? Still, God did not destroy me! He allowed me to live and to raise my family. I knew I was the black sheep and everyone held me at arm's length for killing righteous Abel. What can you do when you make such a terrible mistake? I could not take my life. That was not what God wanted. Many times I would have been glad if God had slain me for my sin. However, I learned that I must live it down and become a kind and loving human being like my brother whom I slew.

"Now, God has brought me to this day, a humbled and chastened man. I am so incredibly thankful for Christ's forgiveness. No one could have more godly sorrow than I. Abel was dead, and I could not seek his forgiveness. On this most wonderful day, I heard from his own lips that he has forgiven me and does not wish to hear anymore about my sin. At last I am free to rejoice and be glad. Praise God for his mercy that endures forever! And thank you, Abel, for lifting the burden from my heart."

Abel Speaks

At last Abel stood to speak. His human perfection was in stark contrast to the rest of the family. While they were all whole and physically well, they were not raised in physical perfection like Abel and the rest of the Ancients. When he began, everyone sensed the glory and majesty of a great man of God.

"My dear Mother and Father, and all family members—you were sad at my early departure. I hope you will be equally glad in my blessed station of having a 'better resurrection.' When I awakened, it was not at the altar where I had offered a lamb, but I awakened in the New Jerusalem. The joy of serving the King of glory has been the greatest joy of my life, and the second joy of my life has been receiving my mother and father back to life.

"When the time came for your return, all the Ancients agreed that this should mark a turning point in the great work of regeneration. Our dear parents are the very last to return to life. Everyone else has been regenerated. It staggers the mind to understand how massive this project has been. Every human being that ever lived was to be brought back to life and graciously provided for. Under the leadership of Christ not one day or hour of labor has been wasted. All plans were perfect and all human resources were husbanded for this great work of regeneration.

"On this day we have come to the culmination of the great work of regeneration. It is hard to understand why so many overlooked Jesus' teachings on this subject, but now every human being is a living witness to its effectiveness. Billions of homes had to be built, hundreds of billions of the trees of paradise had to be planted, clothing provided for all, and everyone shared equally in the wealth of modern computerized households. For the first time in human history, no one has more than anyone else. No one is unwanted or unloved. There is room for all at God's altar. And Cain, now that the Lamb of God has atoned for all our sins, your offerings at God's altar will no longer be disregarded."

Eve Speaks

Eve stood up, her eyes still red from tears of joy for her happy reunited family.

"My dear Children—when your father gave me the name Eve, the mother of all living, I thought it was more kind than true. I felt I was really the mother of all dying. However, no matter how I longed to undo what I had done, it was not possible. I rejoiced with every child God gave us, but I believed that possibly one of my children would be the 'seed of the woman' that would 'bruise the serpent's head.' I rehearsed that promise every time a child was born, but the serpent that deceived me remained to mock me.

"Our life was very hard compared to when we lived in Eden. Adam worked by the sweat of his brow tilling the soil that was stingy in yielding its increase. It was not like in the garden of God where we lived in fragrant surroundings eating all the luscious fruit and drinking the nectar of all living fruits. The beauty of that garden was too majestic to describe, but whoever re-created this garden has approximated it very well. We lived most graciously, enjoying life without a worry or a care. There was no fear, sorrow, sadness, guilt, shame, or regrets— only happiness every day.

"When that serpent deceived me, it was very tempting. I thought that if I ate the forbidden fruit, worlds of knowledge and wisdom would open to me. I thought I would be lifted higher and have a place among the angelic hosts, and become wise like God,

"I was totally deceived. Oh, I gained knowledge, but it was the knowledge that brought sin. Suddenly there was guilt, shame, pain, regret, and the loss of contact with God. This was the beginning of a dreadful nightmare. It would have been total disaster but for God's grace.

"The only ray of hope we had was God's promise that in childbearing, someday and somewhere, a promised 'seed' would come. Little did I know that through Mary, as I have been told this morning, the Christ of God would come. God mercifully allowed me to think that in my lifetime the promised seed would come. I did not know *when* the Messiah would come, but I died still believing in God's promise that the 'seed of the woman would bruise the serpent's head.'

"We labored long and hard, but our life was still happy and blessed. In Eden we did not fully understand how generously God had provided for us. We lived as royalty without a burden or care. It was not until we lost everything that we realized how extravagantly rich our lifestyle had been. Not a day passed without our longing for the fruit of the trees of life. Eating it today was like a dream, only better. Standing here, I realize that the billions of people that have returned to life are all my children. I can scarcely imagine how great was the gift of procreation.

Little did we realize that the whole human race was in our loins and that in God's mercy and grace we could pass on the gift of life.

"I suppose I will have more to say when I learn what my children did. In our time, we had no wars. I still do not really understand what that means. I hope to learn how my children conducted themselves. It has been whispered to me that I really do not want to know how they behaved. I almost fear to inquire, lest I should find that my children forgot they were created in the image of God. I understand that I must learn how far they strayed from God's image.

"Standing here, I realize we have triumphed over death and the grave. I am told that one of my children was Christ, the Savior of the world. I want to know him and render to him the homage due his name. I trust my children will do the same. Praise God for our great deliverance. Being restored to Eden is like receiving the gift of life again. The darkest day of my life was when we were driven from Eden as criminals. Today is the happiest day of life, standing here before you truly as the mother of all living. Thank you, my dear children."

Hope Over Tragedy

Abel stood up and kissed his mother on her cheek.

"That was a wonderful testimony of faith and trust through the long and dreary night that you lived through, Mother. You never lost hope. In your heart you believed you could find your way into God's favor once more, and at last you have. Today you face a happy beginning all over again, but this time you possess the knowledge of good and evil. When the serpent is loosed from his prison, you will not be inclined to listen to his delusions. God bless you, Mother! God cause his face to shine upon you and give you peace. Now let us hear from our earthly Father."

Adam Speaks

"My children, I am glad that no one has renounced me for bringing all the pain and unhappiness upon this world. I have not yet learned how badly our children behaved through the centuries, but I understand it has been dreadful. Our sin seemed so small at the time. It was only a simple matter of eating a piece of forbidden fruit. That seemed such a small transgression, but I know now there is no such thing as a small sin. When one disobeys his Creator, it is like opening a dark cave with poisonous vapors. Once those vapors escape, they cannot be brought back and contained again. The toxin of sin results in death, and it quickly spreads over the earth.

"Our life after Eden was blessed. Our greatest joy was being able to share the gift of life with our children. However, there was always a note of sadness. We knew our children must die as we would. Your mother and I lived in Eden without the knowledge of sin and death. How happy and simple our life was together!

"I knew when I ate the forbidden fruit that I would die, but I was determined not to let Eve stand alone in the transgression. I knew what death was. I pruned trees and saw what happened to branches that were cut off. I saw big fish swallow small fish in the crystal clear waters emanating from Eden. It was not death that I feared. I ate the forbidden fruit with full knowledge that death was certain. What I did not know was the corrupting power of sin. If mankind had only died, it would have been sad but tolerable. I could not imagine in my wildest dreams how some of my children would behave, just from the few things you have told me today. I have not yet reviewed the events that happened while your mother and I slept, but I understand we shall be reviewing a very sad history.

"There were also beautiful children who went on to demonstrate an amazing faith in God and an incorruptible sense of righteousness. If we had evil children, we also had good children who pleased God, one of whom is right here, our lost and now found son, Abel. It is humbling to know that some of our children managed to please God where Eve and I failed. That proves that God made us with inner strengths that many of us failed to exercise. It was easy to let down one's discipline for a moment, and that was all that was needed to plunge us into the raging torrents of human passions. Your mother and I failed God, we failed you, and we failed ourselves. However, it is comforting to know that some of our children, whom we now call the Ancient Worthies, did not follow in our footsteps. Then there are those who now are living and reigning with Christ because they followed the Master in life and in death. Yes, as I have just learned, some of our children made heroic efforts to please God—and they succeeded.

"This inspires those of us who did not put forth greater effort in trying to retain the image of God in which we were created. Now we have the opportunity to put in a stellar performance, where before we just drifted along. My life with Eve was fruitful, and you beautiful children are witnesses to God's grace and favor that blessed our life together. This was a triumph after our failure. All I can say is that I am determined to overcome in my second endeavor where I failed in the first. Thank you."

Lev and the Obadiah Family Given Honorable Mention

The last feature of the blessed day was a tribute to Lev and the Obadiah family. Abel announced, "We did not want to let this day pass without thanking Lev, Rebekah, and the Obadiahs. We wish to thank Lev and his staff for re-creating a suitable home for Eden. We did not want our first parents to live in houses like we live in. We asked Lev to design homes that would be very much like their first home in Eden, but with every comfort of our time. Lev has served in so many different assignments, but I do not think he has had a happier one than this.

"The Obadiah family is well known for their accomplishments in horticulture. With great care, Rebekah and her parents re-created these Edenic surroundings. We know that this garden cannot equal the first Eden that God planted, but they did a magnificent job. If our first parents were present to advise them, they probably would have been more accurate, but they depended on me, and I was never in Eden. All I could do was remember some of the things our parents told us. I am responsible for anything that is lacking."

Adam spoke up, "There is no lack, Abel. The Eden that God planted was, without a doubt, more expansive and beautiful. However, our desire to return to Eden is fulfilled with splendor this day. Eve and I thank Lev, Rebekah, the Obadiahs, and all who assisted them for such a perfect arrangement of plants, shrubs and flowers. It is absolutely exquisite. We never had such an elegant home as this in Eden. We thank everyone! Our longing has been fulfilled!"

Abel continued, "We will show the whole world our parents' first embrace, which we recorded. Tomorrow at the chapel in Eden, the program will be televised. Everyone wants to see our first parents, so the entire human family will be tuned in. Because of the different time zones, people will be viewing our parents at various hours. However, should anyone miss the program, it can be replayed at any time. In time, our parents will be taken on a world tour to visit their children. Before they do that, however, they will be educated in human history so they will have a good idea of how their children behaved in their absence."

The World Chapel in Eden

Lev had built a chapel in Eden knowing that a steady throng of people would want to visit a simile of the garden that God planted. It was more conventional in construction in order to accommodate a steady flow of people. That morning, the chapel was filled to capacity with Adam and Eve's immediate family and many of the Ancients, who wished to greet their first parents. It was "by invitation only" on this first day.

Abel was chairman of the program and had asked several of the Ancients to lead in worship. The music was extraordinarily beautiful in reverence and praise. The whole world watched in amazement to witness Adam and Eve in living reality. A great landmark had been passed, but it was not the end, rather a greater beginning. Though all humanity had returned from the grave, they still had not been fully reconciled with one another, and much less had they all been reconciled to God.

After the prayer, Abel spoke. "We have passed a landmark now that our first parents are back. It is an unspeakable joy to have them with us, and the whole world is watching us honor our original forbearers. We owe our lives to them, but what we make of our lives will depend on our love for God and for our fellow man. Those who do not love God supremely, more than they love self, stand in danger of having been brought back to life in vain. Those who failed in their former life can now succeed in attaining characters that will please God. It is possible, however, to fail twice—both in the past and in the present. This places responsibility for attaining everlasting life upon overcoming the selfish propensities that have dominated us for so long. We are able to be free of this selfishness if we choose to be. Now I present to you our first Mother, Eve."

Eve stood with her extraordinary grace and beauty, speaking in a clear, strong voice.

"Thank you for providing everything for my return to life. I know great work went into this regenerating process of bringing life into this world and caring for it. When we finished rearing our children, we had the joy of helping our grandchildren. Now it is hard to believe that through us, life came to the billions on earth. This was a great honor and privilege. However, I am painfully aware that I failed God under the test, and that I failed you, my children. I failed Adam also, and I failed myself. I stand humbled before you to ask your forgiveness. If I have learned anything, it is that I have vowed within my heart that I will not fail again. This is a new beginning. I am determined by God's grace to triumph. Thank you—and I hope you will join me in living this second life to win. May God bless you, my children."

Adam then stood next to her. "Eve has said much of what is in my heart. I awakened to find myself alive again, as most of you did. This is an extraordinary experience to be given life again for a purpose. I, too, failed God. I failed you, my children, and myself as well. Could I have done better? Yes, of course. If I had seen the outcome of my sin, I am sure that would have given me pause. I did not know what evil was like, nor could I imagine the terrible and painful results that were to follow. I was still a child in my comprehension of reality.

"Yet after we sinned, God did not leave us without hope. We were given a promise before being driven from Eden. 'I will put enmity between thee [the serpent] and the woman, and between thy seed and her seed; it shall bruise thy head, and thou shalt bruise his heel' (Genesis 3:15). True to His Word, we have the opportunity of triumphing over that serpent, knowing that its head will be crushed. When we awakened yesterday to find ourselves back in Eden, it fulfilled the longing desire of our hearts. Originally, we were to spread Eden over the world, but that work has been done while we were sleeping in the grave. Thank you for doing that.

"I would like to believe that reconciliation is going on in families and between families. My sons Cain and Abel are reconciled with one another and with our whole family. This is the great work of the present — reconciliation between parties that were at enmity. When this great work is accomplished, the greater work will be for mankind to be reconciled to God. We must now consider that we have violated nearly every law that God has ever given us. It is going to be a staggering undertaking to come back into His fellowship. No one said it would be easy, but it is certainly necessary. It can be done if we will it in our hearts. Unless we make a determined decision though, reconciliation will not happen. God bless you, my many children. I am determined by every power within me to be reconciled to God."

It was a great moment of renewal. If only every human heart was so committed, but alas, it was too much to hope for universal reconciliation.

Adam and Eve Learn the History of Their Children

That evening and the following week Lev was privileged to take Adam and Eve on a journey in time, passing from their death all the way to Armageddon and the establishment of Christ's power on earth. It was with a sense of sadness that he called up the various chapters on the history of the human race on the screen.

Adam and Eve learned of how evil had multiplied on earth when the angelic sons of God materialized as men and took the daughters of men. This happened after their death, so it had been hidden from their eyes. They were appalled at the flood that destroyed the evil that had gotten totally out of control. After the flood, they saw how the world was given a fresh start, and iniquity was curtailed for a season. Then they watched the record of the evil forces that resulted in the Tower of Babel and the quest of men to organize for world domination. They saw how God intervened again by confusing the languages that resulted in the division of nations.

At the same time, they observed that men and women of faith distinguished themselves by walking with God. This was their first history lesson, and Lev closed the evening promising that during the following week they would be given history lessons on how various groups of their children conducted themselves. A few would make Adam and Eve happy, but the conduct of many would make them mournful. Lev wanted to break them in slowly to the evils contained in history and reinforce the lesson that God always had someone who pleased Him on earth.

The week passed in intense examination of the highlights and shadows of history. Adam and Eve both wept as they saw scenes of unimaginable cruelty. Repeatedly they said, "If we had known what our sin unleashed upon this world, we would surely not have disobeyed our God and eaten the forbidden fruit. We ate of that fruit totally ignorant of the forces of evil that would spread throughout the world."

"The Seed of the Woman"

When they finally saw "the seed of the woman"—Christ, they were overjoyed. Then when they saw him suffer and die, they were horrified beyond belief. They realized the tide of evil would continue unrestrained. Lev had to show them these scenes over and over again. They learned that Christ arose from the dead invested with all power in heaven and earth and was in control of the present earth as a glorious spiritual being. It was with a mixture of sadness and happiness that God moved majestically toward the fulfillment of His purposes.

Lev noticed Adam and Eve were very near to human perfection, and they learned and retained every bit of information easily and completely. It was easy to see that they had been created in God's image, for they conducted themselves with dignity and grace very much like the Ancient Worthies. They were focused and intense in their determination to please God. They were not badly damaged by their fall into sin. They were only one step removed from God, whereas, some of their children had fallen to the bottom of the pit where the journey to return to God would be long and difficult.

Finally, Lev showed them how the age closed in the great Armageddon conflict as the world assembled against God's chosen people in the Holy Land. It looked grim, and Lev did not tell them the outcome. So Adam and Eve were very tense when watching the last great battle on earth. It seemed so hopeless. Lev told them of his own death in that last battle, and they were grateful for the living testimony of what had happened. When they realized that God destroyed the entire army of millions of people the very next day, as sad as that was, they knew it was the turning point. From that time forward, the greatness of the Kingdom would be given to Christ and his followers.

Adam and Eve were shown the world in ruins and the return of the Ancient Worthies with seeds from the trees of life. Now they understood the massive program of regeneration. They watched until they saw themselves alive again. The overview of history had a very sobering effect. Nothing had been sugarcoated—they saw the world the way it really had been and was now. So much was very ugly, yet still there was nobility in many hearts that gave them hope that most of mankind would make a heroic effort to return to God.

There was a long silence when Lev concluded the quick overview of human history. Adam sighed. "Never did I think so many of my children would become so mean and degraded. Where did they learn to behave in such depraved ways? They even justified their diabolical treatment of others with either a religious rationalization or some other so-called higher good. We certainly had set a very high standard. Even when Cain murdered Abel, it was not premeditated murder, but manslaughter. We were so devastated with that. Our hearts were broken, but we did not demur at the punishment God laid upon him. We knew that it was just, even though it pained us to see the hardship Cain faced."

Lev responded solemnly. "You must try to understand, Satan and his angelic followers whom we refer to as 'fallen angels' contributed to human degradation. After you died, the fallen angels 'married the daughters of men,' beginning a reign of violence and debauchery. That is why the Lord destroyed all but eight people in the flood. This had a braking effect upon the raging wickedness in the world. Men learned that God would intervene when the limits of depravity were pushed. They saw it at the Tower of Babel and again with Sodom and Gomorrah. But nothing deterred the efforts of the devil or the fallen angels. At the end of the age, however, the judgment and destruction of the fallen angels took place. Satan has been restrained in the abyss until the thousand years are ended. After that time has elapsed, God will use the devil as a final test and development of His people."

Death Limits Suffering

"I am glad I did not live through all the years of horror you have depicted," Eve shuddered. "God was merciful in limiting human suffering by death. When we fell asleep, we did not know what evils would be experienced by the world. How kind of God not to allow the great increase of knowledge and wealth until the end times. When men finally had the means of helping all of humanity, selfishness was so great that those who amassed wealth separated themselves from the poor and downtrodden. Only now do I see an equitable distribution of the world's wealth. God has done what we should have at the beginning. We should have spread the Garden of Eden over the whole earth. We failed so miserably, and we even lost what God had planted. I thought about that garden every day of my life. You cannot imagine my joy to awaken there again! Even then, I was afraid to blink lest I should awaken outside of Eden."

Abel added, "We all had those feelings when we returned to life, Mother. Be assured, you have been restored to your former estate and are expected to assume lordship of the fish of the sea, the fowl of the air, and over every living creature. You are to subdue the earth and bring it back into harmony with God. That was your original commission, and you are back to take up where you left off. The Lord has returned to you your first dominion."

Lev continued. "You will be traveling to various countries to see your grandchildren, especially those closest to you in time. Obviously, it is easier for you to go into their territory than for all of them to come here."

"Eve and I both know that most people are good and want to be better. However, when I saw the cruel and terrible things that were done by my children, I was absolutely horrified. Some of our children turned into murderous monsters. How can that be? Human compassion should have prevented such evils from taking place. It is my greatest sorrow to learn how dreadfully my children treated each other. I am at a loss to comprehend it," Adam sighed.

Trying to Understand

"Maybe later you can ask some of those who were once in power how such atrocities were carried out under their authority," Lev suggested. "I doubt if you will ever get a direct answer. The power of the human mind to rationalize and minimize responsibility is unbelievable. Many of those who returned have not been making normal progress in the regeneration process. When they get weighted down with their obnoxious past, it is very difficult for them to own up to the pain and death for which they are responsible."

"I am not eager to talk to these tyrants of history," Eve announced. "As a woman, I know the value of human life. Every human being came into the world at a great cost to women. We brought the human family into this world, and we nurtured them to adulthood. Everyone is a precious human being—no one has the right to torture or kill.

God or men of noble character do not accept such conduct. If I must meet with those who disgraced the human race, I would prefer to meet with those closer to my time such as Nimrod, who charted a wrong course, and the Sodomites, who were self-destructive. The fallen angels desecrated the earth before the flood, but these people felt they had a license to do whatever they pleased. When people thought they had license to sin, it seems that it became impossible to prevent human deterioration."

Lev replied, "Well, when the two weeks of festivities end, perhaps you can select those places you wish to visit first. It will be good for people to meet their first parents and learn how human beings should have conducted themselves from the very beginning."

An Interview with Adam and Eve

During the festivities the nations were enthralled with Adam and Eve, who appeared for an interview televised before the entire world. At last the gap between the young and the old was being bridged. Their words were wise and informative, as they appeared in the likeness of nearly perfect humans, very similar to the Ancients. One interviewer asked them to describe life before and after their fall.

Adam said, "The contrast was painful. In Eden, we lived in complete comfort with absolutely no concerns. Perfect food was within arm's reach. The climate was perfect. We had no wants or fears. Our lordship over earth was complete. All the animals behaved and our tasks were very light. There was no sweat or labor, no thorns or thistles. You have scenes from Eden and they are lovely, but the Garden that God planted for us was even more spacious and grand. However, we did not have a temperature-controlled house with all the modern amenities. Actually, we are more comfortable now than we were then. We were perfect then. Only the Ancients know how that feels. It's wonderful to be completely free of sinful inclinations. That is something we desperately want to regain."

Eve joined, "Yes, the difference between perfection and imperfection is the difference between night and day. In our perfection, we never had a sinful thought enter our minds or unkind words pass our lips. We had no selfishness, suspicions, pride, vainglory, or pomp. No ill will of any kind ever entered our thinking. Our thoughts were pure and our conduct always had God's approval. The minute we sinned, everything changed. We came under a dark cloud, and only now is it beginning to lift."

"We had no fear of God," Adam continued, "because we had nothing to hide. Every day, God's Word, the Logos, would come to speak with us. Those were the most stimulating moments I can remember. We looked forward to his visits with more anticipation than any earthly pleasure. His thoughts were always so uplifting and filled with love. We lived for those visits. We are the only two people on earth who had no parents. Communing with the Logos who made us was much more exciting than having earthly parents. Those were holy visits, moments when time stood still for us. Our hearts burned within us at each visit. When they stopped, we had nothing to look forward to at the end of the day. The door that only sons of God could enter closed the day we sinned. Our last visit with the Logos found us ashamed, fearful, brokenhearted, and very lost."

"I was completely deceived," Eve explained. "I had never known anyone who told a lie. Adam only told me the truth. He did not even know how to lie. He was so pure and genuine! I assumed that only truth was spoken. I knew no other language. However, the serpent convinced me by suggestion that if I ate the forbidden fruit, worlds of light and knowledge would open to me. I would become as wise as God. The forbidden fruit was tempting—it had enormous appeal. I concluded anything that looked so good could not be that bad. I ate, fully believing my charmed existence would be further enhanced. I offered it to my beloved Adam. From the look on his face, I knew he did it only to share my fate. It was like falling hard and having the wind knocked out of you. The only knowledge I gained was the knowledge of shame, guilt, fear, and dread—anxieties I had never known, and I was devastated."

"And it didn't end there," Adam added. "When the sentence was pronounced against each of us—the serpent, Eve and I—we realized we would die a slow death. From that day forward, we had to toil with the sweat of our brow on an undeveloped earth that brought forth thorns and thistles and did not yield its increase. We struggled to have enough food for our children and ourselves. Nothing was easy. We soon began to feel the loss of vitality as the vigor of perfection left us. The only consolation was in seeing our beautiful sons and daughters, and subsequently our grandchildren and great-grandchildren. That brightened our lives. As we ourselves faced the certainty of death, it was consoling that our children would carry on. Somewhere, somehow, there would be the 'seed of the woman' that would bruise the 'serpent's head.' We did not know how long it would take before that 'seed' would come into the world. If we had known how long it would be, we would have been *very* discouraged."

Violence Was Hidden From Our Eyes

"Yes, that is true," Eve agreed. "We had no idea that violence would overtake the world as it did. In our time there were no wars. Life was difficult, but it was relatively peaceful. There was no time for mischief. We worked from dawn until dark providing the necessities. Only Adam and I knew how easy life in Eden had been, but none of our children had any concept of it except as we occasionally mentioned it. Our children never knew what it was like living from the trees of life, or how good the fruit was. Fortunately, it was not until we were gone that the fallen angels left their heavenly estate and came down to earth to marry the daughters of men. That act turned our difficult world into a world of violence full of wicked passions. God enabled a pure lineage, uncorrupted by these fallen angels, to continue up to and after the flood. He never lost sight of His end design, even though we did. Nothing was allowed to interfere with His majestic plan of the ages that was moving systematically toward an irresistible fulfillment. Now that we have arrived at a point where God's plan is visible to the whole world, it is so easy to see. However, in our lifetime we only clung to certain promises, believing that somehow they would come to fruition."

The interviewer asked, "What kept you going through all the dark days, when you realized that you and all your children were condemned to death?"

"I think both Eve and I clung to the slender hope that somehow the human family would be restored to God's favor. We knew that the 'seed of the woman' would 'bruise the serpent's head.' That did not tell us much, but it was enough to know that, ultimately, we would triumph over Satan. He lied to Eve making her believe she would not die. He then perpetuated that lie with false religions that taught man that he had an immortal and undying soul, as though anyone can live without a body. Even angels have bodies — not bodies of flesh and blood, but spiritual bodies. Angels, mankind, and animals cannot exist without a body. Every false religion claimed a fictitious afterlife, which gained them control over the people. Do what they told you to do and they would assure a pleasant afterlife — untruths, all of it.

"The truth was that death is real. Our only hope was that Christ would raise the dead and give to each a new body as it pleased him. Some would be given a spiritual body so that they could live and reign with him, but the majority would receive a terrestrial body such as we now have. This is the whole truth, and finally, everyone who has returned to life again knows they were not alive while dead. We were all *very* dead and knew nothing until we awakened."

The interviewer said, "Well, we all know that now, but I guess most people preferred to believe Satan's lie, 'Thou shalt not surely die.' We were better at make-believe than with the truth."

After the interviews and festivities had ended, the immediate problems of being reconciled with one another continued to dominate human relations. The Ancients were relieved of much of the pressure of keeping the regeneration program at top efficiency. They were engaged in resolving personal problems and were free to travel and exert their influence over society. Now that everyone was returned to life and amply provided for, the workload for all mankind leveled off to a maintenance program. There would be more relaxation and more time to expand the human mind. But expanding the human heart was still the top priority.

"But of the tree of the knowledge of good and evil,
thou shalt not eat of it"
(Genesis 2:17).

Chapter Fourteen

As Adam and Eve traveled to meet their children in various nations, one of the most asked questions was about the tree of the knowledge of good and evil. If it was in Eden, *why* wasn't it restored? *Will* it be restored? If it were to be restored, *when* would it be? People wanted to know why it was placed there in the first place, seeing all the harm it had caused. Why were Adam and Eve entrusted with this tree, while their children had not been granted the same privilege?

When asked on one occasion why God had not provided the tree of knowledge for the world, Adam replied, "I am not the one to ask. Christ is in complete and total charge. For whatever reason, the tree of knowledge has not been given to men to add to their responsibilities. Will it be placed here? Possibly, but remember, this tree proved more of a test to us than we were prepared for."

"Well, tell us about it, then," many inquirers demanded. "What kind of knowledge did it bring? What was so bad about having that knowledge?"

"I must tell you, first, that this tree was a controlling mechanism for human procreation and sexuality."

"You were given instructions to 'fill the earth,' so what was wrong with that? It was perfectly normal, and we are all glad that you began the process of procreation."

Adam answered, "There is a time and place for everything in God's plan. Eve and I were not mature enough to begin procreation when we did. God did not want us to fill the earth on some supercharged program. It was more important that we learned to obey Him first. Perhaps if we had shown the strength and discipline He was looking for, He would have permitted us to eat of this tree on a controlled basis. Then it would not have been sin, for God would have lifted the prohibition. After men and women had chosen their marriage partners, they would eat of this tree to begin procreation."

Nimrod Seizes the Moment

One of the men stepped forward as spokesman for many on this issue. His name was Nimrod. He said, "We have learned to control procreation, so what harm would there be in allowing this fruit in our society now?"

"You have been engaged in a tremendous task of receiving billions of people back to life," Eve responded firmly. "Making provisions so that all came back to the highest standards of life ever dreamed of could never have been possible while men and women were pursuing lifestyles similar to those of the past."

Nimrod felt that the crowd was sympathetic to his position and became more confident. "You obviously were drawn to that tree yourself, Mother Eve. Maybe, since we are your children we have the same desires that you once had. You were eager to change your position. Isn't it reasonable that we should be also?"

"Just one minute," Adam asserted. "Why are you making your desires known to us when we have no authority on this matter whatever? You would do well to accept that far greater wisdom than yours has kept this tree from being among the trees of life. It existed in our garden, yes. If Satan had not deceived Eve, she probably would have been perfectly content to wait to be introduced to the use of this tree. Eating from that tree caused enormous trouble, pain, and death. We are still struggling to undo all the evil effects of sin that we activated back in Eden."

"Here you are, telling us that we should be content," Nimrod spoke defensively. "We all suffered because of *your* mistake. It might be easier suffering for our own mistakes, but we are not suggesting rampant promiscuity. Control would be exercised in structured marriage patterns."

Eve stood her ground. "Sin can never be controlled in structured patterns of any kind. Once passions are awakened, it is all too easy for them to exceed the limits. That has been the pattern of history. Society wisely advocated rigid marriage controls, but at the end of the age, we know that promiscuity became a great source of misery. Most of all, it was absolutely intolerable and inexcusable for the problems it brought to children. If I may speak truthfully, I would be glad if the tree of the knowledge of good and evil is never brought back. I remember vividly what pain it has caused all my children and me."

"Thank you for your opinion, Mother Eve."

Adam spoke directly on the issue. "This tree is best left in the hands of Christ. The tree itself is not evil. Everything has its place in God's purpose. When Mother Eve ate of that tree, she did not know how it would affect her, nor did I for that matter. All we knew was that it was forbidden to us. That is all we needed to know. Yes, we knew something else, or at least I knew it. I knew that the death process would begin once I ate of it."

"Ah," Nimrod exclaimed, "but you ate of it anyway. At least tell us, was it really delicious?"

Forbidden, but Good Tasting

Eve replied, "Yes, in all honesty, it was good for food, every bit as good eating as were the trees of life. However, we only ate one piece of fruit each, and then we were driven from the Garden of Eden to die for lack of the nutrients of the trees of life."

It was apparent that there was some quiet resistance to the way things were being done. Adam and Eve were being used as a sounding board to make hidden desires known. They were both surprised at the intensity of these desires and distressed that they were the ones being badgered on this matter.

Eve seized the moment, saying, "Nimrod, aren't you the one who was the great builder of cities?"

"I am glad you remember my abilities, Mother Eve."

"Are any of the cities standing today?" Adam asked. "Especially, could you explain the motivation behind building the Tower of Babel?"

Nimrod blushed. "Cities were not built to last forever. I knew that. However, I made them very well, and my genius for building cities was well known. Some of the finest workmanship went into those cities."

"Oh, I don't doubt your ability. But can you explain the Tower of Babel to me?" Adam repeated.

"Looking back, I must admit that it apparently did not please the Lord, because He ended our efforts by confusing the languages of the workers (Genesis 11:7-9). I remember the very day it happened. I had planned for the final phase of building. I had all the materials provided and everything was ready to go. When I spoke to my men that morning, no one understood me. When they spoke back to me, I did not understand one word of what they said. It was total confusion. I tried to continue, but it was hopeless. Even worse, the people knew that God was displeased with our efforts, so the whole project was scrapped. It was heartbreaking to me, because it would have been a masterpiece of construction. However, yes, if you wish to know, I believe now that this effort was a mistake."

"Well, I am glad to know that we weren't the only ones to make a mistake," Adam said. "Could it be possible that you might be making another mistake now by insisting on access to the tree of the knowledge of good and evil?"

"I don't think so. Remember the tree brought the knowledge of good, didn't it?" Nimrod asked. "Why do you imply that it only brought evil?"

"You are right," Adam replied. "The good was the gift of procreation that God gave to man. That was a good and holy gift. However, when we partook of it before we were given permission, it resulted in great evil. It was a two-edged sword cutting both ways. It could have been used only for good if we had waited on the Lord. So, my advice is, wait on the Lord in this matter."

"Can anyone answer one question?" Nimrod inquired. "Are the seeds of this tree available, or are these trees existent in any form?"

"I am just back from the grave a short while, but perhaps Lev Aron may answer your question as he has been around a long while," Adam replied.

Lev gave the answer. "Yes, perhaps the seeds of the tree of the knowledge of good and evil are in possession of the Ancient Worthies. However, they will have these available when they choose, and that will only be when Christ allows them to be released."

"That is what I wanted to know, thank you. Everyone has to accept Christ's decision in these matters. We will wait until then," Nimrod replied.

Lev decided to close the discussion.

Adam and Eve Meet Bera, Former King of Sodom

In meeting various nations and groups of people, Adam and Eve were on a goodwill mission to foster a family relationship among the peoples of earth. Not that all the descendants of Adam and Eve behaved in a way that would honor their parents; however, the time had come for reconciliation among men. It was difficult because some had little discipline in their lives and had developed a rationalization for their actions—that everything they liked to do was their own choice and no one else's business. However, sin was everyone's business. Sin was what created unhappiness. Pleasures brought by sin could not be justified because of the pain it brought to others, and ultimately it boomeranged on the initiators. Sin certainly concerned God, and He dealt with it forthrightly. "The wages of sin is death" (Rom. 6:23). To say that sin should be "no one's concern" was not reasonable. Anything that created unhappiness must be everyone's concern. Sooner or later sin would exact its price without exception. Eve found the forbidden fruit good for food, but it brought bitter results.

In the vicinity of the now extinct city of Sodom, some of its residents had returned to life. Due to the kindness of others, provisions were made for their return. They had been cut off when Sodom was destroyed, and so they had no children to receive them to life. Many generations had been cut off for various reasons this way, but Sodom had been cut off by God to prevent corruption from becoming indelibly stamped into their characters. There was such a thing as total depravity, but thankfully in the case of the Sodomites, God intervened before that point was reached. It was a kindness that they could not appreciate then, and, regrettably, some were not even prepared to appreciate it now.

Adam and Eve met with the people of former Sodom. Adam spoke in his usual brilliant manner. "We are hoping to meet our grandchildren who are spread throughout the earth, but we wished to meet first with those closest to our home and our time of living. Most of our children lived as we did for nearly six thousand years until the age of knowledge burst upon the world. We ourselves need to understand what changes all that knowledge brought, but it is easiest for us to meet those who lived basically as we did."

Eve added, "We have an opportunity to live again, and this time our goal is to live forever. I know I shall take valuable lessons learned in my past life to insure that I do not make the same mistakes again. If we learn from our past, it will help us to have our names written in 'the Lamb's Book of Life.' If we do not learn and apply those lessons, we will be condemned to make the same or even worse mistakes this time around."

Bera, the former king of Sodom, tried being the spokesman for some of his former citizens. "Well, we certainly welcome you and wish to pay honor and respect due our first parents. I hope you will not look with disfavor upon us as many do today. We almost have to apologize for being from Sodom."

Adam interjected, "From what I have learned in reading the biblical account of your life, your subjects might have fared better being taken captive by the five kings who invaded your land. At least you would have had to live by disciplines they would have placed upon you, and that might have preserved your life. When the two angels of the Lord entered Sodom, some of its citizens put on their worst performance and sealed their own end."

"The citizens of Sodom were free spirits who enjoyed life," Bera replied. "Perhaps they behaved badly that night, but they did have redeeming qualities. The Lord in His tender mercies has brought them back to life, and they appear no different than other men."

Adam was surprised by the relaxed attitude Bera took respecting his citizens' conduct. "Everyone has not come back equal in virtue and honor. Some bear the image of God very well, but with some that image has been badly marred," he said.

Bera Speaks on Behalf of the Sodomites

"I hope you do not think too unkindly of us. I found our citizens a fun-loving people, and I do not suppose that was evil. You know we did not have any jails in our city. We had no murders or robberies, so by common standards the citizens of Sodom were generally law-abiding."

Eve asserted, "You cannot surely mean their conduct didn't merit the punishment that came upon them. You know that if God found ten righteous people in that city, he would not have destroyed it."

Bera momentarily lost composure, but it was quickly regained. "I, a mere mortal, cannot sit in judgment of God. How could anyone say that God's actions were not just or unwarranted? However, from what I read in history, God permitted more vicious and violent people than the Sodomites to take tens of thousands, and in some instances, millions of lives. They were not stopped. Why were the Sodomites singled out for punishment?"

Adam said, "I am recently returned to life and cannot answer many things, because I only have a very perfunctory knowledge of what has taken place in this world. If God chose to take them away quickly, or whether they died or lived longer or took their own lives, the fact is that all did die and have now returned to live down their sins and show godly sorrow."

"I must tell you my former subjects are very happy to be alive again, however, they feel that some of the pleasures of the previous life are being withheld from them. They often speak about the tree of the knowledge of good and evil, and they wonder why it is not available to mankind generally now."

"All I can tell you is that Christ is in control of all affairs. The Ancients are only servants of the King, so you must wait for Christ to reveal his purpose in this matter or seek an answer from Christ himself," Adam said in a stern voice.

Eve chimed in, "Don't you think we have enough problems trying to untangle the web of sin created by mankind in the past without providing for new problems to emerge?"

Someone from the crowd stood up, saying, "We are not rebelling, we simply want answers. What is wrong with having our questions answered?"

At this point Lev intervened. "It strikes me as strange that suddenly we believe the tree of the knowledge of good and evil is being withheld unnecessarily from you. Why not ask Mother Eve if she now thinks the tree was withheld unnecessarily from her?"

Eve took her cue. "I was deceived into partaking of that fruit. I felt God might have been withholding from me worlds of light and beauty. I was very wrong. Another thing I learned was that at that moment, there was an urgency to partake of the forbidden fruit. It could not wait until tomorrow after I spoke to Adam about it. It could not wait until I spoke to God's spokesman, the Logos, in the cool of the evening. I had to have the fruit immediately, and I have lived with sorrow and regret because of my foolish haste."

Bera answered, "Wait, please, we have no forbidden tree to eat from. It is simply kept out of our reach. Our question is, why?"

Eve replied, "That is what I wondered, too. Why was that tree forbidden? It was because of my burning quest for forbidden knowledge that I became victim of Satan's deception. I did not have to eat of the tree. My stomach was full of good fruit from the trees of life. I was not hungry. I had no need to eat of the forbidden tree. My curiosity led me into temptation, and soon without much effort I was the victim of Satan's lie. I had been totally deceived. Remember, I was perfect before I sinned. I was pure and innocent. I had never heard a lie, never an unkind word, never did I know anyone would speak untruth. I had no unholy ambitions or desires. I did not know what sin was until like a thunderbolt I found I had crossed over the line. If it could happen to a perfect and pure human being, perhaps God in kindness is keeping temptations out of reach."

Why the Tree of Knowledge Is Withheld

The same person who had been so vocal before stood up again. "Thank you for your solicitude. We appreciate both of you as our first parents, and we do not wish to make your visit an unpleasant one. However, please do not confuse our question with rebellion. If there is a reason for the absence of the tree of knowledge we are mature enough to accept the answer."

Lev answered very forcefully. "Instead of seeking the tree of the knowledge of good and evil, there is much knowledge to be gained by remembering the mistakes made in your previous life. Do you remember when you were taken captive by the five kings (Gen. 14:8-16)? If Abraham and his servants had not risked their lives to save his nephew Lot, who was living among you, your lives might have been spared. True, you would have been taken as slaves, but as such you would have lived under rigorous discipline. There would have been no time for corruption. You would have risen early in the morning and worked until the last hue of light. The life that you lost by your uninhibited freedom, you might have saved being slaves with the whip on your backs. You would have learned discipline, which you did not know by living in freedom with corruption. You would possibly have lived to have offspring, and your generations would not have been cut off. Perhaps your offspring would have learned the disciplines necessary to go on to greatness."

"Thank you, again," the same vocal person exclaimed. "You make an interesting point. If I had a choice, I would choose being taken when fire rained down from heaven. There was no pain in the grave, no whip on my back, and no working from dawn until dark. We were well provided for without having had offspring. We were better supplied on returning to life than we had been in Sodom, and certainly much richer. I am not sure that I agree with your conclusions, however. We do not seem to be disadvantaged in any way since our return. Contrary to what many have thought about the people of Sodom being such wicked people, we are very much in harmony with conditions today. We are not worse than other people and perhaps better than many whom we have heard were responsible for taking millions of human lives."

In the conversations that followed, it was becoming increasingly clear that resentment was building in the minds of some people. Perhaps these thoughts and feelings had been in the back of people's minds, but few were so bold as to demand answers. It was becoming obvious that the return of their first parents, while being an occasion for joy, was also a time when hidden thoughts and reflections were starting to surface.

The Atonement Did Not Free From Personal Sin

The prevailing belief had been that the atonement for sin would free people from the consequences of their previous sins. It had been easy to accept what religious teachers had taught, that upon accepting Jesus they would be transported to heaven at death, and none of their evil deeds would be remembered or brought to mind. Hence, there was the idea that there were no consequences for sins flagrantly committed. All one needed to do would be to call on the name of Jesus or commit to some religious rite and be acquitted from all responsibilities for any pain that may have been caused.

It had given people a false sense of comfort, and even religious leaders had not concerned themselves with following after that "holiness without which" no man would please God. It had also added to the burden of reformation, when the largest effort required would be in reconciling the whole human race to God. Quickly forgotten and laid aside were Jesus' words, "I say unto you, that every idle word that men shall speak, they shall give account thereof in the day of judgment" (Matthew 12:36).

Now that it was known that the deeds of the former life could not be erased and forgotten but must be acknowledged and repentance demonstrated, a certain feeling of resentment persisted. Adam and Eve, in their naive benevolence, could not understand why everyone wasn't joyful and happy in the most fulfilled way. They were so filled with joy to have recovered the Paradise of God, and were so committed to making sure their names were found written in the "Lamb's Book of Life" that they expected others would automatically feel the same.

After this last encounter Adam said to Lev, "Perhaps we should inquire of the Ancients as to why the tree of the knowledge of good and evil is being withheld, and that way we can at least answer these questions."

Lev answered, "Why should we represent them in their request? They are just as capable as you or I to ask the Ancients. They obviously have not chosen to do that but want you to do it for them. If they didn't have qualms about this matter, they would have done it long ago, but they hesitate to ask the Ancients because they realize they may be rebuffed. It is neither their responsibility nor ours to question Christ through the Ancients. We must always remember that Christ is an infinite Sovereign who does not need to be reminded or prodded as to what course to follow, or what is best for the human family in their still-weakened condition."

Accepting the Present Status

"I see, Lev, you have a very wise answer. They are free men and women, and if they carry resentments, let them air these with the

Ancients who are perfect and full of the Spirit of God. If they deem it worthwhile to pass the information to Christ, fine. If not, they will know what to do. However, Christ knows everything without being petitioned by anyone.

"I am glad you came along as our guide, Lev. You have more experience and a greater understanding than we do. Things are so wonderful now. I cannot imagine where this undercurrent is coming from. If the devil was still free, I could understand it. It must be from some of the latent sin still clinging to mankind. Eve and I must be very careful not to become spokespersons for special interests."

Adam and Eve Meet the Pharaoh Who Died in the Red Sea

Continuing their journey, Adam and Eve visited Egypt. They were received with great enthusiasm and excitement, and people seemed not only eager to meet the ones to whom they owed their life but also whom they seemed to cherish, as they should. There was a grand turnout and the mood was festive and joyous.

The former Pharaoh of Egypt, who perished in the Red Sea, was the spokesperson for the gathered Egyptians. Adam and Eve already knew of the history of that time and were pleased to see this former ruler so graciously receiving them.

Pharaoh said, "We welcome you, our dear first parents. It is our wish to honor you with love. We are not worthy of your presence among us, but we want you to know we love you and thank you for the gift of life. I, more than others, did not regard human life when I lived before. A man can become crazed with power and that was my situation. You know, having slaves do the work for you was a form of wealth. However miserable it was for the slaves, the practice was economically desirable for those who possessed them. I have to apologize to you for using some of your children, who really were our brothers, as slaves. In the day of my pride I could not bear the thought of losing such valuable advantages slavery provided us. Even as I endured the various plagues, the moment the effects of the plagues ceased, I hardened my heart until the tenth plague of the death of the firstborn of Egypt. Strangely, I knew our firstborn would die, yet I could not yield to letting our slaves go."

Adam replied, "You and the people paid a high price for resisting the Lord's will. How could you jeopardize your precious firstborn?"

"It was not easy, but I could not bring myself to letting the Israelites go. My mind was set in stone, and not until I saw the people ready to rebel against me did I repent of my position. Even then it was not for long. No sooner did the Israelites leave than the realization of our huge loss of this large labor force set in. It seemed impossible to get anything done without them. Soon, the people were behind me again, and I thought I could salvage our situation by going after Moses and the Israelites."

Adam responded, "So it was then that you decided to bring them back into slavery, even trying to follow them through the Red Sea?"

"Yes, exactly. As I looked at the situation, I was confident our swift chariots could reach the other side before the waters closed in on us. What I did not count on was that the ground, which was actually dry when we started to cross the Red Sea, quickly became quicksand. It was hopeless. Our chariots became mired, and the horses were rearing up trying to escape. We could not jump off our chariots, because the horses would trample us. As the waters advanced, the chariots pulled closer together with wheels locking into each other. What seemed an easy quest turned into tragedy with the quicksand sucking us under. I foolishly tried to resist God and lost. All my men and horses lost their lives because of my folly."

A Learning Experience

Eve said, "Well, if you learned not to resist God's will, it was worth it."

"Exactly! I was a fool and deserved my punishment. My poor subjects did not deserve that kind of treatment. I am now in their debt and am committed to trying to serve in any way I can to show my repentance for what I did. I have determined to put forth a double effort to serve, for I am in debt to many people."

Adam replied, "This is so gratifying to hear. It is exactly how Eve and I feel. We owe our children extra devotion, for we brought so much trouble and evil upon them. We did not understand how a little thing like eating a forbidden fruit could have such baneful results, but having returned to life, we are appalled at the events that occurred while we slept. It is very sad indeed. Had we known how exceedingly evil the results of our eating the forbidden fruit would be, we would have resisted it with our very lives."

The former Pharaoh replied, "Yes, by God's grace and mercy, we can look back with hindsight and see how wrong we were. We don't deserve the kindness we have received. I marvel I was not brought back in chains and made to feel the whip on my back for all the pain I caused the Israelites in keeping them in slavery. It was only after I had been punished that I decided to mend my ways and not go astray again."

Eve said, "This has been a happy reunion for us today. I don't find any seeds of resentment and that warms my heart. We all sinned in some way or another, but now is the time for turning things around and making them right, not only with our family members, but with God."

The orchestra played beautiful music as Adam and Eve mingled with the crowd. There was warmth everywhere during this love fest. More than the happiness all felt, there was a bonding together as a human family and a realization that life in its fullest sense could only be achieved in harmony with God and the rule of His dear Son. The meeting bode well for people grasping the need to accept the discipline of living according to the law of love.

Meeting People Who Remembered Jesus

Adam and Eve asked Lev to take them to meet with people who lived in the days of Jesus, the Savior of the world. This would prove to be an inspiration to our first parents to realize the promised "seed" which would "bruise the serpent's head" had come. Many would tell of the Savior with the sweetest of memories though some who secured his death might be uncomfortable with their visit.

Nazareth Visited

Arriving in the area called Nazareth, Lev's aircraft touched down by the Sea of Galilee. A crowd awaited the arrival of the first human pair with awe and reverence. Adam and Eve remembered how their child of promise walked along these shores and preached to the multitudes. They knew the common people loved Jesus, the man who spoke as never a man spoke and who went about doing good. Even as they walked among the people, they could see many heads bowed in prayer. Yes, happiness everywhere was being expressed in an atmosphere of holiness and reverence. It was not only a gala event, but hearts tried to catch the inspiration of the hour.

Speaking to the crowds Adam said, "My dear children, we have come to visit you and your area that has been touched by the feet of our child of promise—the Christ of God. We were over three thousand years removed from it in time, but standing here we know our Son once stood here among you. If you have any memories of his walk in the midst of you, please tell us how his life touched yours."

One lady came forward. "I remember Jesus the boy, the carpenter's son. One look at him and you knew he was different. He was not a flippant child as children sometimes are, but loving, joyous, reverent, and serious. He was gentle and kind in his demeanor. He was a serious worker, and no matter what he worked on, it turned out beautifully. Even as a lad his workmanship was superior to his father, Joseph's. I noticed that his brothers did not accept him, and they left him out of their circle. They knew that he was a special child whose birth was announced by angels, but they did not see how he could succeed in accomplishing anything staying around Galilee. They were eager to have him go to Jerusalem, thinking perhaps he might find a following there. I spoke to him on several occasions, and he was the most gracious child. After Joseph died, he took over the business and supported Mary and the other family members. Many times when I brought him a broken chair or bench, he would fix it without charge. He knew I was a poor widow and needed every shekel to survive. You could not be in his presence without sensing that he was a righteous person."

"Yes, yes," a man asserted. "He used to read the Scriptures in the synagogue. He had never gone to school, but he read fluently and made every word he read come alive. When he explained the verses he read, he made them very clear. Often we would speak about the Scriptures he read, and inevitably we would speak about him. He was a person that commanded your respect and attention without any effort on his part. We loved it when he was there to serve us. Oh, Mother Eve! You were blessed to have given us such a child, by God's grace."

"My dear parents," another man said, "I was there the day he came to John the Baptist. John was baptizing people to repentance, and I was among those repentant ones. Jesus came to him seeking to be baptized. John said, 'I have need to be baptized of thee.' However, when Jesus still requested that John baptize him, he did so. I was there and saw the heavens open and the 'Spirit of God descending like a dove, and lighting upon him: And lo a voice from heaven, saying, this is my beloved Son, in whom I am well pleased' (Matthew 3:16, 17). I shall never forget that moment. It is emblazoned in my heart and mind. I knew he was the Holy One of God."

"I am so honored to meet you both and speak to the father and mother of us all," spoke a woman who was standing in the line that had formed to tell what they recalled of the Master. "I was at the home of Jairus trying to comfort the family in the illness of their daughter. I suggested that Jesus be found and told of her illness. However, while they went to find Jesus, the child died. We tried everything to save her, but all our efforts failed. I could not stop weeping, because I thought if I had only had them seek Jesus earlier, he might have arrived in time to save her. When the Master appeared, we told him that the child had died. He said, 'Weep not; she is not dead, but sleepeth' (Luke 8:52). That seemed strange to us, because we knew the child had died. She was cold and lifeless by the time he arrived. He took the parents into the room of the dead child and soon appeared with her, alive and well.

Our weeping turned to tears of joy and happiness. I shall remember that forever."

Blind from Birth

"My dear grandparents and father and mother of the human race, I am pleased to meet you. My name is not important, but I was the man who was blind from birth, given my sight by Jesus. Blind people would have perished from the earth if those with sight did not provide them some help. It was terrible being dependent upon others. People have their own burdens and are weary of the extra burden of caring for the blind. I had to sit and beg for food. I often found that it was the widows and the very poor who needed food themselves who gave the most generously.

"That is how I lived, and many times I wished I could die and not have to beg for a living. I lost my dignity and honor. Many would have been pleased if I had gone away and not bothered them anymore. What could I do? I was blind and not capable of earning a living. I did not have proper facilities to bathe often, and sitting in that dusty place I was also dirty. My clothes would become soiled and occasionally my mother would provide freshly-washed clothing, and then even that service made me feel more like a human being. Every day was the same. Some days I received enough money to add to the family's needs, but most days I did not collect anything. However, my parents managed to keep me alive.

"The day Jesus passed by, I did not know how my fortunes would change. A blind man sees with his ears, and I knew by the sounds that someone important was passing. I held out my cup hoping for someone to drop in a coin. That did not happen. They were discussing among themselves whether it was my parents or I who had sinned. I was embarrassed. I had not done anything wrong. I was born blind. My parents were very good people and certainly were good to me — caring for me as best they could. They could not support me forever, so they taught me to beg. What I brought home helped to feed me and my other family members sometimes.

"Jesus answered, 'Neither hath this man sinned, nor his parents: but that the works of God should be made manifest in him' (John 9:3). The next thing I knew someone was putting warm clay on my eyelids. I had heard of Jesus before, how he healed the sick and the lame, but never did I believe anyone could restore my sight. Yet this man spoke almost as an angel, saying, 'Go, wash in the pool of Siloam.' That was all. A good man led me to that pool, and when I washed my eyes were opened. I could see! It was a totally joyful shock. I could not believe it. Suddenly the world was full of light and beauty. There were people, flowers, trees and everything that I knew but couldn't even imagine were there. In a moment, I was made to see perfectly and I danced for joy.

"This caused a stir in the community. Those who knew me affirmed that indeed I had been the blind man at the gate. Others contested it. I told everyone what had happened, and how I had gained my sight. Then they brought me to the Pharisees. I thought they would share my joy in having sight. From the looks on their faces, I saw they were very disturbed. In all the years that I sat at the gate, never did one of these alleged holy men stop to talk to me, and I am not aware that any of them ever put a coin in my cup. They were actually dismayed that I had been healed. They said, 'This man is not of God, because he keepeth not the Sabbath day' (John 9:16). They wanted me to renounce Jesus. How could I do that? I was so blessed with sight, and suddenly I found myself being treated as a criminal. I could not believe what was happening.

"Most of the people I knew rejoiced with me. My parents were overjoyed. Now I was strong and could work hard to earn my bread with my own hands, and I knew I would earn enough to feed others also. I had a sense of dignity and purpose. These religious leaders kept questioning me, implying that the man who had healed me was a wicked man. I finally said, 'Whether he be a sinner or no, I know not: one thing I know, that, whereas I was blind, now I see' (John 9:25). I confessed my belief in Jesus no matter what others thought of him. I know now that Jesus was the 'seed' of promise. Unfortunately, I did not live long enough to become a consecrated follower of the Lamb. I died in an accident before Pentecost."

Moved by the Blind Man's Story

"The praise belongs to God. Jesus came only by God's mercy and grace," Adam said with tears in his eyes. "When the promise was given concerning 'the seed of the woman,' I thought that was strange. Why was it not 'my child' instead of being the 'seed of the woman?' We both puzzled over that. We did not know that God would use our daughter Mary to bring this child into the world. Now that we know the whole story, how beautiful it is."

The day passed while people lined up to tell their little stories about their contact with the Master. Everyone's heart burned as they listened to story after story of those who had their lives touched in some way by Jesus. As the day closed, the people still thronged about their first parents.

Lev said, "It is time for us to leave. I am sorry that all of you could not tell your stories. Remember, however, we have forever to fill in all the pieces. This was a glorious day, and I am sure our first parents were overwhelmed with your love and all the precious memories you shared. We must let them rest for the night. Tomorrow they will meet with those in Jerusalem, some of whom may have been the ones who managed to kill our Lord. So good night, 'The Lord bless thee, and keep thee: the Lord make his face shine upon thee, and be gracious unto thee: The Lord lift up his countenance upon thee, and give thee peace.'"

The Nazareth Chapel Meeting

The next morning Adam and Eve led the chapel services in Nazareth. The audience was most excited at having the origin of the human race standing before them. Other nearby chapels closed, and as many as possible were packed into this one. Speakers were placed outside and thousands took in the service standing or sitting on the grass around the building. Music was specially written for this occasion and was transporting.

Adam began the service. "Our hearts are full from yesterday. It was as though we lived in the days of the Master hearing your stories. However, last night I read Luke's account of Jesus' visit to Nazareth. I read how pleased you were to have him in your midst, and how soon after he refused to perform miracles for your gratification you wanted to cast him down headlong over the ledge of a hill (Luke 4:18-30). I was not surprised that no one mentioned this yesterday. I would have been ashamed to confess such conduct, too. We, your first parents, must also take our fair responsibility for opening the door to sin in this world. No sin can be considered small or insignificant. The smallest of sins leads to other sins, and soon it gets totally out of control. We know what it was like to be perfect, and how after we fell sin affected our lives. We opened the door to all the darkness, and we openly apologize for what we did. However, if we had not sinned, God's mercy and grace in all of its majesty might have been hidden from us. Little did we know that God would have to send His 'only begotten Son' into the world as a sin offering for us."

Eve joined in, "And as a result, we have the opportunity to learn about real love. Love can turn to hate in a moment. It is easy to love those who love us; sinners manage to do this quite well. To love those who do not love you in return and may persecute you takes the kind of love that Jesus showed. That is the kind of love we must all attain if we would be reconciled to God. When Adam read to me of how some were full of admiration for Jesus one moment and next they wanted to cast him over a cliff, I could see that sin was present in the human heart at all times. I must tell you, though, that originally we did not know what sin was. Never could we have imagined what we unleashed in this world. Christ managed to lift the judgment of death standing against us, and now we must with great effort remove sin from our hearts."

Everyone crowded around the first pair when the services ended to at least see them if they could not get close enough to personally greet them. People have always been fascinated with their roots, and nothing was more fascinating than meeting the source of human life.

Adam and Eve were leaving for the outskirts of Jerusalem, where they hoped to meet others who had known the Master, both those who loved him and those who had conspired to kill him. They would see the best and worst of what mankind was capable of doing in this visit.

Adam and Eve Set Down Outside of Jerusalem near Bethany

A crowd waited as Lev set his aircraft down in a scenic spot near Jerusalem. People pressed near to get their first look at the original human pair. As Adam and Eve stepped out of the plane, they waved to the crowds, accepting bouquets that were handed to them.

Eve said, "Thank you for your warm greetings. It is wonderful to be loved and appreciated. I am sad to come to this territory knowing that here, Jesus, who was the 'seed of the woman,' had been hated and crucified. We all know the story and we have not come to condemn anyone, but we are interested to know how the only man who was 'holy and harmless and separate from sinners' should come to be hated so savagely. All who have read those pages recording the Master's death have wept. It was so sad, so evil, so unacceptable, yet it has turned into our redemption. Only God could make something so wicked turn into the greatest blessing to mankind."

Adam stepped forward. "We wanted to meet and talk to those who knew Jesus while he walked here on earth. We want to talk to both those who loved him and to those who feared him and in jealousy wanted to kill him. We have not come to censure anyone, only to understand how righteousness and sin played out in the closing moments of his life. We spent yesterday learning of the love people felt for him. We know how sin operates, and we accept that our children inherited sin from us. We will be spending the day here and ask that any of you who knew Jesus, either his friends or his enemies, please come forth to tell us your story."

Caiaphas Tells His Unfortunate Story

Caiaphas, the former High Priest in Israel and largely responsible for Jesus' death, was standing far in the background. He was hoping to be unnoticed, but someone in the crowd shouted, "Here is Caiaphas, the former High Priest; maybe you would want to talk to him."

His face turned red, stunned that someone had betrayed his presence.

Adam waved to him, "Please come forward. Yes, we want to talk to you, Caiaphas."

Caiaphas couldn't escape, so with great embarrassment he came forward. "I am not sure that you want to see the likes of me."

"If you saw the Master, you must have some opinion about him now that is different from what it was before. Tell us, please, how you saw Jesus then and now," Adam requested.

"Well, I cannot justify myself or my previous conduct. As a matter of fact, I do not wish to be here, but I was singled out. You must understand that I did not know, nor did others know, that he was the 'Lord of glory.' If we had known who he was, we would not have crucified him. However, I came from a long line of the Aaronic Priesthood. That was an august and venerable office that continued in Israel until its overthrow. God through Moses instituted the Aaronic Priesthood, and we believed it would continue forever. We were jealous of anything that threatened our office. Needless to say, we saw Jesus as a threat.

"You know, only the Priests in Israel were authorized to make sacrifices for people's personal sins. This man, who was no son of Aaron, came along claiming to forgive sins. This was outrageous to us. Try as we would to find some fault with him, we could not match his wisdom and brilliance, which frustrated us even more. We sat in Moses' seat, and this man, only a carpenter's son, was going about the nation healing the sick, casting out demons, restoring sight to the blind, and causing the lame to walk. He outperformed and outshone us almost every day. The people loved him and thronged about him whenever he appeared among them. We were not loved, and probably we were not as lovable as we should have been. We represented a venerable tradition in carrying out the services of the Priests of the Temple. Yet, every day we realized we were sinking lower in the eyes of people, while this Jesus seemed to be growing in popularity."

Eve gently said, "We are not asking for a confession of any kind from you, Caiaphas. Forgiveness can only come from God in this matter. We can understand how you felt overshadowed by the Nazarene. Having said that, what could make you seek to have him crucified? You know crucifixion was an awful way to kill a man. Certainly, it was not God's method of putting anyone to death. Why would you use the terrible Roman method of torture?"

"When you ask the question that way, I am speechless. How can I justify it now, knowing that he was the very 'seed' of God's promise to you? I did not have to wait until I returned to life to realize something was wrong. Things in Jerusalem started to deteriorate soon after Jesus' death until the collapse of the Jewish nation in 70 A.D. I sensed that I had failed to live up to the ideals of the Jewish Priesthood. Since I have come to life, I have faced endless shame and contempt. Yet, my detractors do not know the positions that we occupied and that the power we had was being threatened. We were desperate. We could not outperform him, so the next best thing was to kill him."

Pilot Wanted to Release Jesus into Your Hands

Adam commented again. "Yes, but Pilate offered to turn him over to you to do with as you pleased. You could have stoned him to death, which was a more merciful death. Why didn't you accept Pilate's offer?"

"Remember, the crowds did not love us, whereas Jesus had many friends. If all the people he had helped and healed heard that we were to stone him to death, they would have thrown stones at us. We knew that. We needed the Romans to kill him. The people were afraid of the Romans. You know, Jesus stayed in Bethany during the week preceding his crucifixion. That is where he had raised Lazarus from the dead. The people there were completely behind Jesus. They would not have allowed us to take him away to be stoned. However, no one dared lift a hand against the Roman soldiers, because you could be crucified for that. That is why we took the course we did."

Eve then said, "This is the saddest news to us. Why did you have to take matters into your own hands? Didn't you believe in God? How could you do such vile things to the Son of God? I am so appalled! You knew what you were doing was wrong, but all that mattered to you was to hold on to your power and office, which you lost anyway. Doesn't it seem strange that the High Priest of God could be so out of harmony with God so as to kill His dear Son?"

"You are correct, dear Mother, but speaking with hindsight. You are in the same situation as I am. If you had known what evils would follow eating the forbidden fruit, would you have eaten it anyway? I am sure you would not! If I had known the Jewish Priesthood was ending with Jesus' death, and that he was making an offering of himself that could forever take away sin, we would not have done as we did. We crucified him in ignorance. I am not saying that we were not guilty or that our hearts were pure in this matter. We sinned greatly. Please understand, we were bitterly punished for what we did. We are still kept out of power or any influence."

An Unfair Comparison

Eve remonstrated, "It's not fair to compare my sin with yours. I was absolutely ignorant of evil. You, on the other hand, were seeking to have a man crucified, one of the cruelest ways that a man can die. You knew what you were asking for in seeking his death. Not even a dog should suffer that way, yet you conspired to secure this cruelest of all deaths. It makes me shudder!"

"I am sorry, my dear Mother. You are right. Our sins aren't comparable except that neither of us knew where our sins would lead."

Adam stepped in again. "Tell us, you saw the man Christ Jesus. How did he look and what kind of man was he?"

"I must tell you the truth. He was absolutely handsome with not a blemish of any kind. He was soft-spoken and very intelligent. We were doctors of the law and well studied in the Scriptures, but never could we prevail in any discussion with him. We engaged our brightest lawyers to catch him in some misstatement, but every attempt was futile. Even at his trial, Jesus was in command. When we made a mistake, he spoke up and embarrassed us for our violations of the law. At times, when he could easily have secured his freedom, he said nothing. He was a man in total control of himself at all times. How much we envied him! We were driven by our fears and jealousy, but Jesus had an empire over his passions. I now know that he allowed us to secure his death. He could easily have secured his freedom before Herod or Pilate. He fulfilled what the Scriptures prophesied of him."

Adam said, "You have had plenty of time to think about this matter. Is it true that many of the priests who demanded his death became followers of Jesus?"

"Yes, it is true that many of the 'priests were obedient to the faith' (Acts 6:7). We found we were arguing amongst ourselves endlessly. His death did not bring us peace or security. Soon, large numbers left our priesthood to join Jesus' disciples. While Jesus lived, he had no more than five hundred followers, but after he died thousands became his disciples, including many priests. He was still winning, and we were falling apart. We tried to stop his disciples from preaching, but they were unstoppable. When we persecuted them at Jerusalem, they simply scattered abroad like burning brands of fire, spreading their gospel as they went. Christianity was triumphing. We tried to kill it, but it would not die. Even Saul, one of our most gifted sons, became a turncoat to the Jewish faith and joined the Christians. He became a thorn in our side, for he was too brilliant for us to meet in open discussion. Nothing went well for us after we killed Jesus. We are to be pitied more than hated."

"Seed of Promise" Killed

Eve sensed that Caiaphas was not showing a repentant spirit but only admitting what he could not deny. She said, "I am not sure that you feel any remorse for what you did, Caiaphas, but are merely acknowledging the inevitable. Your sorrow seems to be that you lost and that your treatment of the Son of God brought no advantage to you or your cause. No one deserved to be treated as Jesus was, not even the worst criminal. It was cruel and inhumane, even diabolical. I feel a righteous anger that my own offspring should have deliberately killed my child."

"I understand your anger, Mother Eve. However, it was prophesied that the Son of Man would be lifted up as the serpent in the wilderness upon a pole. Then he would draw all men unto him. So, we were merely actors on the stage at that time. You must know that we were punished and so were our descendants. We paid for our crime, so please do not expect us to pay it again."

Adam quickly interjected, "We are not involved with punishment of any kind. We, too, were punished as were our children for our crime. The punishment endured is sufficient. Anyway, that belongs to God and not to us. What we love to see in those who erred grievously is godly repentance and a will to write a new chapter in their lives demonstrating a love of God and of humanity. It is easy to find nice words that do not indicate the right condition of heart or mind. Obviously, you did not love God if you did not love His Son. It cannot be otherwise. Love for God would have prevented your wicked and ruthless conduct. Even a little compassion and kindness in your heart would have prevented you from taking the course you did. You must have been open to the suggestions of Satan to do what you did."

Poor Caiaphas! His face turned ashen. He had tried unsuccessfully to make his conduct appear as one of those unfortunate human mistakes. Regrettably, his explanations bordered on hypocrisy and an unwillingness to accept the enormity of his responsibility. He threw up his hands as he left, saying, "I had hoped for a happier meeting, and I am sorry you found me such an unworthy child. Shalom."

Martha's and Mary's Friend Recalls Jesus

An adoring audience thronged Adam and Eve. A woman appeared that had been a neighbor and friend of Mary, Martha, and Lazarus

(John 11:1-44). "I was there consoling Mary and Martha when her brother had died. I knew they had sent for Jesus seeking his help when Lazarus fell ill. Much to their sorrow, Jesus did not come until after Lazarus had been dead four days. When news that Jesus and his disciples had come at last, it gladdened everyone's heart, because Jesus was such a strong and comforting figure at all times. I went with Mary where we met Jesus. His disciples and a crowd of people were gathered around him.

"The crowd opened to let Mary come to Jesus, for they knew if anyone could comfort her, it was he. I held Mary's arm as she fell at Jesus' feet, saying, 'Lord, if you had been here, my brother would not have died.' She sobbed so filled with sorrow that all the women and even some of the men had tears running down their cheeks. I noticed, too, that Jesus wept. He was very sympathetic. Most people realized that Jesus loved this family. His tears ran down his beautiful face to his beard. Someone gave him a small cloth to dry his tears. Then he asked, 'Where have you laid him?'

"The crowd knew that Jesus had performed many miracles, but no one believed that he could raise a man who had been dead four days — no, not even Martha. When he arrived at the tomb and commanded the men to roll away the stone, a hushed silence fell over the crowd. It was so quiet that only a songbird was heard singing in the trees near the tomb. Then with a loud voice he said, 'Lazarus, come forth!' Everyone watched with pent-up emotion. Could this man actually call forth the dead? Suddenly Lazarus, wrapped in his grave clothes, appeared at the door of the tomb. Everyone was dumbfounded. Then Jesus said, 'Loose him and let him go.'

"Mary ran to embrace her brother and Martha followed. A cheer went up from the crowd. The tears that flowed because of death were turned to tears of joy and gladness. Little did we know that this same Jesus, in his resurrection glory, would one day call each of us forth from the grave; and never did we expect you, our dear first parents who were dead for thousands of years, to come forth and stand before us as at this day.

"When news of Lazarus was heralded about, friends and neighbors came from all over the community of Bethany. They brought food of all kinds and soon an open-air banquet was held for this man who could raise the dead. Jesus mingled easily with the crowds, but seldom spoke. When he did speak, everyone immediately quieted so they could hear him. Never did a man speak as this man, and never did any man have power over death as he. I never forgot that day—it is engraved in my mind and heart. If I could only re-create those few hours spent with him that day so you could share it with those of us who were there, I should be thankful, my dear first parents."

"You have turned that moment into one we can share," Eve assured her. "That is why we came here today, to hear those touched by Jesus' life in some way. It is more wonderful to have living people tell of their moments with the Master than reading it from records. You shared that beautiful moment in time with us, and its magic burns within our hearts. Thank you."

A Money-Changer in the Temple Testifies

Another man asked to speak to the supreme patriarch and matriarch of the human family. Having secured permission, he began, "My name is not important. I must tell you about Jesus. That is what you wanted to hear and he is the one of whom I shall speak. I was a money-changer in the temple. We had a very lucrative business, and we took advantage of our situation, charging unreasonable rates for our services. We could do that because people came from many nations to Jerusalem with different currencies. We would exchange their money so they could buy animals to sacrifice and pay for the temple services. We, of course, had to pay the former High Priest Annas handsome royalties for our privileges. He dismissed us of our privileges if he suspected we had cheated him out of a coin. We had to account carefully for all our dealings; otherwise he would thrust us out of the temple.

"I was doing a fine business one day when a handsome young man entered, wearing a pure white robe. People thronged around him, and instantly I realized this must be Jesus. I must have stared at him rudely, but I could not take my eyes off of the majestic man. He strode directly toward my table, and standing before it he cried, 'My house shall be called a house of prayer; but ye have made it a den of thieves' (Matthew 21:13). I was frightened, for he looked angry and I had always heard that he was gentle and kind. To my utter dismay, he grabbed my table and overturned it, spilling my money all over the floor.

"Normally, I would have been worried about collecting my money, but I just stood there speechless and frightened. I would have been furious if someone else had done this to my table, but I wasn't angry. He then drove out our animals and no one even tried to stop him. The crowds cheered him. They knew we really were thieves of a sort. I always knew in my heart it was an unsavory business, but that day I realized I was part of a corrupt system. Jesus' words burned into my mind. Others helped collect my coins, but for the first time I had lost interest in them. When I went home that evening, I told my wife what had happened and that I could no longer work there. She worried, 'How will you make a living then? We have it so good, why would you give up your station?'

"I told her, 'I don't know how I am going to make my living, but when Jesus overturned my table, I knew I was guilty of sin against God. I cannot return. Somehow, the Lord will provide. I will work honestly to make my living. Other men do, so I can, too.'

"That day the Master changed my life. Yes, I was guilty of being a thief in the house of prayer. Those words have never left me, and thankfully it changed my life."

Adam responded, "My son, that kind of testimony warms my heart. You did not try to rationalize your situation, but seeing it was wrong you stepped out boldly in faith to do the right thing. Tell me, did you go hungry or did your family go hungry for taking the right step?"

"No, I was able to earn an honest living by hard work and stepping down from our high lifestyle. I was no longer tormented by the visions of poor people that I exploited. They say, 'the poor man's bread is always sweeter,' and it was true. I did not become his follower, but he helped me change my course in life. Later when the temple was destroyed, I was spared by living outside of Judea."

A Former Chief Ruler Speaks Up

Next a distinguished man stepped out of the crowd wishing to speak to Adam and Eve about his experience with Jesus.

"If I may, my dear first parents, I have a sad confession to make. I sat in a position of power and influence in Judea. I had many friends like myself who heard Jesus speak and saw the wonderful miracles he performed. I believed in him. However, hear my confession. I was a weak man, one without courage. For fear of the Pharisees, I did not confess him out of concern of being put out of the synagogue (John 12:42). The Pharisees were very powerful. If I had followed my heart, I would have followed Jesus, but I did not have the courage to stand up for what I knew was right.

"If my powerful friends and I had stood up for Jesus, the Pharisees might have been forced to treat Jesus more fairly. Actually, they were very much like us being more fearful than courageous. However, they outnumbered us and we found that intimidating. To be put out of the synagogue would have been to suffer financially. We were successful merchants, but we depended on the common people who attended the synagogues for our business. I hate myself for being such a coward. I knew he was the Messiah of promise. I loved to hear him speak. He did not force himself upon anyone, yet when I heard him and saw him, I knew without question that he was one sent of God. I must confess with tears my failure to be the man I should have been."

Eve spoke comfortingly to him. "Well, at least you are honest, if not courageous. However, now is the time we must all be courageous. Let others do what they will, but those who love the Master must be loyal to him. We can no longer yield but must stand up to be counted for what is right and what is true. While at the moment that may be easy—for truth is all that is available now—the time is coming when Satan will be let out of the abyss, and undoubtedly he will assail the truth and make error appealing. Courage will once again be a necessary virtue to overcome in the final test."

"Yes, yes, dear Mother, weak men have been known to be courageous when motivated to be so. If I have learned anything from my former life, it is that I cannot dodge my responsibility because of fear. I lost everything when Jerusalem fell—my life and that of my family. The Christians fled from Jerusalem before its fall. When I spoke to them, they warned me to flee the city with them, but I lacked the courage. I thought, how could I give up my business, and how would I make my living as a vagabond in strange places. For my cowardice, ultimately my family and I perished. The first time, I spared myself grief by not showing the courage I should have. The second time, I lost my life for lack of courage. Yes, you are right. Every person must be courageous for the truth and for righteousness."

The Infirm Man Made Whole

Soon another man stepped out of the crowd surrounding our first parents. "May I tell you my story about the Master?"

Adam replied, "Nothing would please us more."

"I was the infirm man who tried for thirty-eight years to be healed. I would have someone take me to the pool of Bethesda, hoping that I could be first into the water after an angel supposedly stirred it up, as the legend had it. I saw the waters stirred many times, but I was lame and could not reach the pool for others managed to get there first. One day I was lying there, probably looking hopeless and sad, and a stranger appeared. At the moment, I did not know who he was, but soon afterward I learned it was Jesus. He asked, 'Wilt thou be made whole?' I explained my sad efforts these many years. Then Jesus said, 'Rise, take up thy bed, and walk' (John 5:6-8). I felt a surge of energy in my body and suddenly strength came into my feet, and I could get up and walk. Strangely, not having walked for so long, I was afraid to take a step, knowing that I had forgotten how to walk. However, Jesus commanded me to walk, and to my surprise I had the strength in my legs to rise, and then I was able to walk without stumbling or falling. You have no idea how overjoyed I was. He told me to take up my bed and to my amazement I could do that also.

"Everything would have gone well, except some Jews saw me carrying my bed on the Sabbath day. They said it was not lawful to be doing that. They did not seem to care that I was able to walk again, but only that I was carrying my bed on the Sabbath. I explained that the man who healed me told me to do what I was doing. That did not matter to them. The law was the law and that was that—I was breaking the law! They wanted to know who it was that issued those instructions to me; but truthfully at the time, I did not know. I thought for a moment that they were going to stone me, but I knew their anger was directed toward the one who healed me. However, later I met this same man Jesus in the temple. He said to me, 'Behold, thou art made whole: sin no more, lest a worse thing come unto thee' (John 5:14). That proved to me this man was a prophet, or more than a prophet, for he knew how I came to be lame.

"I thought that now I knew who it was that healed me that I would tell the Jews, thinking they would respect this great man of God. However I learned, to my dismay, that they persecuted Jesus because of the healing he had done for me, and that they really wanted to kill him. I could not believe it! No one cared that I lay lame for so long and was suddenly healed. Some of these same people had given me alms through all the long years of my infirmity. I could not understand why they could not enter into my joy. If they had a son or daughter healed, it might have meant something to them, but me? I meant nothing at all. I knew that I meant something to Jesus. Here was a man of great compassion and love. One thing about Jesus was that once you saw him, you never forgot him."

A Little Window Opened

Eve commented, "Thank you! Your life opened a little window for us to see Jesus. Every story we hear of him thrills our hearts. It is not that we do not know him. Actually, we knew him in Eden. The Logos was the spokesman of the Lord, the Word of God, that would visit us every evening. That was always the brightest part of our day. He had an angelic form, but he was a treasure house of knowledge. Everything we wanted to know he would explain to us. If we asked what he was not authorized to reveal, he would simply tell us that. He was so gentle with us. The only time we were uncomfortable with him was after we had sinned. And that was our last visit with him. That is what we missed most when we were driven out of Eden. Of course, we also missed the fruit."

The man who had been lame said, "Having tasted of the trees of life, the perfect food God made to perfectly fulfill our needs, we would all miss eating that fruit if it were taken from us."

Eve agreed, "Yes, I couldn't believe it when the angel with a flaming sword motioned to us that we must leave our beautiful home. We found common trees with which the world is familiar outside of Eden, and we ate vegetables and certain herbs so our stomachs were full, but we were not happy. Thank you for telling us about our Son of promise. We know we will never see him, but we savor every story that acquaints us with his loving heart."

Going to Golgotha with the Soldier Who Helped Crucify Jesus

The following day, Lev took them to see where Jesus was crucified, which was called Golgotha, the place of the skull. Adam and Eve wanted to place a wreath of flowers there. They had watched scenes of the crucifixion the night before, and as they left early that morning with the wreath, a large crowd followed them. The mood was solemn as they walked the via Del la Rosa, slowly contemplating each heavy step of the way.

The morning was very quiet, far different from the day when Jesus had carried his cross. Some in the crowds had wept for Jesus, but others had jeered and mocked him. Because he was so weak from the beatings he had received, Jesus began falling under his heavy cross.

The soldiers beat him mercilessly, urging him forward. Finally they realized he was not feigning his weakness; he could not bear the load. Then they seized Simon of Cyrene to help Jesus bear his cross.

It was an ugly business the soldiers were in, and no sensitive human being could do this grisly work. The crowd followed Adam and Eve, sharing their tears as they relived the saddest day of human history. They arrived where the cross was now known to have been, for one soldier who had crucified Jesus was there to identify the spot. Eve laid the wreath of flowers on the location while her eyes filled with tears. They knelt in prayer, as did everyone who followed their first parents that morning.

After they arose, the soldier who had crucified Jesus said, "My dear Mother and Father, I am ashamed to tell you that I was the one who drove the nails into his hands and feet. I have tried to stay away from this place. However, knowing you would be here, I had to come and tell you who I was. I had crucified many people, and I thought this was going to be just another day in my grim work. I never allowed myself much emotion. With the two criminals, it was business as usual. One never really got used to doing this gruesome task. The Romans knew it was dehumanizing for soldiers, so they wouldn't keep us on this assignment too long. Most men hated it.

Jesus Was Different

"When it was time to nail Jesus to the cross, he was different from the others who would struggle with us, trying to avoid being nailed. He just laid down and put his arms and legs in the proper place, not even pulling his hands or feet back from the nails. I didn't understand how he could have such control over his movements. The body naturally recoils at the pain, but he only groaned without resisting. It was like killing a helpless lamb, and I had a very strange reaction to it. Usually the criminals we crucified would try to strike us or wrestle with us to avoid being nailed to the cross. I can't say that I blamed them. Jesus, however, didn't resist or vilify us but quietly accepted the torture.

"From that moment, I knew Jesus was extraordinary. I was in the army, so I knew about death and cruelty. I saw men suffer and die, but never did I see a man such as Jesus. It almost seemed to me that he took charge of his own death. I wondered why this man was so hated. He had done nothing wrong. No one reviled the two thieves on either side of Jesus. I am sure they felt even as I did, 'Poor fellows, they are paying a supreme price for their crimes.' No one deserved this kind of death. But with Jesus it was different. The crowds taunted, spat upon him, made sport of him, and would not allow him the dignity every human deserves. We soldiers could not do our task with compassion. We had to strengthen one another in our cruelty.

"However, at noon the sun grew dark, and an eerie feeling crept over us. We knew Jesus was not a criminal. We had heard that this man had healed the sick, given sight to the blind, and had even raised the dead, and we worried that heaven might break out in fury against us. Why would such a man as this be hanging on a cross? The soldier who had taken Jesus' robe was very nervous. We were superstitious in those days and worried that some curse would come upon us.

Jesus Died Suddenly

"He died at three o'clock in the afternoon and that was very uncommon. Usually, men lasted up to three days on the cross, and this frightened us even more. Because of the Jewish law that no one could be on the cross on the Sabbath day, which was the next day, we had to take the victims down. It was customary to break the victim's legs, and Pilate gave us permission to do that; but because Jesus was dead, we did not break his legs. Actually, this was to fulfill the scripture, 'A bone of him shall not be broken' (John 19:36). I was glad that I didn't have to break his legs even though he was dead. Breaking the legs of anyone was cruel beyond words, especially for those who had already been brutalized with excruciating pain. After a day like this, our custom was to numb our brains with drink.

"However, when Jesus died there was an earthquake, and later we learned the Temple curtain had been rent in two. That day, everyone who left the crucifixion scene was beating their breasts because of the horror of it all, and even the centurion said, 'Truly this man was the Son of God' (Mark 15:39). Somehow I could not do what I normally did on that horrible day. I did not go and get drunk with my fellow soldiers. I spent several sleepless nights recalling events of that day. I realized I had become brutalized and asked for removal from that branch of service in the army. My captain thought I was foolish, for I was already an older soldier and could not compete anymore on the battlefield. Whatever my risks, I could not stay in what was supposed to be an easy station.

No One Should Be Employed in Crucifixion

"I want to express to you, my first parents, my humble apology for what I was forced to do to your very special Son. Men should never have had a job like mine. I hate myself for it. Every memory of that day fills me with anguish. If I did not know that the Savior we crucified that day was now exalted to spiritual glory and reigning over earth as our Lord and King, I would be terribly oppressed in mind and heart. However, he has forgiven me, bringing me back to life. That is how he has repaid me for my cruelty to him. Can you also forgive me?"

Adam replied, "If Christ has forgiven you, there remains nothing for us to forgive. Thank you for sharing your heart with us. We intend to learn every piece of information we can obtain from all who knew the Savior. Not only so, we want to learn of his disciples that followed in his footsteps. However, we have eternity to do that, but this day was a blessed beginning in our search to come as close to our son in his life on earth as possible. We yearned for this day, not realizing how sad and tragic it would be. Yet he died for our sins and is now a satisfaction for the sins of the whole world. From this saddest of all stories comes a very beautiful ending. None of us deserves such kindness."

Adam placed his hand on the soldier's shoulder. "My son, I know you will never be employed in anything evil again. Annas and Caiaphas would not have done what they did if they had to personally crucify Jesus. It was easier to get Pilate to do it, who, in turn, had you do it.

And now you are left with haunting memories. I am afraid I began the chain of evil, and it was because of my sin that Christ died at your hands that day."

The day ended with many stories and many tears, both of sorrow and of joy. One thing was certain—happiness was not going to end or ever be diminished.

"For a day in thy courts is better than a thousand"
(Psalm 84:10).

Chapter Fifteen

The following day had been set aside for Adam and Eve to spend with their most honored sons and daughters at Jerusalem—the Ancient Worthies. It was to be a festive day like the others, with the whole world looking on at this venerable assembly of humans who had pleased God.

Abel welcomed his mother and father. "I would like to introduce everyone here personally to you, but that will have to wait until later. I have had to limit the time you can spend with the generations that led up to your beloved son, Jesus. These are the men and women whom God honored to be of the royal line that would lead to Christ. Not all are Ancient Worthies who are in the lineage of Christ, but many are, and it is these you will meet.

"First, let me introduce Noah and his former wife. They, like you, were the forebearers of the race of mankind after the flood." Noah and his wife came to Adam and Eve and greeted them each with a holy kiss.

Adam greeted them with sincere appreciation. "My dear ones, you saved the world from extinction, for God saw you were righteous and allowed you to save what was salvageable of that old wicked world. God bless you! Your task of building an ark was enormous, and only the Lord could have prospered your work. I know you preached righteousness in a world that scorned it, but that is why you are here today among those most worthy of mankind."

Abel continued, "Noah and his wife had three sons and daughters-in-law, but only Shem followed the bloodline to Christ. He was the one that secured that holy genealogy and passed it on for the Holy Record, the Bible."

The Next Holy Generation

Eve addressed Shem, "Bless you, my son, and your dear wife. You carried the torch of life to the next holy generation."

Abel then introduced Abraham and Sarah, the father and mother of the faithful believers. "It was to these two people that God confirmed his promise seven times, finally swearing by an oath, 'And in thy seed shall all the nations of the earth be blessed' (Genesis 22:18)."

Eve sparkled with enthusiasm. "Yes, this was following the line that would lead up to the 'seed of the woman' — through Mary to Christ. I know of your life of faith and devotion! God bless you forever!"

"And now I present to you Isaac, the child of promise born to Sarah and Abraham. And here is his former wife, Rebekah. The promises made to Abraham were confirmed to Isaac. They knew that through their bloodlines would come the promised Christ."

Adam smiled warmly. "God be praised for giving us such a blessed family. I thank you for never forgetting the promised 'seed.'"

"Next I present to you Jacob, the Father of the nation of Israel who had twelve sons."

Eve responded, "It is an unspeakable joy to meet the father of that great nation, Israel, but more importantly, the father of Judah, from whom the royal Son would come."

"I present to you Salmon and Rahab in the royal lineage. Rahab joined God's people after Jericho fell. Her faith saved her from destruction and preserved her to be a mother in the lineage of Christ."

Adam said, "Bless you, Rahab, for being a heroine of faith. God rewarded your faith not only by saving your life, but honored you with being of the royal line and has given you a place among the Worthies."

Ruth the Moabite

"Here are Ruth and Boaz among your honored descendants," Abel said. "Ruth gained the privilege of being of this royal line by faith. She left Moab to be with her mother-in-law, Naomi, and married Boaz to give us Obed, and Obed gave us Jesse, and finally, Jesse gave us David, to whom God promised a King upon his throne forever."

Adam said, "God has blessed your faith, Ruth, to become a part of the royal lineage. Welcome, my Daughter, to the hall of the faithful."

"I now give you David, who is of the royal line and of the Ancient Worthies. He needs no introduction, only to say that he was a man after God's own heart."

David seized the moment to kiss both parents of the human race. "Oh, this day is so blessed! We toiled without ceasing to hasten it, and now that you are here in our midst, we intend to honor you for being the father and mother of us all. We have all this wonderful food to celebrate your presence with us. As we eat and share God's bounties, there will be time for personal fellowship. This is only a small beginning. One day, I hope you both live to meet and hold each of your children in your arms, for you are the father and mother of us all. Thank you. After the prayer of blessing on the food, an orchestra will play music honoring this great occasion while we continue our fellowship."

The day proved a beautiful experience for their first parents. To actually meet the people who eventually brought the promised Christ child into the world was thrilling. It was so gratifying to know that some of their children actually pleased God even while around them the world degenerated.

That evening, they told Lev they wished to end their last day of the world celebration visiting one of the World War II death camps in Poland. Adam said, "We have today seen the best, and now we are prepared to see the worst. Can you take us to Auschwitz? We understand they still have this site intact as an odious memorial of man's inhumanity to man. We know it is painful, but we wish to see firsthand how evil, once enthroned, seems to have no limits to depravity."

Lev agreed, "Yes, I will secure passage to the former Poland on a large aircraft. Once there, we can use a small craft."

"Thank you, Lev. We are too new in this world to find our way around by ourselves. It is still a blur to us."

"Well, thank you for the honor. The whole human race has labored and dreamed of this day, and now that you have arrived, those dreams have been realized."

Some of Your Children Served the Devil

"I must warn you, what you are going to see will tear your heart out," Lev continued. "It is hard to believe that some of your children turned out so noble and others seemed to be in league with the devil. I have often thought about this, and it is very difficult to understand. The people that did these atrocities were not savages steeped in ignorance and superstition, but supposedly intelligent, educated men and women. I do believe you should see Auschwitz, because it will round out your education on what happened while you were in the grave. It was a blessing for you to sleep through those evil years when men carried out a diabolical scheme to destroy Jacob's children. Of course it failed, as has every evil scheme, but that did not end the attempt of the world to destroy Jacob's children. It was in my day that the final attempt was made to destroy us and wrest the land from God's chosen people to try to prevent God's Kingdom from being established on the earth. However, no one can prevail against God."

"Yes," Adam acknowledged. "We are getting a fast education, but we are gratified to see that most of our children prefer good to evil and will make serious sacrifices to stop it."

"True! The great majority are good and decent people who are distressed with evil. However, if you start teaching children hatred and a willingness to die in killing those they have been taught to hate, you can train people to be very evil. Religion has been used notoriously in this way. In the worship of false gods such as Baal and Chemosh, people sacrificed their children. The same conditions apply when parents teach their children to destroy themselves for God's glory. This is the sad state of things that went on in the world."

Lev continued, "I believe there is a flight before noon, so you will need to be ready to leave by nine in the morning. Shalom."

The next morning, Adam and Eve were ready at the appointed time, and Lev flew them to the Jerusalem airport. When they arrived, a crowd was at the airport to greet them. Their celebrity status was well deserved, and what could be more exciting than to greet the original parents of the human race? Additionally, being both very near to human perfection and bearing their original likeness, they were exceptionally beautiful. People wanted to see them personally as well as talk to them.

As they approached their plane, the crowd thronged around them. One person asked loudly, "Tell us, are you disappointed to have us as your children?"

Eve answered with her usual charm and bright countenance. "No, because all children are God's gift. We love you."

A Solemn Protest

That brought loud applause. Adam waved his hand for everyone's attention. "We are traveling to Poland to visit Auschwitz. That will be a sad visit for us. We have had joyful visits everywhere, but we felt we must go there as a solemn protest to what some of our children did. From what I have heard, I can hardly believe that those who did these things were a part of the human race. Possibly they sold themselves to the devil during those terrible days. At any rate, though it may break our hearts, we are going there to see and to feel what some of our dear children experienced. Certainly, when we disobeyed God, we never dreamed that such things would be possible. God bless you, our children."

They turned and boarded the plane. As they entered the aircraft, the flight attendants presented them with flowers and the promise of a piece of resurrection cake and tea for everyone on the flight. The trip was short, but everyone was thrilled to share it with Adam and Eve. Lev sat by them to answer their questions, because they were rather lost with all the modern wonders.

They soon arrived in Poland without incident and with Adam and Eve being thoroughly fascinated by modern technology. They had envied birds flying about before, and now they flew great distances in just a little more than an hour's time. This was incredible for two people who had only walked before.

As they disembarked, another large enthusiastic crowd greeted them. When they learned their destination, some said, "Why do you want to see such an awful place? That will only bring you sleepless nights and sadness."

Eve answered, "Yes, we understand that. However, it is our children that died in these death camps. We are determined to feel the pain of our flesh and blood. We must stand as monuments against such treatment. Obviously, most people did not like what was happening, but the death machine intimidated them."

As promised, Lev acquired a smaller aircraft, and soon they were on their way to Auschwitz.

When they stepped out of the aircraft, Adam said to those gathered to greet them, "Thank you for being here. Eve and I have landed feeling great sorrow and anguish of mind for what happened in the death camps. Forgive us for not being joyful this day. We have come to honor those who died here."

Anna Lebowitz Offers to Be Their Guide

Lev carried a beautiful wreath of flowers that Eve would place by the now quiet incinerators. The crowd, sensing the sobriety, quieted and no one spoke. However, one lady came up saying, "My name is Anna Lebowitz. May I be your guide? My children and I died here."

"Yes, by all means," Adam replied. "There is nothing like having someone who was here to tell us the facts."

"Let me show you the boxcars we came in, traveling in stifling heat in the summer." They walked to the tracks at the entrance of the camp.

"These cars were filled with people allowing standing room only. There were no facilities for humans, and no one could lie down. The cars smelled from human waste, and people who fainted did not fall but were held up by others. We received no food or water and traveled for parts of three days. A woman gave birth to a child in our car; it was grievous because the baby was doomed to die. Our feet ached from standing; we were thirsty, hungry, and exhausted from lack of sleep. Some died on the way, not being able to survive such treatment. This was 'Nazi efficiency.' When we arrived, we were told to leave our belongings at the landing site and they would be taken care of for us. We never saw them again."

They walked through the iron gates that connected triple electrified fences topped with barbed wire and adorned with the ironic camp motto: *"Arbeit Macht Frei"* (Work Brings Freedom). Taking them to the brick block buildings, she continued.

"We were then marched to these dormitories where the men and women were separated. We shed our soiled garments and were given coarse, striped pajamas. We received water to drink and a dry, moldy crust of bread and were allowed to rest in the flea-infested bunks. We were so tired that we could have slept anywhere. The next day, we were roused at about four o'clock in the morning and forced to appear before the Nazi officers who decided who would live and who would die. Women with small children were sent in one direction, and the strong unencumbered ones would go in the other direction. The aged, infirmed, and women with children were marked for death in the gas chambers and then incineration. It was cruel, but efficient.

"Those who first went to the gas chambers were told they would be taking a shower and were told to disrobe. To prevent hysteria, they had forced a few Jewish musicians to play pleasant music. No one would think they were being sent to a gas chamber. People could not believe what was happening, even though they sensed something was wrong.

"Once inside the chamber, the doors were slammed shut. Gas was then dropped into these chambers, and the people would panic, piling up by the door trying to escape from this horrible acrid gas. When enough time passed to kill everyone, they would open the chambers, and Jewish workers dragged the bodies with hooks to the incinerators. But first, they would break out all gold teeth and fillings, cut off hair, and then fill the incinerators with bodies, sending up the stacks the black-stinking smoke.

"The most unfortunate ones were those selected to serve for medical experiments. They were sent to an insane doctor to become live experiments. I shall not tell you about them only to say that no anesthesia was used, and the basest of acts were committed in these medical halls of shame."

Piles of Children's Clothing

Passing down the halls of memorabilia, Anna showed them piles of shoes and clothing—including children's—all piled up and left as a memorial to those who lost their lives at Auschwitz.

"Yes, there is even a room of human hair, one of suitcases, and another of eyeglasses. Every person who was allowed to live and labor was tattooed with a code number on his or her arm. Now all of these victims have returned to life with vivid memories of how they were cruelly and unjustly put to death. The perpetrators of these crimes and the victims have not had an easy time being reconciled, although many have."

Eve sobbed quietly, and most visitors were either drying their tears or trying to hold them back. Anna continued, "This was the most carefully orchestrated killing process ever conceived by man. To accomplish this, seeds of hatred had been sown and nurtured. The victims were dehumanized so that they were not considered worthy members of the human race. Of course, the devil, who is now in the abyss, was the father of the whole diabolical process. I hope everyone realizes he will one day be freed to deceive the world again. But only those who sympathize with sin will hear him."

They soon arrived at the gas chambers that had been rigged up with a phony shower apparatus—a decoy to lend credence to the thought that they would be having a nice warm shower. The guard towers still stood as ominous silhouettes, and the little stand where the musicians played was retained. Their only escape had been up the black smokestacks. Anna said, "The guards watched day after day as new groups of victims were sent to their death. That was their job, and they did it meticulously. Compassion or kindness was closed out of their hardened minds and hearts."

Arriving at the gas incinerators, they saw how this ingenious system cremated the corpses of millions. Bone fragments, ashes and soot were all that remained. The Nazis had hoped all traces of their victims would be obliterated, but now everyone had returned to life. What was done in darkness was now being shouted from the housetops.

Both Adam and Eve kneeled before an incinerator, and all the company did likewise. Lev handed Eve the beautiful wreath of flowers that she laid at the door of the incinerator. Adam prayed, saying for all to hear, "Dear Heavenly Father, we are bowed in grief and sorrow trying in vain to understand the depths of evil that took place. We cannot and will not forget such depravity and wickedness. We lift up our hearts in thanksgiving that You have brought to life every individual who was destroyed. Praise be to Christ for the great work of regenerating the whole human race. And now, in your tender mercy, may the work of reconciling the perpetrators of these evils with the endless list of victims be carried out to completion. Give those who suffered, a compassionate heart of mercy, and those who participated in this awesome destruction a heart of true repentance and godly sorrow. And please give the victims the courage and compassion to forgive. In Jesus' name we pray. Amen."

They all arose still unable to comprehend the enormity of it all. Only God and Christ knew each life lost and faithfully returned everyone. If this tragedy were not followed by the resurrection of the dead, how hopeless and sad it would have been. Thank God, however, that life had triumphed over death, righteousness over evil, and joy over sorrow. Yes, the ransomed of the Lord had returned with "songs and everlasting joy upon their heads" as it was foretold: "and sorrow and sighing shall flee away" (Isaiah 35:10).

A Sorrowful Education

As they turned to leave, Adam said, "We knew that we had to come to this place when we heard of it. Being here today gave us an education in how far sin had gone in destroying the image of God in the human heart. It all seems unreal and we could wish it were only a bad dream that would go away once we awoke. However, the site must remain a monument forever, so that everyone may remember this grim reality. Thank you, Anna, for reliving those darkest moments of human history with us."

They left with an unusual sense of sobriety, deeply impressed by the grim scenes of that dark time when inflamed passions of hatred precipitated such beastly orgies of death. Why and how could such things have taken place in an intelligent and knowledgeable society? How comforting it was to know that God would reveal the hidden things of darkness and make known the counsels of the heart!

They returned that evening to the airport having cruised over the beautiful land that hid its scars from human eyes. The following morning, they took a flight back to Israel where Lev had left his aircraft, and from there to Eden. From the air they could see the huge surge of water coming up from the earth and dividing into four rivers, all as pure as crystal. As they landed, Adam and Eve were glad to be home. They had enjoyed their two weeks of visiting with their children in various places, but it was still true, "there is no place like home."

They asked Lev to stay and serve as an instructor for them to learn to use all the modern tools for gathering information. They were fascinated with the television and computer educational potential. Adam said, "Lev, we have a great deal of catching up to do. The world has changed so very much. The curse of working from dawn until dark has been lifted, and now we may settle into the seemingly magical experience of technology and education. I must learn modern writing, the Bible, secular history, science, and how everything works. Eve and I are the farthest removed from the world of exploding knowledge. However, we are both avid learners and will not rest until we have at least caught up in a reasonable way with all of our children.

"You know, Lev, I used to dream of making instruments and devices to make life easier. I learned how to make metal, and from that I designed metal tools. However, I had children to feed and it took long hours of endless work just to feed and clothe ourselves. I marvel to see people whose only job seems to be to create ideas and devices to make life easier, and then to constantly improve upon them. If we had remained in Eden, we would have had leisure time to devote to improving conditions on earth. We had the mental acuity to do this, but once forced to work endlessly, our mental resources were wasted while we labored hoeing the thorns and thistles that never seemed to cease growing. We know there is so much to learn. Please lay out all the courses we will need to take in the weeks and months ahead."

"It will be my pleasure, Adam. That is the exciting thing about life now. Learning is so easy! The Ancients are the first perfect teachers we have had in the schooling process. When you understand something perfectly and explain it perfectly, everyone learns easily. They make it so interesting that you will have to tear yourself away to get some sleep."

Eve chimed in, "As soon as we become competent, we want to become productive people. I have heard that people donate time to factories that produce necessities. We will be eager to do that as soon as we are prepared. We are very backward, so please lay out the programs from the ground floor up."

"I shall, my dear parents, and then I will leave you to learn to your heart's content."

*"There shall be no more thence an infant of days,
Nor an old man that hath not filled his days:
For the child shall die an hundred years old;
But the sinner being an hundred years old shall be accursed"
(Isaiah 65:20).*

Chapter Sixteen

One evening, while Lev was deep into his studies, the phone rang. "Shalom, this is Lev Aron."

"Shalom, Lev. This is Moses."

"Hello, Moses, I am delighted to hear from you! I thought you had forgotten me!" Lev laughed.

Moses responded, "Be assured, Lev, you never have been forgotten, and we appreciate your faithful service through the years. I am calling because we will be passing another milestone shortly, and some people have not made any progress in improving their characters. Many have lived for nearly a century since their return to life, not enjoying all the good things of this age because they will not fit into a world of righteousness. Like a renegade species, they will never be truly happy with God's arrangements. Every day the sun comes up and sets, and life *seems* secure. The need for fixing the fatal flaws in their thinking look as if it is unnecessary. That is the illusion. The reality is, if they do not change their heart condition and show some repentance, time is running out for them.

"A hundred years without genuinely repenting for monstrous deeds of the past and making a start toward becoming loving, caring human beings will result in second death. You know that many have told you through the years they would have been pleased to stay in the grave, and they never asked to be brought back to life. While they have some enjoyment of living, the thought of having to seek personal forgiveness from those they injured has been a hurdle they have been unwilling to overcome. They have only expressed superficial regret and have convinced themselves that time itself will heal everything without effort on their part."

"How well I know that!" Lev sighed. "How may I assist? I know I cannot change people's hearts. Some people want others to accept them as they are, no questions asked. I have worked with people to change their attitudes but without much success, I'm afraid."

"Lev, you did all anyone could do. You succeeded in getting many to see their true situation. However, Christ wants to give others one last reminder of their peril while there is still time for change. Any progress will be noted, and their life may be extended. Failure to respond at all will show they have absolutely no heart interest in character growth. There is nothing more that can be done for them, so they must cease to exist without any hope of life ever again. "

"What can I do to help?"

"A man whom you have never met or dealt with by the name of Klaus von Staub, a former SS man under Hitler, was ruthless and untiring in rounding up Jews and murdering them, but he has not really shown remorse. Oh, he has expressed some verbal acknowledgement that what he did was not the right thing to do and said he was sorry. What else could he say? He can't say he was proud of what he did. But unless there is genuine godly sorrow that seeks forgiveness and unless this confession is followed by loving deeds and sacrifices to indicate a changed heart condition, it is obvious that nothing has changed in that heart."

An Assignment in Germany

"So I suppose you want me to pay him a visit and try arousing him to the peril he faces?"

"Yes, he deserves to be given one last chance to correct his attitude. Many of these people have a circle of fellowship, which strengthens their weaknesses. These circles need to be broken up. After a century of life, they need to include people who seek God and righteousness. We are sending out several thousand representatives to alert these people. Are you prepared to help us, Lev?"

"I would *never* say 'no' to the King! Give me my instructions, and I will be on my way."

"Wonderful! You will travel to Germany by plane, and there you will use a local aircraft. You will be going to an area near the former city of Hamburg. I will fax you all the details of your trip. You will leave Tuesday morning. Thank you, Lev! Shalom."

Lev stopped in to see his best friend and confidant, Rebekah. She seemed more gracious each time he saw her. Her exquisite home was filled with the fragrance of jasmine and wisteria, and she invited him in for some tea. Having matured through the years, she was a woman approaching human perfection. Her demeanor was regal, but she was even lovelier in heart than her physical beauty.

"Oh, Lev, don't tell me you are going away again! I can see it in your face."

"Yes, you're right. I received a call from Moses to visit an individual who has not made progress for nearly one hundred years. This person is beginning to think that all danger is in the past, and that he has successfully resisted change with impunity. He needs to be warned that death may be standing at the door."

"Oh, I don't envy you that task! You will be as welcome as a plague."

"Well, everyone deserves a warning before they come under judgment."

"If you cannot help him, Lev, I don't think anyone can."

"I worry about how I am going to approach him. After so many years, these people think they are safe and the world has finally come around to accepting them. Still, they are never totally happy since they are out of step with the present arrangement."

"Dear Lev, they couldn't have chosen a better person than you. You have made friends out of total enemies. Anyway, thank you for spending this evening with me before leaving. How about some tea now and sharing some of your studies with me?"

The evening soon passed in warm, delightful fellowship. About midnight Lev gave his friend a farewell kiss. "I will miss you, Rebekah. Shalom."

Lev Takes Flight

Klaus von Staub had been notified of Lev's visit. As he touched down on the landing pad, it was obvious Klaus wasn't home. Lev sat in the garden for about a half hour when Klaus drove into the driveway. He was a handsome man, standing tall with polish and self-confidence. He still had the rigid demeanor of an SS man and greeted Lev formally while stepping out of the car.

"I am sorry to have kept you waiting, Lev. I have been expecting you, but I didn't know the exact time of your arrival. Please, forgive me."

"I have just been sitting here enjoying your garden. How lovely it is! You must have a green thumb."

"Well, thank you. I do take pleasure in it. Please come in, and we will have some lunch together. May I help bring in your bags? It has been a long time since I have had any company. Please feel free to help yourself to anything in the garden you may wish. As soon as you wash up, I will have lunch ready."

As they ate, Klaus asked, "May I ask why I am honored to have your visit? Here in Germany, Lev Aron is a name well spoken of. Even my old boss, Adolph Hitler, spoke well of you."

"Have you kept in contact with him?"

"Only on occasion. I was never in his inner circle. He did remember me, however, and spoke of me with generous praise."

"He never mentioned you in all the time I met with him. One thing he has in common with you is that he is quite artistic and rearranged his garden into quite a work of art."

"Now, you did not come here to tell me about Adolph. You must have some business with me, so please, I do not want to be too bold, but what is the reason for your visit? I know a man of your stature does not call without some specific reason."

"Yes, you are correct. I did come here on serious business. However, I first want to become acquainted with your style of life and how things have changed for the better since you returned."

"Well, I know you are a Jew and probably still may have resentment for what we Germans did. I would never have done what I did had I known everyone was coming back to life again. It is very difficult to face all my former victims. I have been extremely uncomfortable since my return to life. It is not easy being a former SS man in a world that loathes them."

"What I am interested in hearing you say is that *you* loathe your role as one of Hitler's gang of murderers. Do you?"

"That is a very direct question. I just told you I would not have done what I did had I known everyone was returning to life. Doesn't that tell you I regret having done what I was forced to do?"

"Were you forced to be an SS man who was one of Hitler's chosen agents to do his dirty work?"

"No, of course not. When we enlisted in his service, we were not sure what we would be called upon to do. I loved the military lifestyle and the efficiency we had. There were no jobs in those early days, so I signed up. How could I know where it would lead?"

"Well, you know now where it led. I understand you were glad to have the power and privileges you enjoyed as a special representative of Hitler. You loved collecting Jews and their children and sending them off to their death. I am told you were very efficient at what you did."

Germans Were Dying From Blockbusters

"Yes, I must confess I never once thought about all these women and children going to the death camps. We Germans were dying on the battlefields. We were being bombed with huge blockbuster bombs in our cities. We were dying, too, you know."

"That was war," Lev countered. "What you were doing to the Jews and gypsies was not war; it was pure murder. Somehow you imagined you had license to kill innocent people in ruthless death camps."

"Yes, I know I was caught up in an evil system." Klaus *seemed* to be agreeing with him, but all the while he continued justifying himself. "I did not enjoy sending people to their death. However, once you started, there was no way out of it. I would have been sent up to the front if I asked to be removed from Hitler's elite force."

"The worst that could have happened is that you would have been killed in battle. If so, you would have died as a soldier, not as a cold-blooded murderer. You wouldn't have to face the countless hundreds you sent to the gas chambers." Lev was stern, but kind. "You do not like facing your victims, do you?"

"I have said I was sorry to those who claim to be my victims. However, if they want me to grovel, they are just going to have to wait."

"How long?"

"Forever."

"Well, you don't have forever. Your hour glass is running very low."

"I thought I had at least to the end of the thousand years."

"Who told you that? I think you heard what you wanted to hear. You have had nearly a hundred years to make some progress toward becoming a loving human being. Nobody expects you to grovel, but every victim has a right to see that you feel genuine godly sorrow for what you did and that you demonstrate a deep desire to become the caring, loving, and compassionate person that you never were. Is that an unreasonable expectation?"

"Well, what makes you think that I am some monstrous ghoul who loves to see people suffer and die?"

"Whether you loved it or not, you once were. You surely do not believe that everyone misunderstands you. They do understand what you were and what you did—all too clearly. But do *you* understand it? That is my question."

"How could I expect you, a Jew, to understand me? You are ready to condemn me no matter how well I performed."

"Oh, please, don't let your prejudice against the Jews betray you," Lev entreated. "An angel from heaven would not give you a different report than I have. Your conduct was a disgrace to humanity. I know the bands were playing and the flags were waving while you marched the Nazi goosestep, but what was the fruit of your activity? Ashes and black smoke! And all you can say is, 'I am sorry'?"

"I told you I was not proud of my activities, but why not ask the bomber crews if they are happy about all the bombs they dropped on German civilian homes in the war?"

"The difference is that they took steps to avoid wholesale killing of civilians. Sometimes bombs were unloaded because planes were crippled trying to make it home. Sometimes the leader dropped bombs prematurely and the rest followed the leader. This was not cold, calculated, deliberate destruction of human beings. It was war. I was a soldier. I know what it is like to kill people. And I know what it is like to ache for my part in all that. But you cannot compare war death to the systematic murder against an entire race. Every person you murdered had a face and eyes you could look into."

Lev leaned forward with earnestness. "Christ understands that you were indoctrinated with hate poison, but that is something you *willingly* learned and wanted to believe. You were *willingly* deceived and that was your rationalization for participating in wholesale murder. Shame on you!"

Klaus Unnerved

Poor Klaus turned pale. No one had ever been that direct with him before.

"All right, all right. I knew what I did was wrong. I knew many of those people I rounded up for shipment to death camps were good people. I have had a troubled conscience at times, but once you were in the Nazi crime club, there was no way out."

"I can understand that, Klaus, but you are not in 'the Nazi crime club' now. You are free to become a genuinely loving human being. If it is death that you want, you shall have it, make no mistake about that."

"It is easy for you to say, Lev. I still am in that club. We former SS men have a fellowship among ourselves. We did not belong in regular society, so we found comfort among ourselves."

"What do you talk about among yourselves? Do you reminisce about the days of your power, when decked up in your murderer's uniforms, and you had privileges and people feared you? Do you discuss how you dragged people from their homes and put them on trucks to be herded into trains all packaged neatly for death?"

"No, no, Lev! You imagine the worst about our fellowship," Klaus defended. "We do not believe that what we did was right or proper. It was a bad mistake, but we were led down this pathway, very slowly to start with. When we first became SS men, our biggest task was not taking care of Jews, but taking care of German dissenters to Hitler's power. Our job was to take out the opposition, and we were rewarded for that. In the process, we were desensitized and soon nothing was out of bounds for us."

"I understand that clearly. However, you have had nearly one hundred years to repair your mental processes. The best thing you could do is drop out of your club and join the human race."

"Oh, now you are speaking of nearly all my friends. We understand each other and enjoy being together."

"It sounds like you're lemmings to me, ready to follow each other over a cliff."

"That is not true! We are individual thinkers not following a leader. People who know our past do not want us in their fellowship. As I said, I am not going to grovel and beg people to receive me into their fellowship. We are marked by our past and rejected by society. You have no idea how it is."

"You can change it if you want to, Klaus." Lev felt frustration. The man should have known all this by now, but he would do his best to reach Klaus' heart nonetheless. "That is what I am trying to tell you. Other people have every reason to reject you when they feel *you* have not rejected your past. That is what you have to do if you want to extend your days on earth."

"That is easier said than done, Lev. You are accepted everywhere in society. You have friends who love you all over the world with no black marks against you. You are the golden-haired favorite of the Ancients." There was bitterness in his voice. "It is easy for you to say, but I am an ugly duckling that nobody wants. People will be glad to hear that Klaus finally got payment for his sins."

"Klaus, you are feeling sorry for yourself, inferring that nobody loves you and nobody cares for you. That is rubbish! Make yourself loveable, and you will be surprised how love will come to you. I am not here because I hate you. You have never done me any personal harm. I understand how you, too, were trapped into a killing business that dwarfs most people. It is not what you were or what you did that will write your last chapter. It is what you *are* and what you are *willing to be* that counts. You can change, but you have be willing to do so."

No Will to Change

"That's a nice pep talk, Lev, but I'm sorry. I am what I am and I accept it. I *don't* have the will to change. I was never a goody-goody person. Why should I be? Death is not all that bad. I never asked to be brought back to life. If I had been asked, I would have said, 'no thanks.' I enjoy living, but death ends all necessity for change and reform, and I don't want to change! I like what I am!"

"If that is your choice, you shall have it. Just keep on as you have been and soon you *will* die. It will be forever. No laughter, no eyes sparkling with enthusiasm, no smiles of love, no gentle hand to touch yours, no beautiful sunrises or sunsets, no flowers or beauty of any kind, no music to fill the heart, and the precious gift of life will be extinguished forever. Is that what you really want?"

"No, I can't say that is what my first choice is. I have been allowed to live this long; why can't I just go on enjoying life the way I want? I am bothering no one. I can't break any laws even if I wanted to, so what harm is there in letting me live peacefully without having to jump through some hoop asking for forgiveness? My presence is a danger to no one. I tell you, I am a decent human being and am seemingly being threatened for being a nonconformist."

"Klaus, you are forgetting that Christ has given you life again— knowing the kind of man you were—for a purpose. He expects that you should distance yourself from past behavior and move toward being a noble person. Most people are *thrilled* with the opportunities to remake their lives into beautiful copies of Christ. You seem to resent making any improvement. You apparently feel you have a right to live however you want, and Christ should look the other way. One of God's purposes has been that the earth is to be populated by happy inhabitants, and you will never be truly happy the way you have been. You know what I am saying is true. Klaus, I must tell you again, your hourglass is running low. You do not seem to understand that all creatures that will have eternal life must have perfect love and reflect the likeness of God and of Christ."

"You make a good preacher, Lev. However, I am what I am. I do not want to be somebody else. If I change, I will no longer be me. You just don't understand. I am what I am because that is what I chose to be, that is what my friends chose to be. We do not preach or teach that everyone must be as we are."

"Klaus, I am not here to play philosophical games with you. You are free to say 'yes' or 'no' to God. He won't force anyone. God lives by the principles of perfect love, perfect wisdom, perfect justice, and perfect power. He *cannot* deviate from these fixed principles—not for Himself, not for His own Son, not for anyone. That is why He does not deal with anyone directly now, for if He did He would have to immediately consume imperfect humanity. Christ has taken us out of the hands of Divine Justice and stands between God and us. This is why we, who still have sinful propensities, are not destroyed already. However, the day will come when Christ will step down from being Mediator, and we must all then stand before the bar of justice. 'It is a fearful thing to fall into the hands of the living God.'"

Disconcerted From His Smugness

Klaus turned a shade whiter and became very nervous. He seemed to be quite shaken, recognizing the severity of Lev's warning. Used to playing all kinds of philosophy and mental games, it suddenly began to be apparent that God was not going to coerce him into changing. He was not going to be forced to be what he was unwilling to be. At this point Klaus really understood he must decide his own destiny.

Lev continued firmly, "Klaus, you have had the same opportunity as everyone else. You have not been discriminated against or denied any opportunities to make progress in reconciliation. True, you numbed your conscience with a hot iron during the holocaust brutalities, but that is not fatal if you *want* to have it healed. All things are possible to those who seek Christ's help and who truly desire to become loving. You have had a long time to make progress in this area, but you have wasted it so far thinking that no one has noticed. You are wrong, Klaus. But it still doesn't have to be that way. There is still time to make good, if you are willing to do so."

"You have made your point very well, Lev. I must tell you that I am not able to change, because I do not *want* to change," Klaus said flatly. "It is too late, it is a bridge too far, and I cannot turn into something I do not want to be."

Lev tried one last time. "Please do not shut the door on yourself. I have been trying to keep it open for you. Remember that God has no pleasure in anyone's death. He encourages us to choose life that we may live. He is extremely rich and can sustain all in life who desire it enough to live by His righteous rules."

The conversation ended here. Klaus sensed he was not going to improve his situation by clinging to his ways, but he was not flexible enough to change. It was a rude wake-up call, but he was stubbornly resisting changing his old self.

That evening after supper they had some small talk about different things, but Lev, with a heavy heart, avoided any further confrontation. He had made his point, and for now that was all he could do. Perhaps if Klaus slept on it he might think differently in the morning. It was a slim hope.

"By the way, Klaus, do you ever go to the chapel services in the morning?"

"I tried that a few times, but that is not for me. I don't belong there. People know my past, and some people that were there lost their lives because of me, so it was uncomfortable for them and for me as well."

"I am going tomorrow. Why don't you come along with me? You are locking yourself away from a fuller and richer life. Why settle for a miserable existence when you can enter into a world of love and light?"

Without directly answering, Klaus crossed his arms. "I do have one more question, Lev. Why is the tree of the knowledge of good and evil being withheld from us?"

"I have faced that question before. They have been kept off limits. I think right now you have enough problems to handle without opening up new ones."

"How come you don't know? You are connected with the powerful authorities. You mean they haven't told you?"

"No, and I haven't asked. It is not my business. I am content to leave everything in Christ's hands. Who am I to make suggestions to one infinitely wiser than I? He knows what he is doing and he does all things well."

"That sounds like the old party line to me. Lev, you are not free to be your own man, and you don't want me to be free either."

"Hmm…that's a new assessment of me! I've never heard that before! Well, you are free to think that if you wish." Lev felt nothing negative toward Klaus, only sadness over his stubbornness. "However, there is no party line—there is not even a party. I do and say always what I believe. The Ancients are towering giants of integrity and honesty. If you knew them, you would love them."

"I cannot and did not say they were bad people. I must confess they have been generous and more than fair with me. We never gave our victims the right to get off the death train when taking them to the gas chambers. In all fairness, they have given me that right to jump off the train that is taking me to second death. However, as much as I don't like staying, neither can I get off."

"More correctly put, you are too weak. It is all a matter of will; if you decide to do what is required, you will be very glad you did."

"Lev, you are a never-give-up person. You are a decent enough fellow. But, no, it is too late for me. In a way, there is something satisfying to know that all the problems of life will be settled instantly and forever for me."

As Klaus had said, Lev was a never-give-up person. "Klaus! You have been given your life again and here you are, throwing it away. Eternity is in sight for you. I can't understand why you want death."

"No, it is not my wish. It is someone up higher that wishes I leave this world. I am content to stay in it. My life is being taken because I will not be remolded into the right shape."

"You are making yourself out to be a martyr, and you are not. I know what I'd do if I were in your shoes. I'd jump off that train immediately and turn my life around."

"You may be right, but you are not me. However, I will go to the chapel tomorrow with you. I did love the music; it was beautiful when I went there."

"Good! I'll see you in the morning."

Lev then retreated to his studies and prayer for the evening. He heard Klaus' phone ring repeatedly that evening and figured it was his buddies trying to learn what had happened that day during their visit. Lev knew as long as Klaus hung around with the old crowd, none of them would ever find the will to change his life around. Fellowship taking one in the wrong direction was very subtle and made one feel comfortable while going the wrong way.

The next morning they both rose early and after drinking some fresh juice departed for the chapel. It was comfortably filled and the music had already started. They found seats quietly, not catching anyone's special attention. After the usual worship, the speaker chose for his topic that day, "Choose life, that both thou and thy seed may live" (Deuteronomy 30:19).

The speaker was brilliant and forceful about making the choices that would lead to life. Klaus listened intently, wondering if Lev had put the speaker up to this sermon. Everyone sat in rapt attention, including Klaus, who wanted to live but with only a few superficial changes to his lifestyle. The speaker made it very clear that life would not be attained on anyone's own terms. Life was God's gift and only those that overcame the fallen tendencies of the flesh would be rewarded with eternal life.

When the services ended Klaus wanted to leave immediately, so Lev went along with him, not stopping to enjoy fellowship, as was his usual custom.

"You know, Klaus, I had nothing to do with that sermon. If you are thinking I put him up to this, you are mistaken. However, he said what I have been trying to say to you better than I could say it."

Klaus Enjoys Flying

Klaus remained silent. Instead of flying home, Lev asked, "Would you like to fly around the countryside to see the good earth?"

"Yes, I would enjoy that. I wanted to be a pilot in the German Luftwaffe. I always loved flying, but I never made it there. Perhaps my life would have been molded in a different way if I had."

"Why do you say that?"

"Because I would not have been involved in the death camps. I probably would have been shot down, because I would not have been such a good pilot. I didn't have the coordination I needed. That is why I flunked out."

"Well here, take the controls for a bit. Just be careful to exert only slight pressure. Have you ever flown before?"

"Yes, but never in such a sophisticated machine. This is truly amazing. I hear you were involved in the production of the prototype for this aircraft. Is that true?"

"Yes, actually the technical features were all worked out in Israel, but we started mass production of this type of aircraft mostly for the less industrialized nations. We didn't wish to build land-wasting roads, so we made this type of craft and it is turning out to serve very well."

Lev spent nearly an hour giving him a flying lesson, and he was an excellent student. When it came time to land, Lev took the controls again and gently put the craft down on Klaus' pad. "Well, how did that feel, Klaus?"

"Ah, that was great! The sight from up there was beautiful! We were floating over the earth so quietly and efficiently. Time and distance seemed to fade away. Thanks, Lev."

"Yes, and we were not in danger of being shot down either, were we?" Lev laughed.

"That made it more pleasant to be sure. By the way, flying this craft around was a better sermon for me than what the chaplain gave."

"Well, that's strange. Do you love to fly more than you love to live?"

"I guess I just don't respond as normal people do."

"Well, Klaus, the fact is that you have to love to live more than you love to fly. You are getting your priorities turned around."

After they landed, Lev decided to make a sumptuous noon meal. As they were finishing, they were surprised to have a small visitor. Klaus had left the door open and a little red fox pup walked in, apparently lost.

Lev said, "He looks hungry! Let's feed the little guy."

"I have a bottle and nipple that I have had around and never used. What will we feed it?"

"Well, he is probably thirsty, so let's whip up some fruit-of-paradise juice and see if he'll drink it. Also, if you have a little honey to add to the drink, he will go after it in a big way. Isn't he cute?"

"Sure is. Great idea! I have plenty of honey. My neighbor has a beehive and gives me more than I can use. Now that they don't spray deadly insecticides, bees flourish everywhere!" Klaus exclaimed.

Klaus Plays 'Momma Fox'

Soon they had a nice warm bottle fixed, and Klaus picked up the fox and fed it. Lev could see Klaus enjoyed playing 'momma fox.' He petted it gently as it drained the bottle.

"I think this little guy is ready for a nice nap until his momma finds him. I am going to put him into a little basket outside in the garden. His mother can't be too far away." Lev found it strange to watch this hardhearted man being so tender to the little creature.

After lunch, Lev said he was going to visit a factory in the area and asked if Klaus wanted to come.

"No, thank you. Some folks know me there, and I would not be welcome."

"You could make yourself welcome with an attitude change. However, I am not going to lecture you. I'll see you at suppertime. Shalom."

When Lev returned, he heard Klaus talking to his cronies. Obviously, he didn't want Lev to notice that he kept such close contact with his former SS partners since he hung up as soon as he heard Lev come through the door.

"I have supper ready, Lev. We still have a lot of those vegetables left over from lunch, so I warmed them up. We are ready to eat whenever you want."

Lev was careful not to be critical about anything. He did ask, "What happened to our little friend? I notice his basket was empty when I came in."

"Yes, the mother came late this afternoon, just as he finished his nap."

After Lev retired to his study, he heard the phone ringing often, as all Klaus' buddies kept their little brotherhood going. He would have liked to take the phone away for a few weeks and to help wean Klaus from his dependence on his buddies. However, Klaus wasn't a child, and he was going to have to make his own decisions. Klaus also declared he wouldn't go to the chapel meetings anymore and that was a big disappointment to Lev.

The next day at lunch Lev felt compelled to try once more. "You know, Klaus, time is running out. I don't know how long you have, but I'm fairly sure your century of probation is coming to a close. I wish I could be more persuasive."

"No one could be more persuasive than you, Lev. You have done your job well, and I thank you for your effort. I am kind of glad to leave this world. I just don't fit in. I am out of step with almost everyone, so I guess I am in the way. The world might be better off without my buddies and me."

The Death Angel

Lev was very sad as he went into his room that evening. He felt somehow that he had failed. He knew that Klaus had briefly considered seeking to change his life but then quickly dug back in to the old ways. The fact that he had survived a hundred years showed that God in mercy had given Klaus enormous opportunities to change, but he would not.

When Lev arose in the morning, Klaus was not up. He decided to knock on his door. There was no answer. That was strange, for Klaus was always an early riser. After another loud knock, Lev opened the door to find Klaus lying cold and still. Examining him, he knew he had died painlessly in the night. Klaus must have known the end was near from his comments last evening. This was a shock. There had been no death in one hundred years. People all returned to life, but no one had died.

Lev stood there in silence. He wondered what he should do. He couldn't call an undertaker, there were none. There were no doctors to make medical calls. No one was ever sick or needed medical attention. He finally decided to call the Civil Center that looked after civil repairs to roads and bridges or anything that needed to be maintained for the general good.

He soon was able to reach someone that had arrived at work early. "Shalom. This is Lev Aron and I wish to report a death."

"What? That's impossible. We have not had a death in a hundred years."

"Well, we have one now. Klaus von Staub is dead. He died during the night, and I am calling because I do not know how to proceed from here."

"Well, I don't know what to tell you. We are not authorized to handle such things. I think I will have to call the Ancients to find out how to proceed. I have your number, so I will call you back if our department is responsible for handling this situation. This is incredible! It sends a chill running up my spine."

Ten minutes later the phone rang, and now the department head was speaking. "Shalom. Is this Lev Aron?"

"Speaking."

"This is Siegfried of the Civil Center. The Ancients have confirmed that many lost their lives last night. All of them had been warned and encouraged to change, but their period of grace had expired without any serious effort made in that direction. They all knew and were forewarned of what was in store for them if they didn't change, but they refused.

"We have been ordered to pick up the bodies in our area and to bury them. I was given the complete list of names and addresses, so as soon as we can, we'll be there. Please be patient, for this is a shock to us all. However, we knew that some people were not going to change and often wondered how this would be dealt with. Now we have the answer. It is grim, indeed!"

No Mourning for Second Death

Lev asked, "Will there be religious services for their burial?"

"I was told, no. Their deaths will be registered, and they will have marked graves for any friends or relatives who may wish to take notice of their deaths. There will be no mourning, because these people chose to live outside of God's mercy and grace. There will be no return to life for those who have perished, so their names will be blotted out in time."

Lev said, "I guess this will start a long series of deaths of people who won't show a willingness to change within a hundred years of full opportunity. Incredible! All they have to do is make a minimal effort to continue living. This is going to be a wake-up call to many who didn't take seriously that death was inevitable."

Siegfried said, " I know several on the list of those who died, and I know they were stubbornly clinging to an unsavory past. Anyway, we plan to dig up old cemeteries and place those who die there. We will have plenty of room that way. However, we have not had any deaths for so long that this comes as a shock to our senses. In the old days, we were always going to funerals of loved ones or friends. We have almost forgotten all that and have been enjoying the return to life. This is quite a reversal."

"Yes, I know. I was sent to see if I could help Klaus turn around, but try as I might, he seemed to desire death over changing his life. Maybe he was right. He locked God and Christ out of his life, as well as most people, and he only enjoyed fellowship with a few of his old cronies. He would only enjoy life on his own terms and would never accept God's. Poor Klaus. I shared a few happy moments with him, but I just couldn't dig him out of the hole he had made for himself."

In League with Death

"I have the list and sure enough, most of his buddies are on it. However, there are some surprises, too. I notice some who seemed well adjusted also died. Whatever their shortcomings, we know that Christ does all things well. No use continuing to extend grace to those who will not accept it."

"Well, I will wait until you come to pick up the body. I will notify his next of kin. He was a very rigid keeper of files. I must say he was more organized than I am. I will tell them to call your office when you assign a day for the interment."

"Good, Lev, I appreciate that. It will save us the trouble. We had a different day's work planned. It is still hard to believe that people chose death over life. Don't expect us there until afternoon. Could you take care of his personal effects? The home will be kept operational for people visiting in the area. We always need extra rooms here and there, so that will work out well."

Lev called Klaus' mother next. "I am Lev Aron, and I am sorry to report that your son, Klaus von Staub, died in the night."

Although she seemed to be weeping, it felt more like resignation than heartbroken mourning. "Thank you for calling, but someone already told me. I suspected this would happen, but when it happens, it is still such a shock. I knew he was finding difficulty trying to adjust to righteous conditions here on earth. All my efforts to change his attitude were wasted. He just would not change."

Lev tried to console her. "Please accept my sympathy. I was sent here to try to get him to change, but he was determined to take the course he did. You will have to call the Civil Center to get the particulars. This is a new chapter for them, taking care of the dead. People haven't done that in a hundred years. I will bring over all his personal effects in my aircraft, if I may, this afternoon. Will you be home?"

"Yes, Mr. Aron, that is very kind of you. I have told his father and other family members, so you need not call them. I hate to tell you this, but sometimes I think Klaus knew he would be happier dead. The idea of having to remake himself was loathsome to him. His circle of buddies seemed to prefer death."

There was nothing more to say. "I hope to see you this afternoon after they pick up his body. Shalom."

Clinging to the Past

Lev collected all of Klaus' things and started loading them into the aircraft. He had kept pictures of all his buddies. He even found a picture of Aldoph Hitler, much to his surprise. Lev could not help but wonder how that man had made out.

After lunch, a vehicle arrived from the Civil Center. They carefully placed the body in the back. Then Lev left to return Klaus' effects to his mother. He was surprised at her composure even though this news had been a shock to her.

Upon seeing some of his things, she said, "I should have told you to destroy some of those. The sooner we bury the odious memories of that awful regime the better. I don't want anything like that around here."

"I am sorry. I'll take them back and destroy them if you wish."

"Yes, please just give me things that pertain to his person. The other odious reminders of his association I would like obliterated. Thank you for your kindness. Life is so beautiful now—I just can't understand why he chose death."

"The soul that sinneth, it shall die"
(Ezekiel 18:4).

Chapter Seventeen

Lev returned home only to find that occasional deaths were occurring all over the world to those who were molded into patterns they refused to change. It was a small but steady trickle that continued during much of the second century of the regeneration. Lev and countless others had made repeated visits to those on the vulnerable list trying to awaken them, but for the most part it was ineffective.

It was not until the third century of the regeneration that death took a holiday again. Most people were reconciled with one another, and all the old wounds were healed and forgiven. There were continued inquiries about the tree of the knowledge of good and evil. There seemed to be a quiet longing for it to be restored by a few. The biggest problem was that now that the pressure of preparing for the human family to be returned to life was accomplished, people had a tendency to indulge themselves only in pleasure.

While it had been difficult for mankind to be reconciled with one another because of the enormity of the sins that had been committed, under the gentle influences of the time of regeneration the work seemed to prosper. Because the work of reconciliation between men had been so difficult and challenging, once it was accomplished many forgot that the hardest part lay ahead.

It was one thing to be reconciled with enemies. Being reconciled with God was going to require the rest of the thousand years, and even then some would come short. The standard was absolute perfection. That is why God's Spirit was poured out upon all flesh. Only those that accepted divine assistance could possibly hope to attain human perfection.

As men improved and the sinful propensities seemed to fade away, it was easy to assume that perfection had indeed been attained. James' stern reminder, "For whosoever shall keep the whole law, and yet offend in one point, he is guilty of all" (James 2:10), seemed extreme. Nearly perfect seemed good enough to some. It was easy to think that as long as there were no sins of commission, sins of omission would pass unnoticed. Little slips and failures could be dismissed.

However, the sins of omission were beginning to add up. The need to strengthen and encourage others to follow after holiness was still necessary. The days, weeks, months and years could easily pass without efforts to reach higher—and this was the danger.

Dangerous Lethargy

Lev and Rebekah often discussed the need to overcome this lethargy—the assumption that we are "good enough" now. As long as the tiniest imperfection remained, the slightest coolness to love was there. If even the least desire for the forbidden remained, the danger was real. Most people shared this understanding and tried with untiring devotion to reach the mark of perfect love for God and man. Every act of devotion inspired someone else to reach higher. In this favorable environment, progress was being made steadily and the last vestiges of sin were being obliterated.

Without awareness, society was undergoing a sifting. Some were behaving as gentle sheep in their love, tenderness and good works for others. On the other hand, the stubborn goats were satisfied with minimal efforts in helping others while trying to enjoy life to its fullest. No one was doing anything deliberately wrong. It was the effort not being put forth that was beginning to mark some as goats.

As the reign of Christ seemed to draw to its close, a remarkable change had taken place on earth. People reflected the image of God in ways never thought possible. Many had arrived at human perfection, while some were still relaxed and philosophically satisfied with their own attainments. They had done well; no one could say otherwise. Considering that many started out quite far from God, they had made great progress.

Society had been transformed into a glorious state. There were neither evil people nor anyone who did not conduct themselves with remarkable discipline. All were eager to praise God and all loved righteousness. In former times it had been difficult to imagine that society could become so transformed. Having been so far away from God and having come back to such lofty heights of character, it was easy to relax. Few felt worried about underachieving.

Satan had not yet been released from the abyss. Perfect men and women ran the government of earth and it showed everywhere. The stature of leadership was awesome and not one mistake had been made. Divine wisdom was manifest in all phases of the earth.

A certain anxiety began to emerge. Matthew 25 had predicted there would be a process of separation between the "sheep" and "goats." How would this take place and how would things change? What would happen when Christ stepped out from being Mediator between God and man? When would Satan be loosed from the abyss? How would his activities affect mankind? Would the tree of the knowledge of good and evil be restored to men, seeing they already knew evil? Who would be deceived and what would be the nature of the deception? All mankind thought about these things and spoke of them to one another.

Lev found himself amazed at his own happiness. These questions would be answered without any panic on his part. Those who loved God supremely were comfortable as the conclusion of this splendid era was wrapping up. Those most burdened with questions and anxieties were those who had lost opportunities to serve the general good of mankind. These sometimes reasoned that Christ had invested so many of his resources in bringing them this far, that surely there was little chance they would be lost now as his reign ended.

When Would the "Sheep" and "Goats" Be Separated?

Questions kept cropping up. Was the separation of the "sheep" and "goats" *before* the "little season" when Satan would be freed from the "abyss"? Why would Satan be loosed anyway? Things had been much better with him out of the picture. What purpose would be served in letting this criminal out of prison? Why not destroy him outright and never permit his return? These questions were being asked, and for some the answers were insufficient.

There were those who argued that Christ had loved them so much that he would never let them fail. That was sweet music reminiscent of the old preaching that all one needed to do was accept Jesus and heaven was automatically guaranteed. That used to be a very popular myth. In this time of regeneration, however, one thing should have been very plain—having a sacrificing and loving character was essential for everlasting life.

Another heated discussion concerned the Ancient Worthies. When would they leave office? Christ, the Mediator between God and man, employed them, so wouldn't their tenure of office run out when Christ stepped down as Mediator? Who would take their place? Men needed some type of central government and authority. Who would fill this vacuum? Would the Ancients possibly overstay the positions they held and should they be encouraged to leave? Where would they go? Would they be content to just live lives as ordinary citizens, or would they expect to be provided for in some special way? These questions kept being raised.

Conditions had flowed easily for centuries. Now as the reign of Christ was ending, there would be changes. How would this all develop? We hope to discuss this in the last and final book—*When the Thousand Years Expire.*

THE END

The titles of the whole *Alive Again* series of books are *Alive Again, From Ashes to Beauty, Fingers Stained with Evil, Adam and Eve Live Again* and *When the Thousand Years Expire.*

www.ingramcontent.com/pod-product-compliance
Lightning Source LLC
Chambersburg PA
CBHW030355030726
47497CB00002B/343